Mel Bay Presents

50 Tunes for Bass
Traditional, Old Time, Bluegrass & Celtic Solos
Volume 1

By Mark Geslison

C0-EFM-853

Additional titles in this series:
99938BCD 50 Tunes for Fiddle • 99939BCD 50 Tunes for Banjo
99941BCD 50 Tunes for Guitar • 99942BCD 50 Tunes for Mandolin

CD contents

CD 1
1. Angus Campbell
2. Arkansas Traveler
3. Aura Lee
4. The Battle Cry of Freedom
5. Beaumont Rag
6. Billy in the Lowground
7. Blackberry Blossom
8. Bonaparte's Retreat
9. Carthage Waltz
10. Cherokee Shuffle
11. Cluck Old Hen
12. Cotton-eyed Joe
13. Cotton Patch Rag
14. Cripple Creek
15. Devil's Dream
16. Down Yonder
17. Eighth of January

CD 2
1. Forked Deer
2. Gardenia Waltz
3. Grandfather's Clock
4. Green Willis
5. Indian's Farewell Waltz
6. Irish Washerwoman
7. La Bastringue
8. Leather Britches
9. Liberty
10. Martin's Waltz
11. Mason's Apron
12. Mississippi Hornpipe
13. Mississippi Sawyer
14. Old Dan Tucker
15. Old Joe Clark
16. President Garfield's Hornpipe
17. Pretty Peg

CD 3
1. Red-haired Boy
2. Red Wing
3. Sailor's Hornpipe/College Hornpipe
4. Saint Anne's Reel
5. Sally Ann
6. Sally Goodin'
7. Sally Johnson
8. Salt Creek
9. Soldier's Joy
10. Swallowtail Jig
11. Temperance Reel
12. Tom and Jerry
13. Turkey in the Straw
14. Uncle Joe
15. Under the Double Eagle
16. Whiskey Before Breakfast

MEL BAY®

1 2 3 4 5 6 7 8 9 0

© 2004 BY MEL BAY PUBLICATIONS, INC., PACIFIC, MO 63069.
ALL RIGHTS RESERVED. INTERNATIONAL COPYRIGHT SECURED. B.M.I. MADE AND PRINTED IN U.S.A.
No part of this publication may be reproduced in whole or in part, or stored in a retrieval system, or transmitted in any form or by any means, electronic, mechanical, photocopy, recording, or otherwise, without written permission of the publisher.

Visit us on the Web at www.melbay.com — E-mail us at email@melbay.com

Table of Contents

About the Author 3
Foreword 4
Preface 5

Angus Campbell 7
Arkansas Traveler 8
Aura Lee 12
The Battle Cry of Freedom 14
Beaumont Rag 18
Billy in the Lowground 20
Blackberry Blossom 22
Bonaparte's Retreat 24
Carthage Waltz 27
Cherokee Shuffle 30
Cluck Old Hen 34
Cotton Eyed Joe 36
Cotton Patch Rag 40
Cripple Creek 46
Devil's Dream 48
Down Yonder 52
Eighth of January 58
Forked Deer 62
Gardenia Waltz 64
Grandfather's Clock 68
Green Willis 76
Indian's Farewell Waltz 77
Irish Washerwoman 78
La Bastringue 82
Leather Britches 84
Liberty 86
Martin's Waltz 87
Mason's Apron 88
Mississippi Hornpipe 92
Mississippi Sawyer 94
Old Dan Tucker 96
Old Joe Clark 98
President Garfield's Hornpipe 101
Pretty Peg 104
Red-haired Boy 107
Red Wing 110
Sailor's Hornpipe 116
College Hornpipe* 117
Saint Anne's Reel 118
Sally Ann 119
Sally Goodin' 120
Sally Johnson 124
Salt Creek 126
Soldier's Joy 128
Swallowtail Jig 132
Temperance Reel 134
Tom and Jerry 136
Turkey in the Straw 138
Uncle Joe 144
Under the Double Eagle 146
Whiskey Before Breakfast 155

*This tune is out of alphabetical order because it is the second tune of a medley.

Appendix 158

About the Author

Mark Geslison, the author and coordinator of this series, is a multi-instrumentalist who plays the mandolin, guitar, bass, percussion, banjo and dulcimer. He has performed traditional music for most of his life and has been an instrumental champion several times since the mid-1980s including: Western Regional Guitar Champion 1988, 1989; Western Regional Mandolin Champion 1988, 1989; Utah State Guitar Champion 1988, 1989, 1992; Utah State Mandolin Champion 1988, 1989, 1992, 1994 and 2002; and Utah State Banjo Champion 2001 (4-string).

Mark has been the director of the Folk Music Ensemble program at Brigham Young University since 1992. The Folk Music Ensemble program includes performing groups that focus on Bluegrass, Appalachian, Early American and Celtic music styles. His students perform approximately one hundred times per year in all parts of the world including the South Pacific, Asia, Europe and North and South America.

Mark is also the founder and director of the Institute of American Music (IAM). IAM is a non-profit, private school of music designed to teach traditional music in an ensemble setting to young people and families. This series originated within IAM where Mark noticed a need for ensemble arrangements.

Visit... www.instituteofamericanmusic.com

for additional products that will assist you with your study of the 50 Tunes series including:

- Curriculum books with scales, exercises, technique and graduation check-off.
- Rhythm tracks (guitar chords and metronome) for practicing all of the 50 Tunes at varying metronome speeds.
- Bluegrass and Celtic songbooks.
- Information on creating and maintaining ensembles, family bands and "communities" of music.
- Free downloads of mp3 audio tracks and pdf sheet music.

Foreword

This book contains 50 tunes from the United States, the British Isles and Canada. The companion CD set includes the recorded version of each of these 50 tunes. The appendix at the back of this book contains instructions on tablature reading and chord charts. These components will help you while learning the enclosed tunes.

50 Tunes Volume 1 is not meant to be the ultimate beginning-to-advanced tool. Rather, it is intended to give a broad tune (melody) base to students and instructors alike. It is also intended to show creative arrangements of basic melodies with stylistic nuances designed to develop left and right hand skills (compare *Old Joe Clark 1*, *Down Yonder 2* and *Red Haired Boy solo*).

Preface

Arrangements

Erik Neilson arranged *Whiskey Before Breakfast 2*. Geoff Groberg arranged *Red Haired Boy solo*. All other parts were arranged by Mark Geslison. All 50 tunes are in the public domain or are otherwise under license.

Tune Order

Since this book is part of a series for various instruments, it is nearly impossible to arrange the tunes in a 'beginning-to-advanced' order that fits every instrument. Although the tunes have been arranged alphabetically, it is not necessary to follow the order of the book. You might want to start with *Old Joe Clark 1* or *Cripple Creek 1* and finish with *President Garfield's Hornpipe 2* or *Leather Britches solo*. In general, the tunes are organized so that "1" represents the simplest variation, "2" represents more difficult variations while "solos" represent the most complex of all parts. *Down Yonder*, for example, contains all three of these levels.

Chords

Most chord sequences in this book are set according to "tradition." However, the author has taken the liberty to set some chord sequences according to how they "sound best" to the ear of the author. Students and teachers are welcome to change chord sequences according to their preference.

Left-hand Fingering and CD Tempo

It is vital to finger the bass correctly in order to develop the speed necessary to play the enclosed bass solos at CD speed. Pay close attention to the left-hand fingering marking found in most parts. It is important to develop well thought out fingering habits when playing solos on the bass. For tunes with no bass solo, you should get to know these melodies as performed by other instruments so as to eventually create your own solos. Ultimately, you will want to gain the ability to play most of these tunes at 120-160 beats per minute. Most of the 50 tunes were recorded at 100 beats per minute. The following tunes were recorded at the listed tempo:

Tune	Tempo
Aura Lee	80
Battle Cry of Freedom	76
Carthage Waltz	108
Cluck Old Hen	120
Cotton-eyed Joe	120
Down Yonder	120
Gardenia Waltz	112
Indian's Farewell Waltz	112
Irish Washerwoman	100-120
La Bastringue	120
Martin's Waltz	112
Red Wing	120
Swallowtail Jig	100-120
Turkey in the Straw	120

Special Thanks

I want to thank Bradley Slade for the photography that has given this series a professional look.

-Mark Geslison

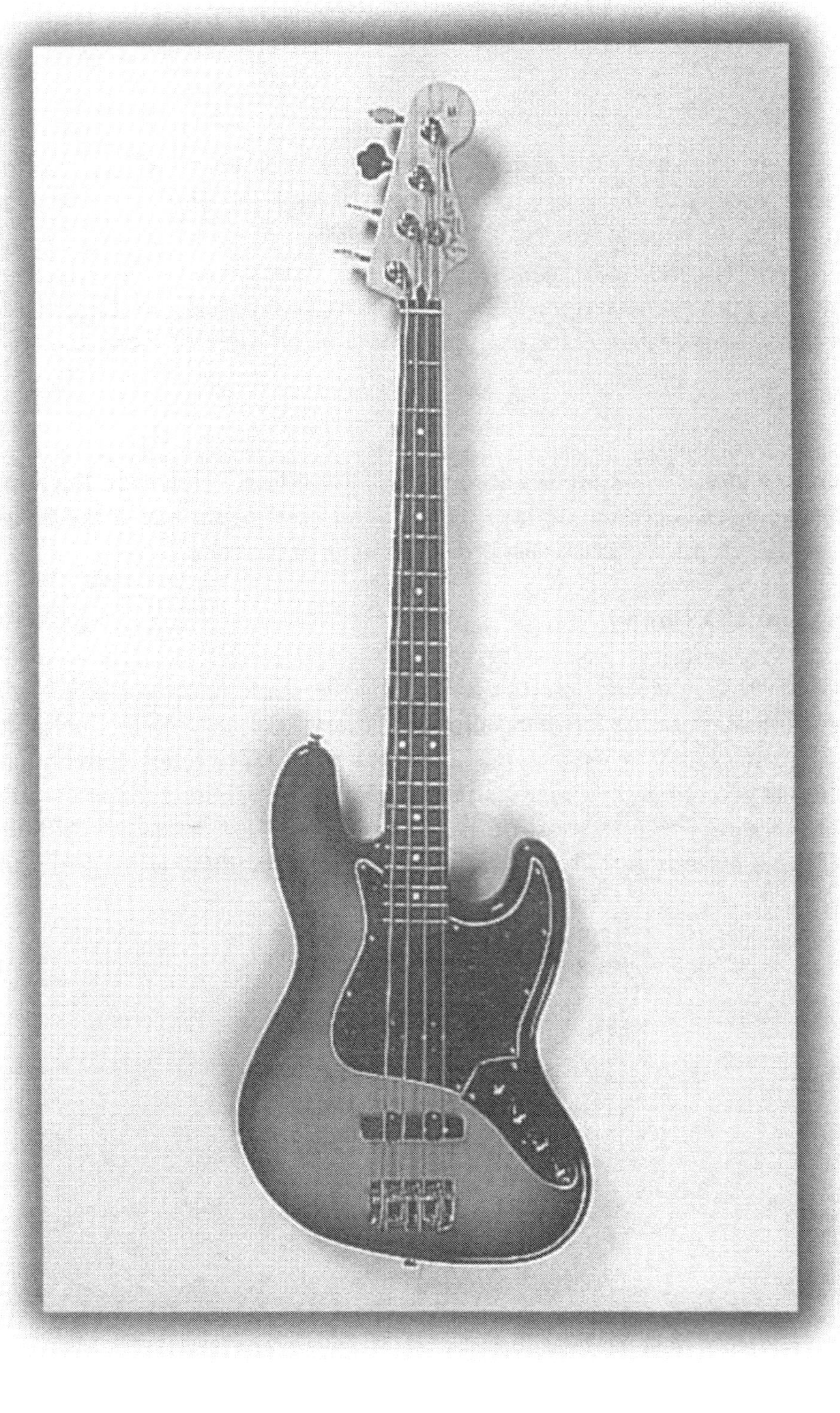

Angus Campbell

Scottish

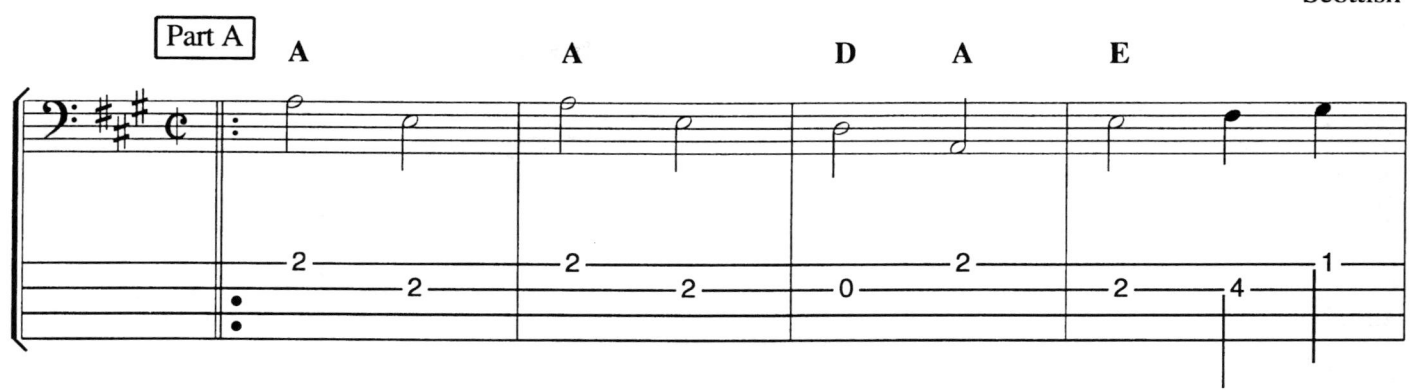

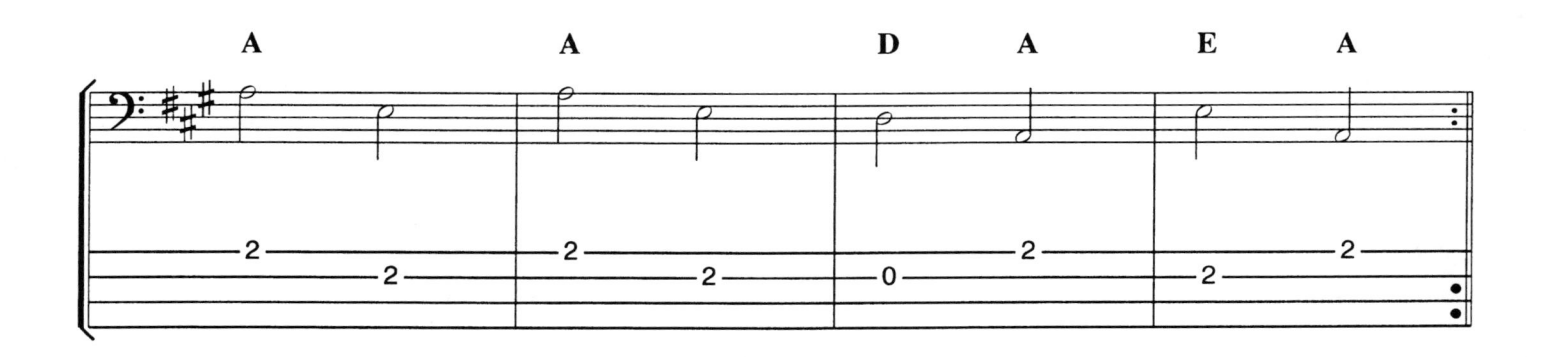

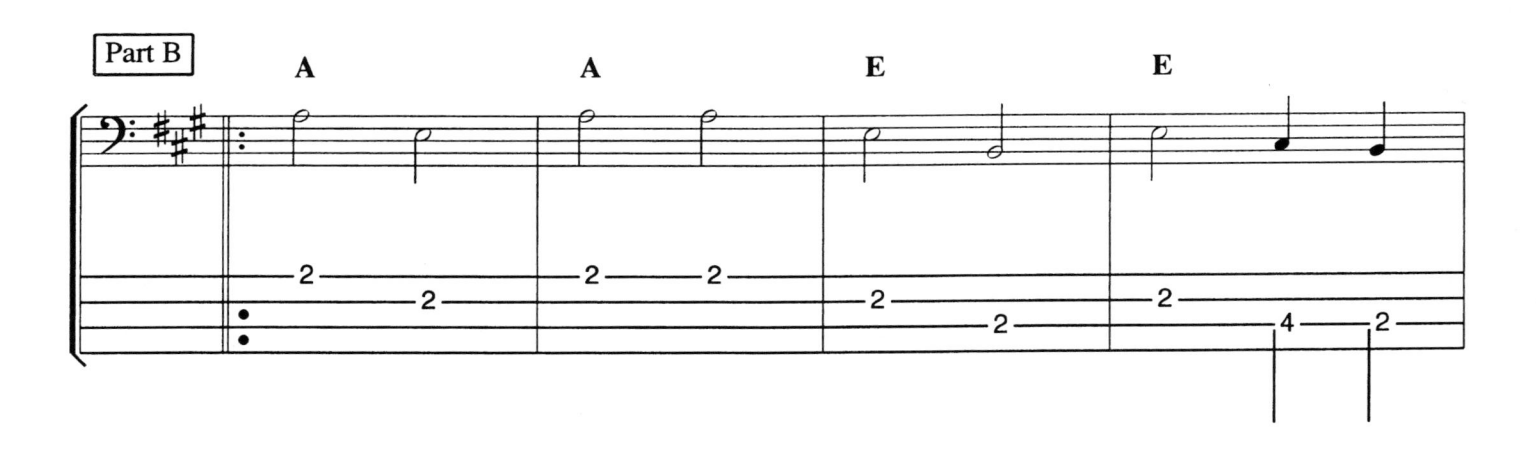

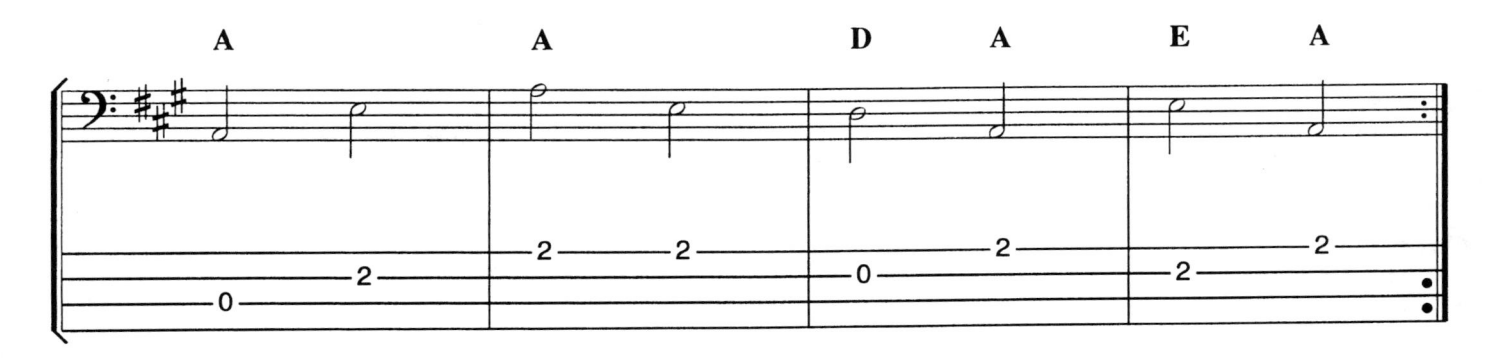

Bass 1

Arkansas Traveler

North American

Bass 1 (key of D)

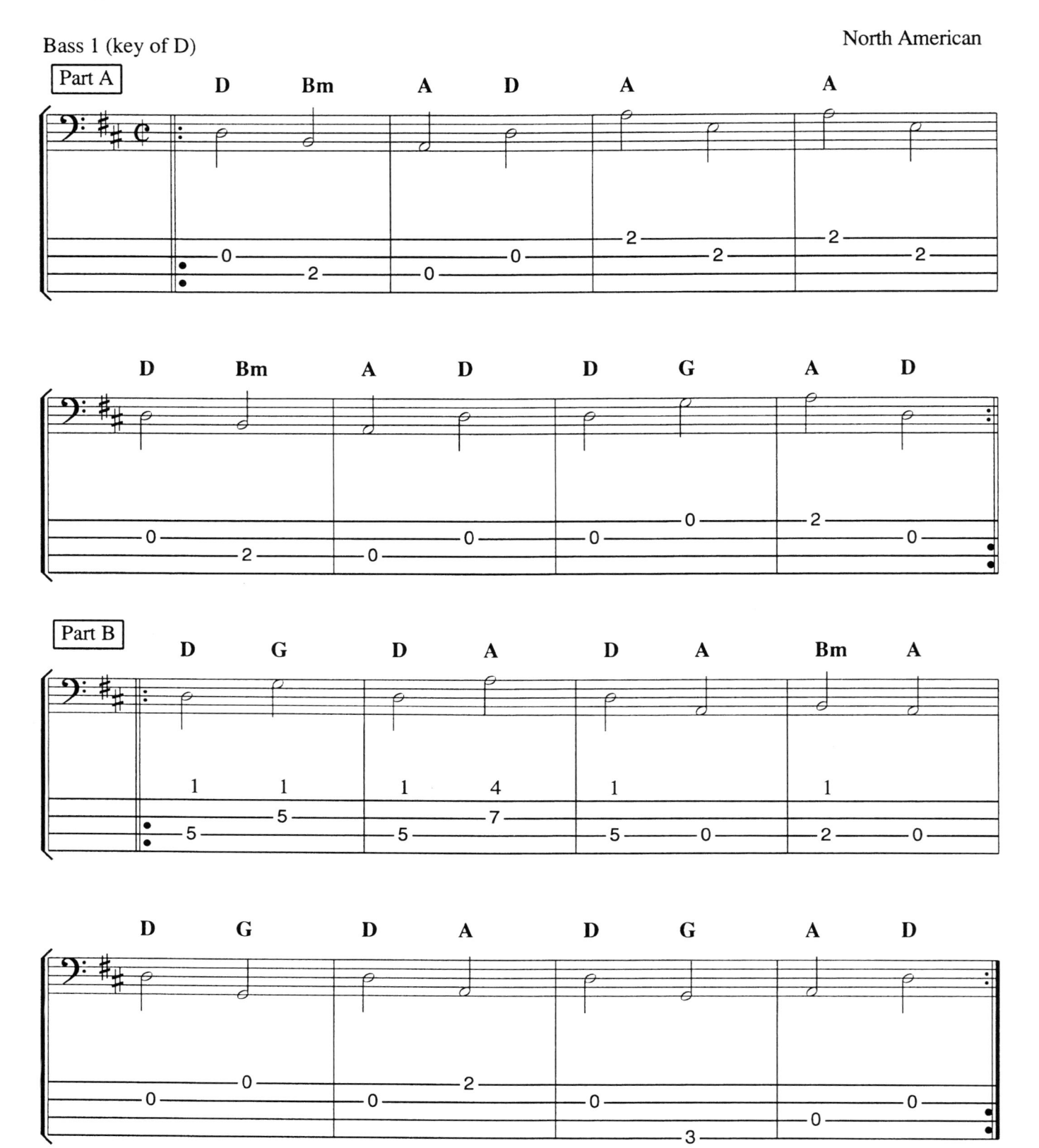

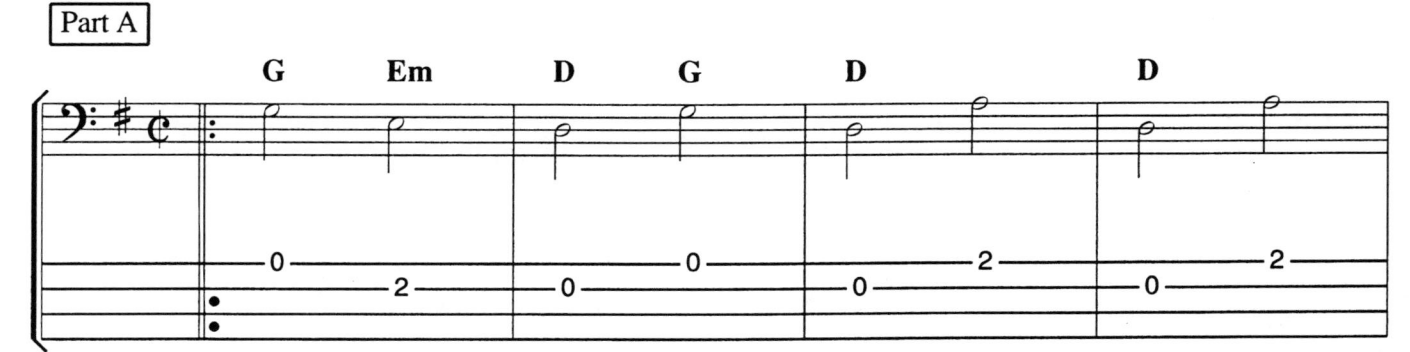

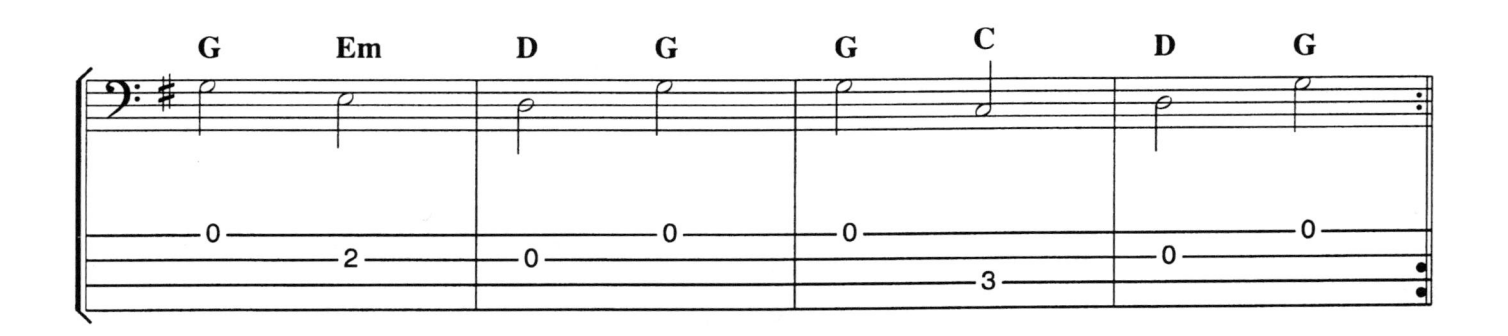

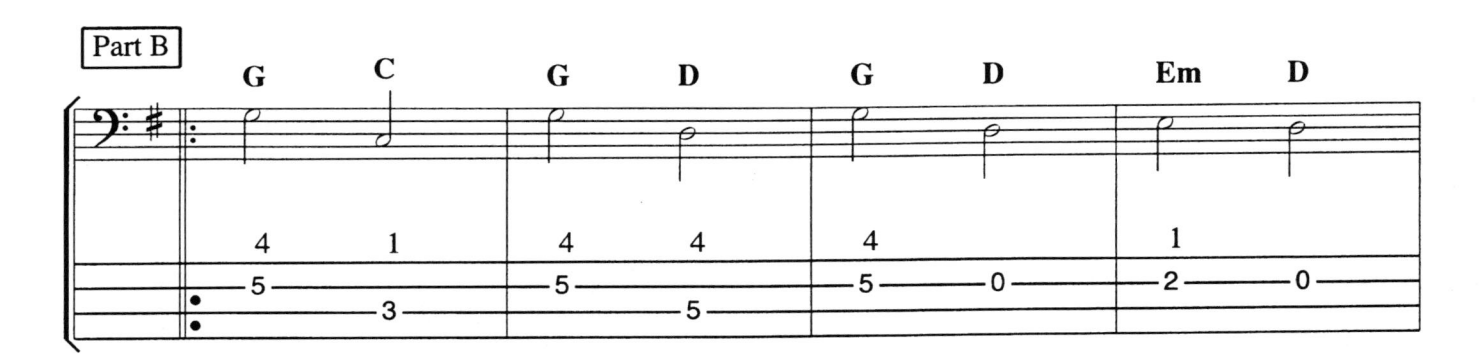

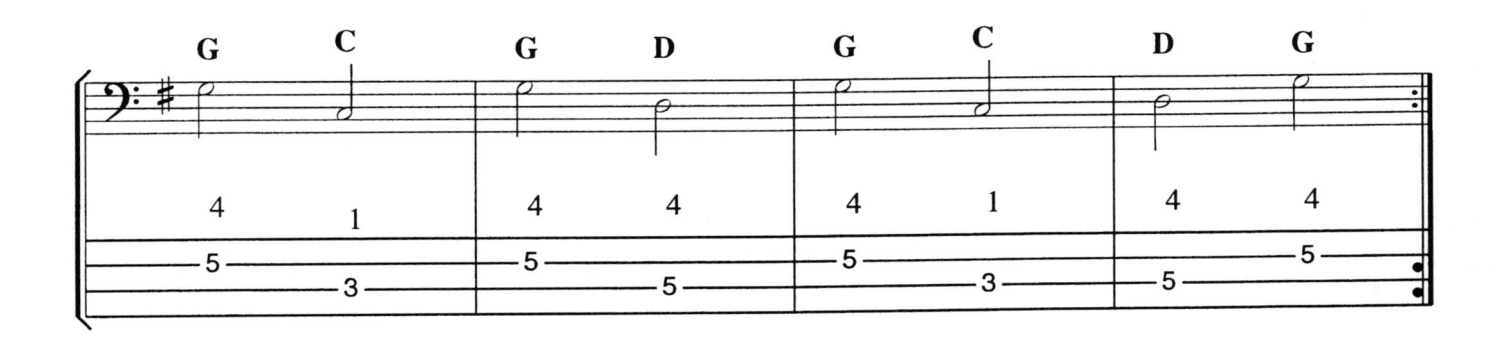

Arkansas Traveler

Arkansas Traveler

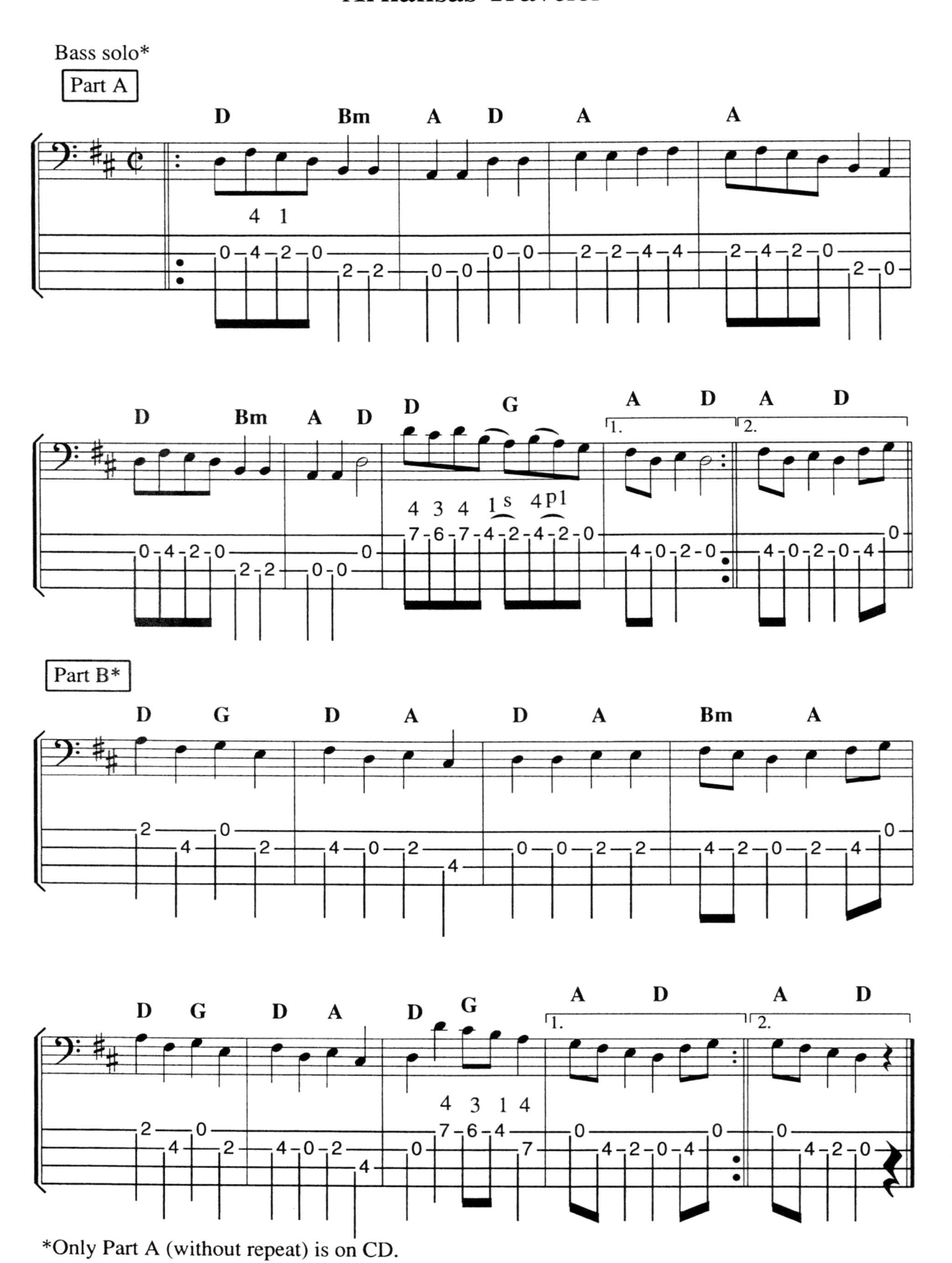

Bass solo*

*Only Part A (without repeat) is on CD.

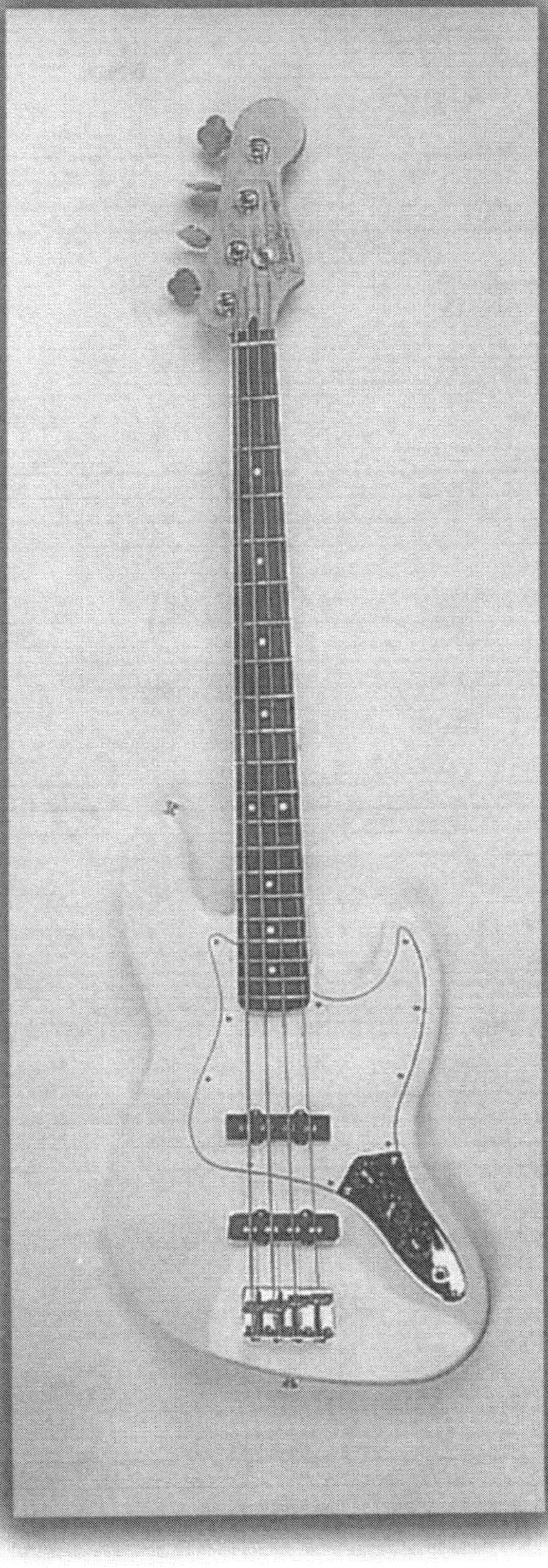

Disc 1
Track 3

Aura Lee

Bass 1*

Irish

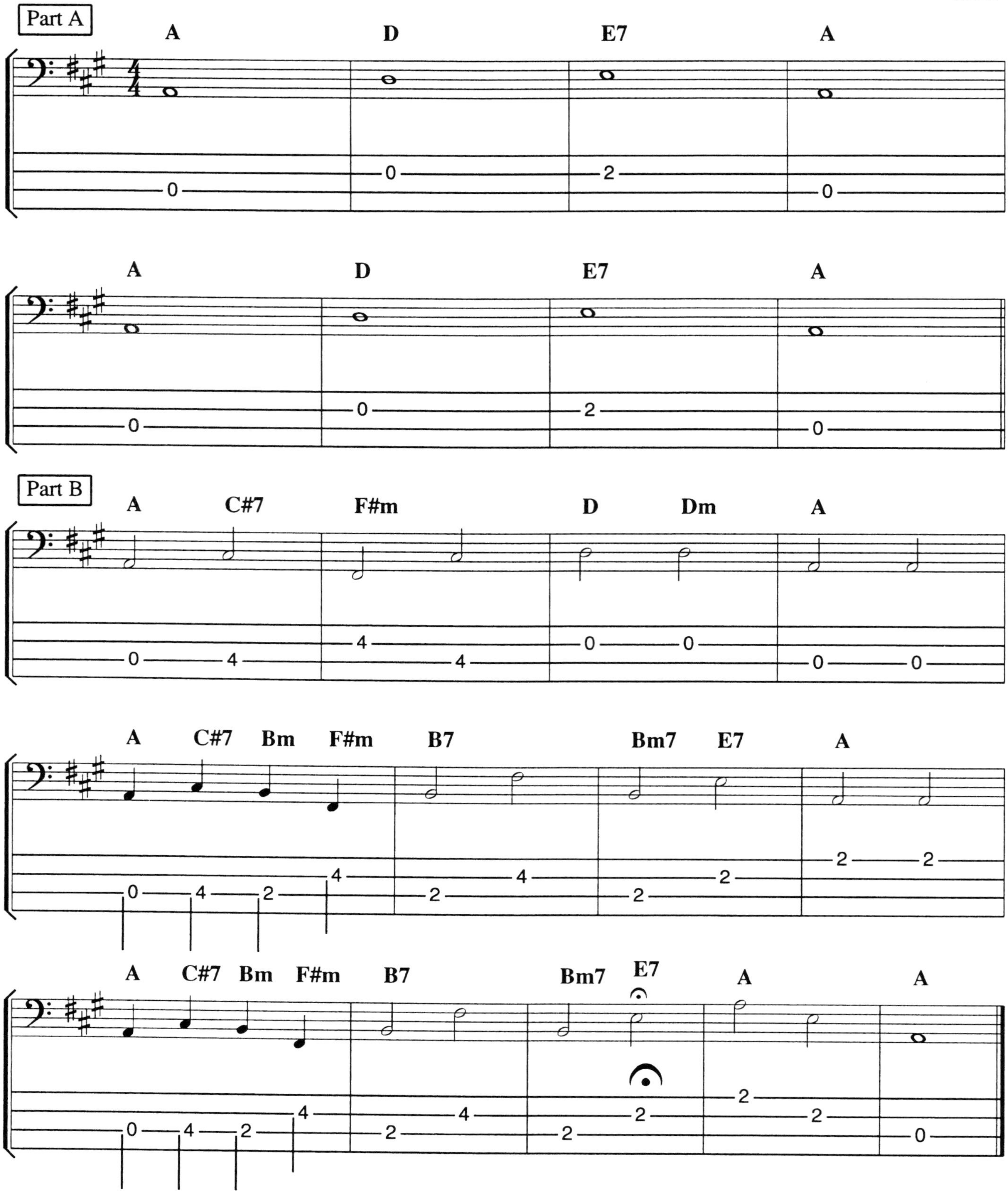

*Bass 1 is not on CD.

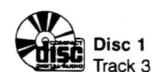

Aura Lee

*Bass solo**

*Bass solo is not on CD.

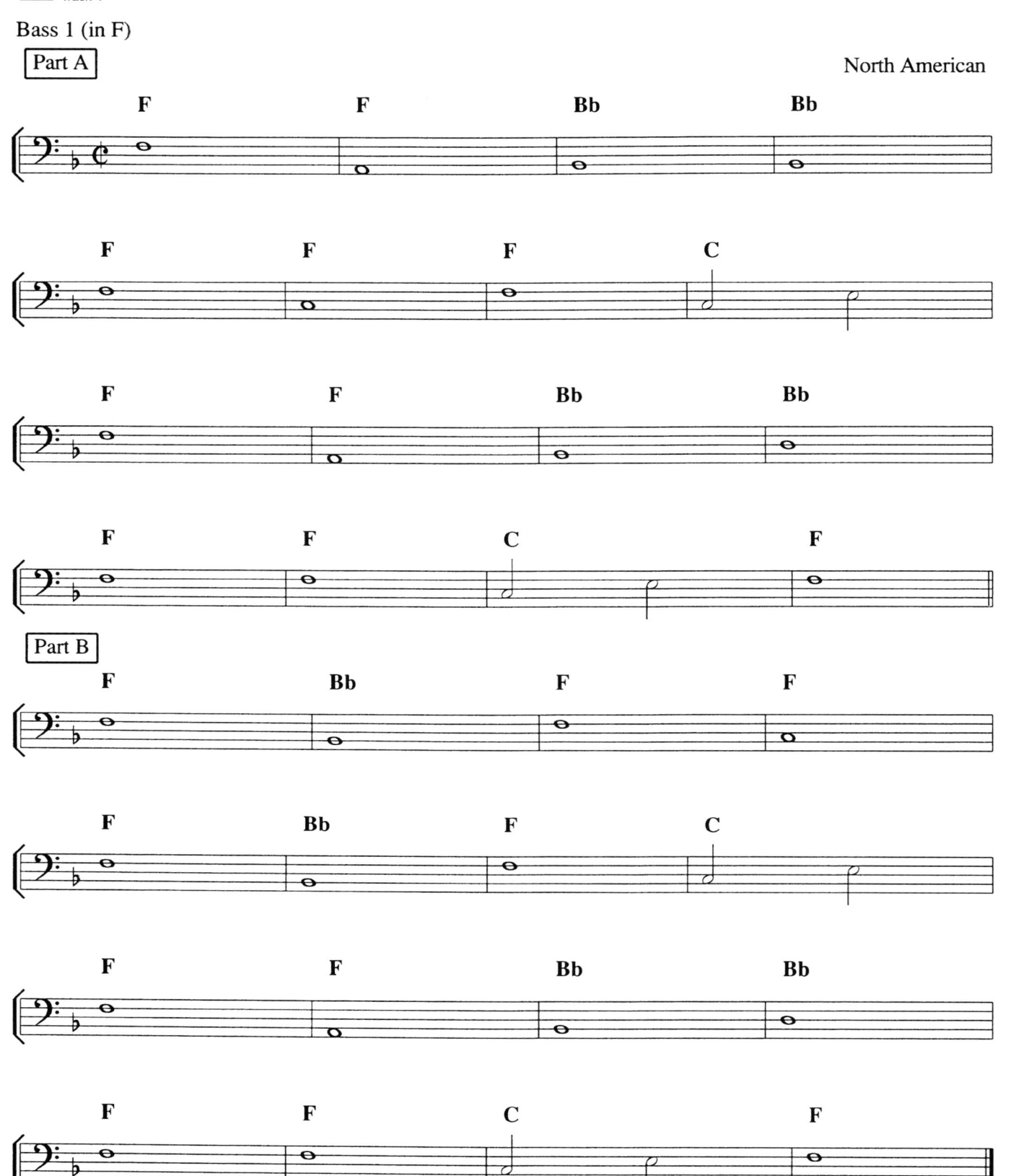

The Battle Cry of Freedom

Disc 1 Track 4

Bass 1 (in F)

North American

Part A

Part B

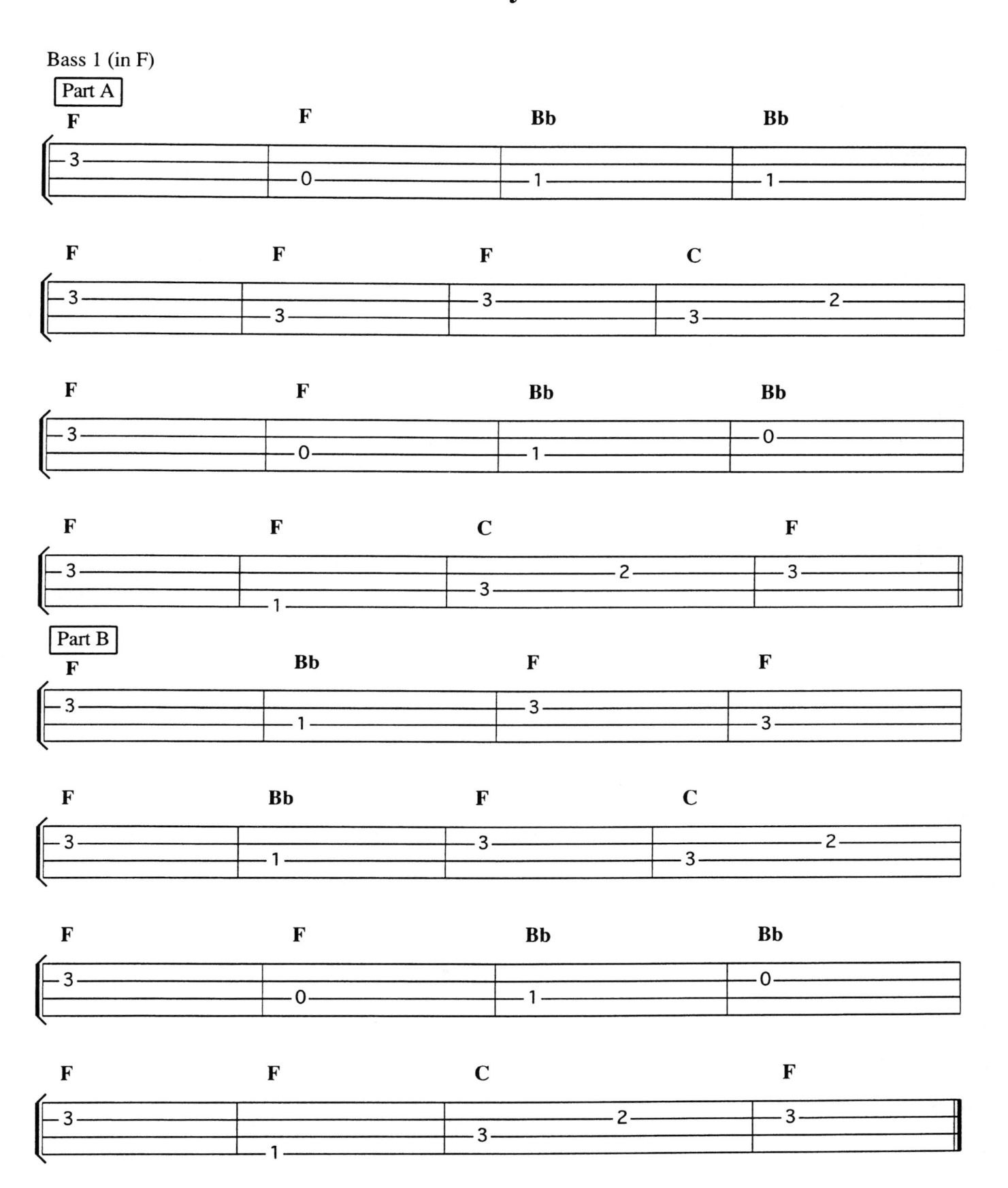

The Battle Cry of Freedom

Bass 1 (in F)

Part A

F	F	Bb	Bb
3	0	1	1

F	F	F	C
3 / 3	3	3 / 3	2 / 3

F	F	Bb	Bb
3	0	1	0

F	F	C	F
3	1	2 / 3	3

Part B

F	Bb	F	F
3	1	3	3

F	Bb	F	C
3	1	3	2 / 3

F	F	Bb	Bb
3	0	1	0

F	F	C	F
3	1	2 / 3	3

The Battle Cry of Freedom

Bass 1 (in G)

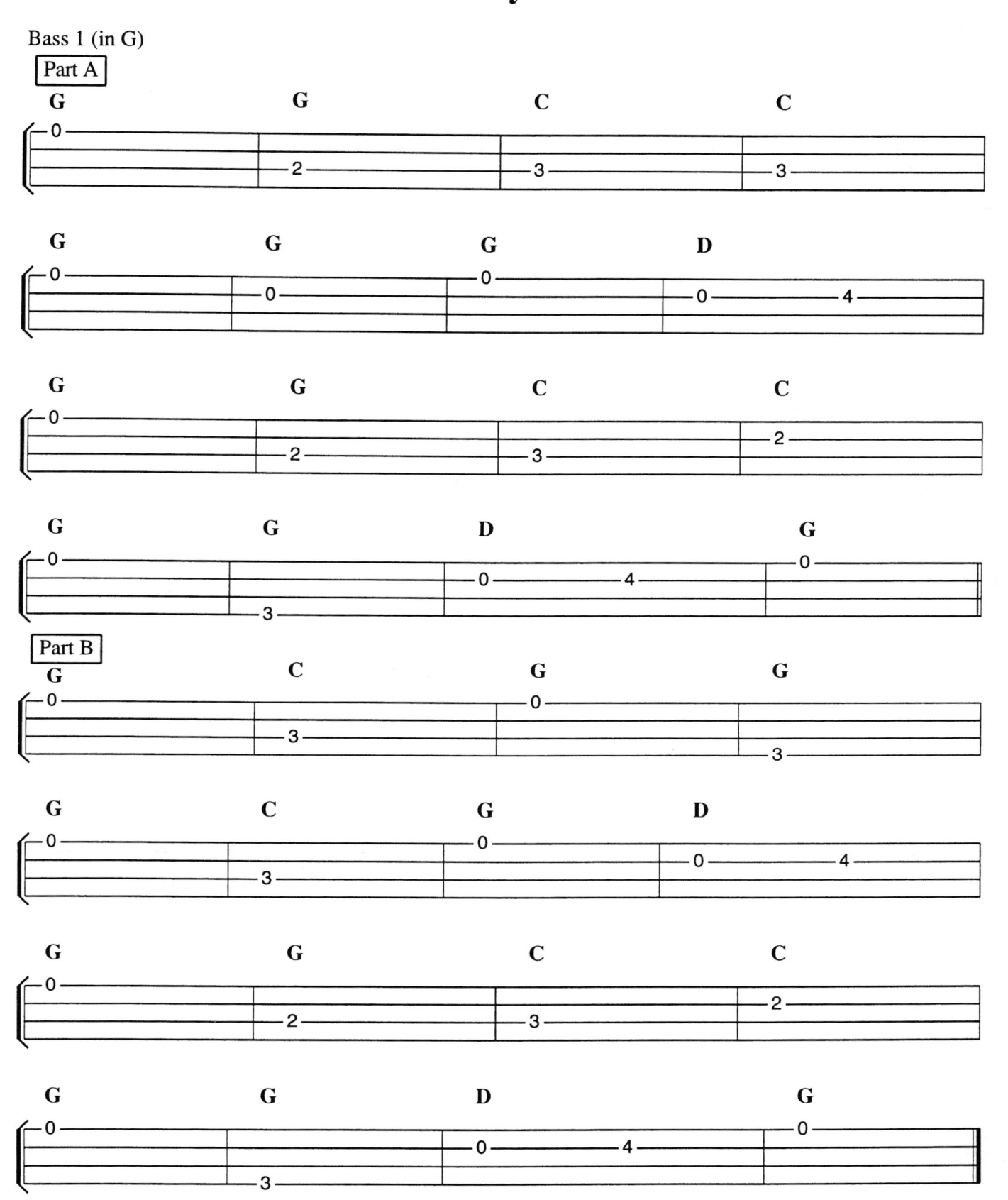

The Battle Cry of Freedom

Bass 1 (in G)

Part A

```
  G                G                C                C
|-0---------------|----------------|----------------|----------------|
|-----------------|-----2----------|-----3----------|-----3----------|
|-----------------|----------------|----------------|----------------|
|-----------------|----------------|----------------|----------------|

  G                G                G                D
|-0---------------|----------------|--0-------------|----------------|
|-----------------|--0-------------|----------------|--0------4------|
|-----------------|----------------|----------------|----------------|
|-----------------|----------------|----------------|----------------|

  G                G                C                C
|-0---------------|----------------|----------------|----------------|
|-----------------|-----2----------|-----3----------|-----2----------|
|-----------------|----------------|----------------|----------------|
|-----------------|----------------|----------------|----------------|

  G                G                D                G
|-0---------------|----------------|----------------|--0-------------|
|-----------------|----------------|--0------4------|----------------|
|-----------------|-----3----------|----------------|----------------|
|-----------------|----------------|----------------|----------------|
```

Part B

```
  G                C                G                G
|-0---------------|----------------|--0-------------|----------------|
|-----------------|-----3----------|----------------|-----3----------|
|-----------------|----------------|----------------|----------------|
|-----------------|----------------|----------------|----------------|

  G                C                G                D
|-0---------------|----------------|--0-------------|----------------|
|-----------------|-----3----------|----------------|--0------4------|
|-----------------|----------------|----------------|----------------|
|-----------------|----------------|----------------|----------------|

  G                G                C                C
|-0---------------|----------------|----------------|----------------|
|-----------------|-----2----------|-----3----------|-----2----------|
|-----------------|----------------|----------------|----------------|
|-----------------|----------------|----------------|----------------|

  G                G                D                G
|-0---------------|----------------|----------------|--0-------------|
|-----------------|----------------|--0------4------|----------------|
|-----------------|-----3----------|----------------|----------------|
|-----------------|----------------|----------------|----------------|
```

Beaumont Rag

Disc 1
Track 5

Bass 1 (for guitar)

North American

Parts A and B*

*First time through = A, 2nd time = B, 3rd time = A, and 4th time = B.

Beaumont Rag

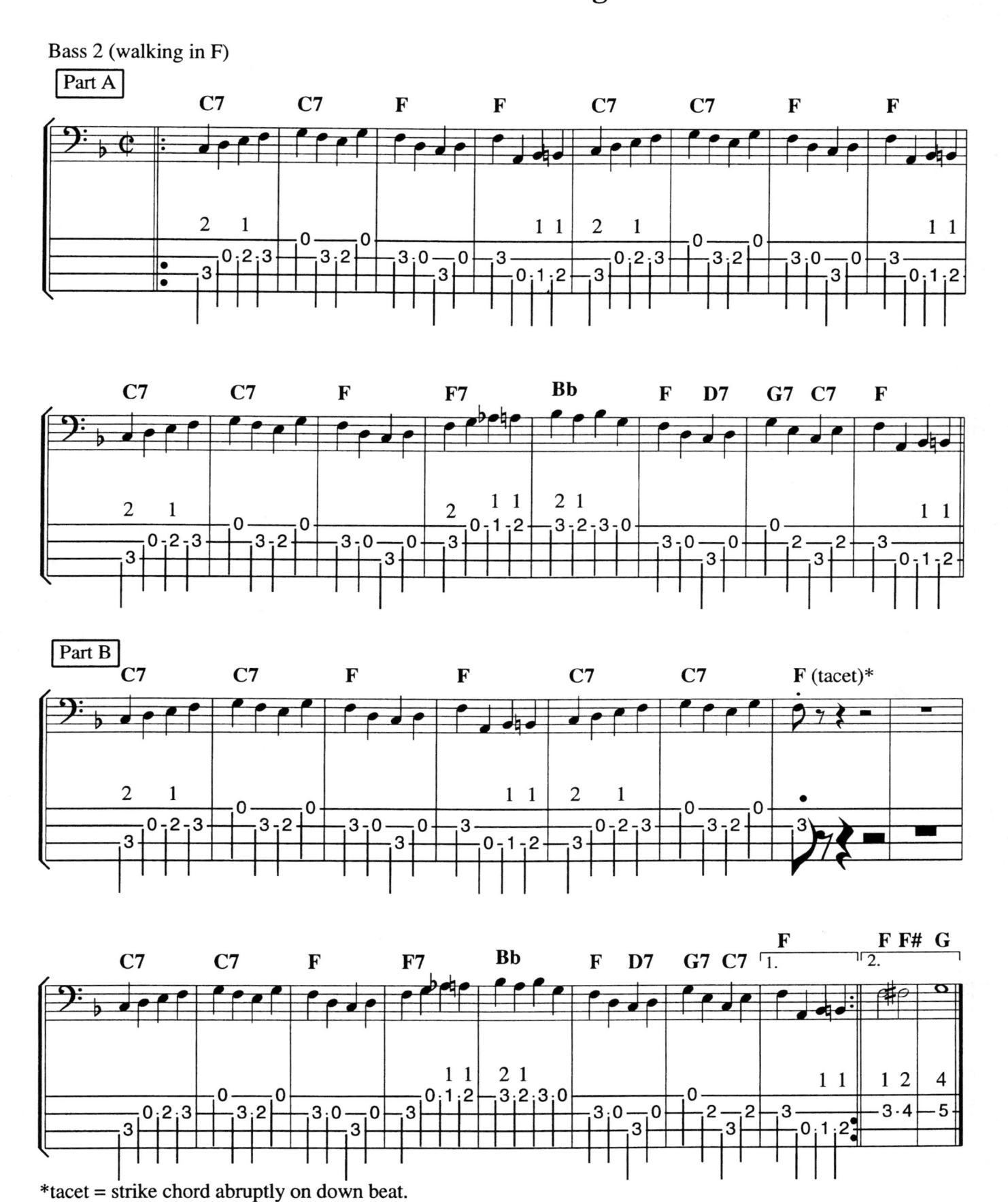

*tacet = strike chord abruptly on down beat.

Billy in the Lowground

Bass 1

North American

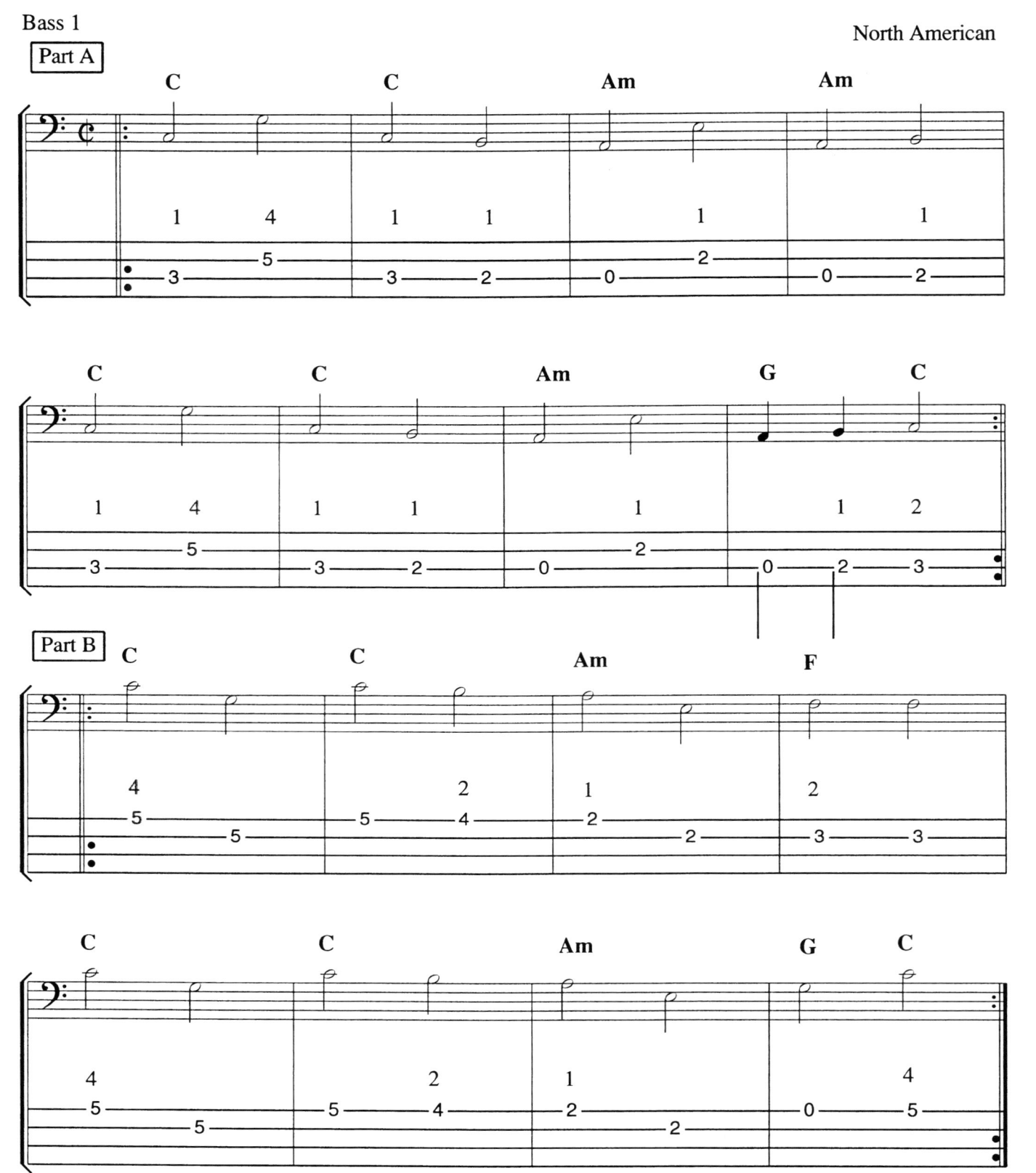

Billy in the Lowground

Bass 2*

Part A

*Bass 2 is not on CD.

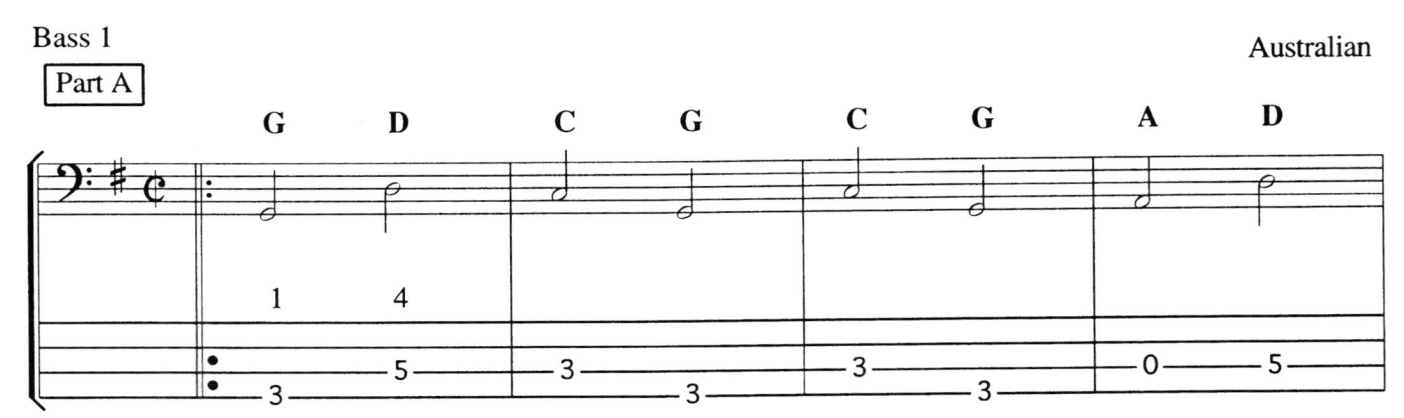

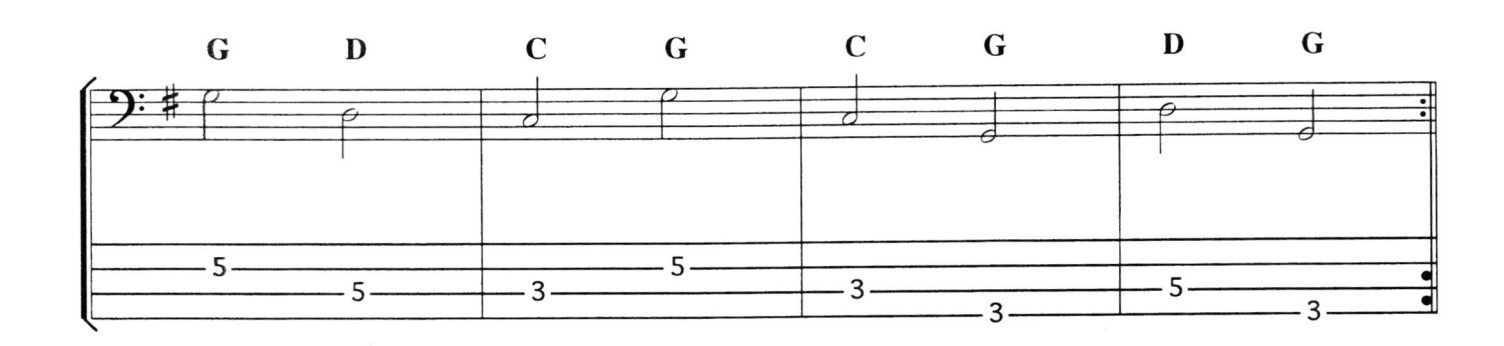

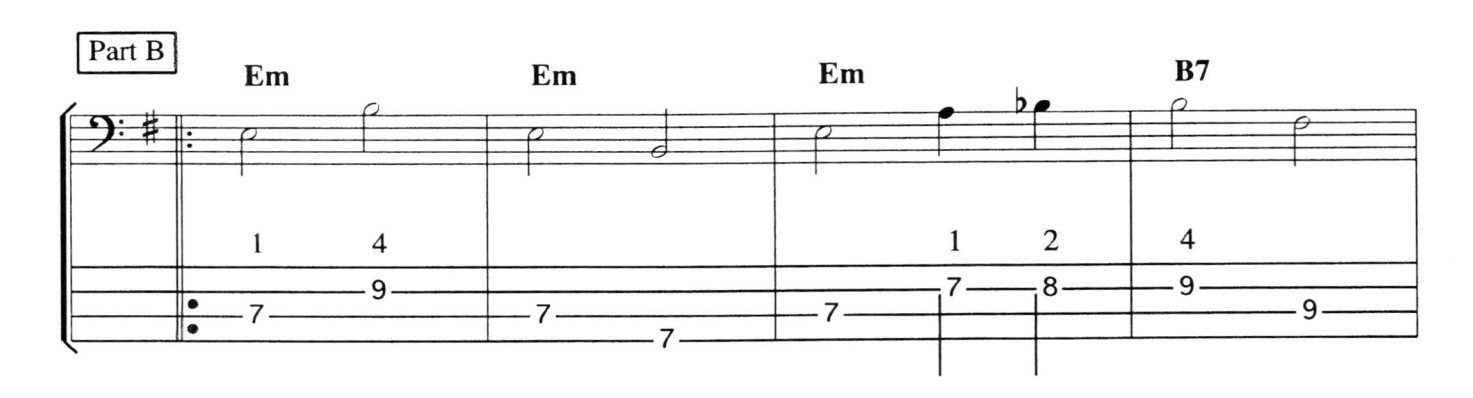

Blackberry Blossom

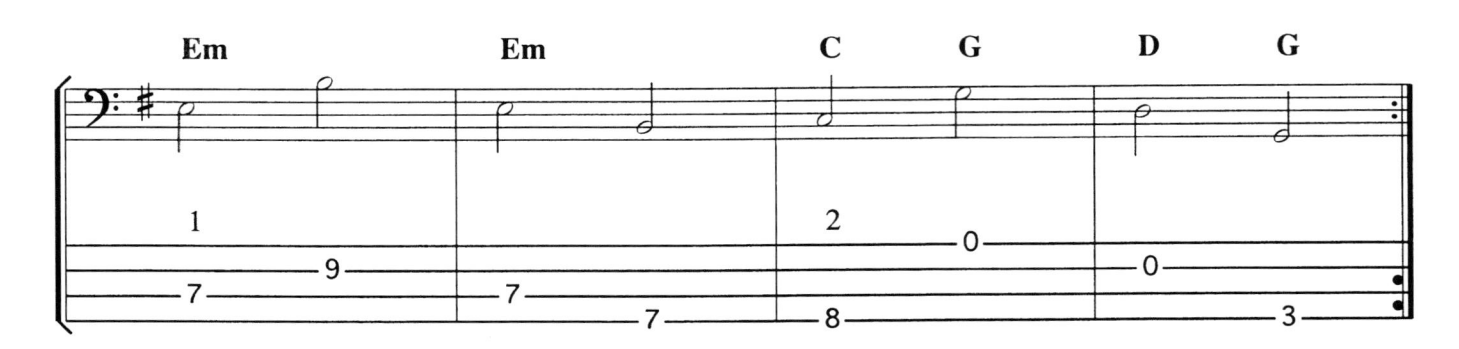

Blackberry Blossom

Bass 2*

*Bass 2 is not on CD.

Disc 1
Track 8

Bonaparte's Retreat

Bass 1 (melody 1)

North American

Part A

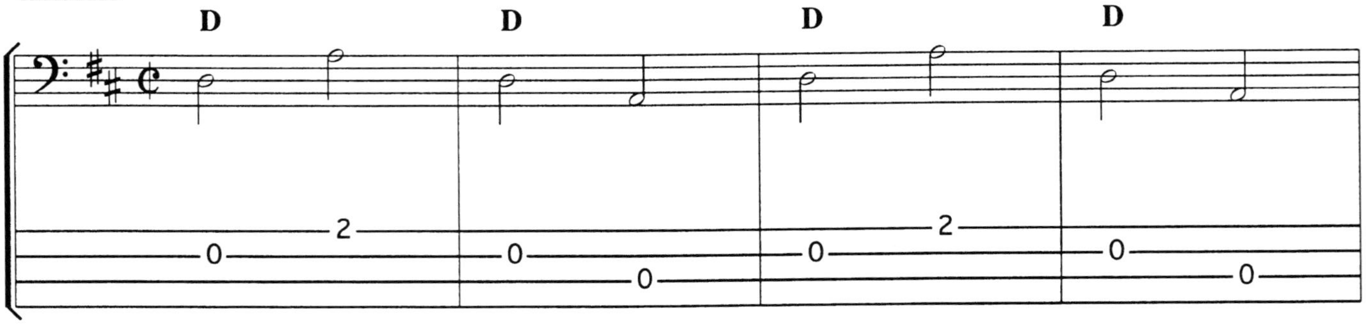

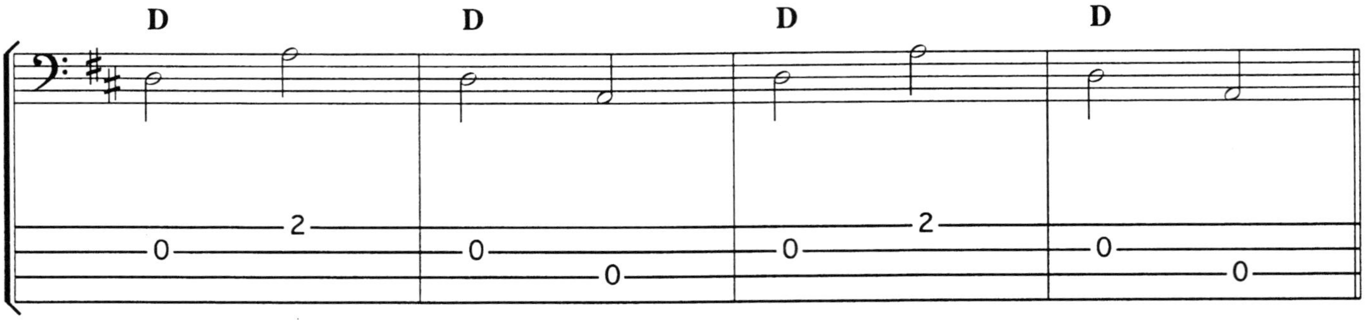

Part B

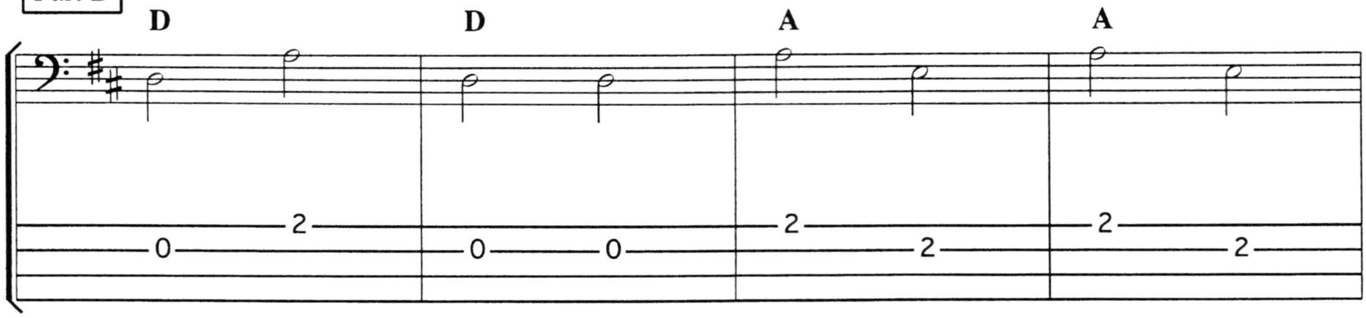

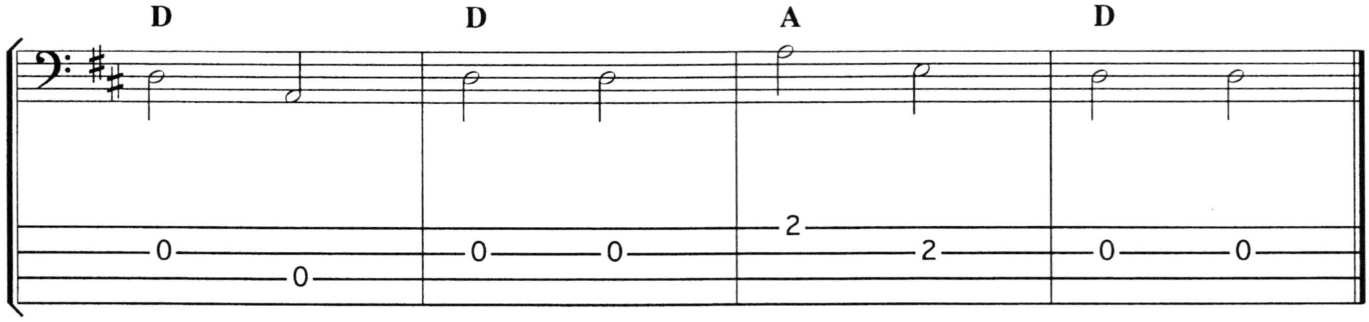

Bonaparte's Retreat

Bass 1 (melody 2)

Bonaparte's Retreat

Bass (solo)*

Carthage Waltz

Bass 1

North American

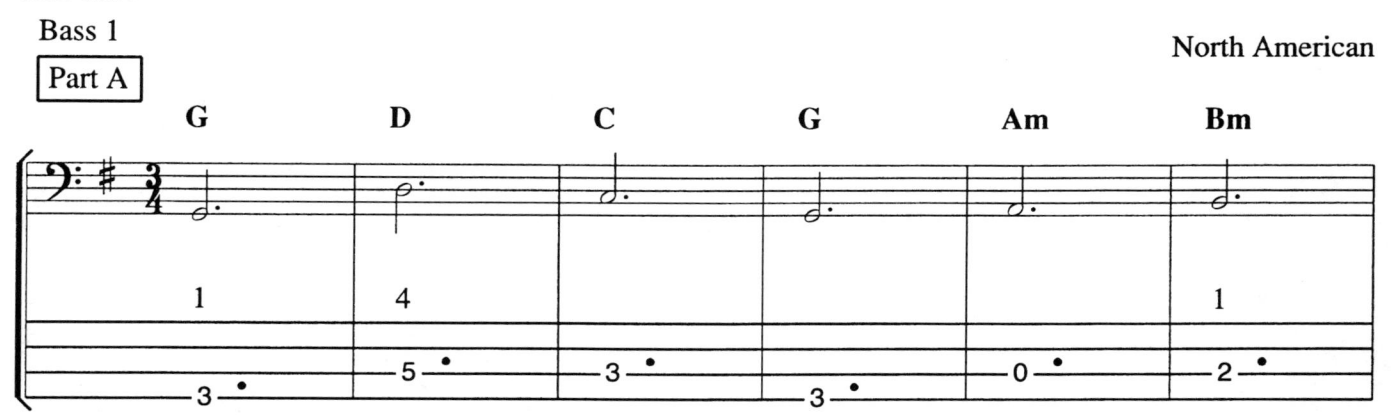

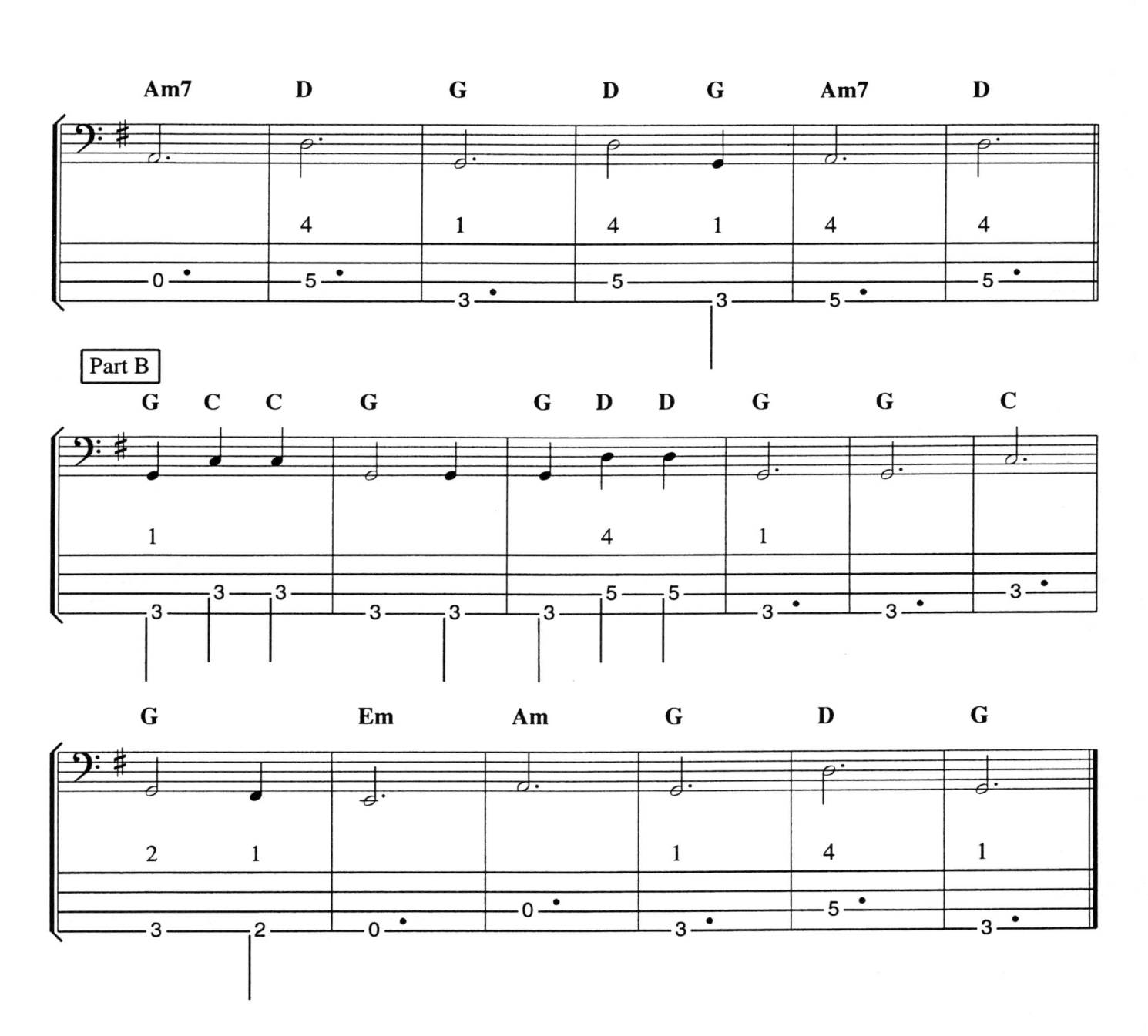

Carthage Waltz

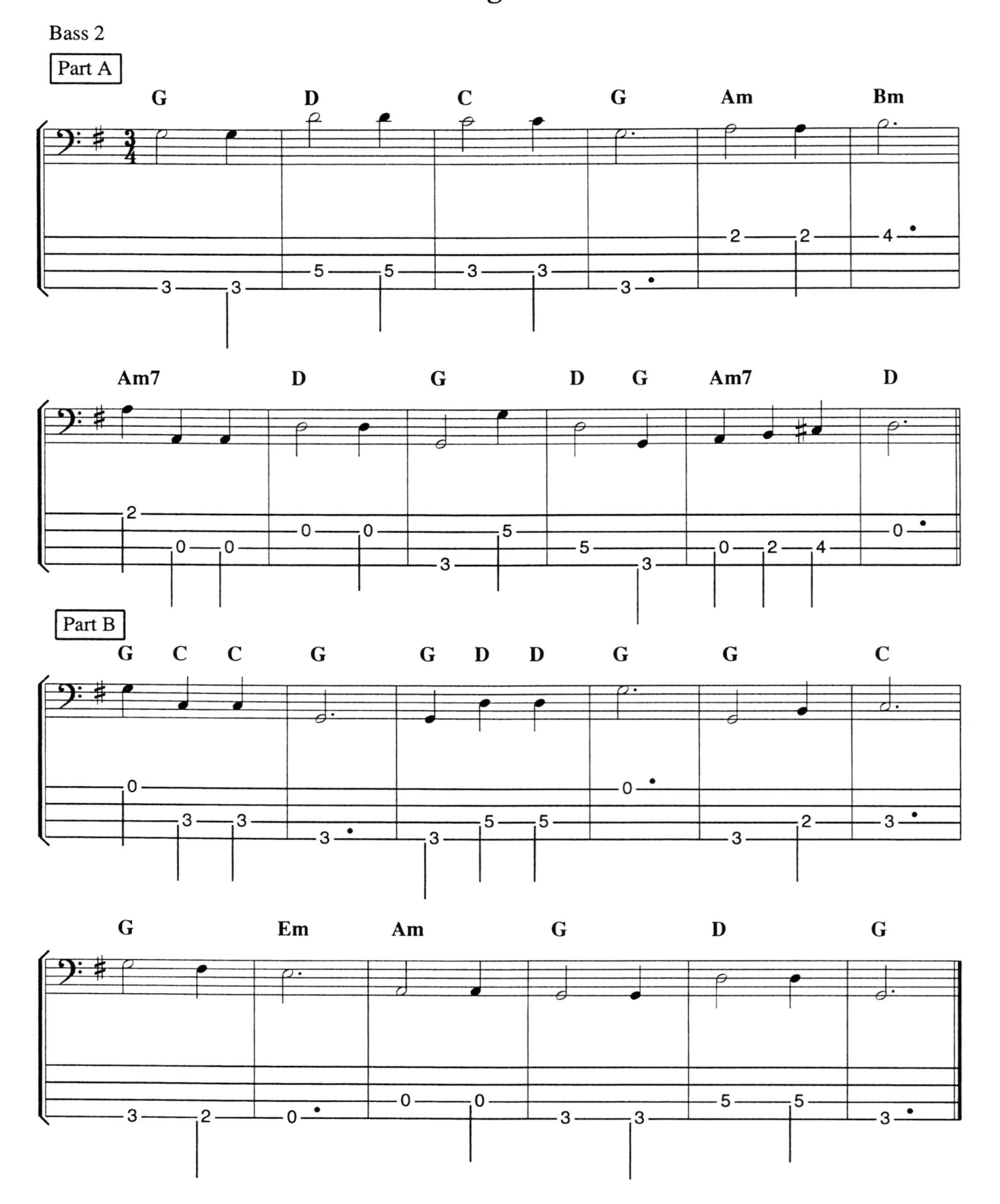

Carthage Waltz

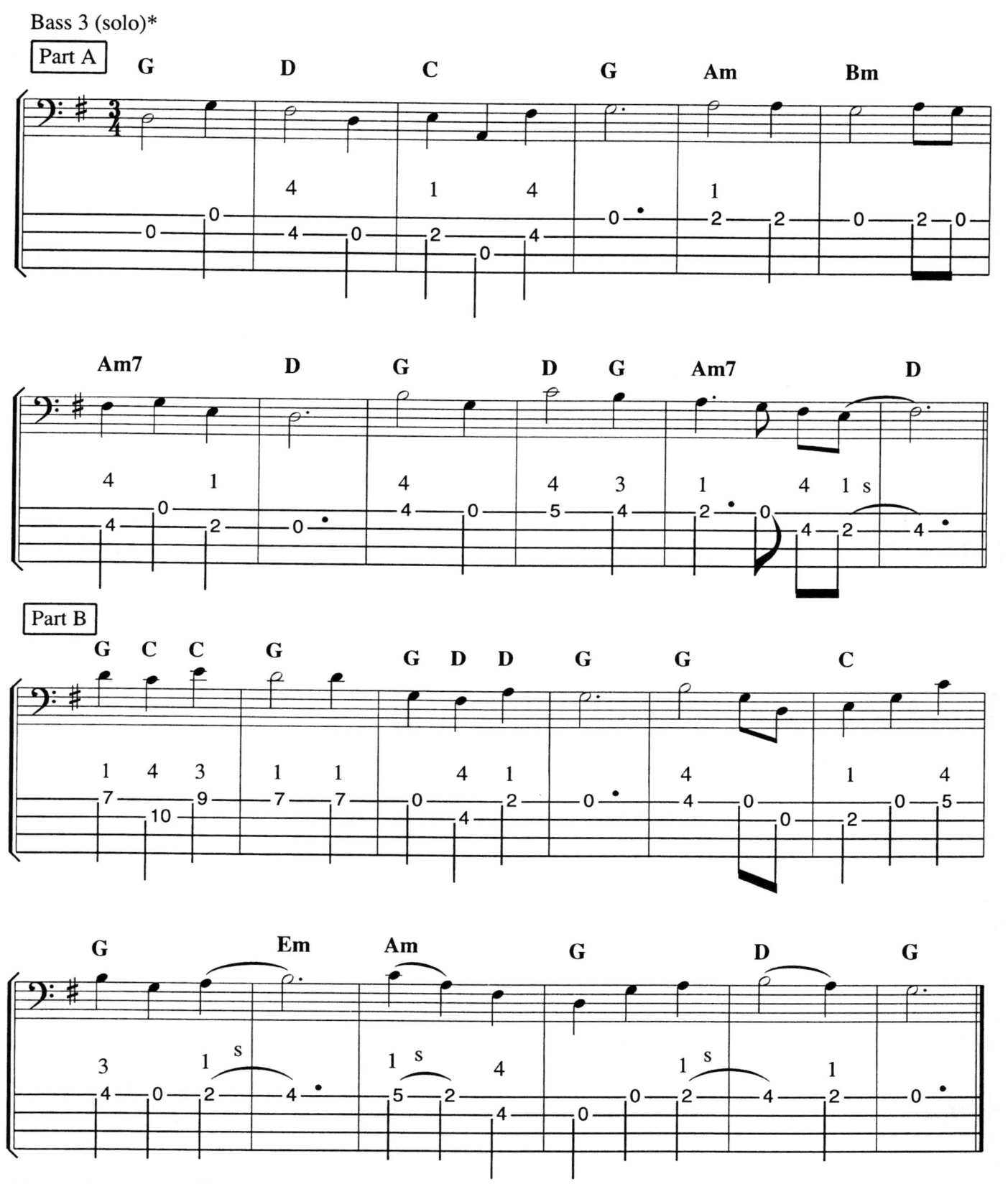

*Bass solo is not on CD.

Cherokee Shuffle

Bass 1

North American

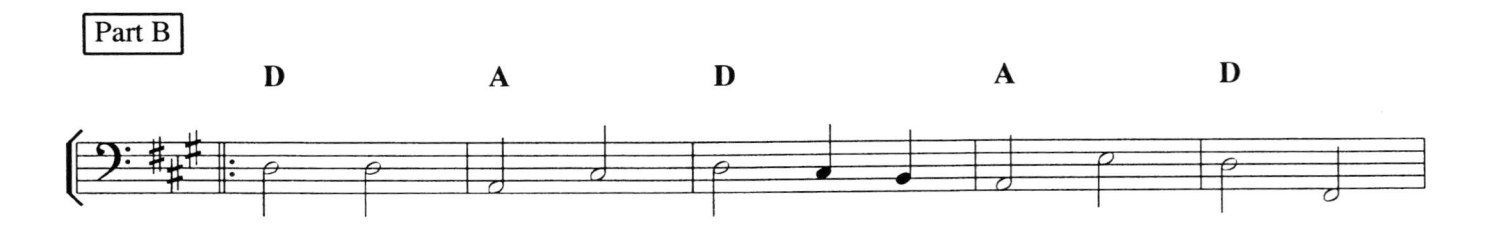

Part A

Cherokee Shuffle

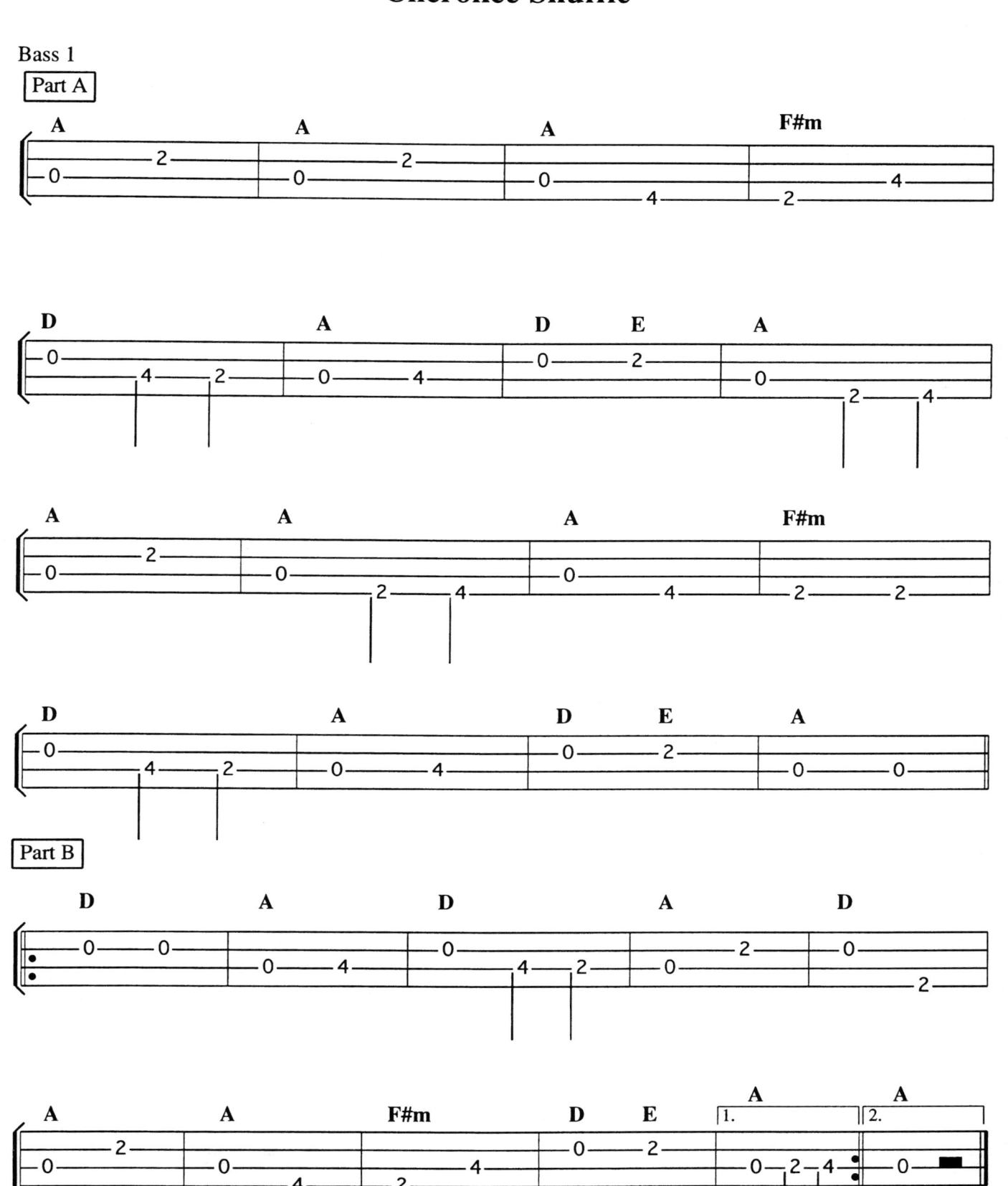

Bass 1

Part A

```
   A              A              A              F#m
|--0---2------|--0---2------|--0----------|-------------4-|
|-------------|-------------|--------4----|---2-----------|
```

```
   D              A              D    E         A
|--0----------|--0----------|--0---2------|--0------------|
|------4---2--|-------4-----|-------------|-------2----4--|
```

```
   A              A              A              F#m
|--0---2------|--0----------|--0----------|-------------2-|
|-------------|-------2--4--|--------4----|---2-----------|
```

```
   D              A              D    E         A
|--0----------|--0----------|--0---2------|--0------0-----|
|------4---2--|-------4-----|-------------|---------------|
```

Part B

```
   D         A         D         A         D
|:-0---0---|-------0--|----------|-------2-|--0----------|
|:--------|--0---4---|--4---2---|--0------|----------2--|
```

```
   A              A              F#m            D    E    [1. A        [2. A
|--0---2------|--0----------|-------------|--0---2------|-----------|--0------|
|-------------|-------4-----|---4----2----|-------------|---0-2-4:--|---------|
```

Cherokee Shuffle

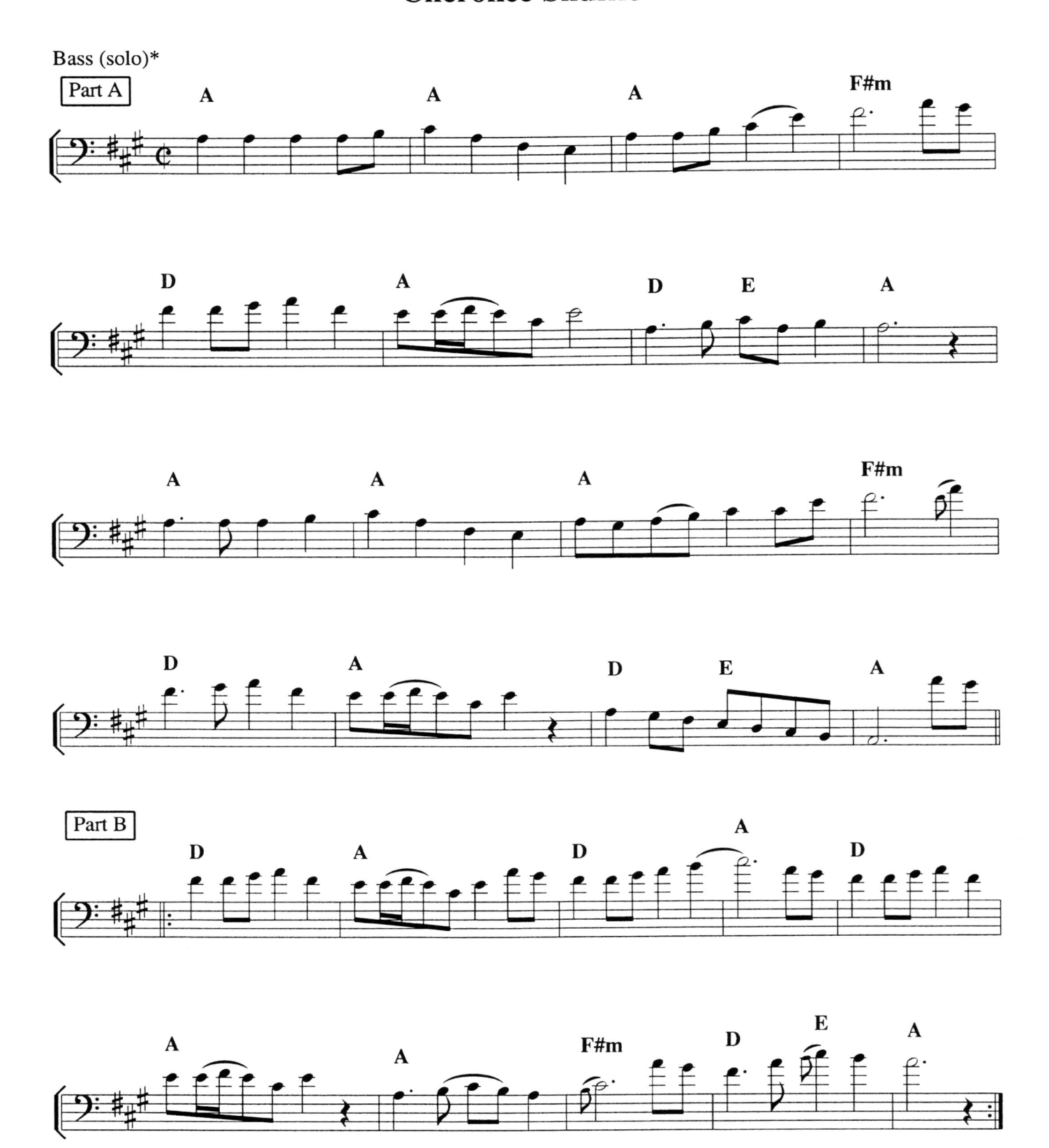

*Bass solo is not on CD.

Cherokee Shuffle

*Bass (solo)**

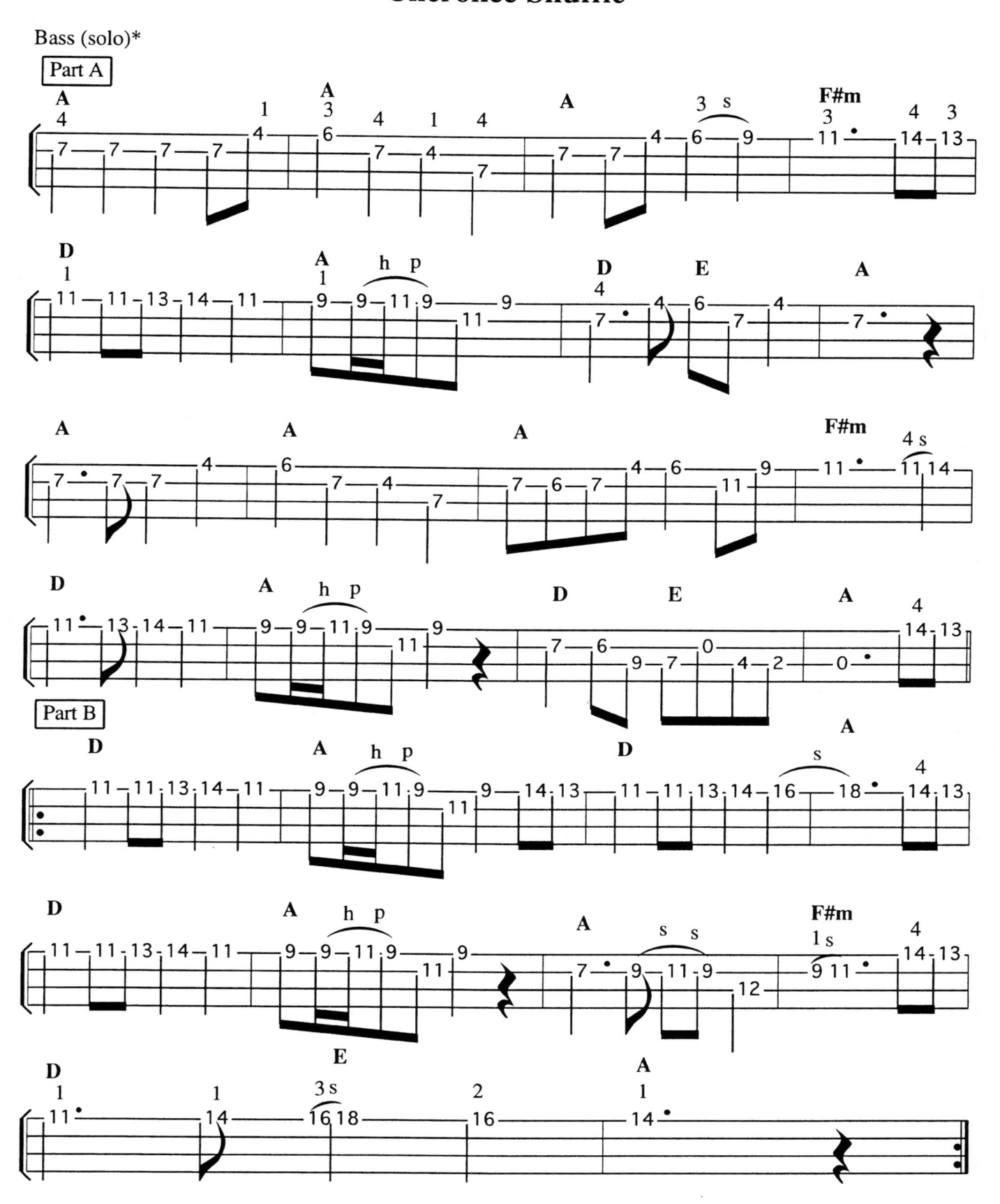

*Bass solo is not on CD.

Cluck Old Hen

Bass 1 — North American

Part A

Cluck Old Hen

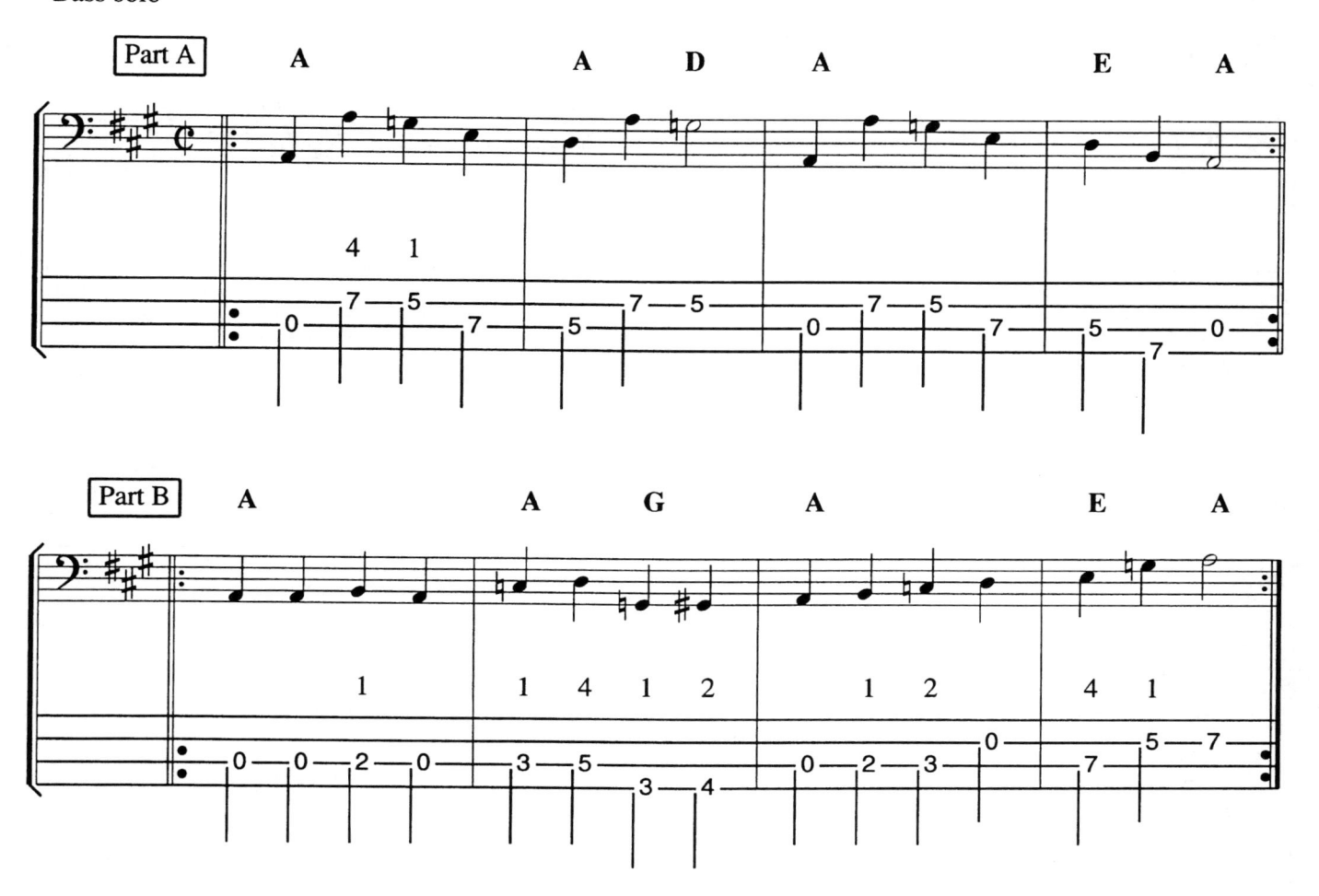

Disc 1
Track 12

Cotton-eyed Joe

Bass 1 (key of A)

North American

Part A

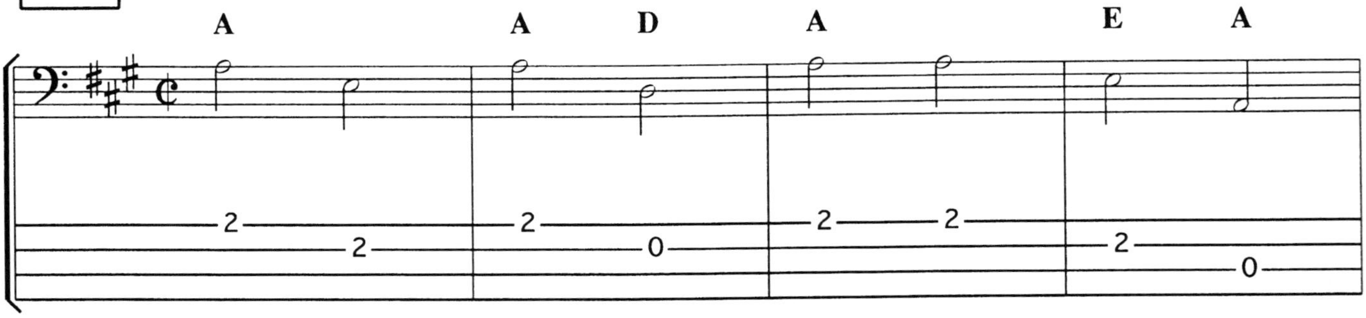

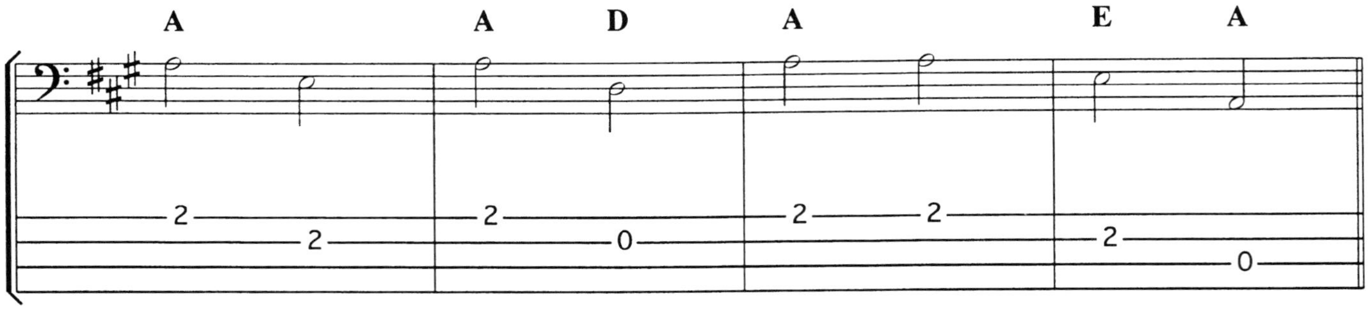

Part B

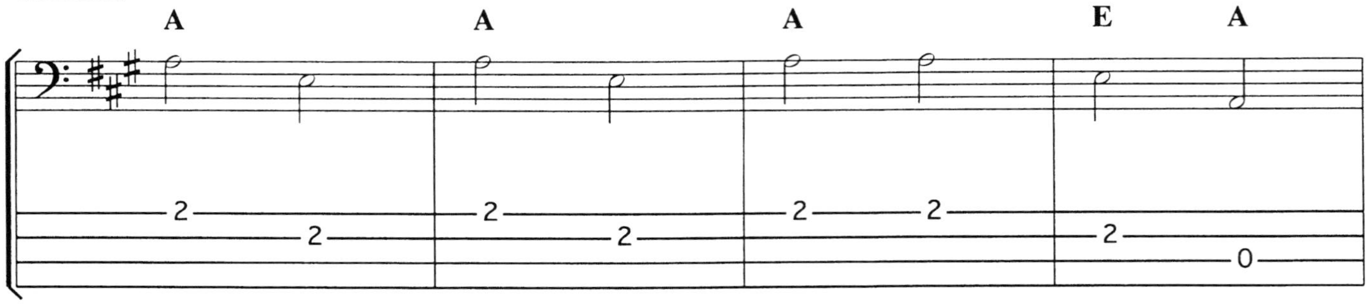

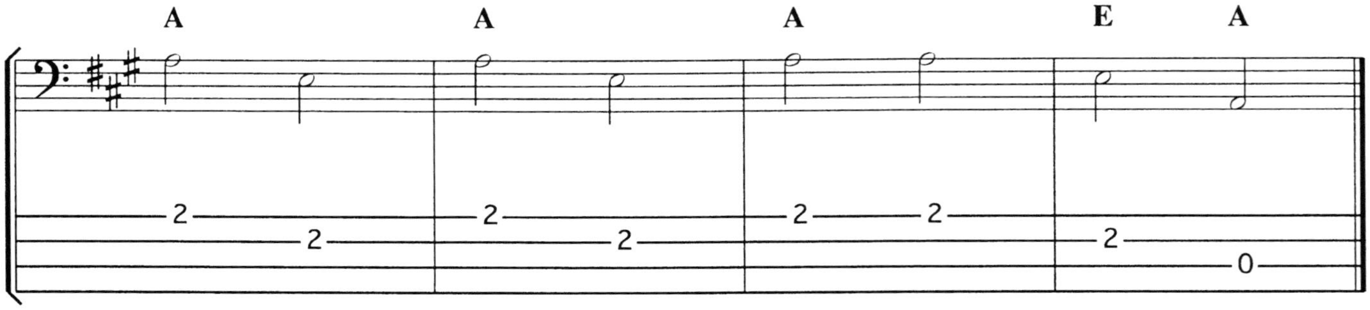

Cotton-eyed Joe

Bass 1 (key of D)

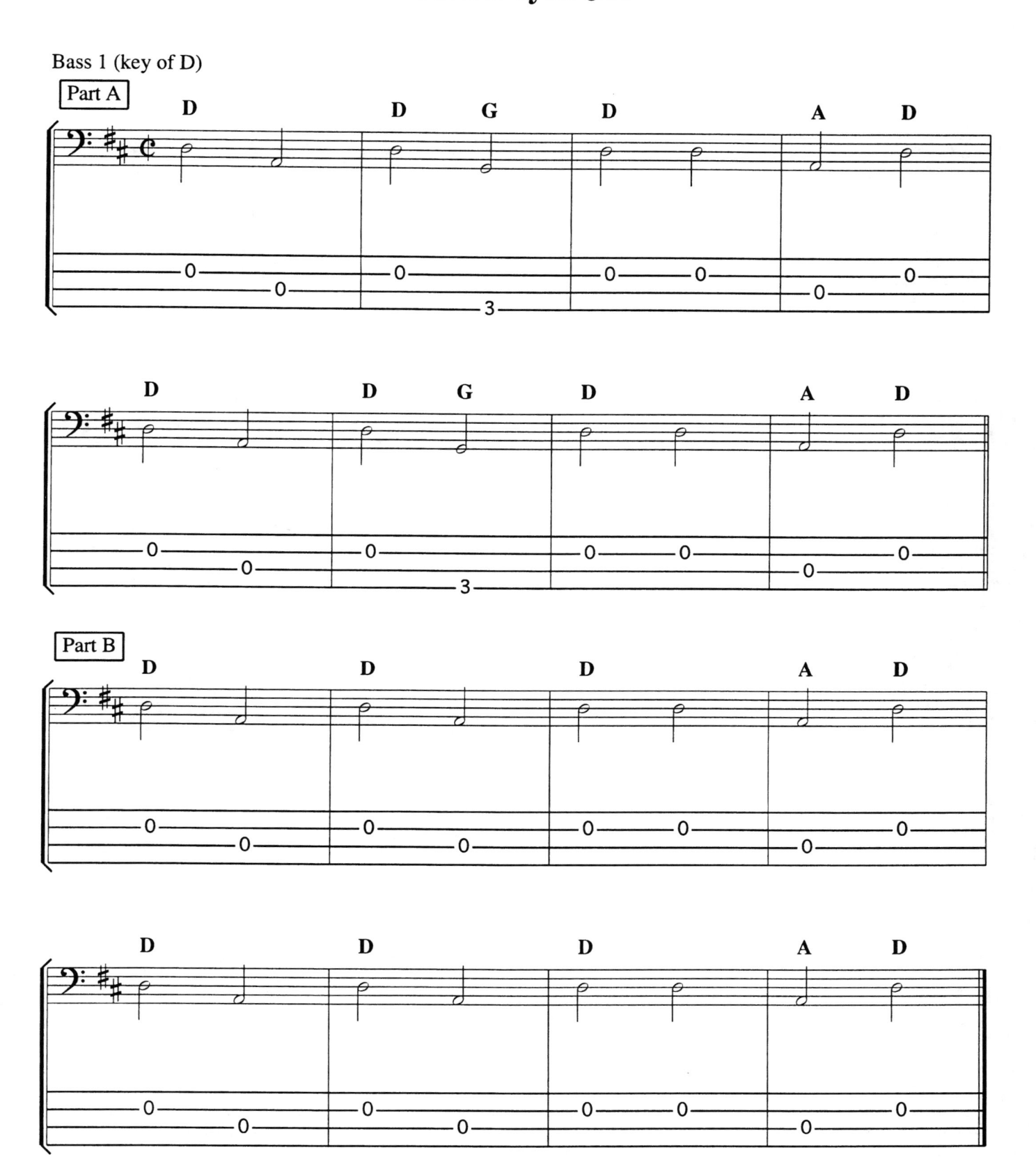

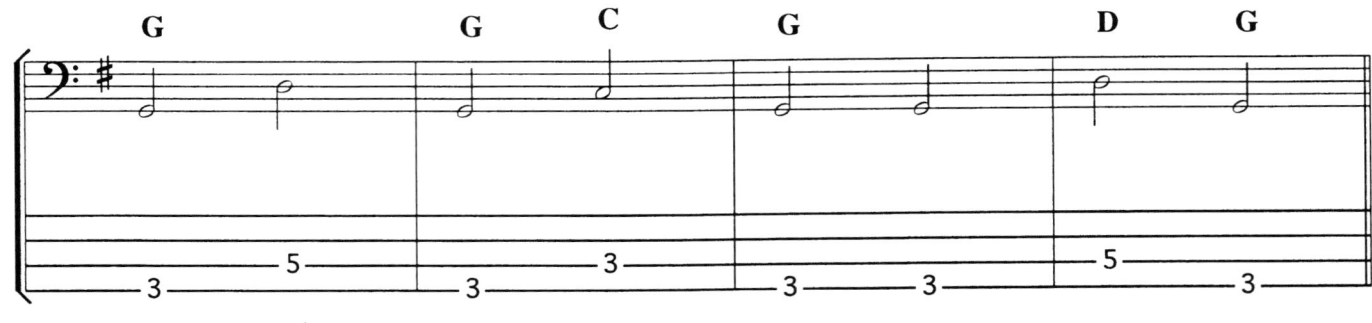

Cotton-eyed Joe

Bass 1 (key of G)

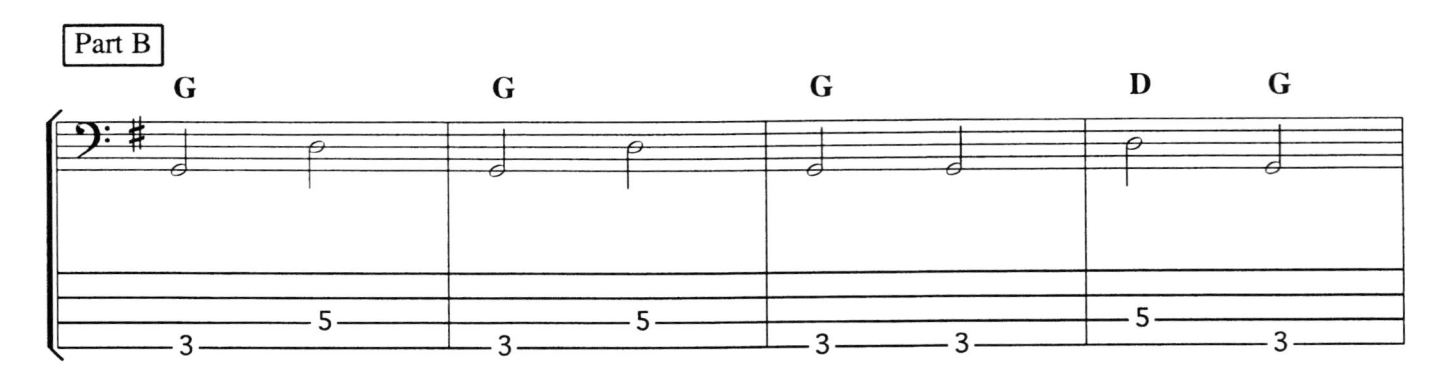

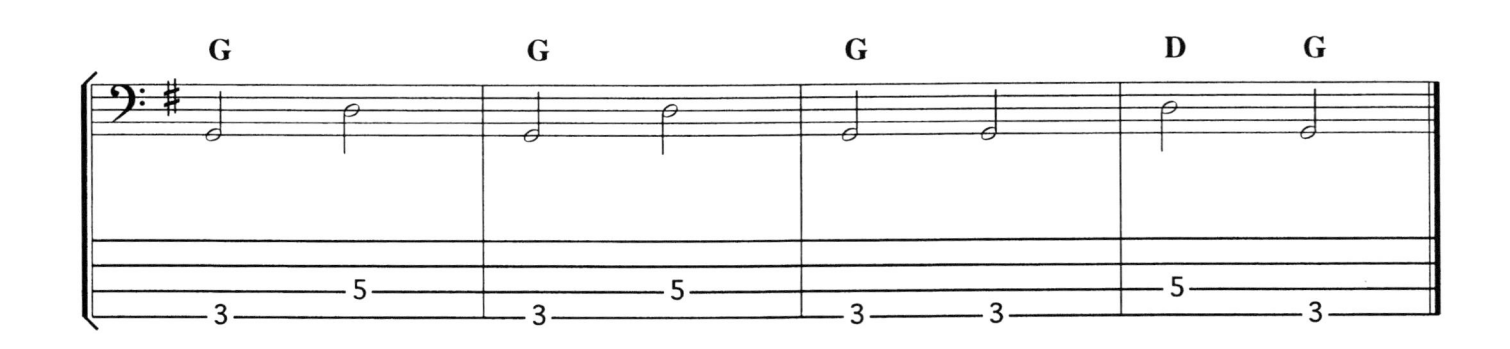

Cotton-eyed Joe

Bass solo* (key of D)

*Bass solo is not on CD.

Cotton Patch Rag

Bass 1

North American

Parts A/E

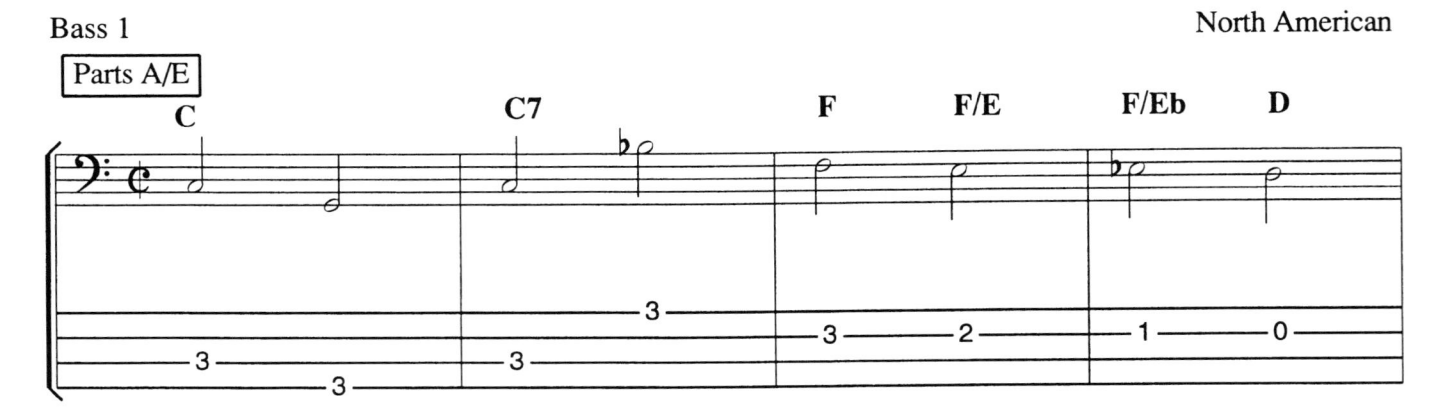

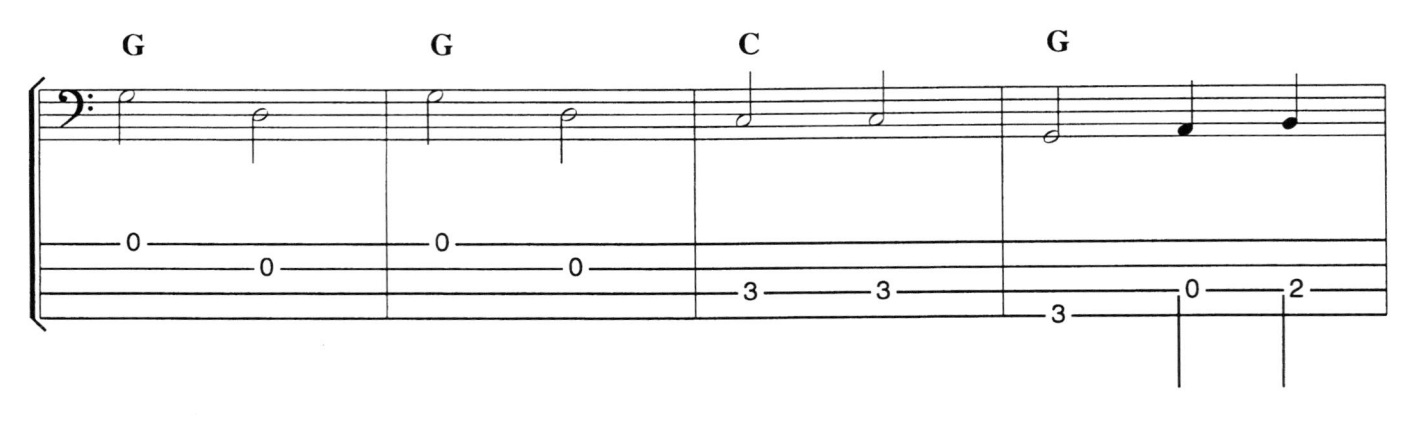

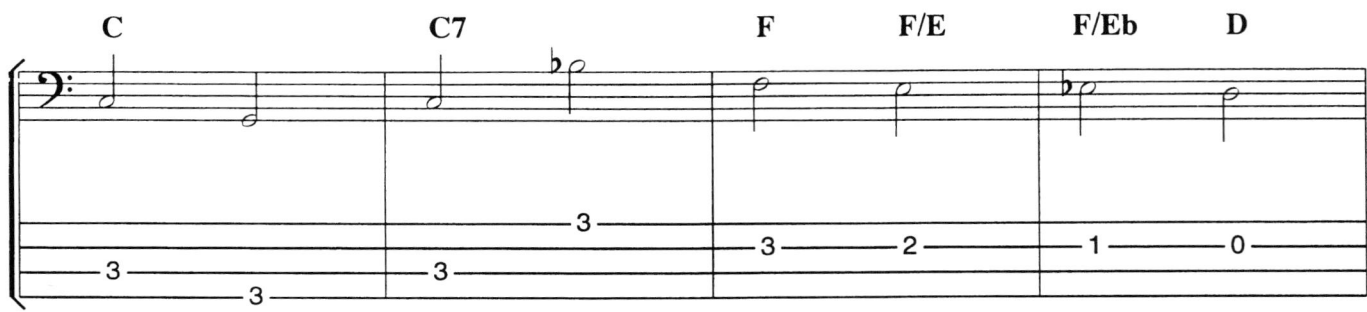

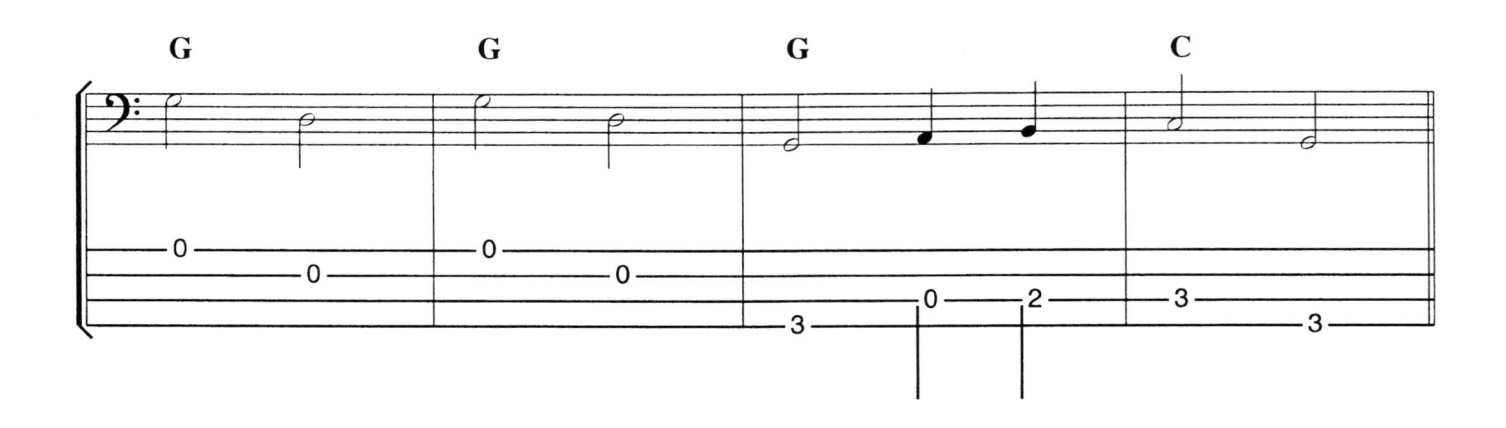

Cotton Patch Rag

Bass 1 (cont.)

Part B

Cotton Patch Rag

Bass 1 (cont.)

Parts C/D

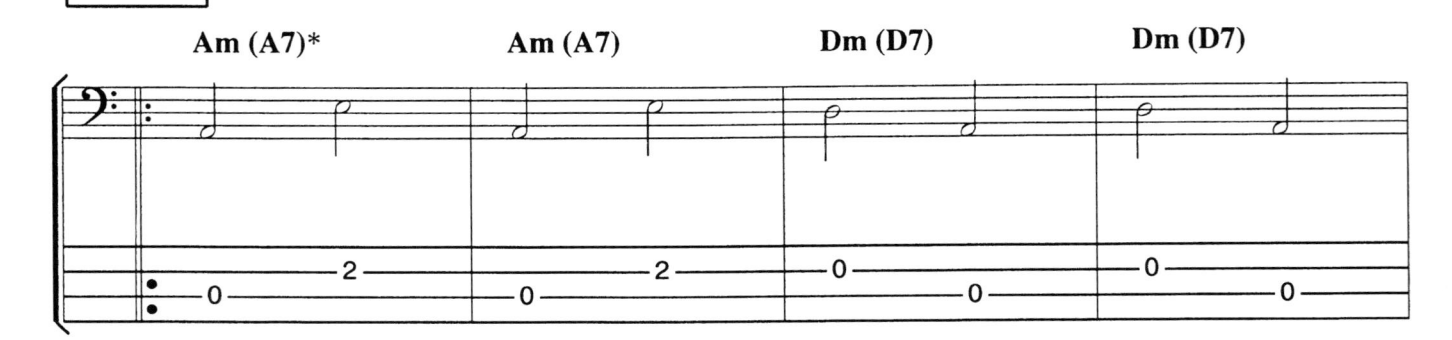

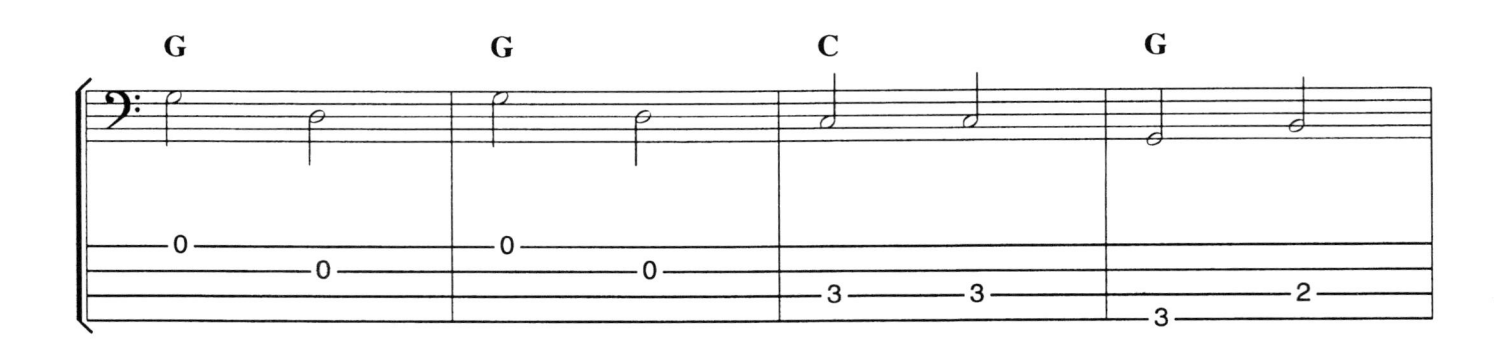

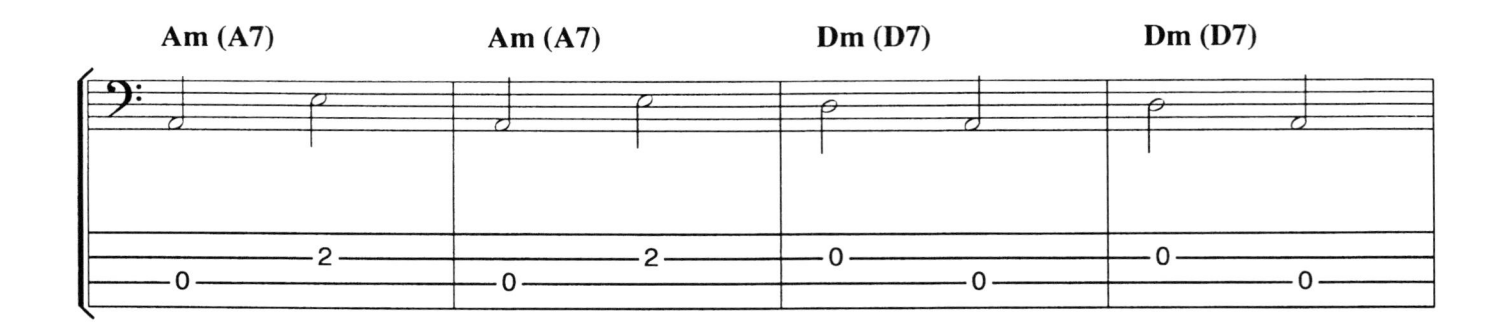

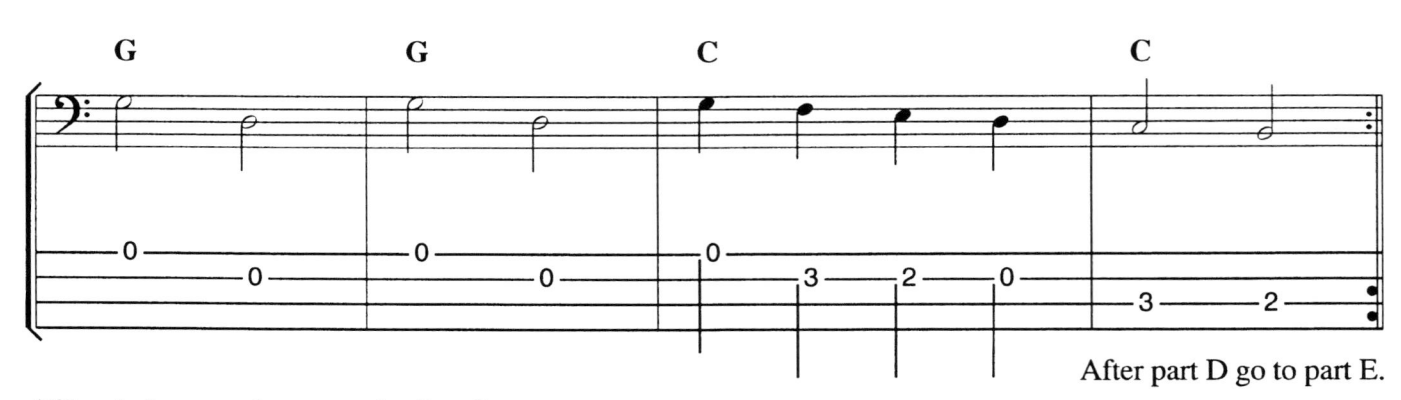

*Chords in parentheses are for Part D.

After part D go to part E.

Cotton Patch Rag

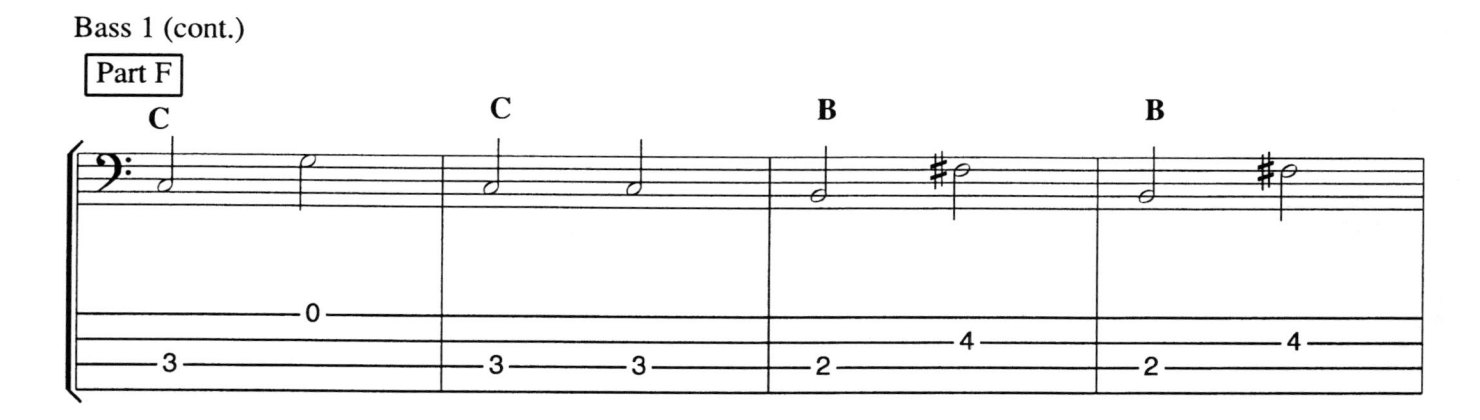

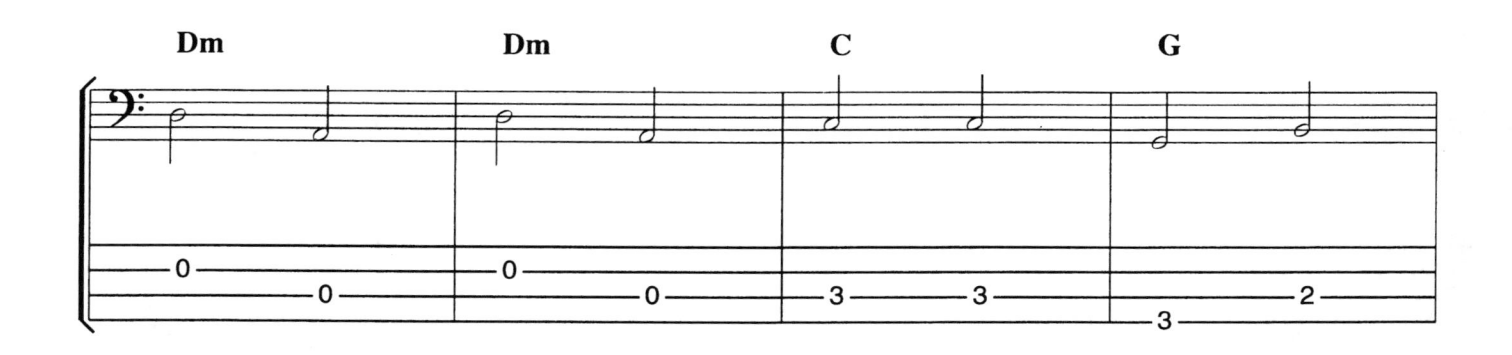

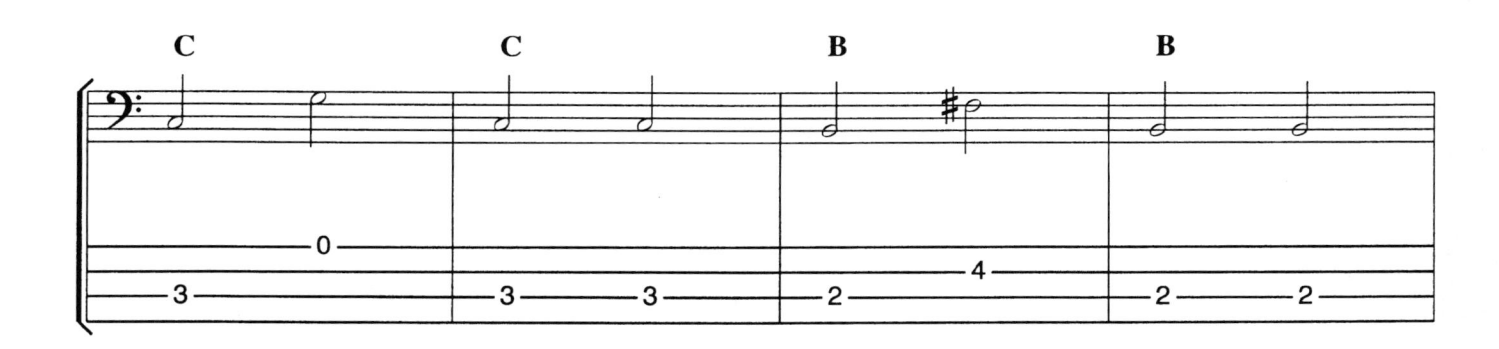

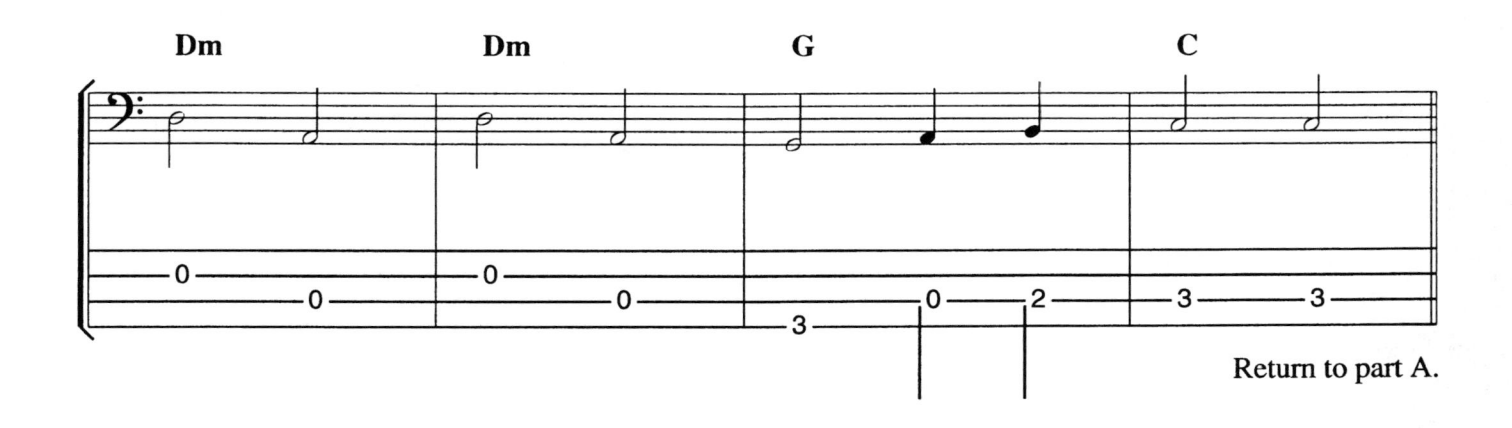

Cotton Patch Rag

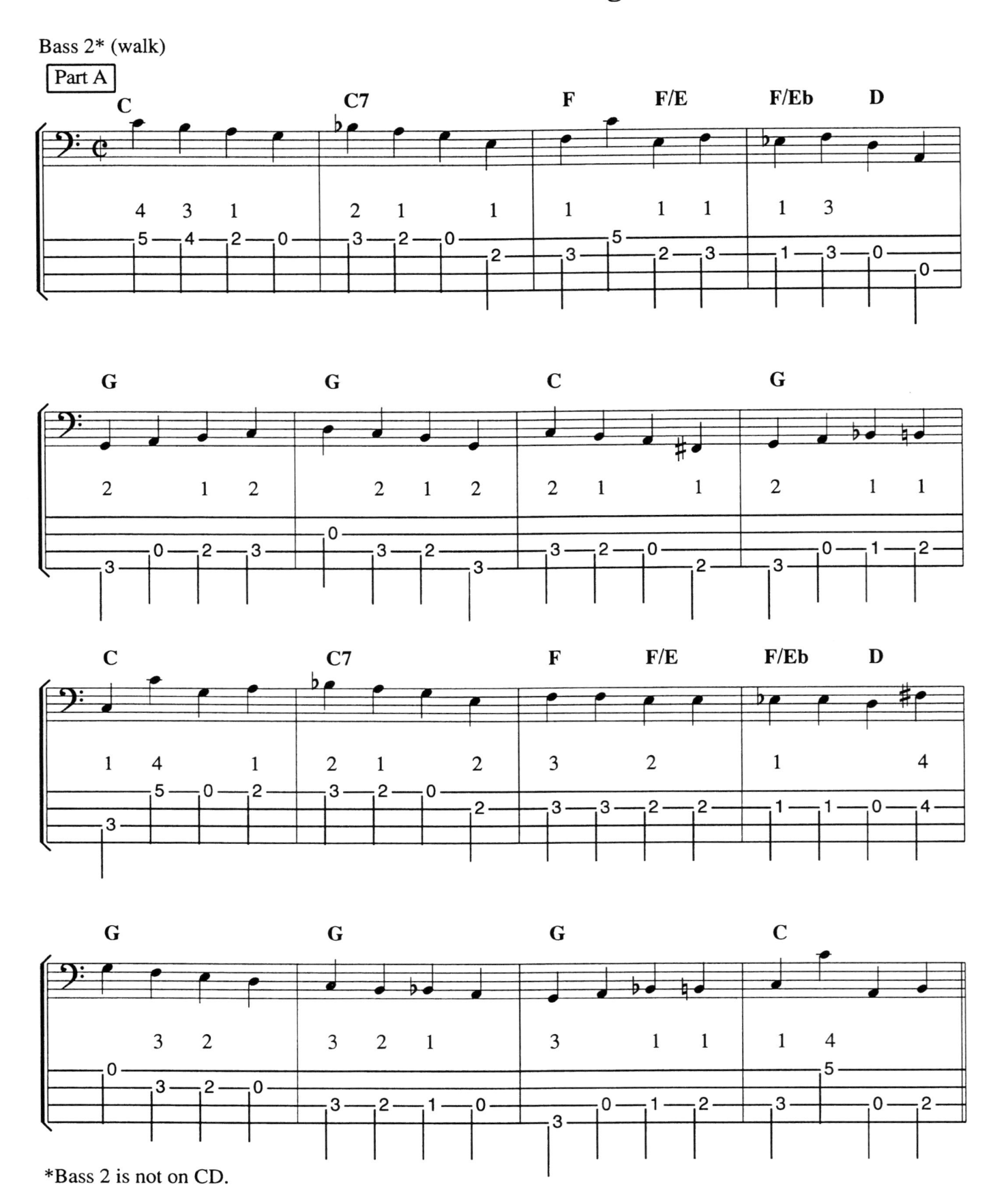

Bass 2* (walk)

*Bass 2 is not on CD.

Cotton Patch Rag

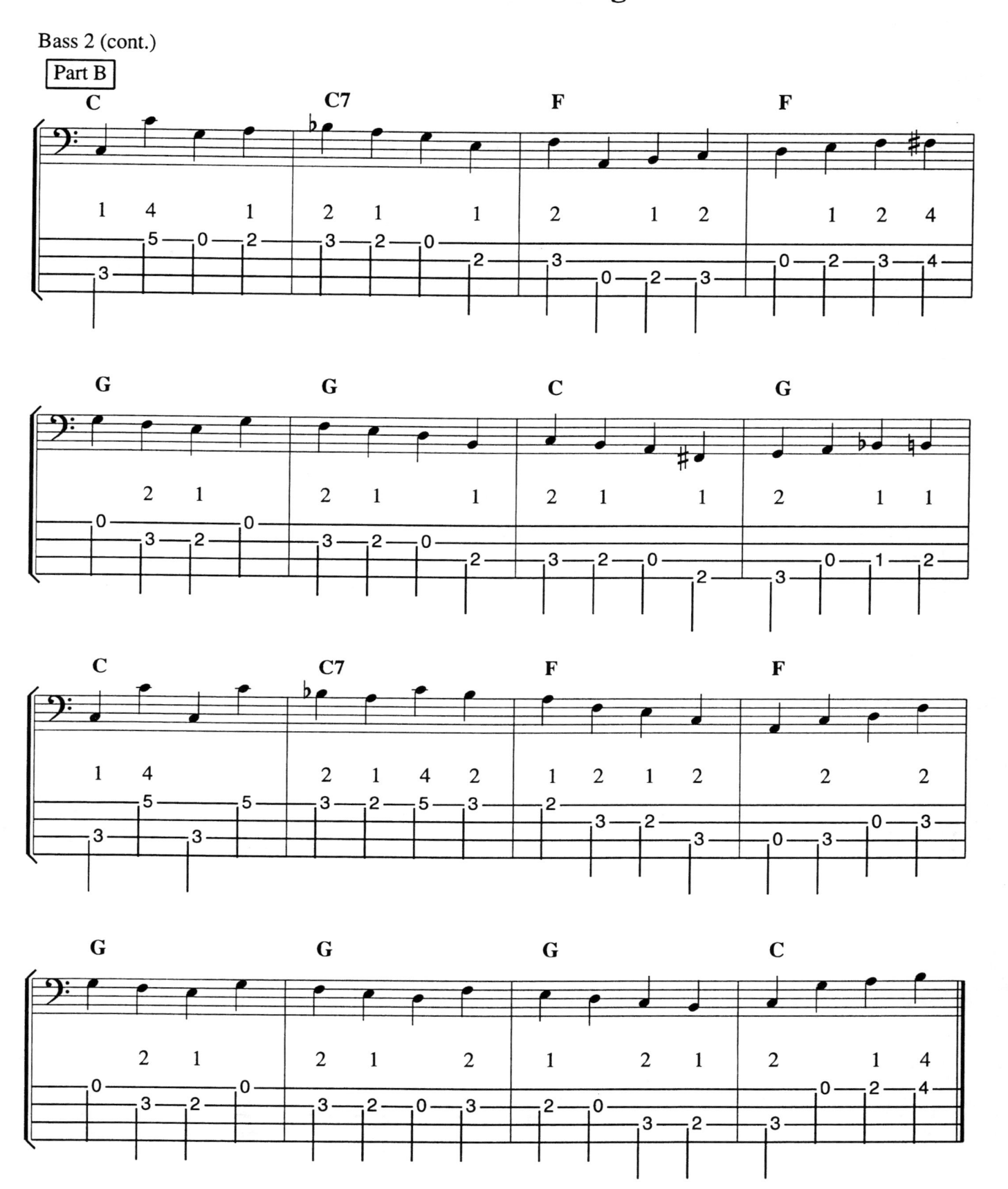

Bass 2 (cont.)

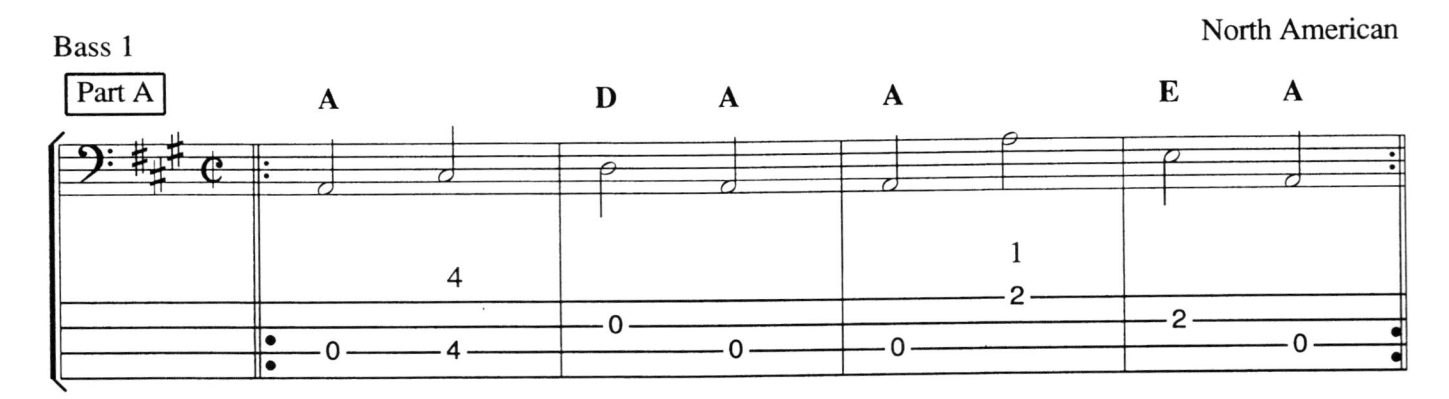

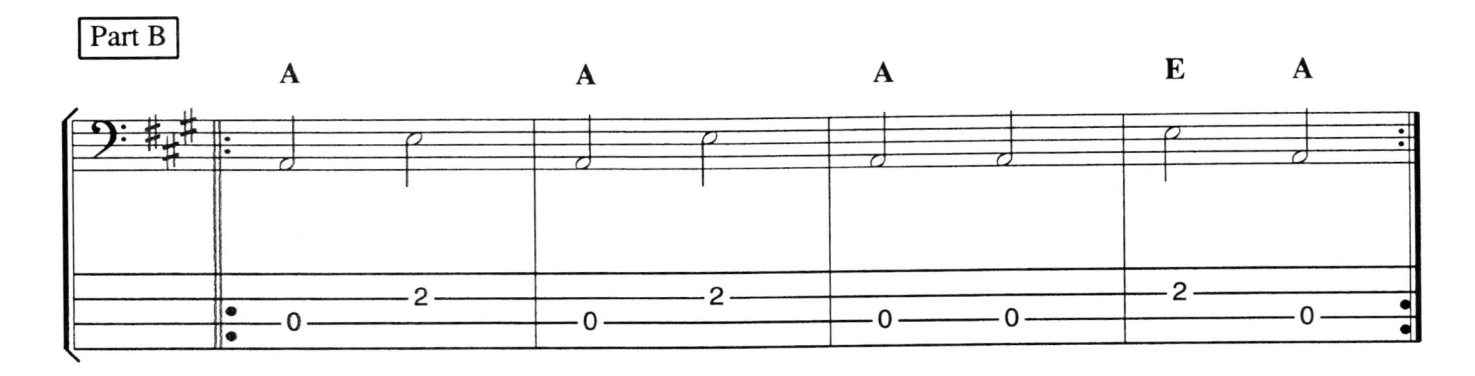

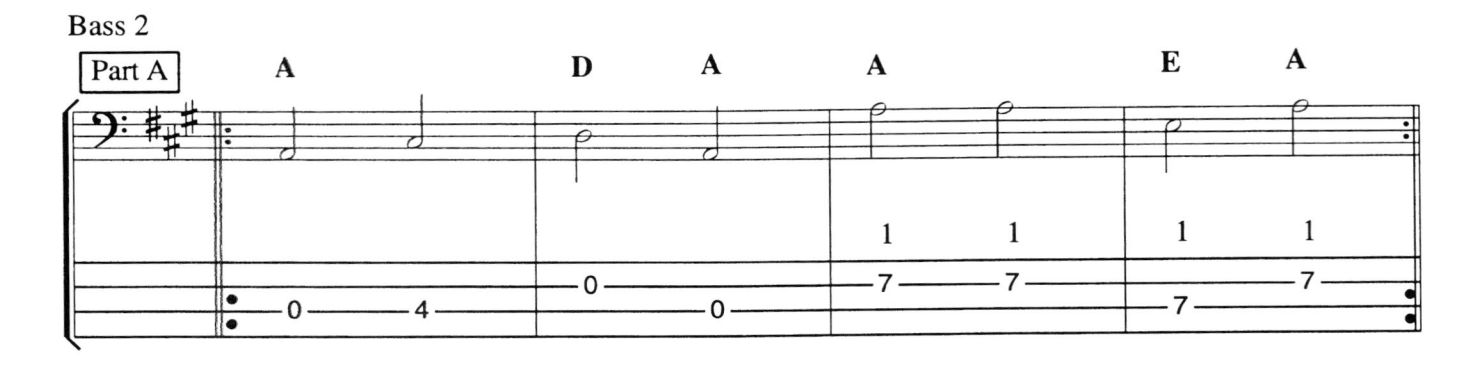

Cripple Creek

North American

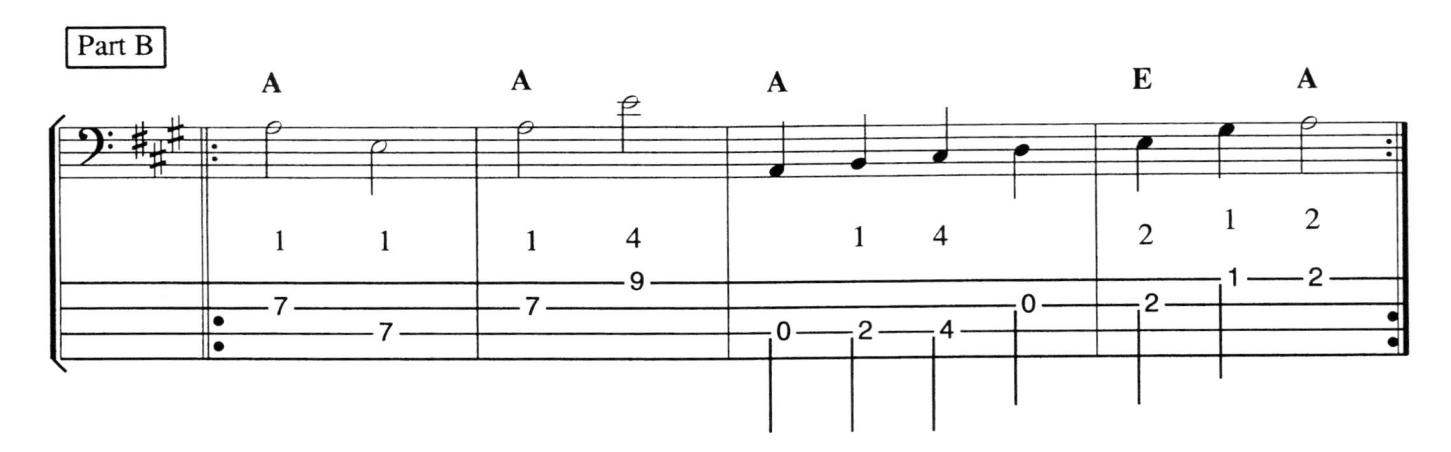

Cripple Creek

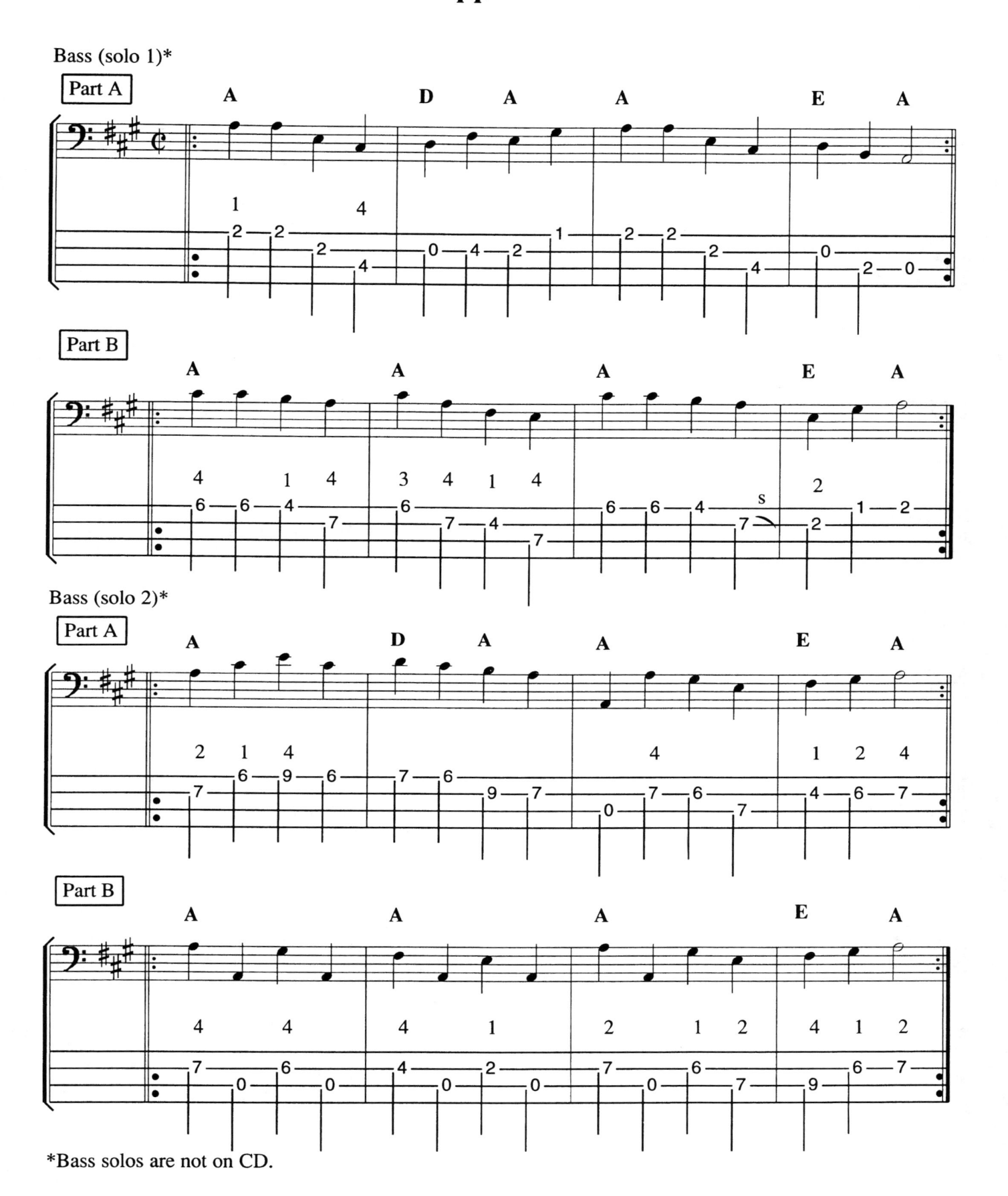

*Bass solos are not on CD.

Disc 1
Track 15

Devil's Dream

Bass 1 (key of D)

North American

Part A

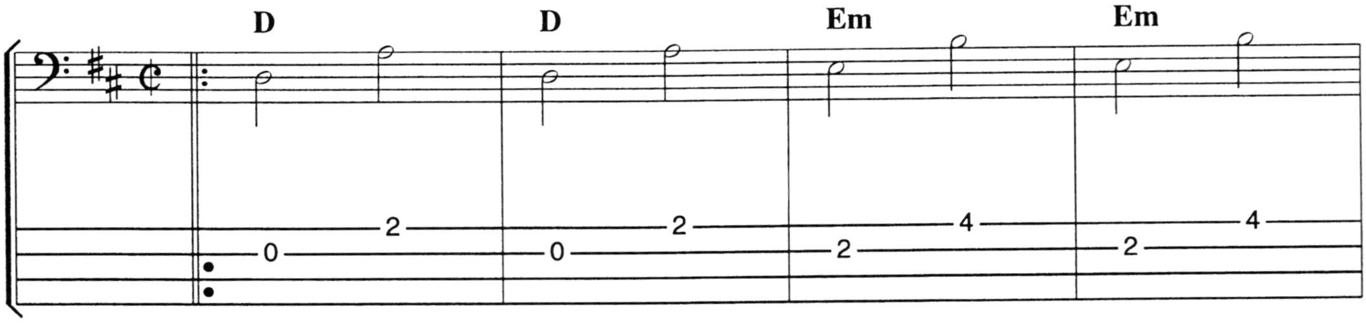

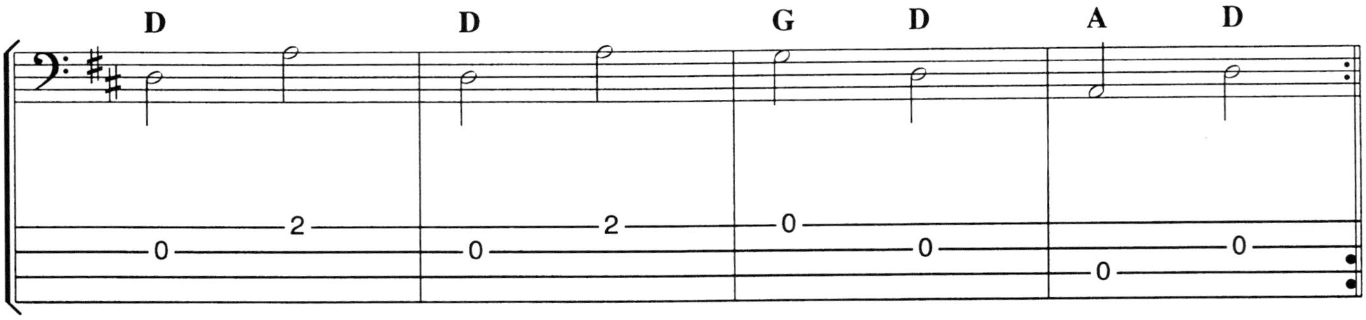

Part B

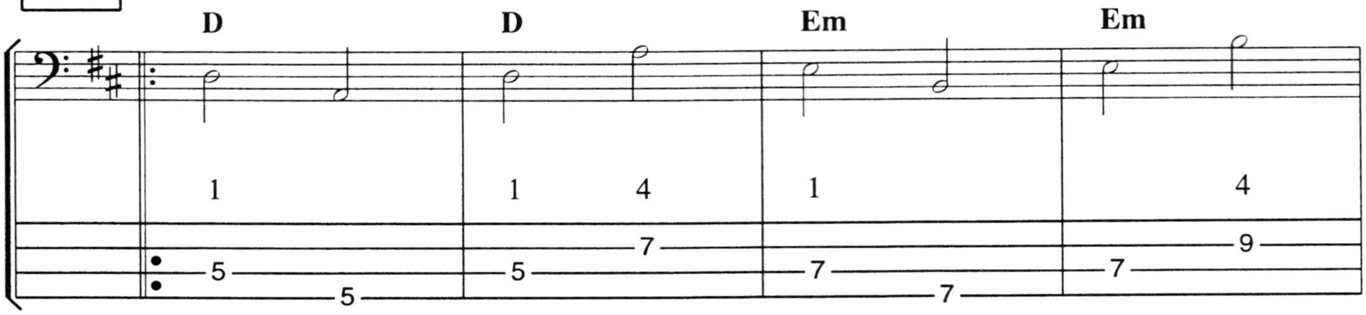

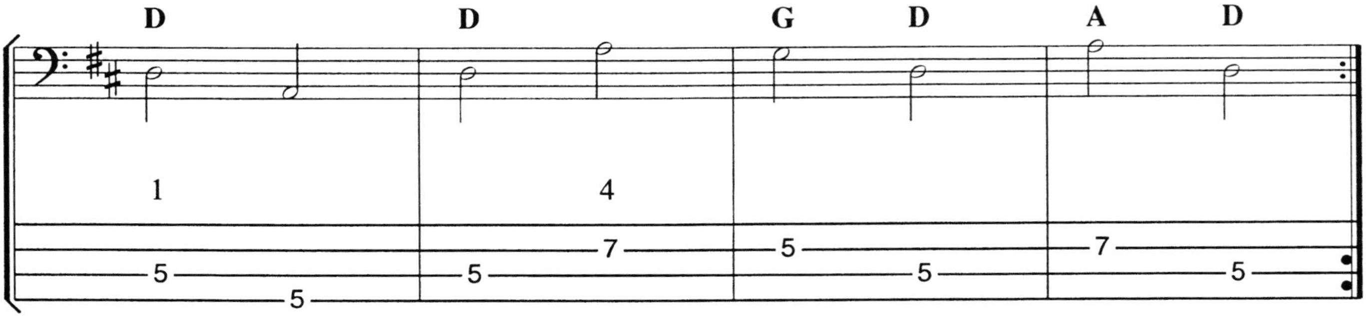

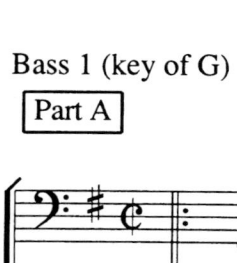

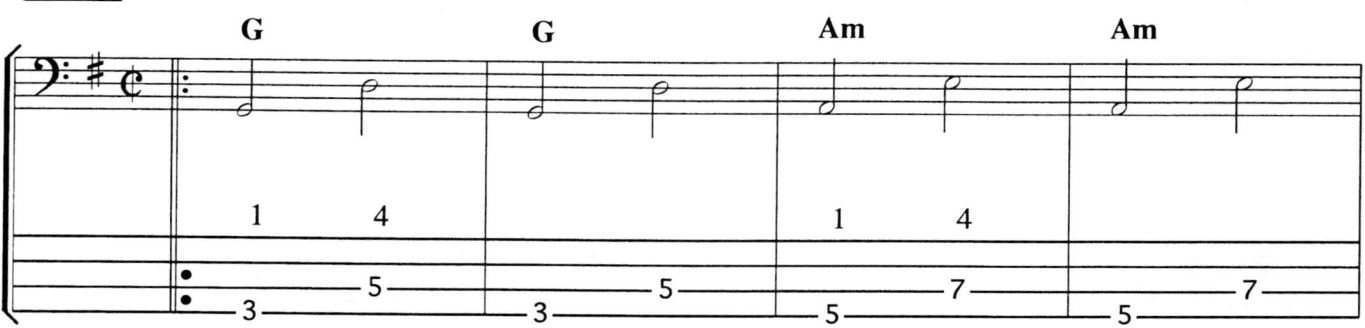

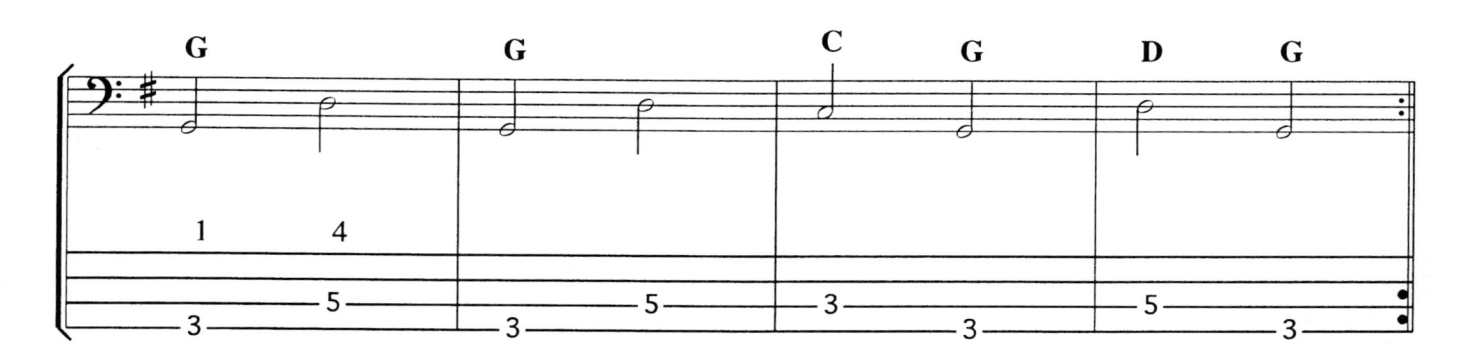

Devil's Dream

Bass 1 (key of G)

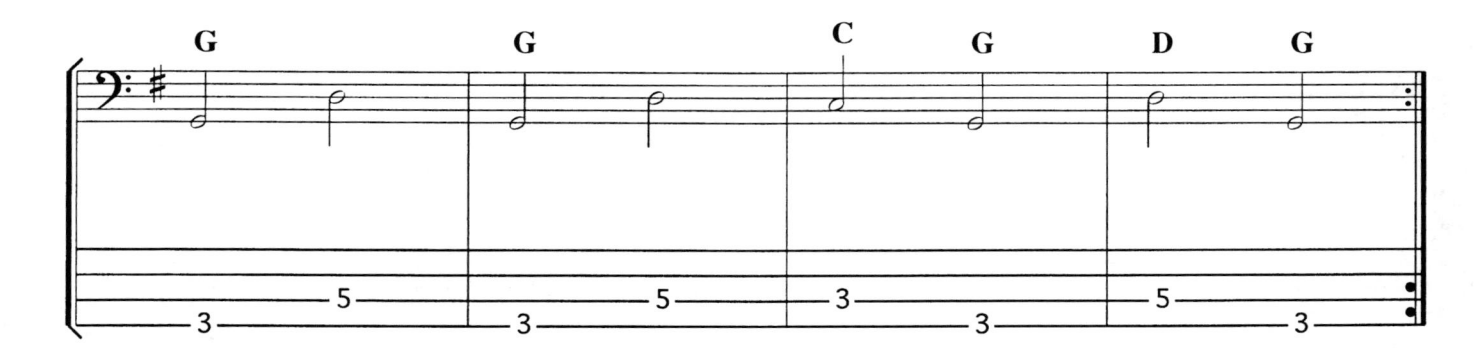

Devil's Dream

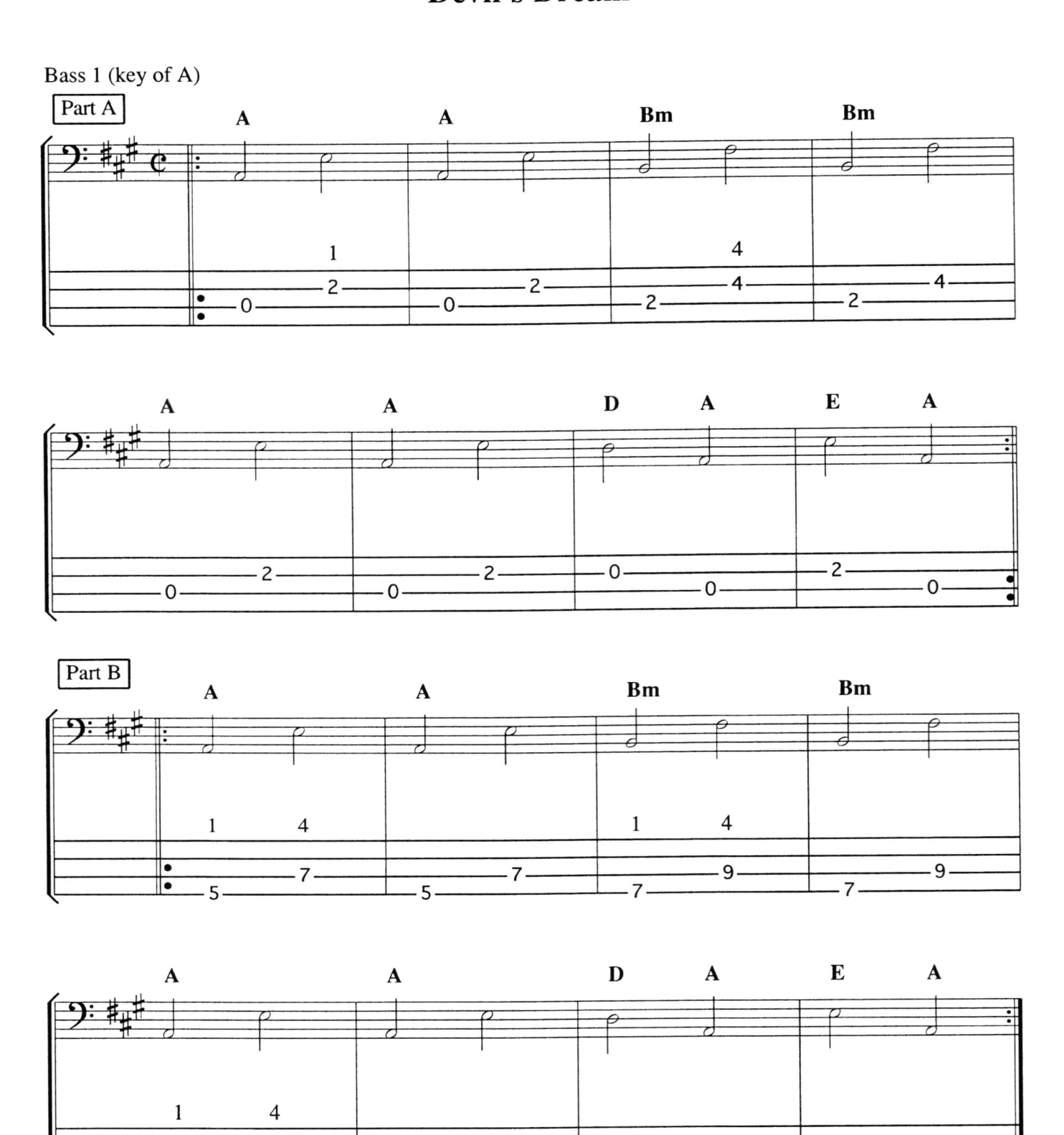

Bass 1 (key of A)

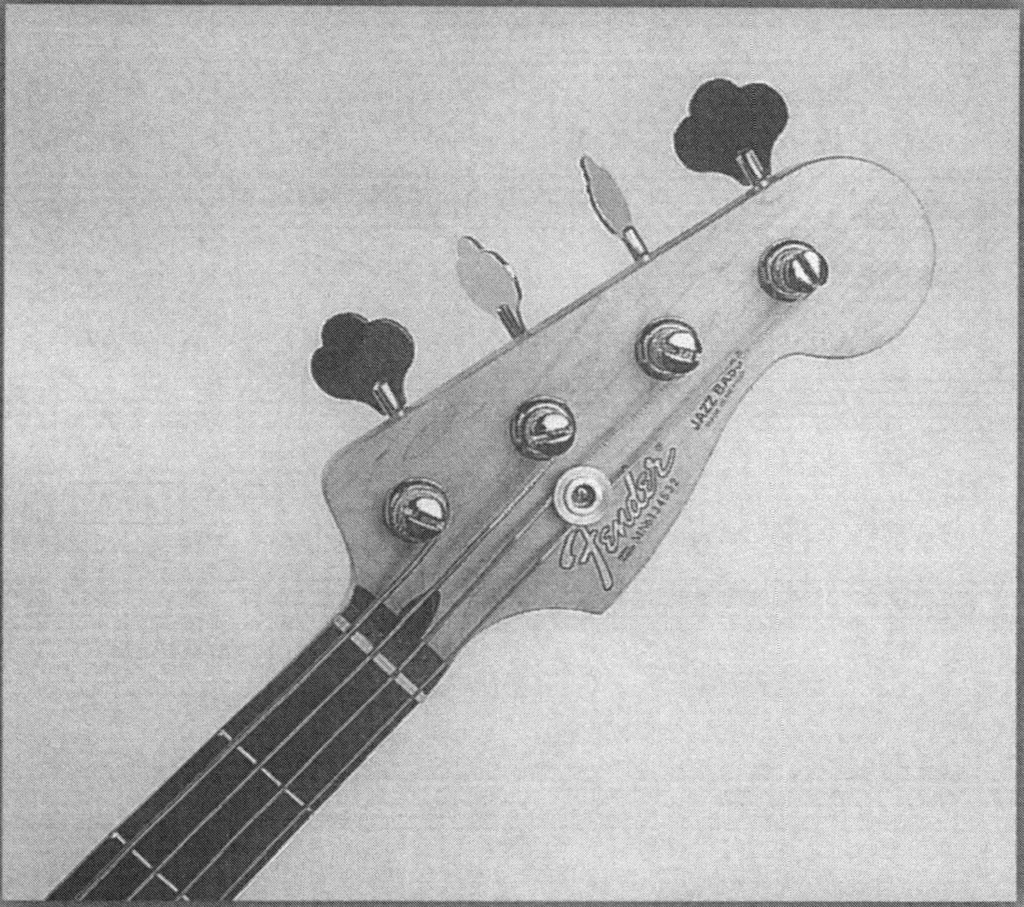

Down Yonder

North American

Down Yonder

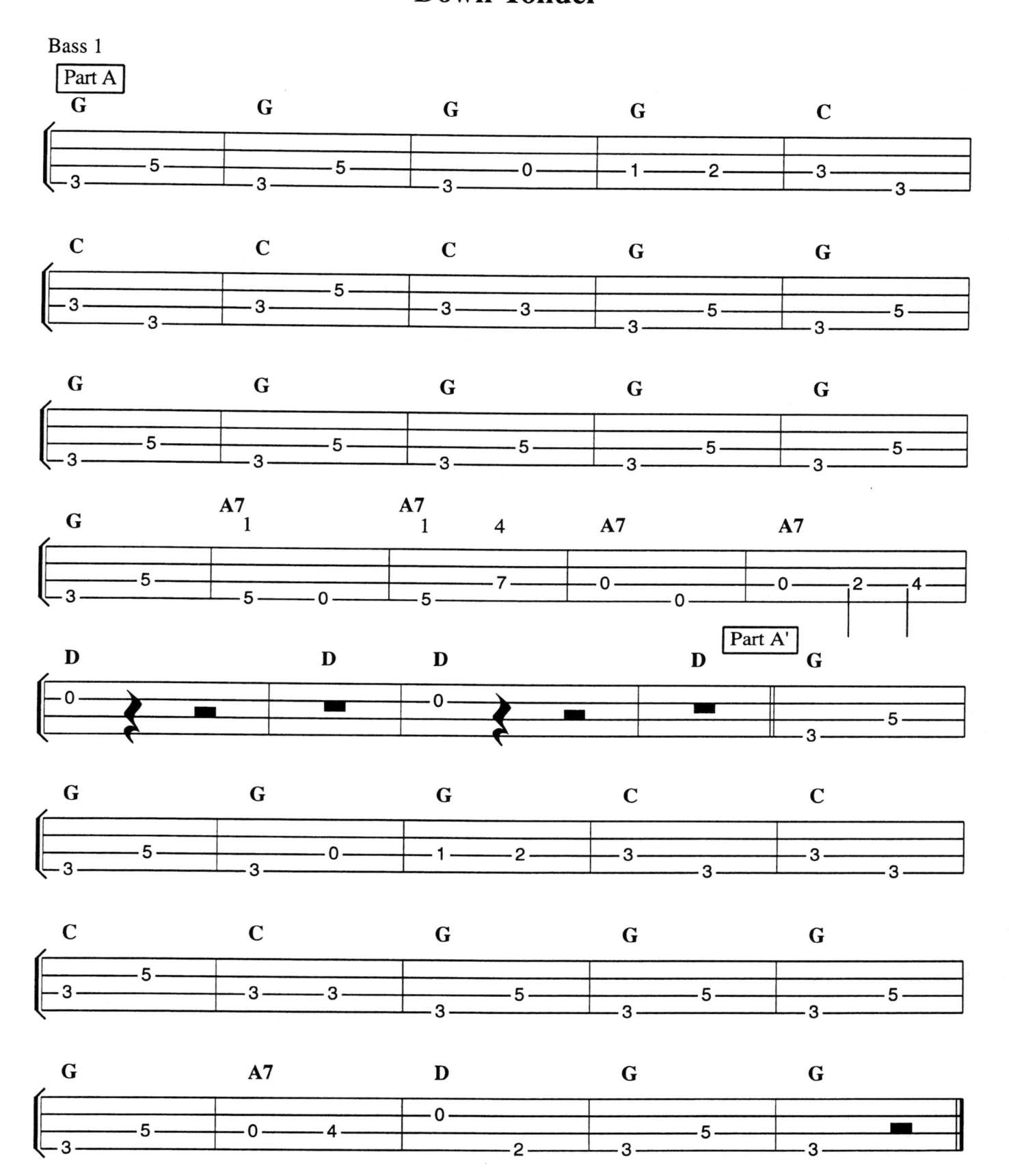

Bass 1

Down Yonder

Bass 2* (walk)

*Bass 2 is not on CD.

Down Yonder

*Bass 2 is not on CD.

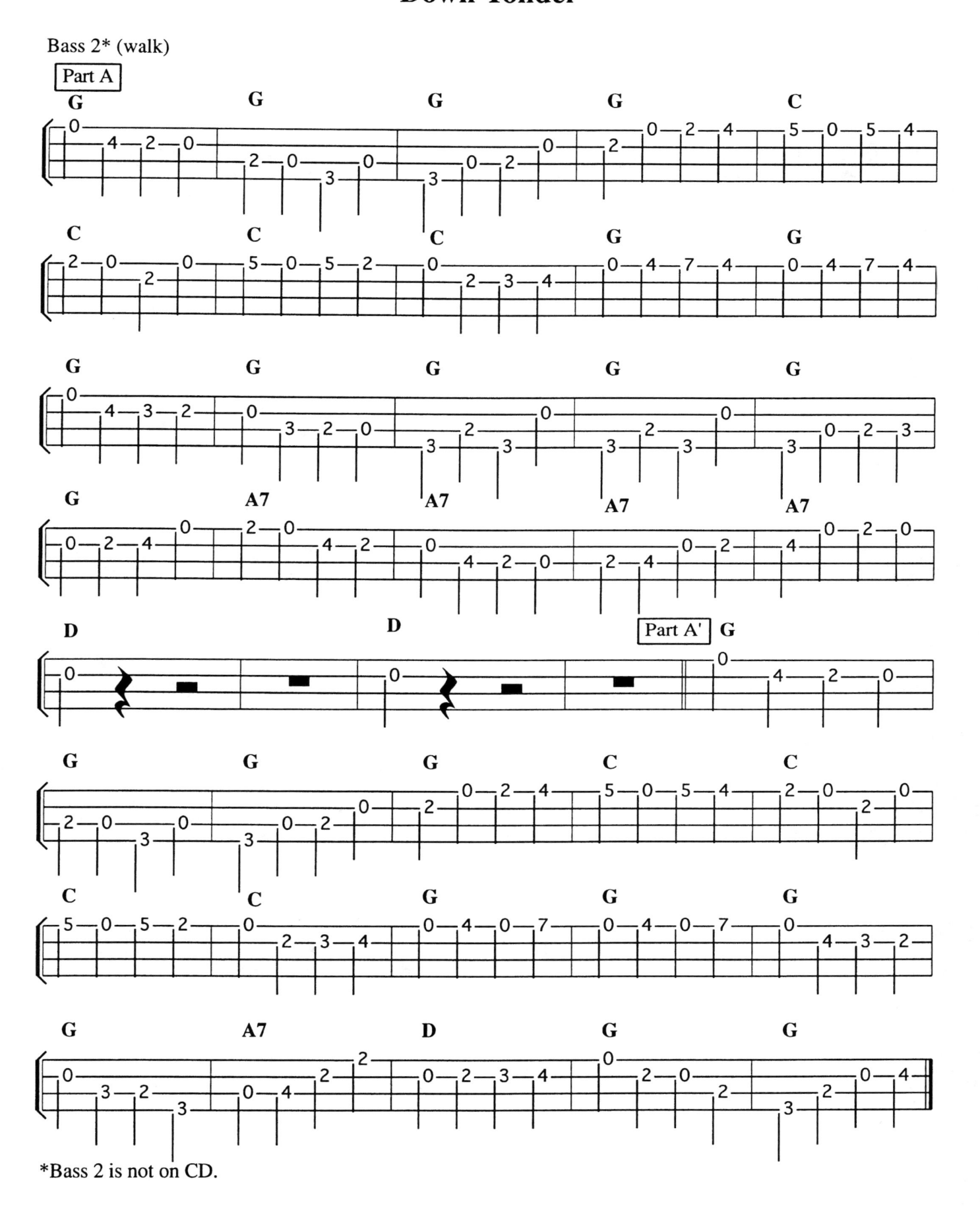

Down Yonder

Down Yonder

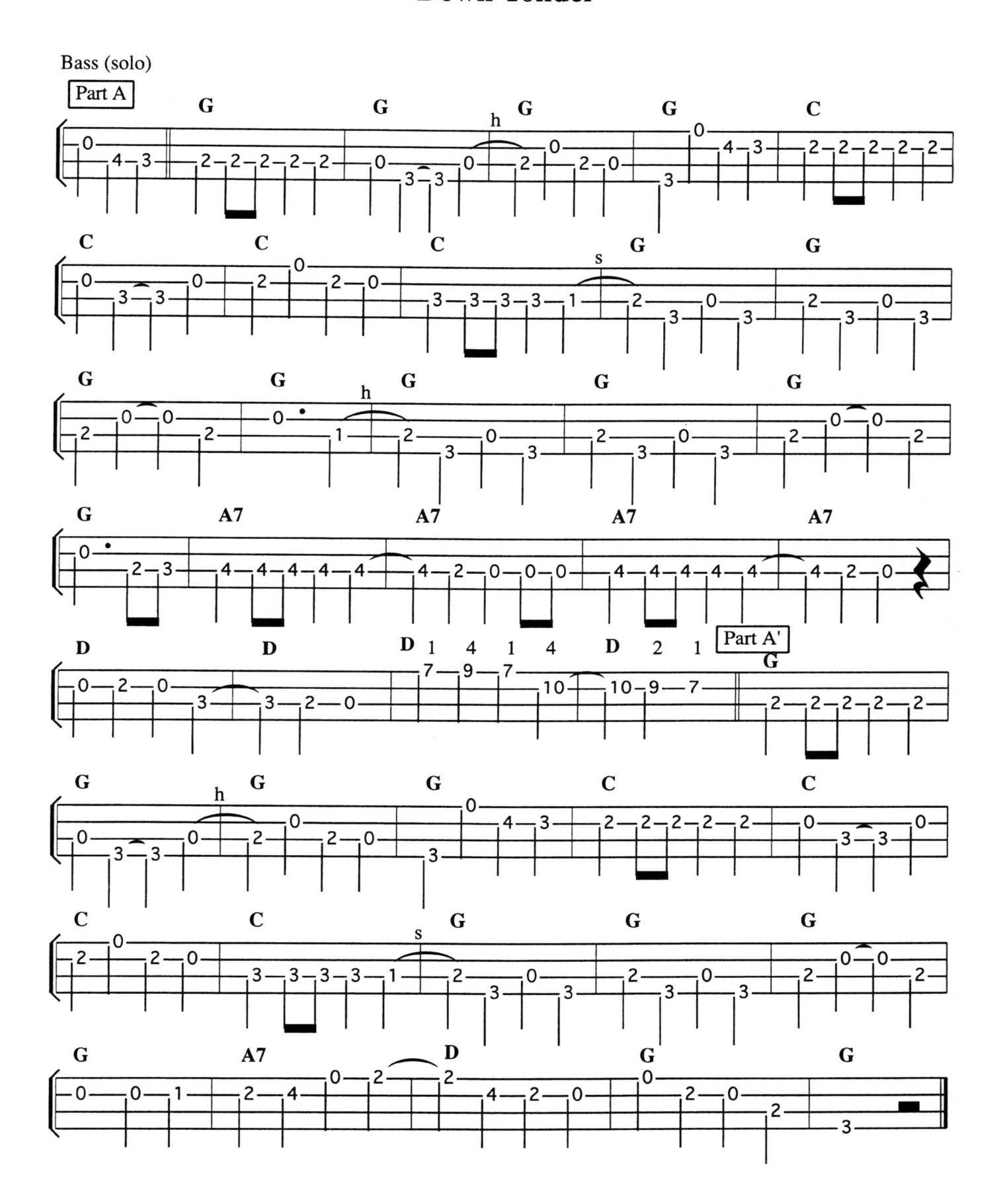

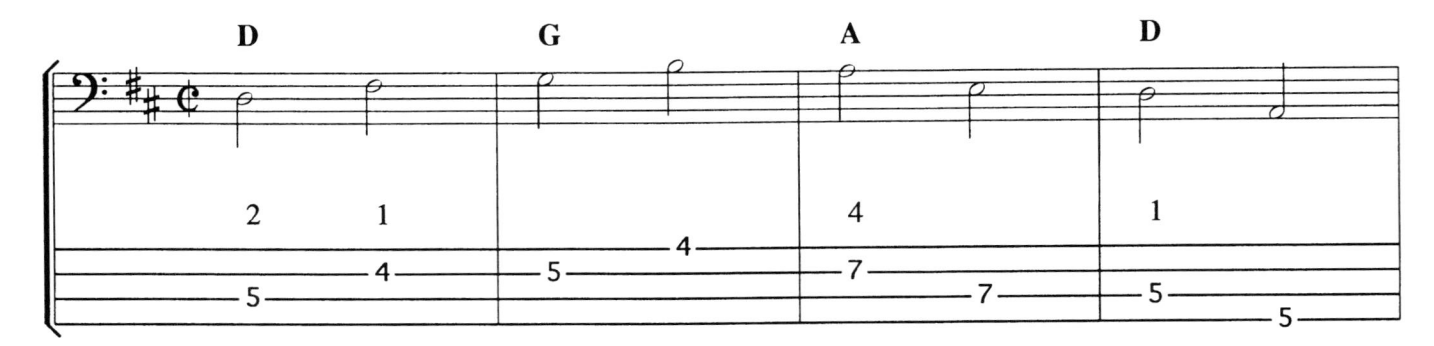

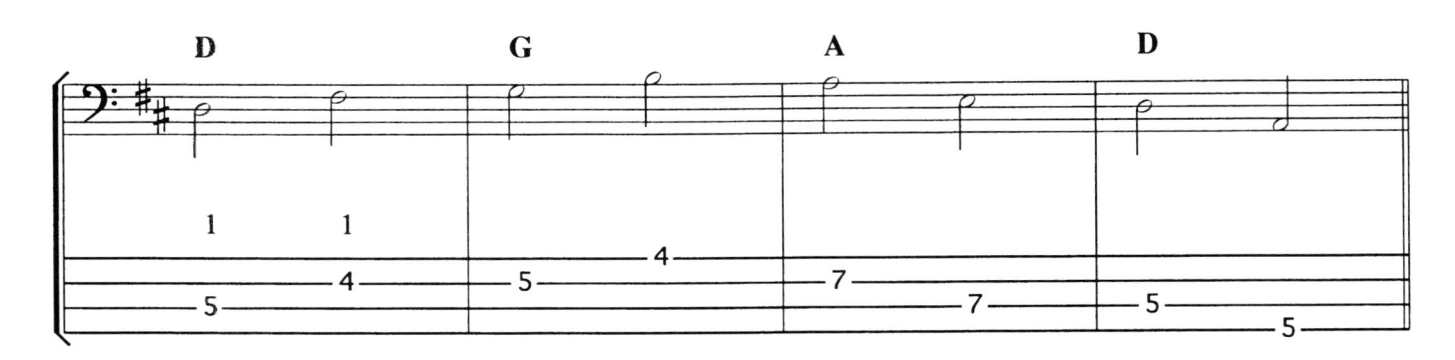

Eighth of January

Bass 1

Part A

North American

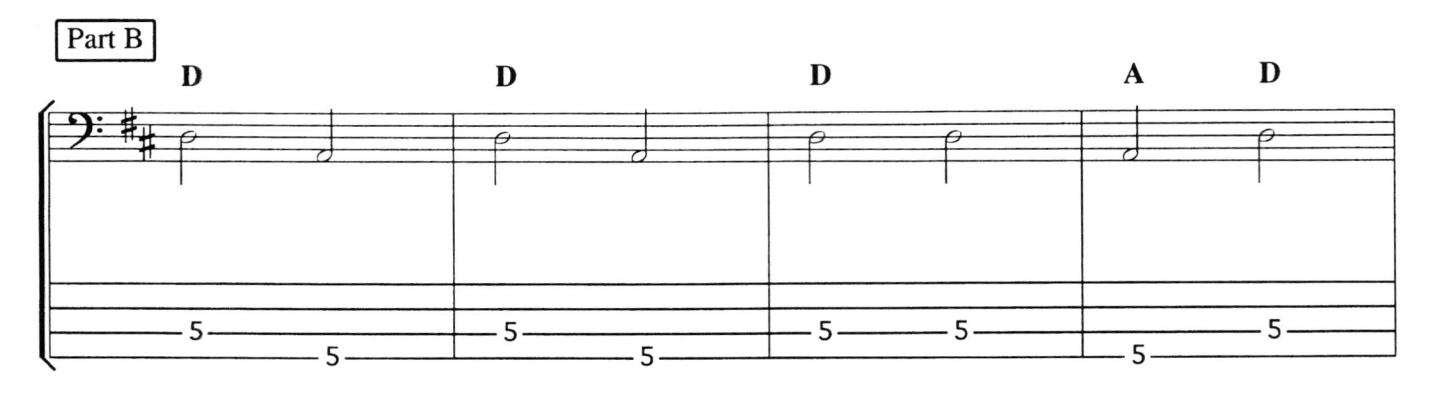

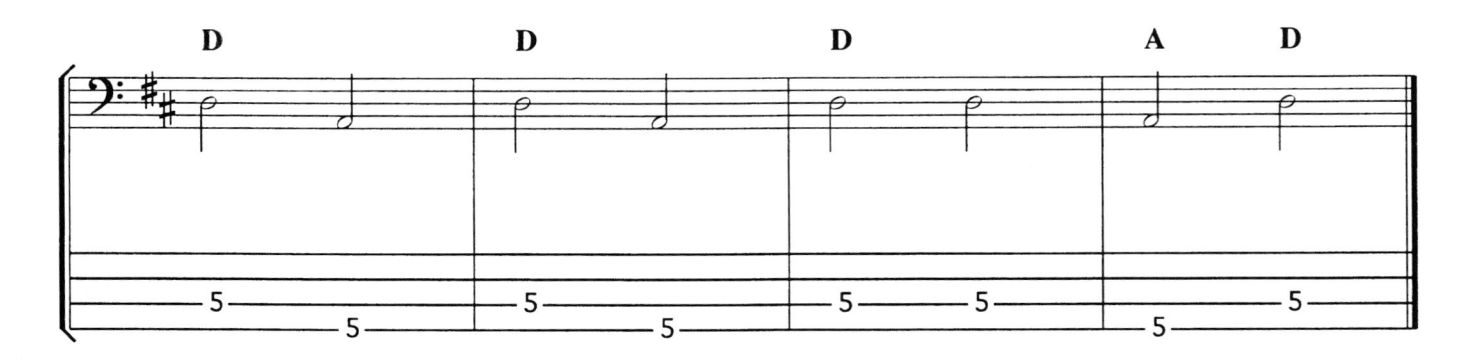

Eighth of January

Eighth of January

Bass 3 (for Fiddle 2)

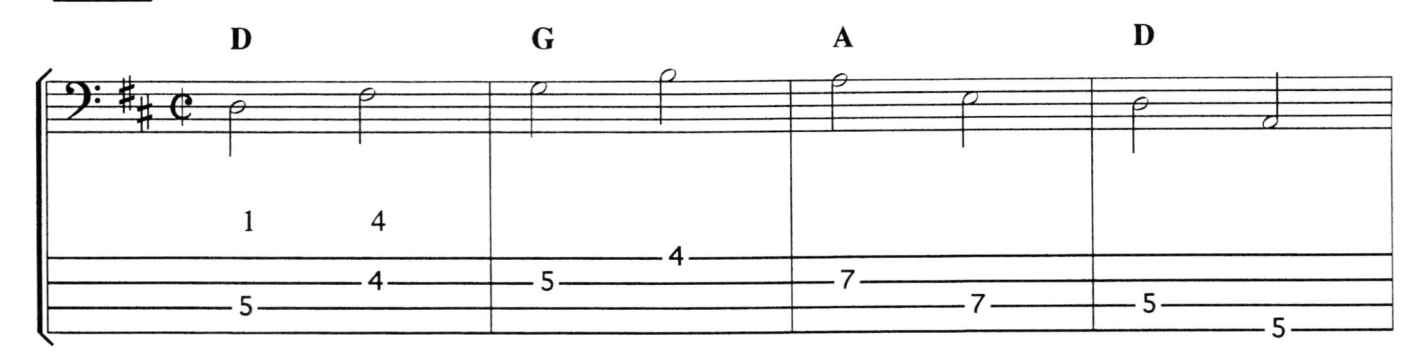

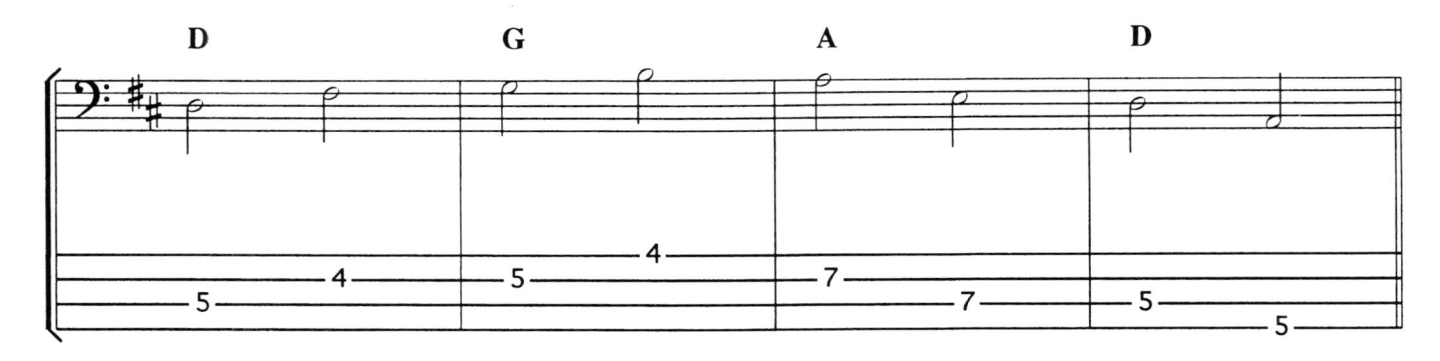

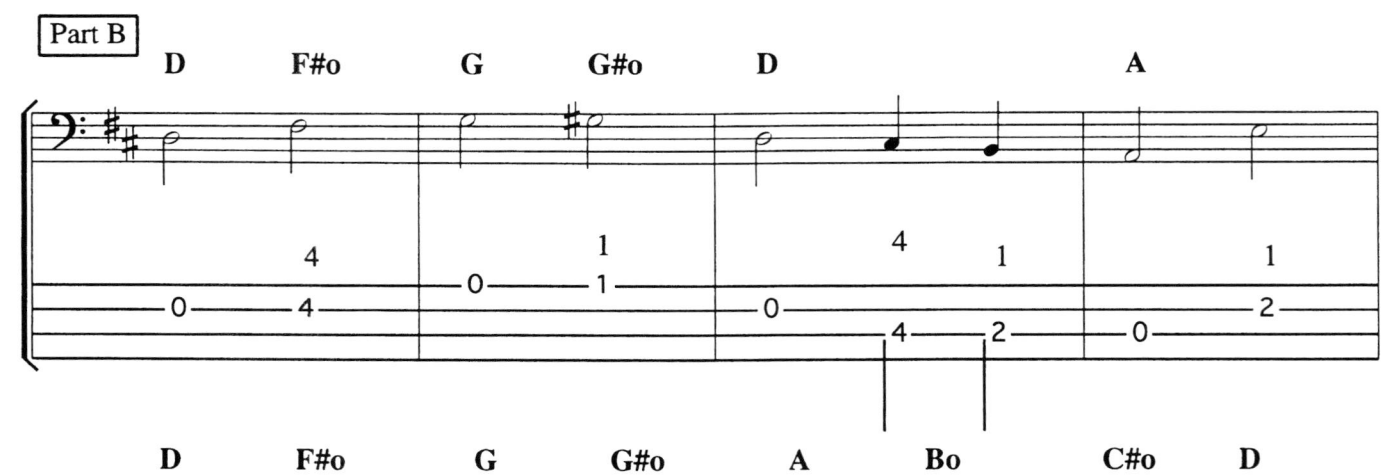

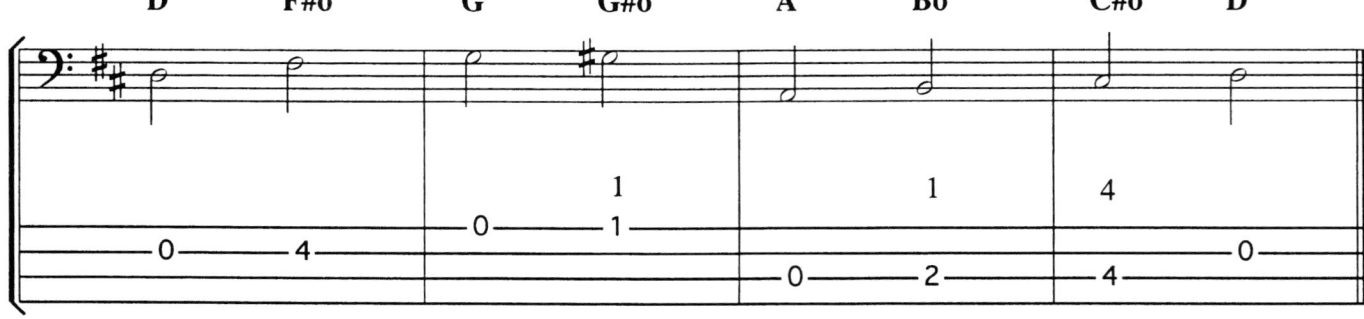

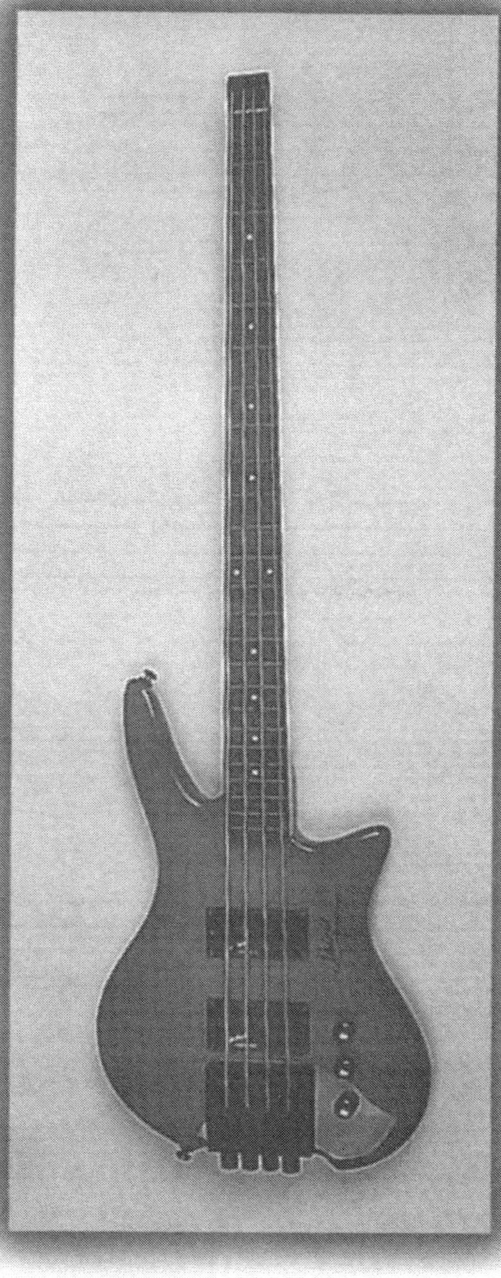

Forked Deer

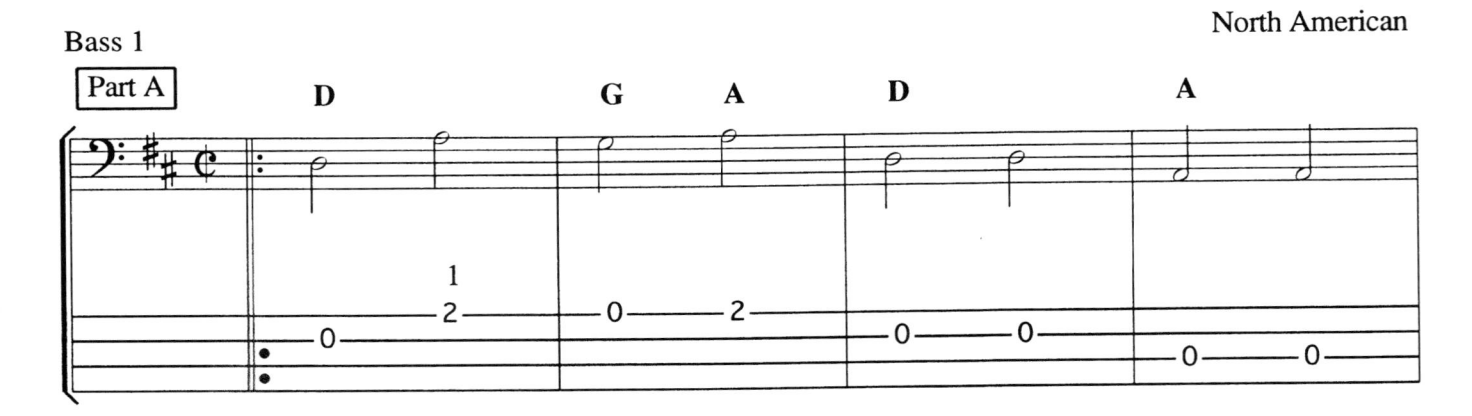

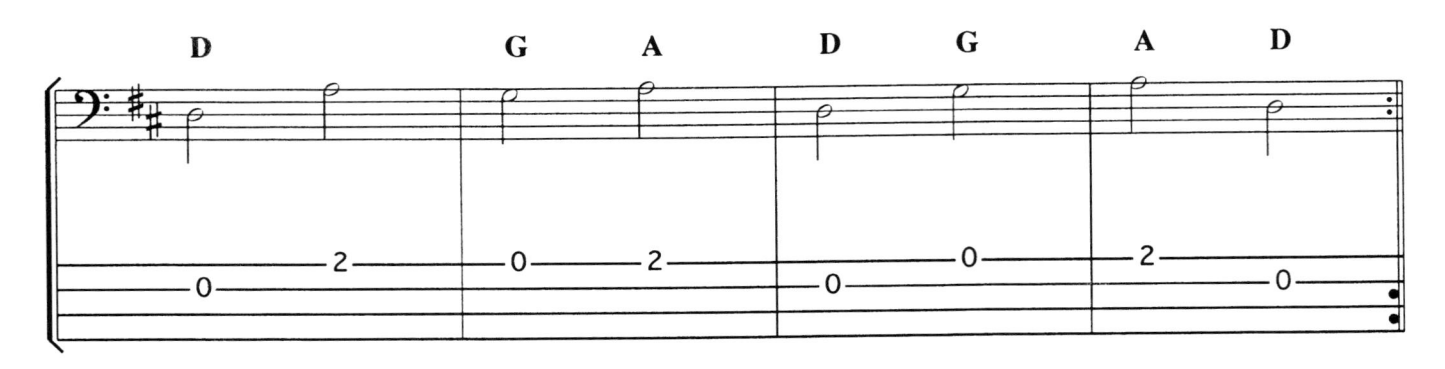

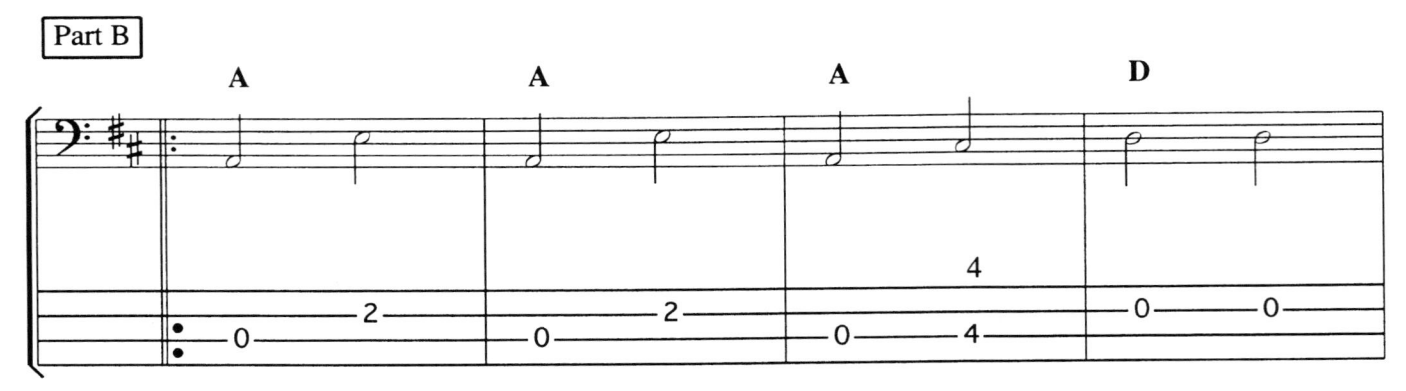

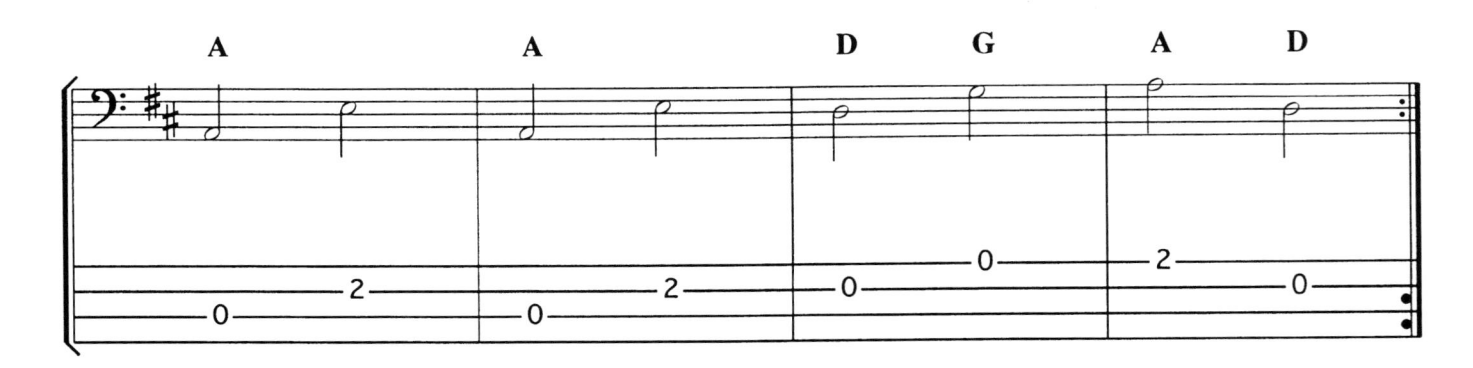

North American

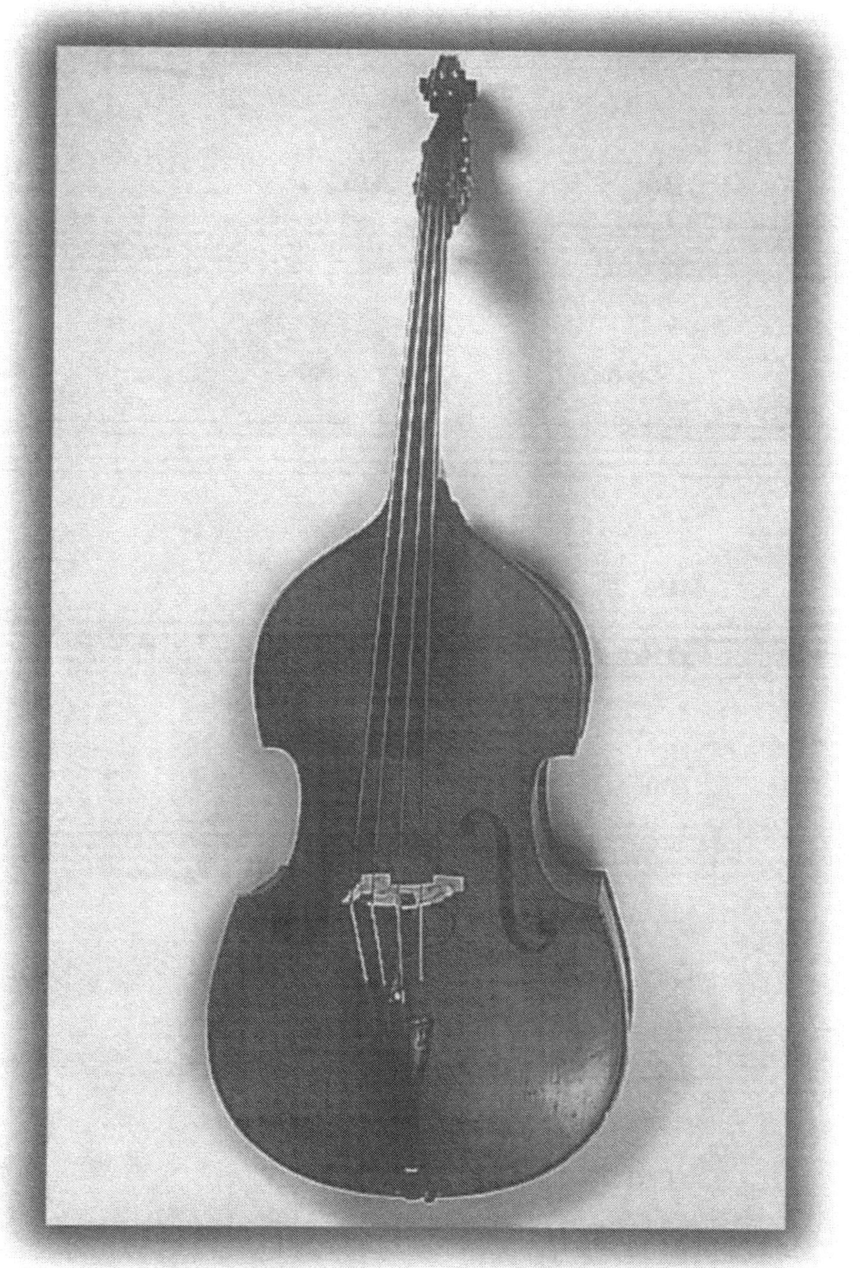

Gardenia Waltz

Bass 1*

Part A

North American

*Bass is not on CD.

Gardenia Waltz by Johnny Gimble
© 1974 by Gardenia Music. All Rights Reserved. Used by Permission.

Gardenia Waltz

Bass (cont.)

Part B

Gardenia Waltz

*Bass is not on CD.

Gardenia Waltz

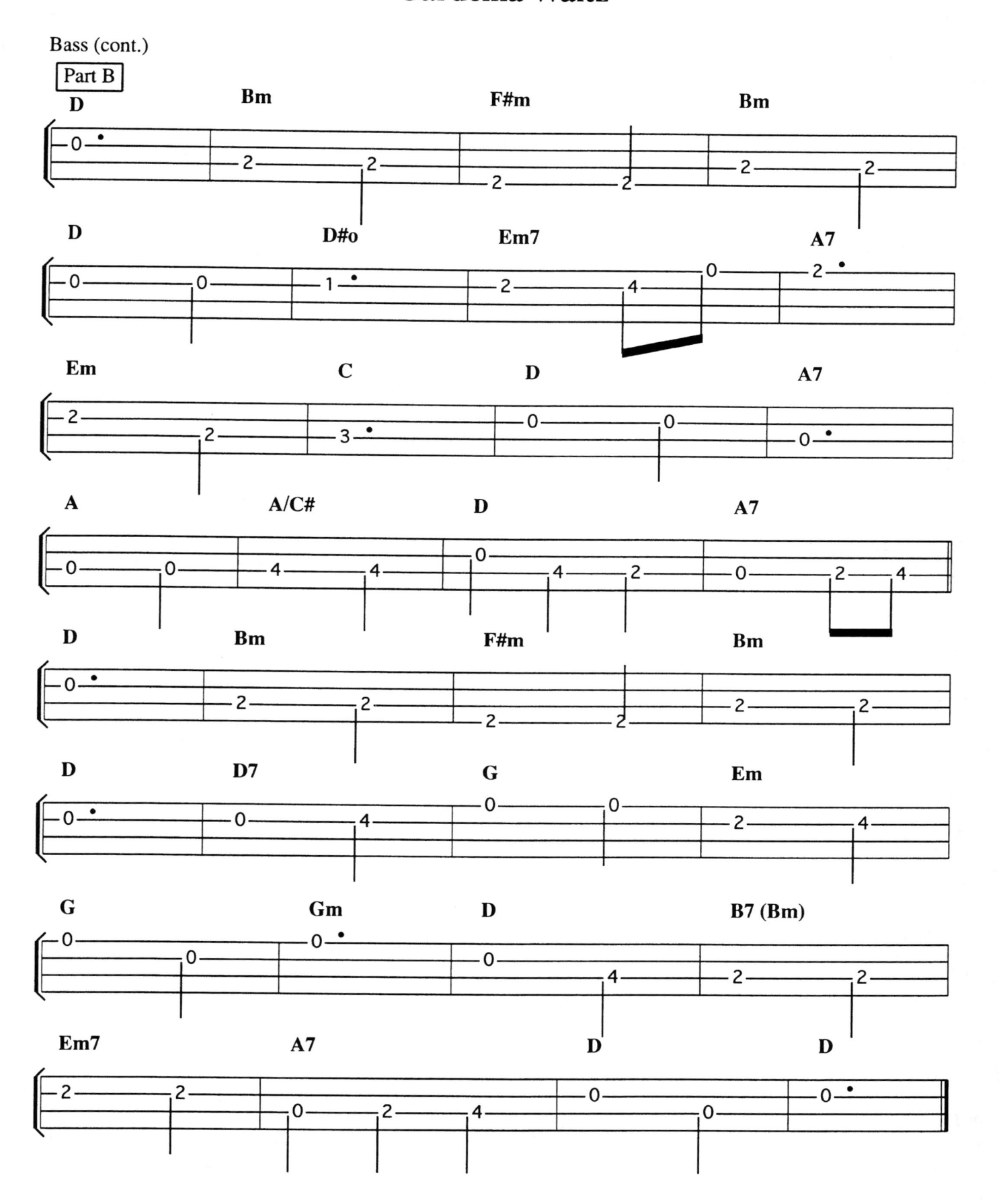

Disc 2
Track 3

Grandfather's Clock

Bass 2 (for Banjo)

North American

Grandfather's Clock

Bass 2 (for Banjo)

Grandfather's Clock

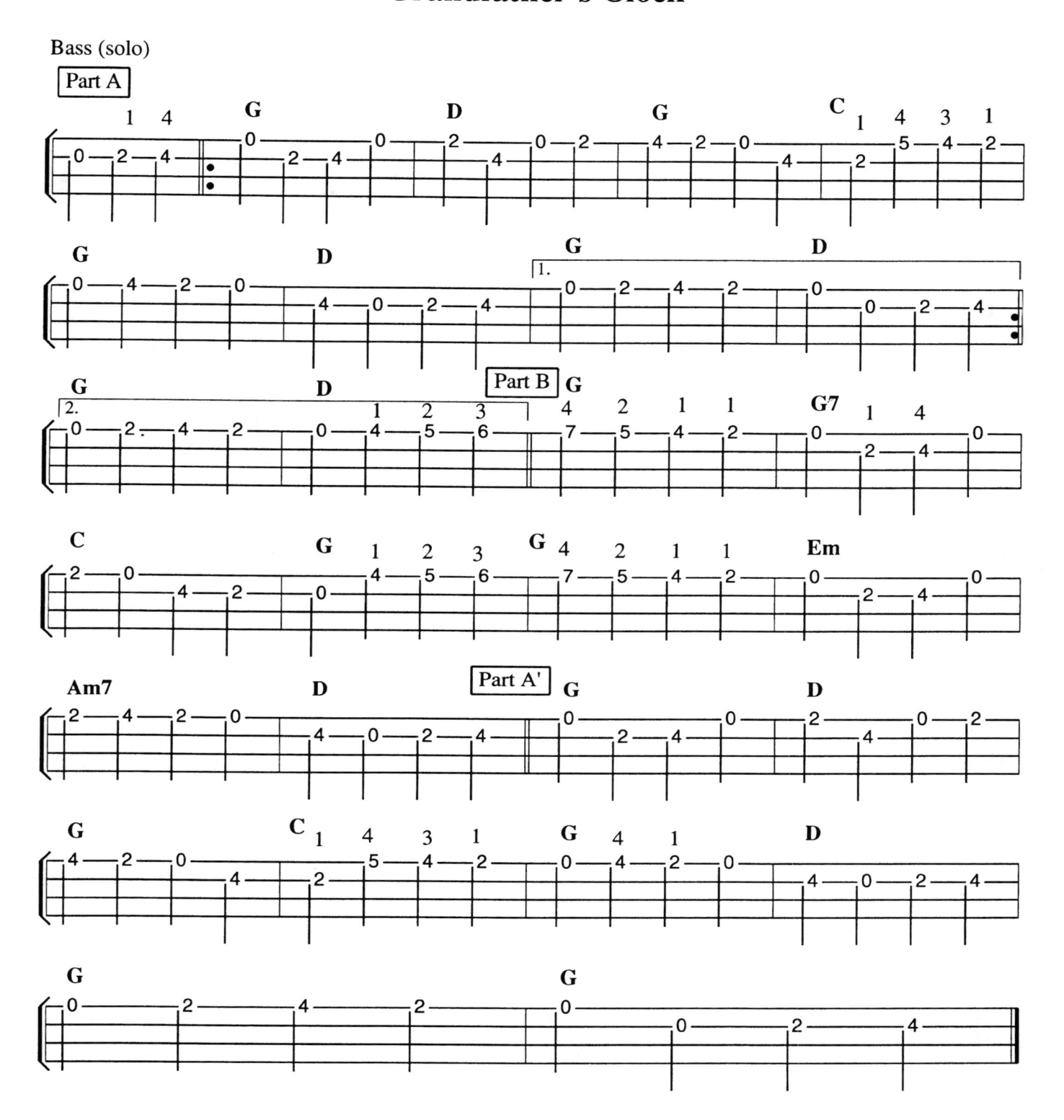

Grandfather's Clock

Grandfather's Clock

Grandfather's Clock

Grandfather's Clock

Bass 3*

*Bass 3 is not on CD.

Grandfather's Clock

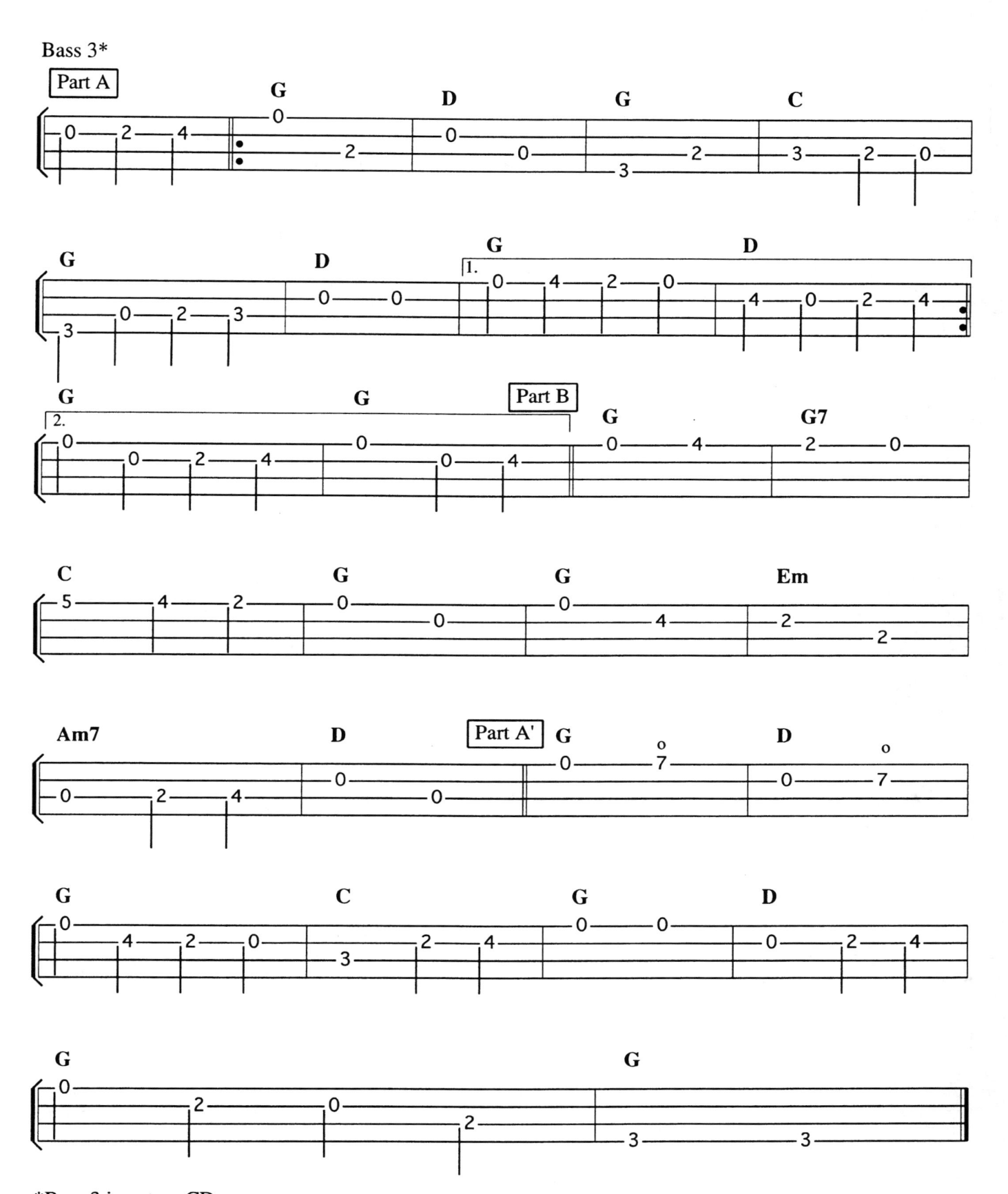

*Bass 3 is not on CD.

Green Willis

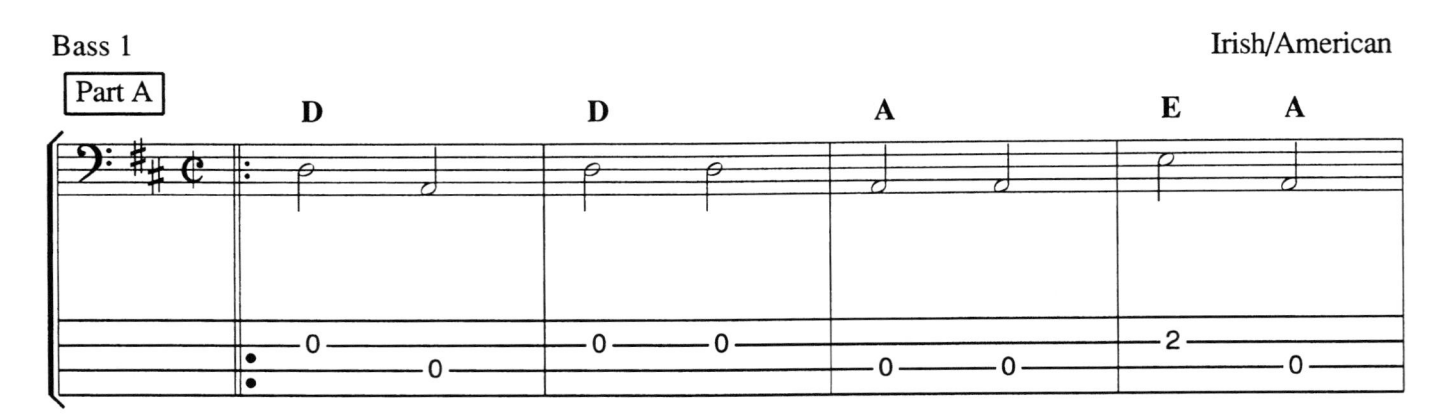

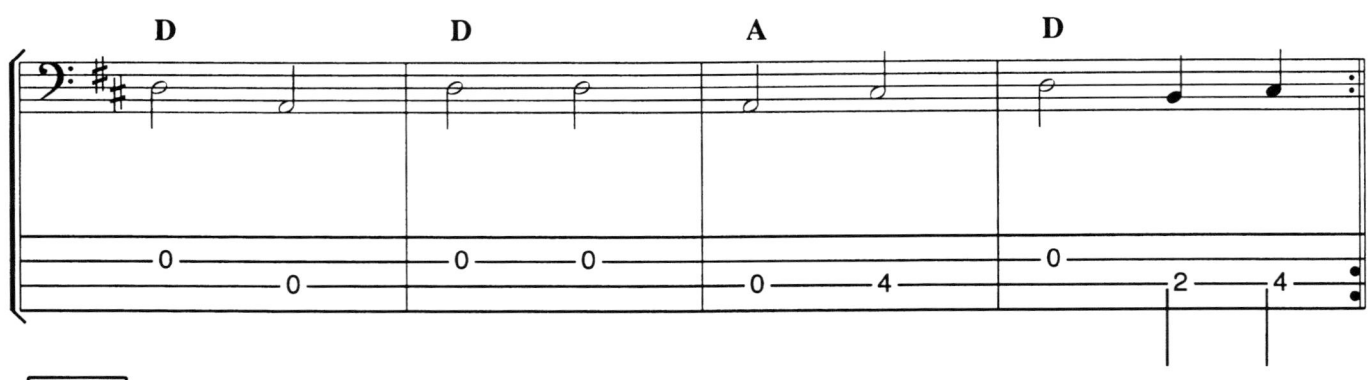

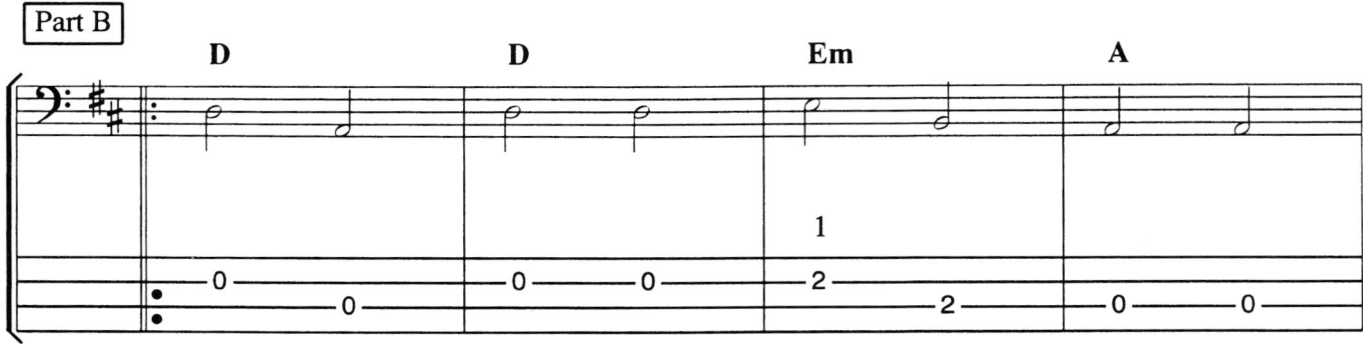

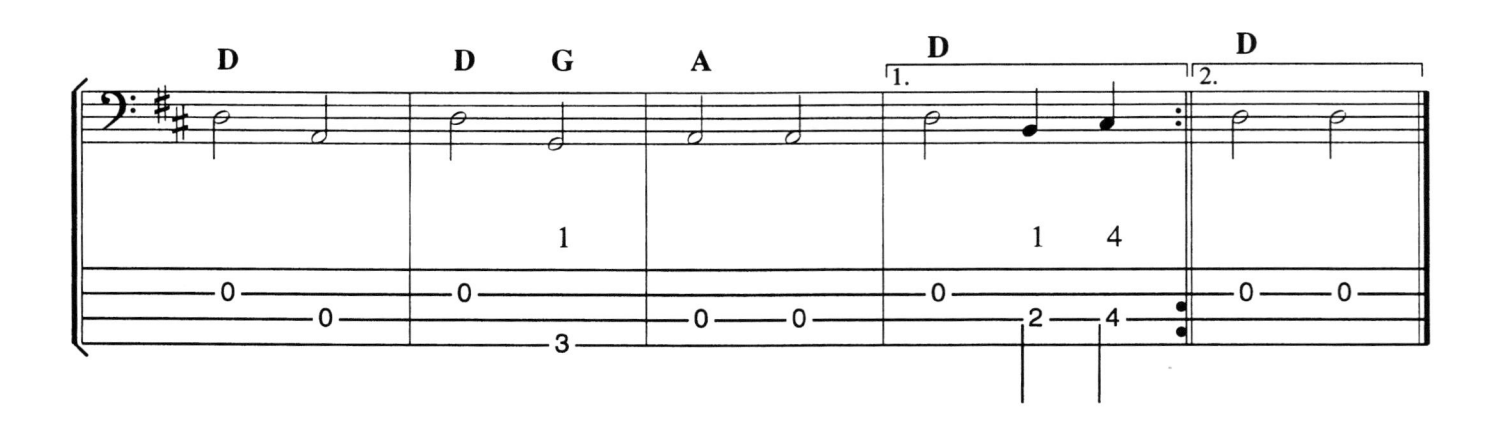

Bass 1
Irish/American

Indian's Farewell Waltz

Irish Washerwoman

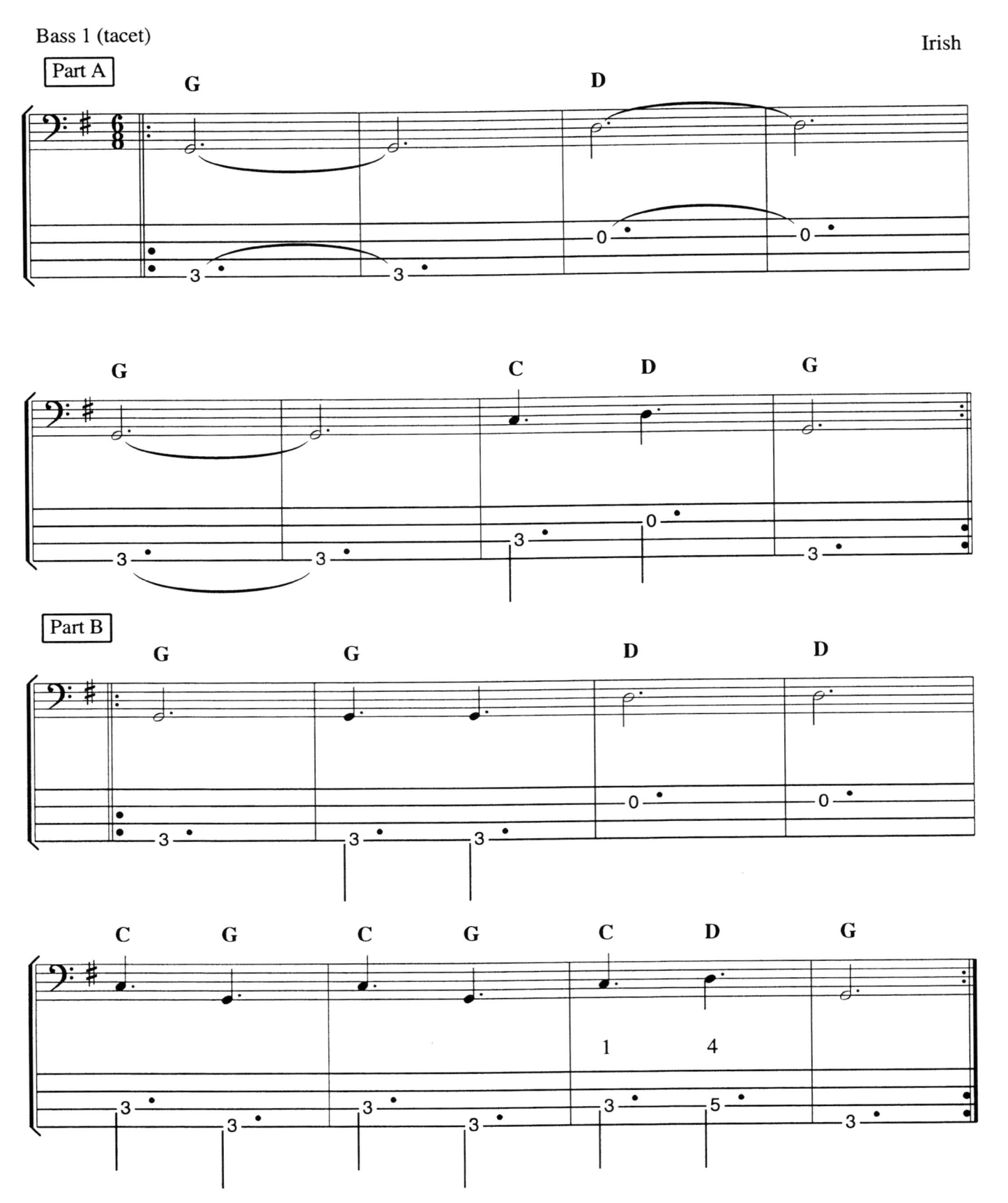

Irish Washerwoman

Irish Washerwoman

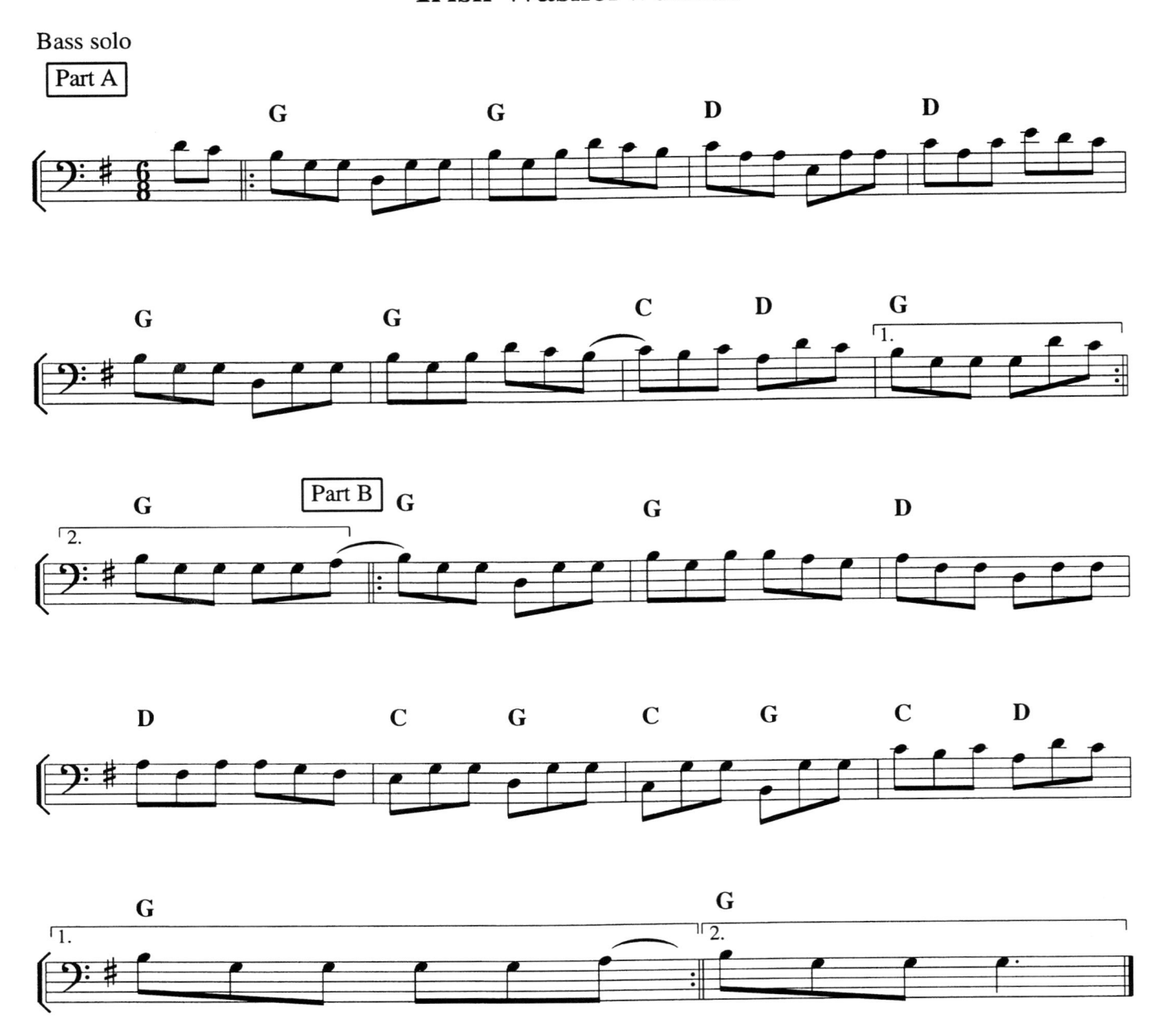

Irish Washerwoman

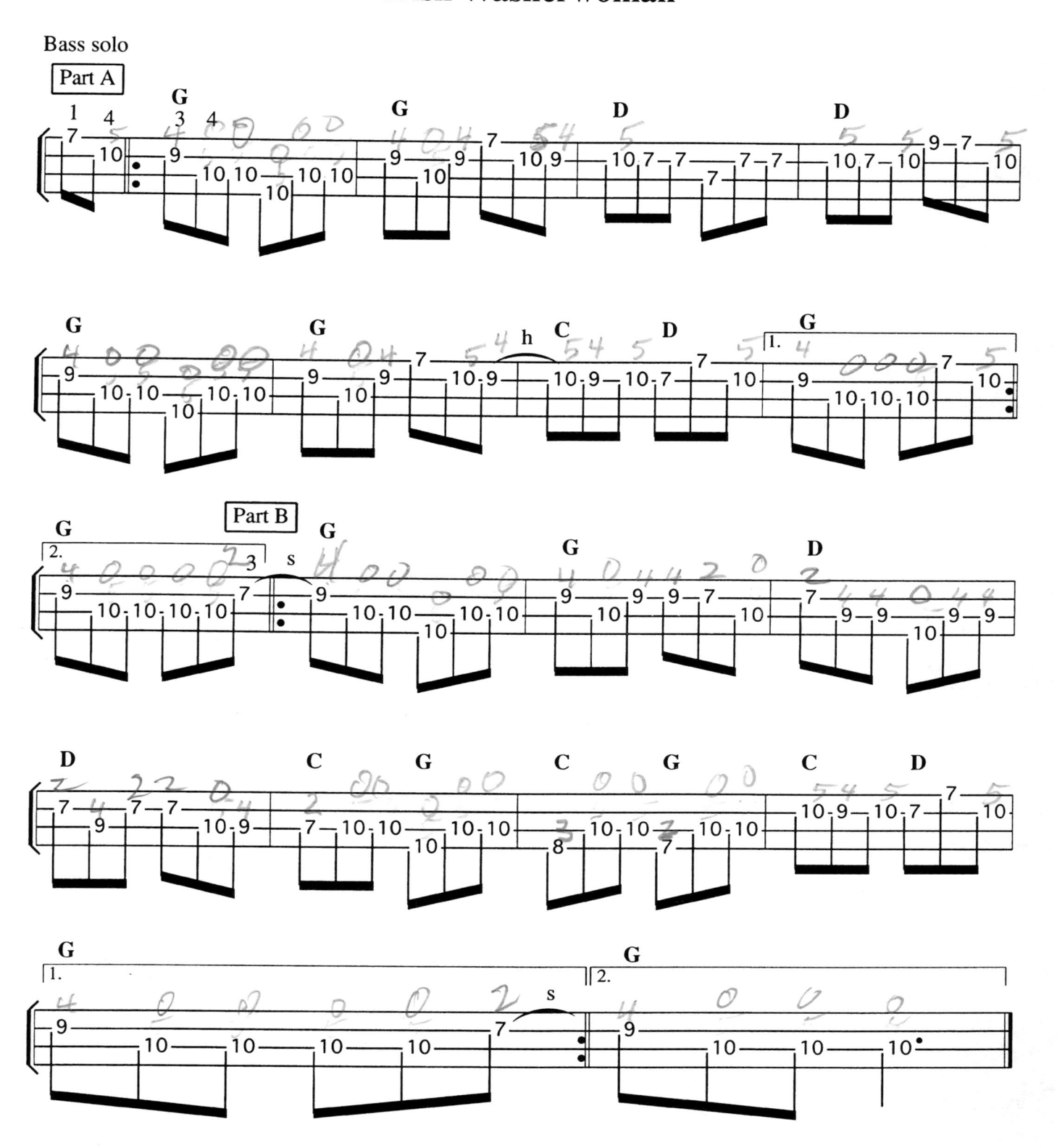

La Bastringue

Bass 1

French Canadian

La Bastringue

Bass solo*

*Bass solo is not on CD.

Leather Britches

Bass 1

North American

Leather Britches

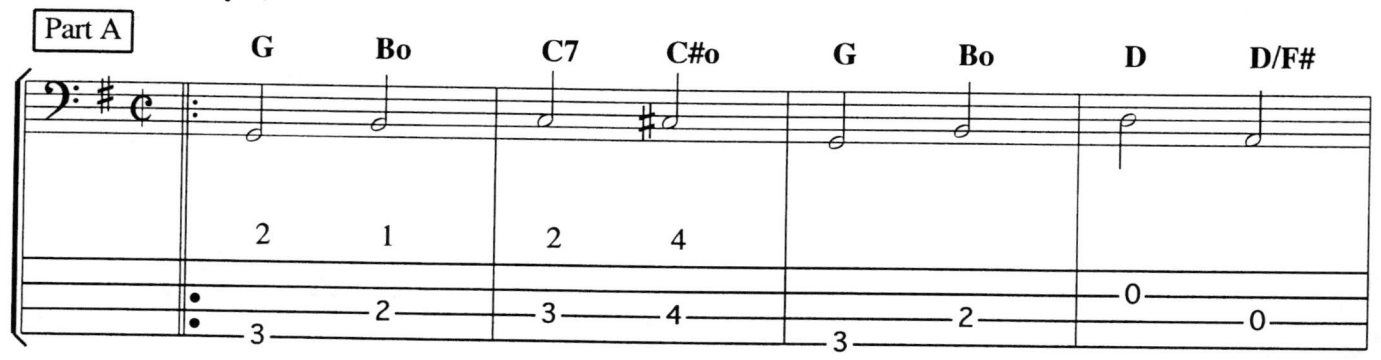

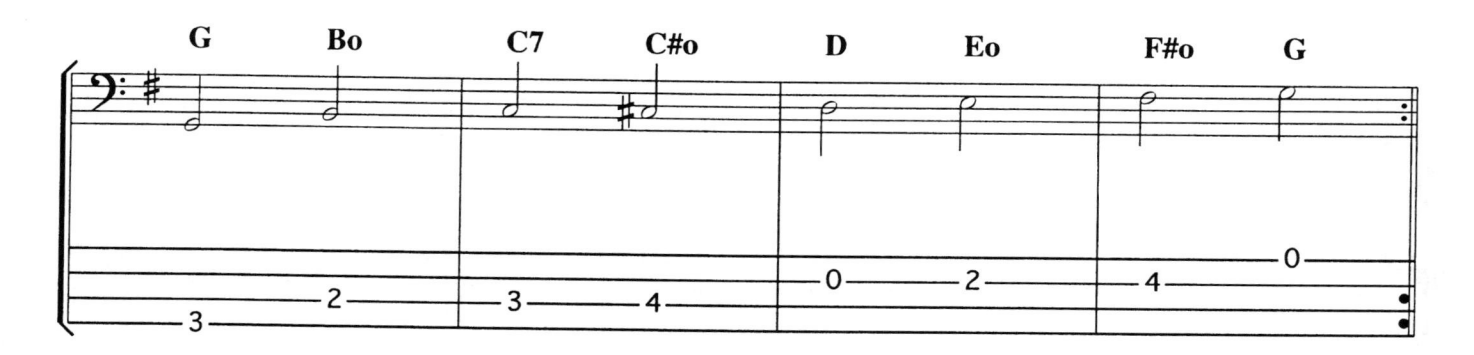

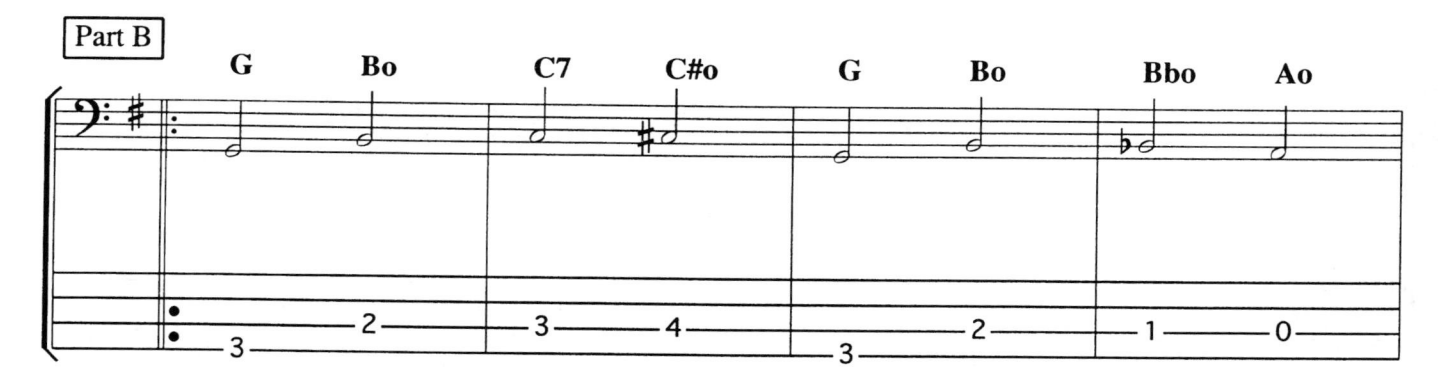

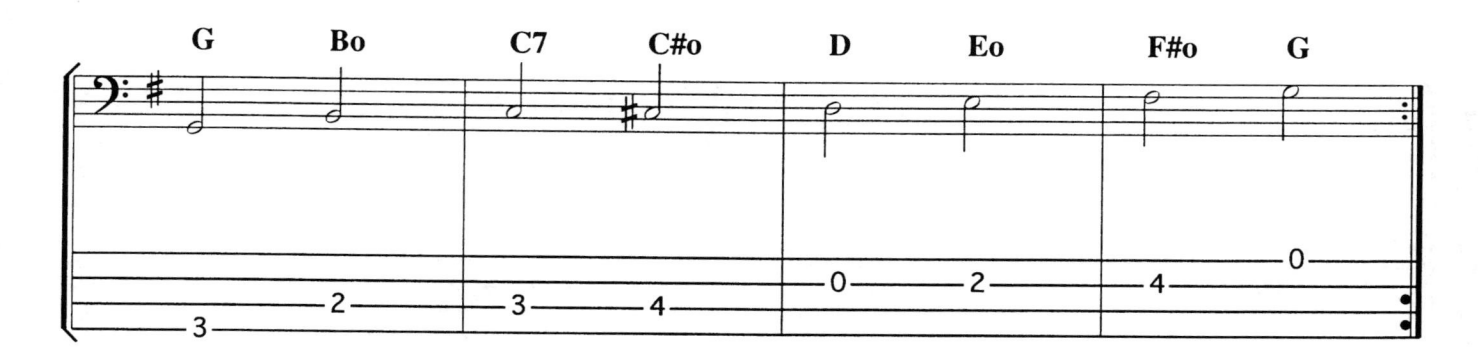

Bass 2 (Texas-style)

Liberty

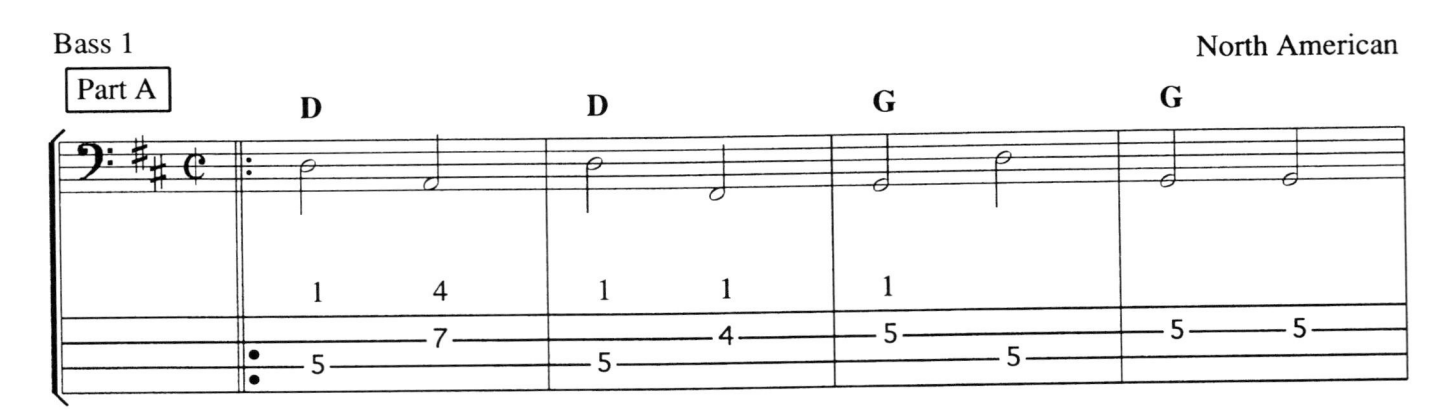

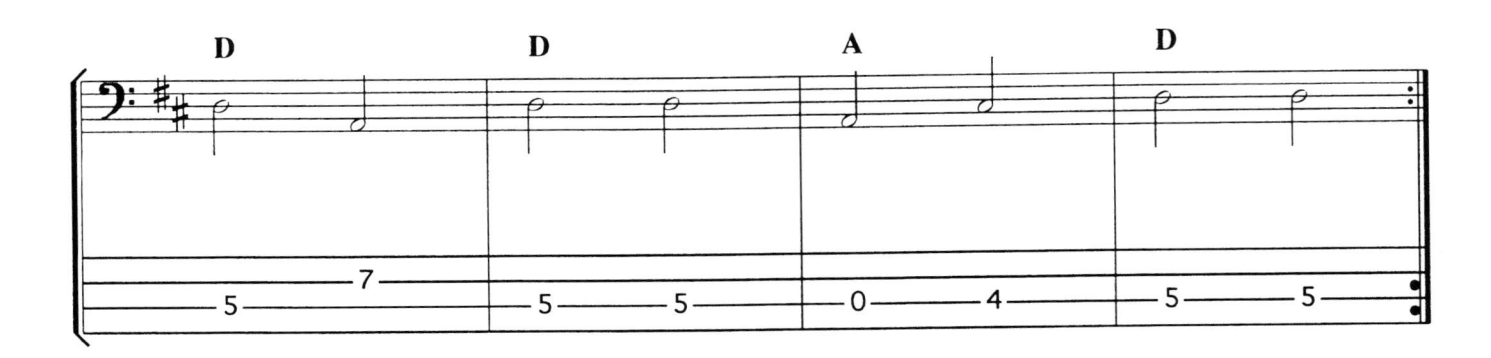

Bass 1

North American

Part A

Martin's Waltz

Bass 1

North American

Mason's Apron

Irish

Bass 1

Part A

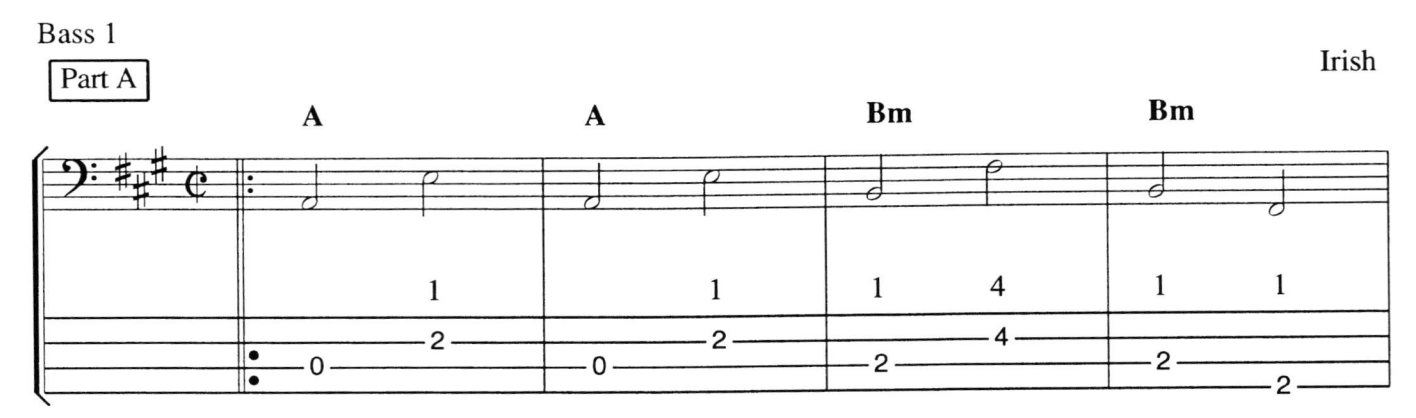

Part B

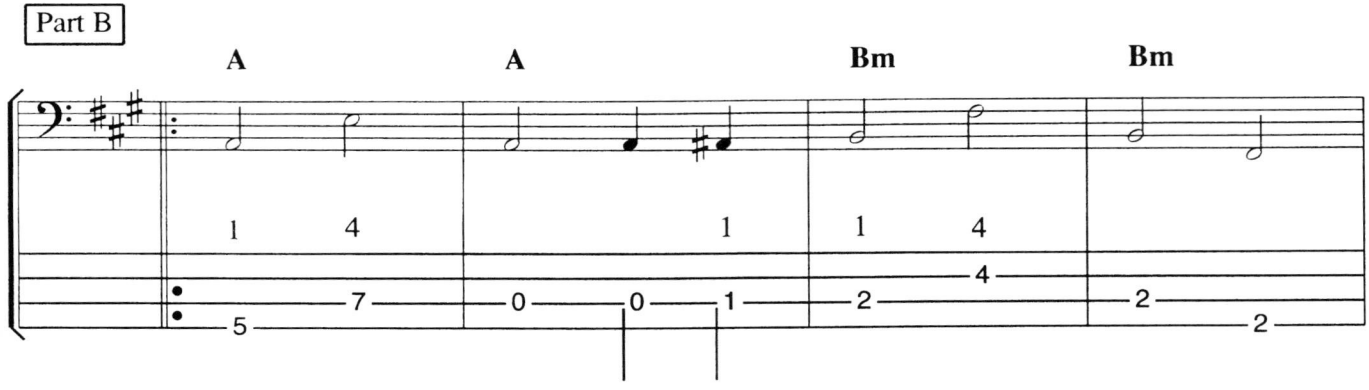

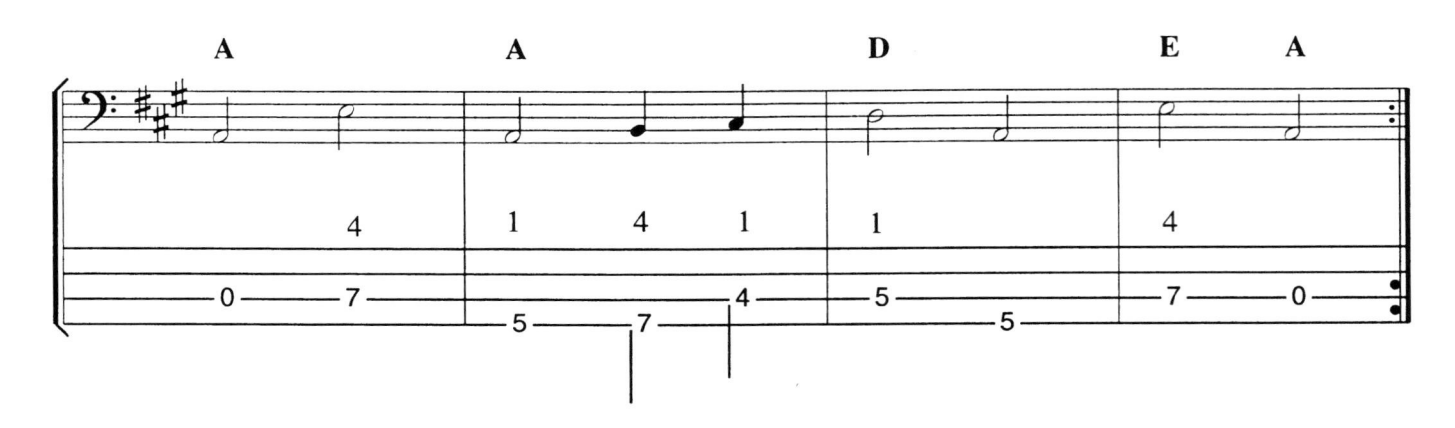

Mason's Apron

*Bass 2 is not on CD.

Mason's Apron

*Bass solo is not on CD.

Mason's Apron

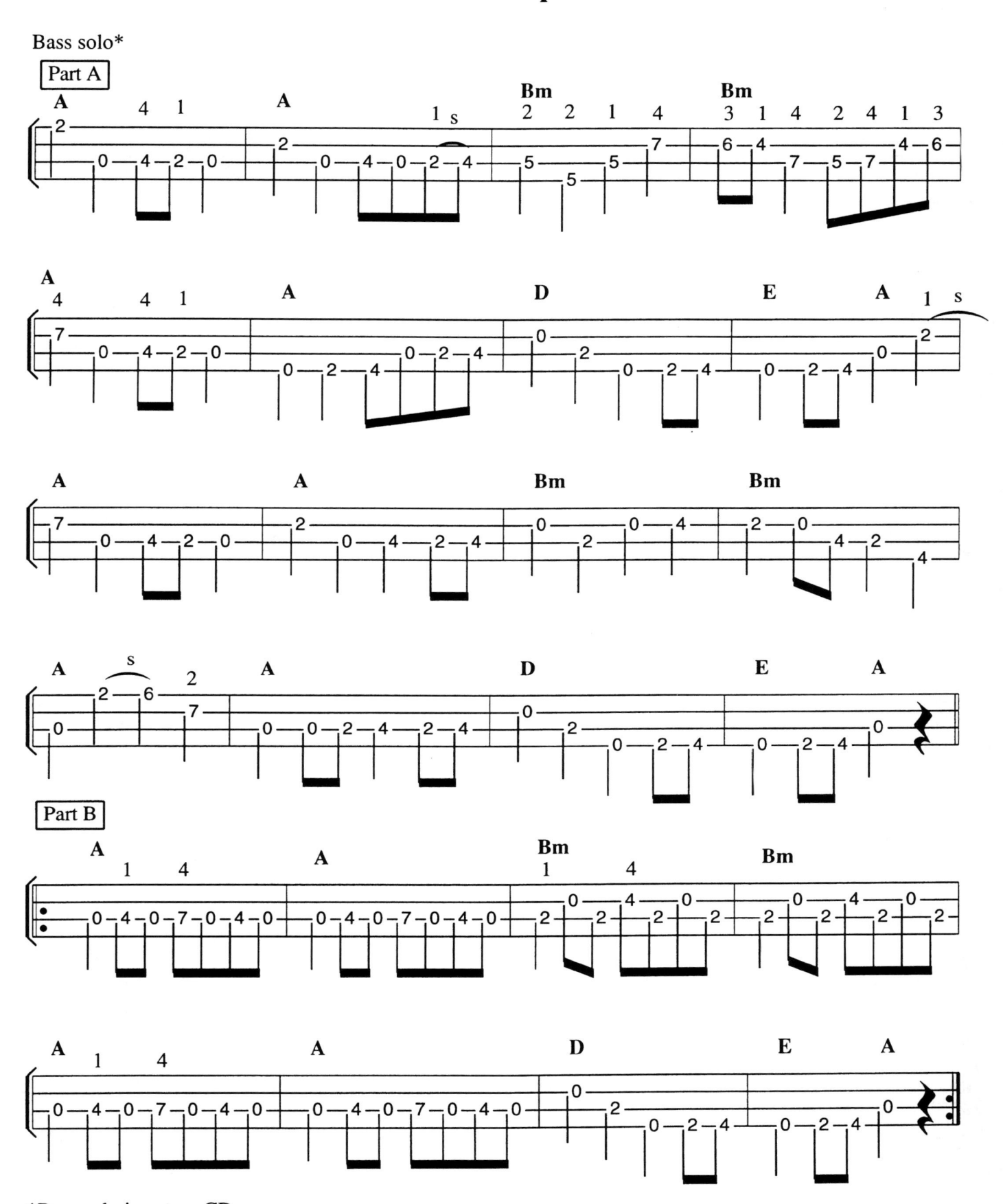

Mississippi Hornpipe

Bass 1

North American

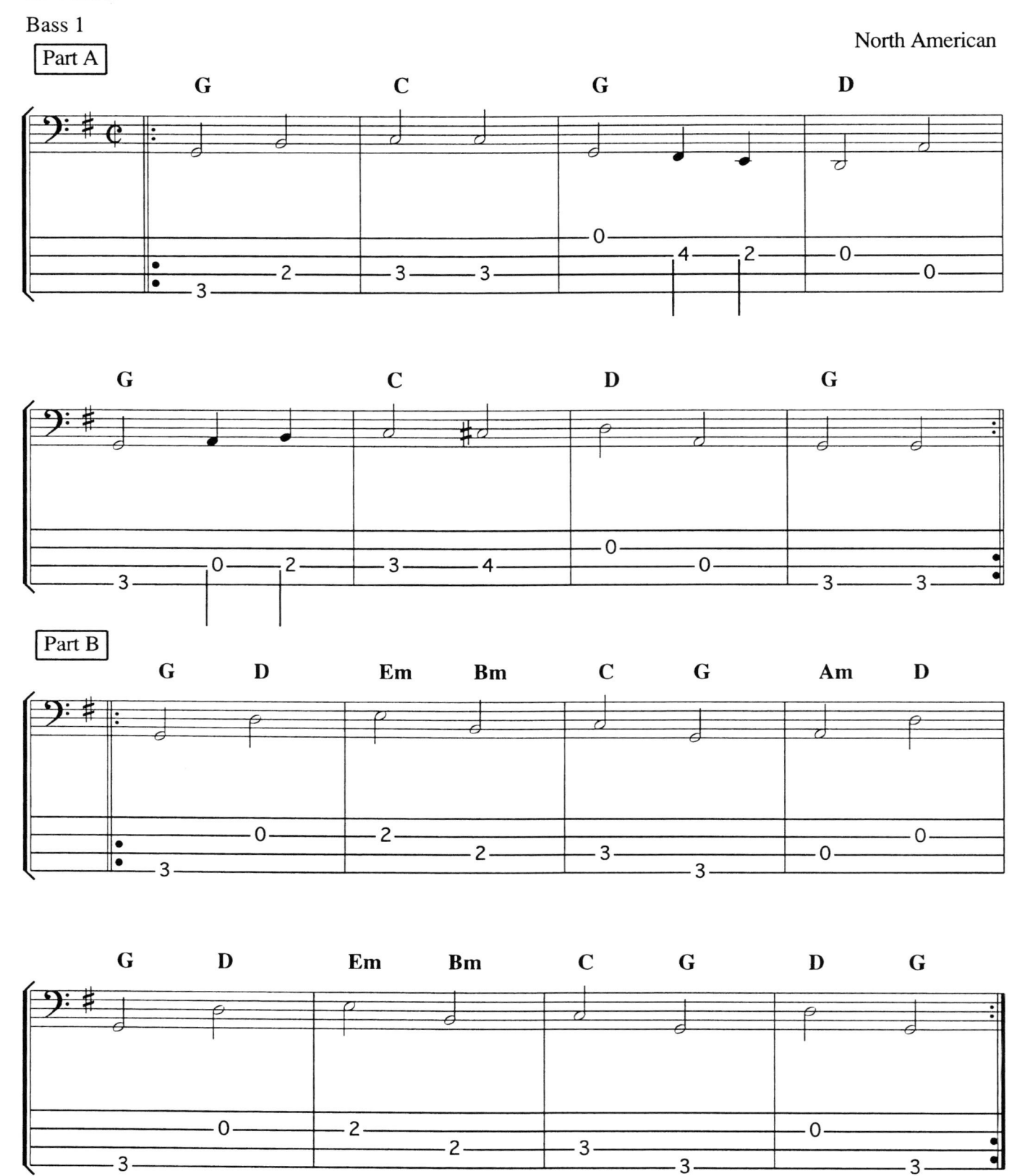

Part A

Mississippi Hornpipe

Bass solo*

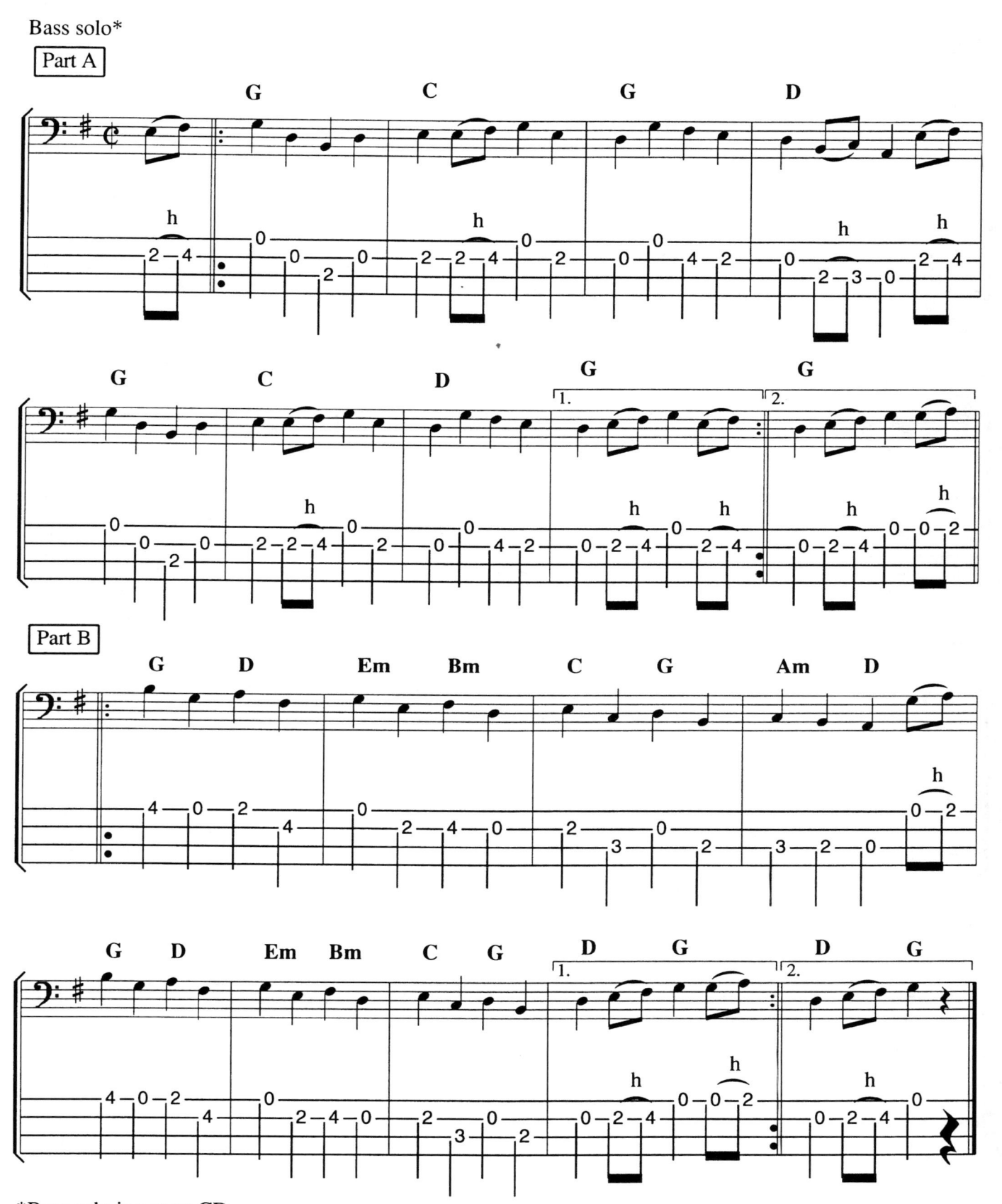

*Bass solo is not on CD.

Mississippi Sawyer

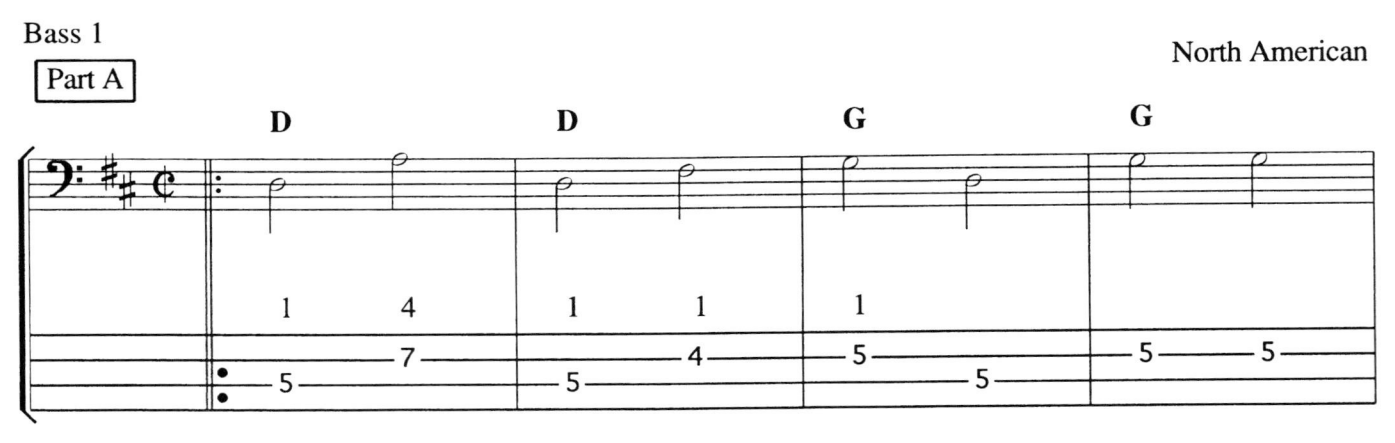

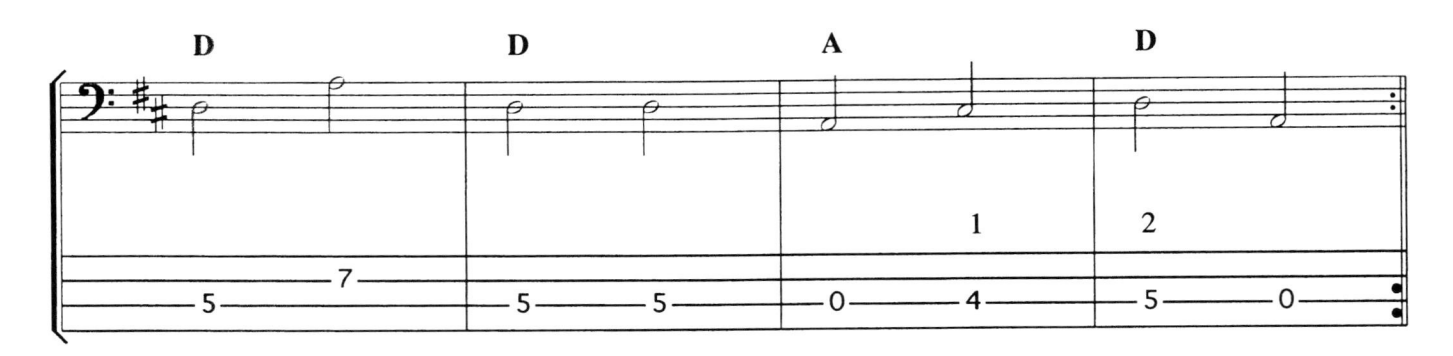

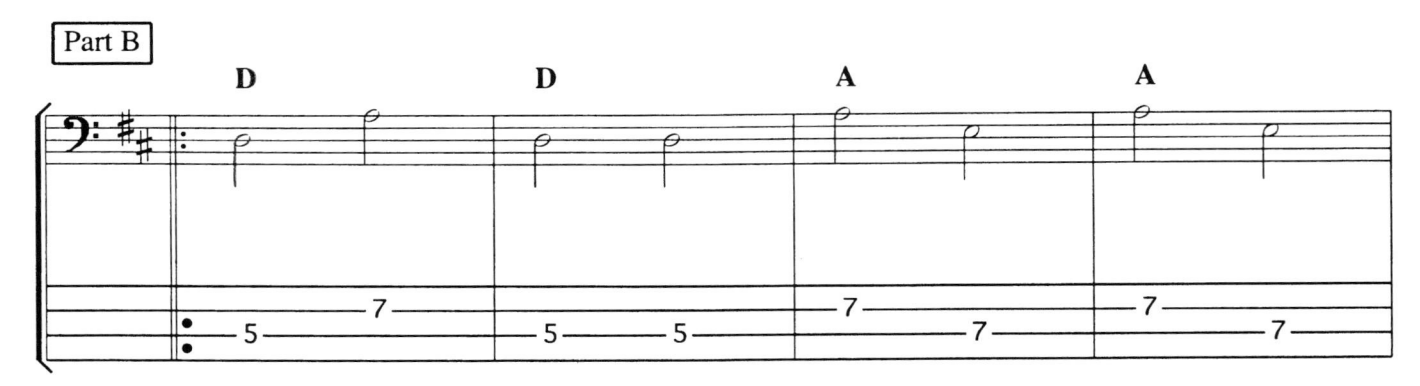

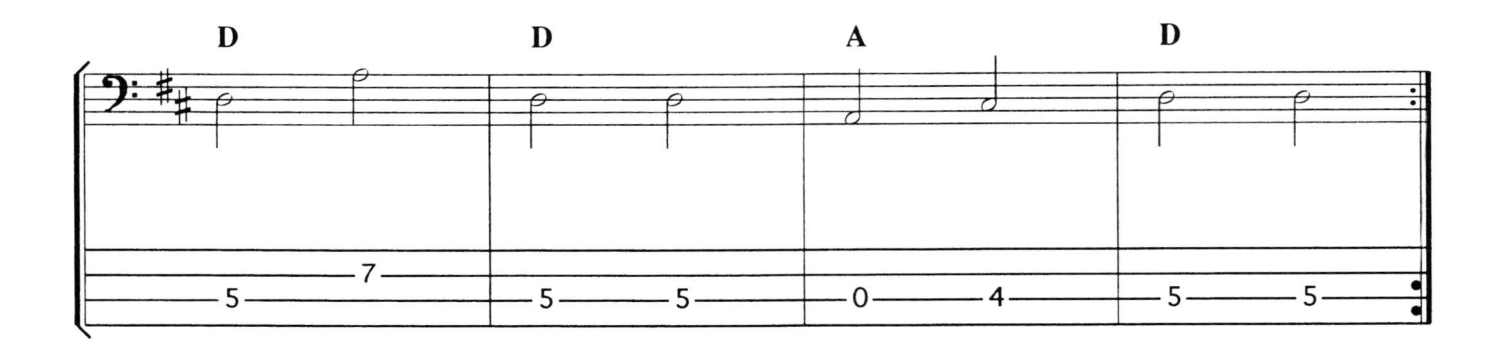

This page has been left blank to avoid awkward page turns.

Old Dan Tucker

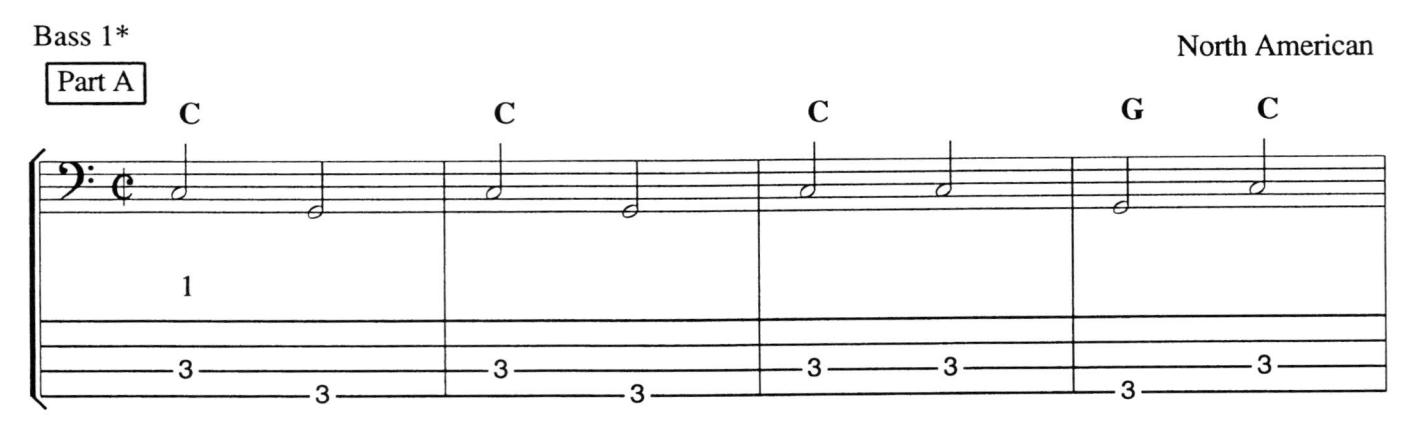

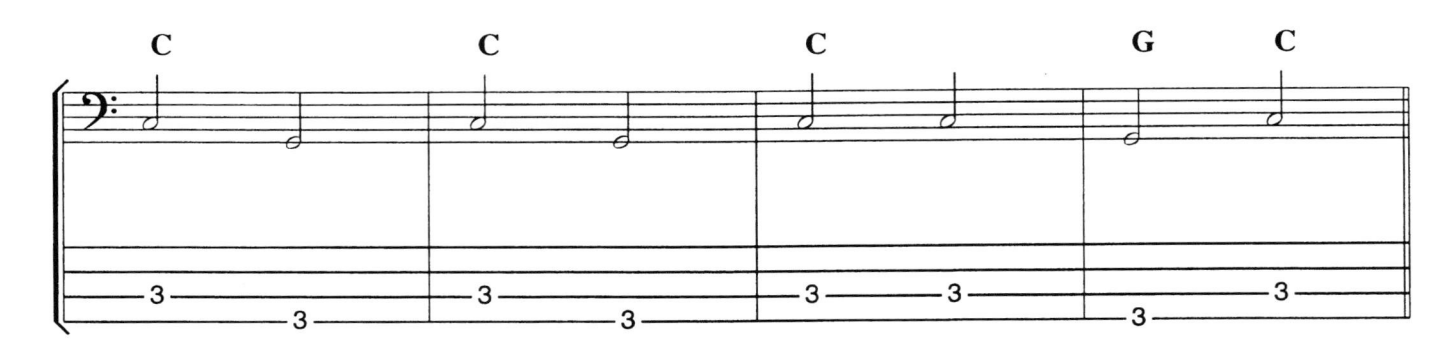

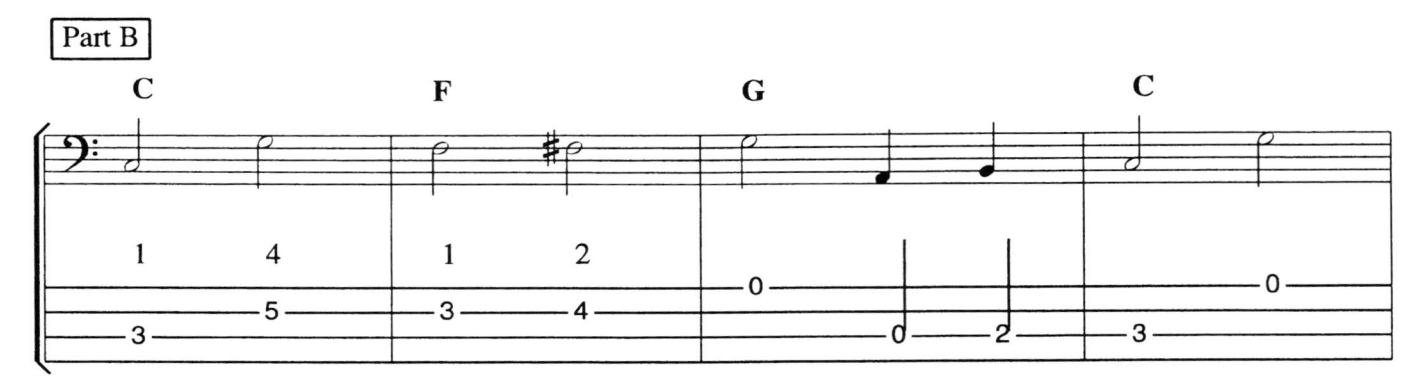

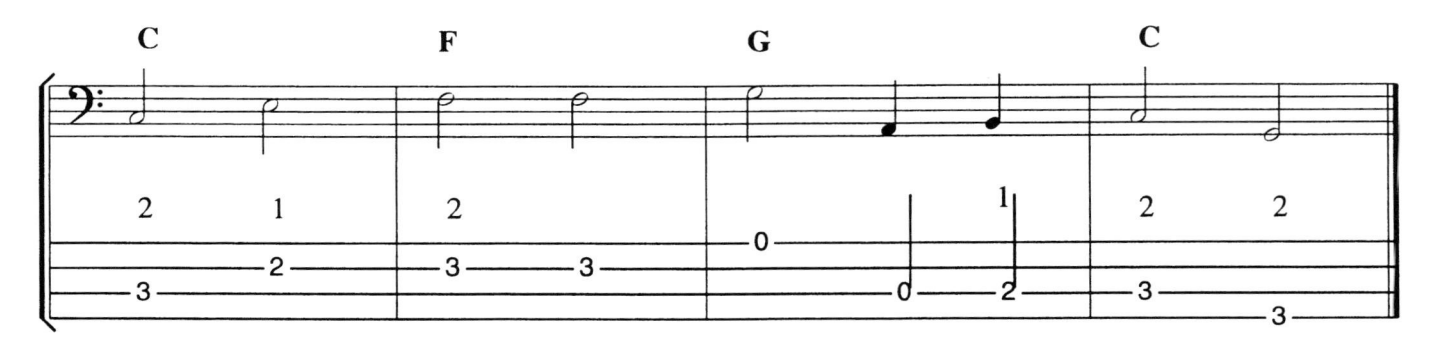

Bass 1*

North American

Part A

Part B

*Bass 1 is not on CD.

Vamp on final measure until part A begins again.

Old Dan Tucker

Bass solo

*Bass solo is not on CD.

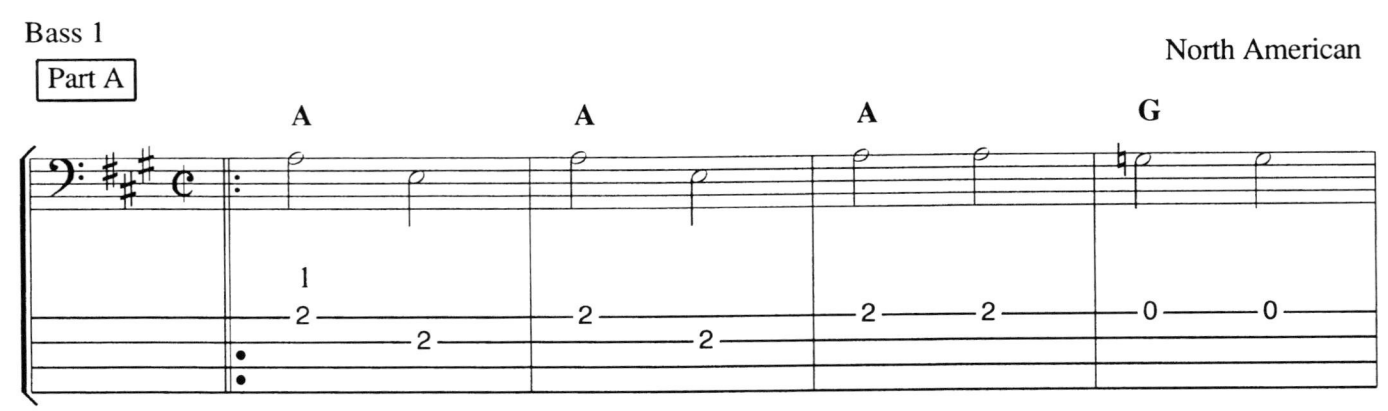

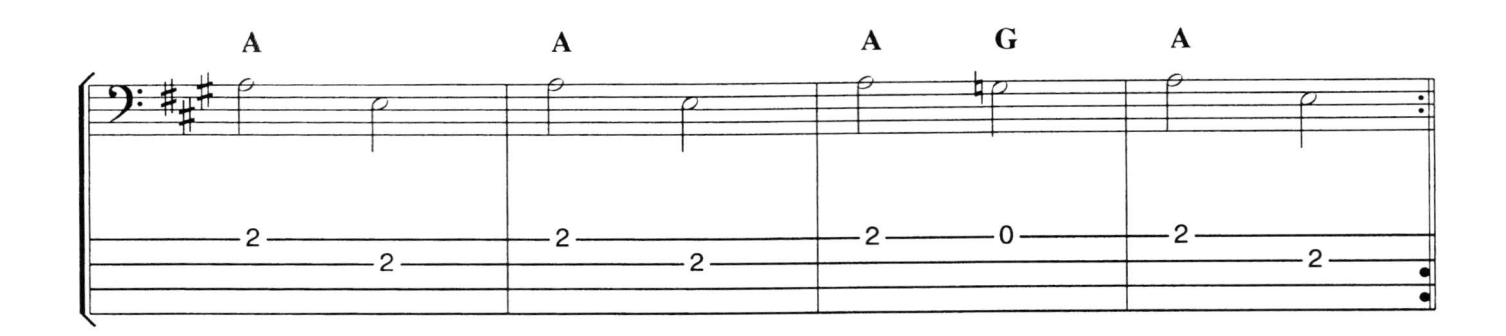

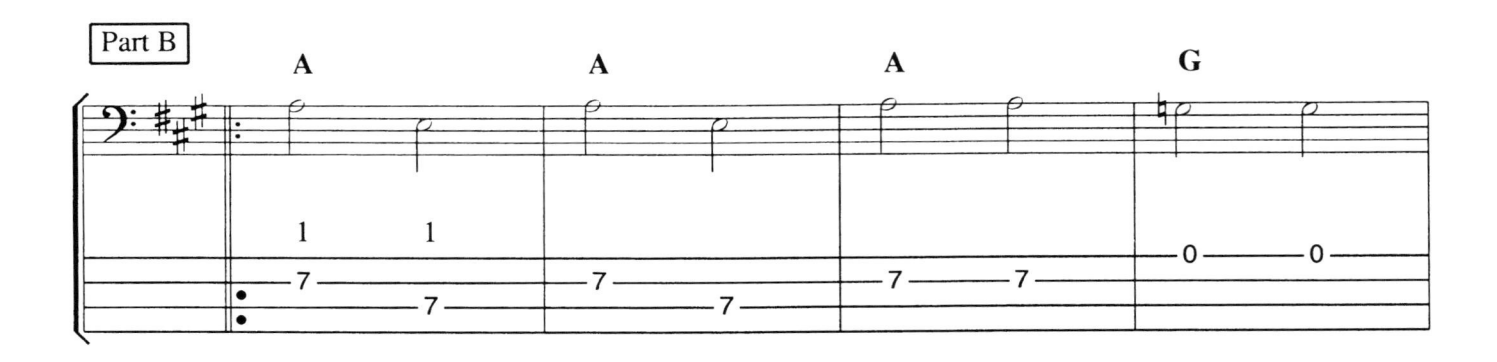

Old Joe Clark

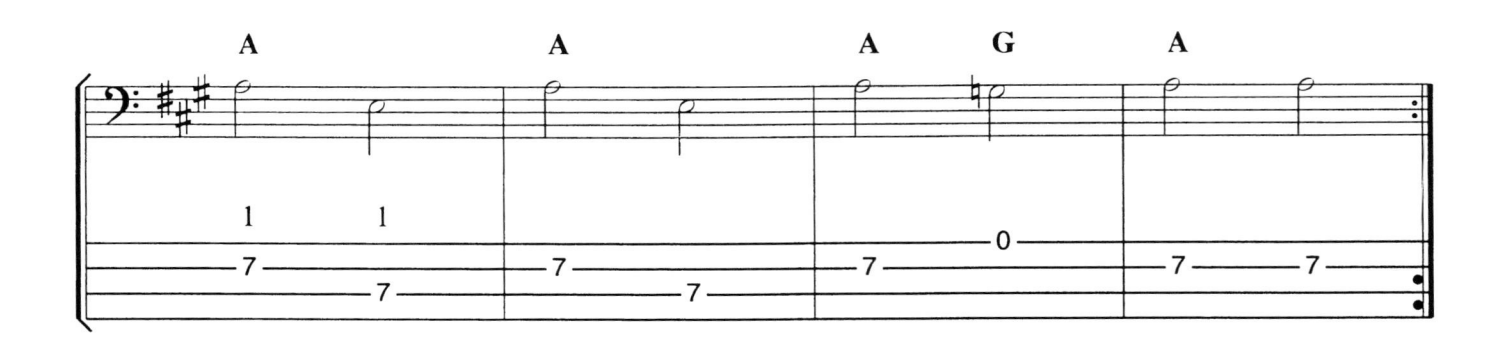

Bass 1

North American

Old Joe Clark

Bass solo*

*Bass solo is not on CD.

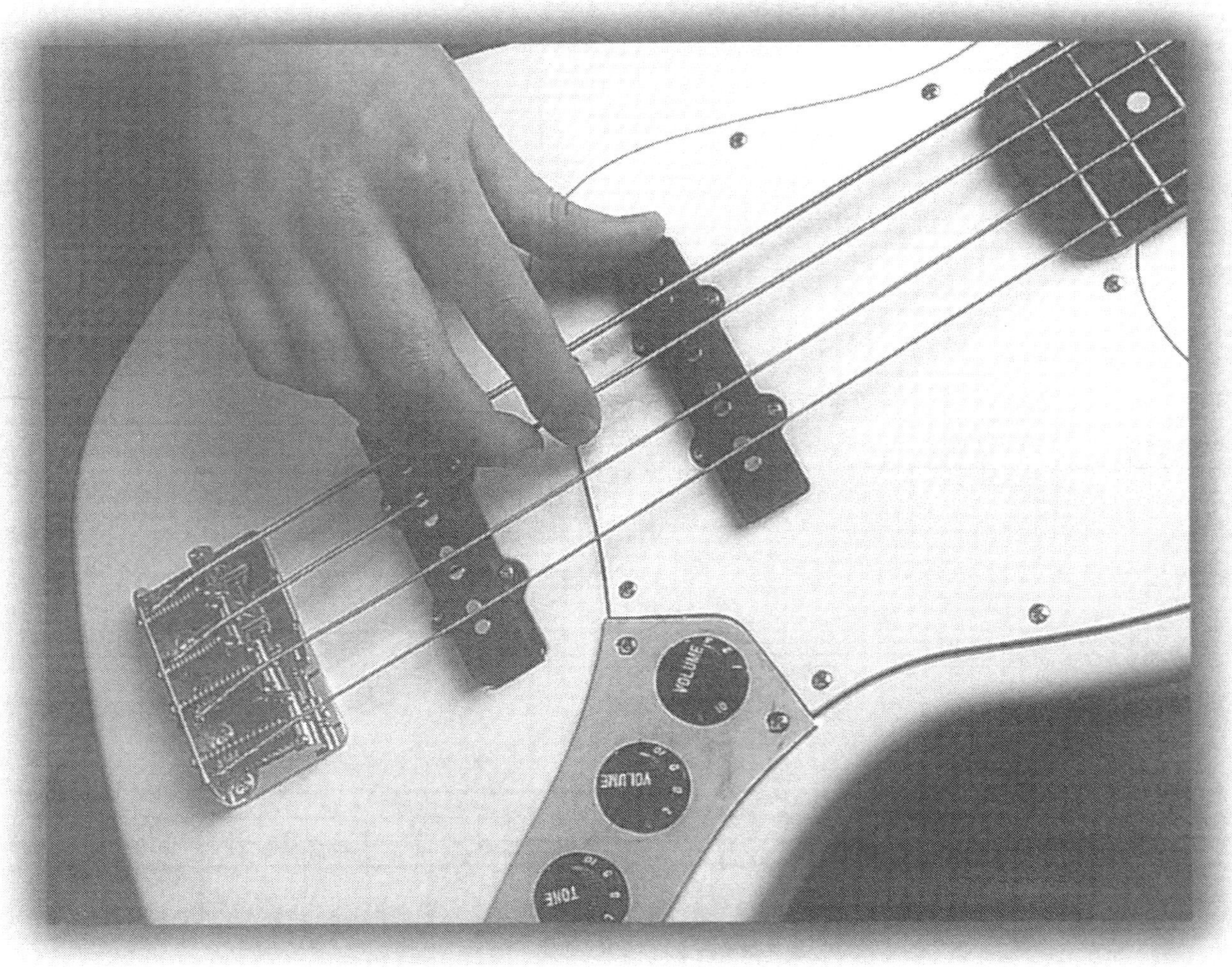
VOLUME
VOLUME
TONE

President Garfield's Hornpipe

Bass 1

Part A

North American

President Garfield's Hornpipe

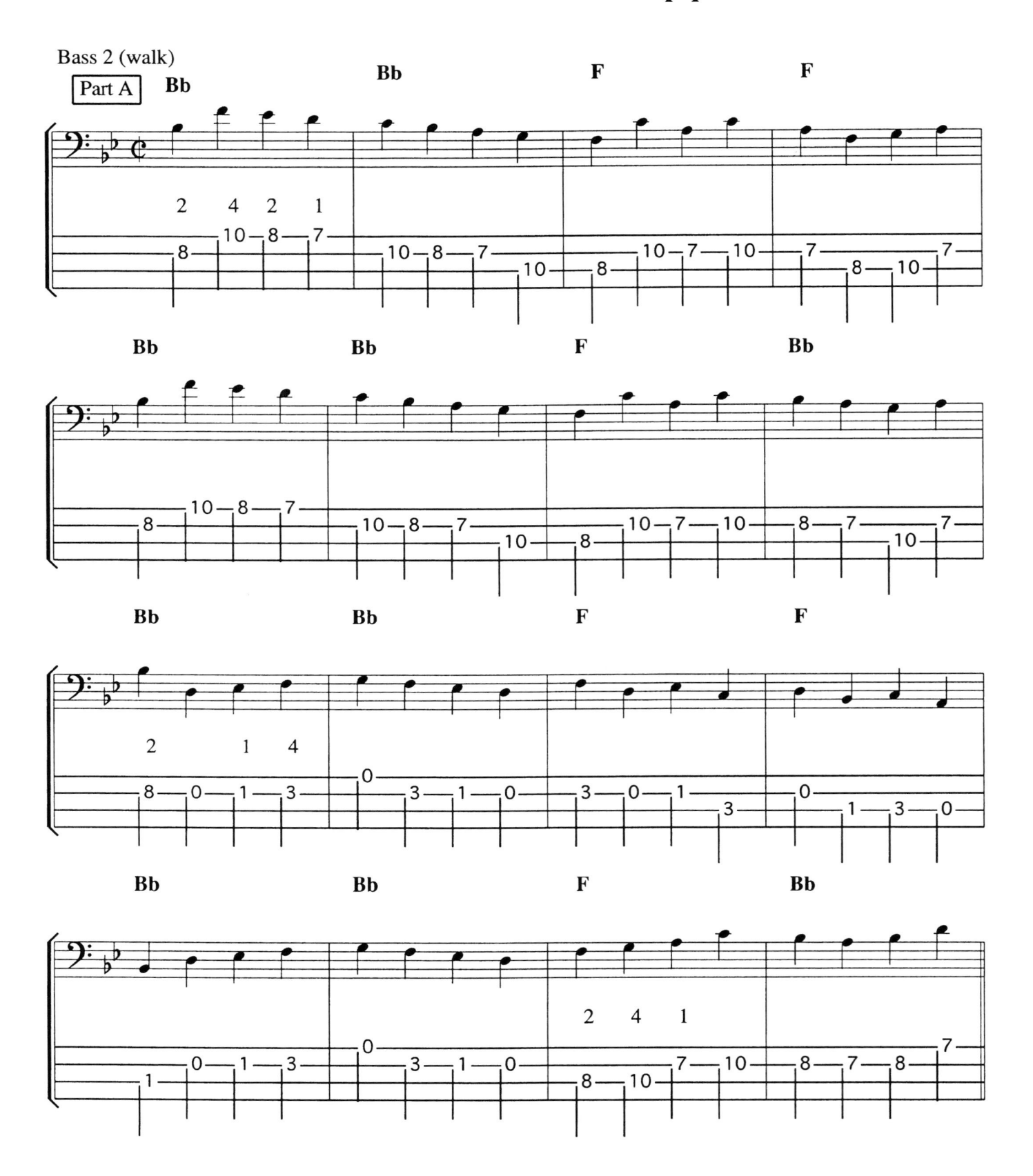

President Garfield's Hornpipe

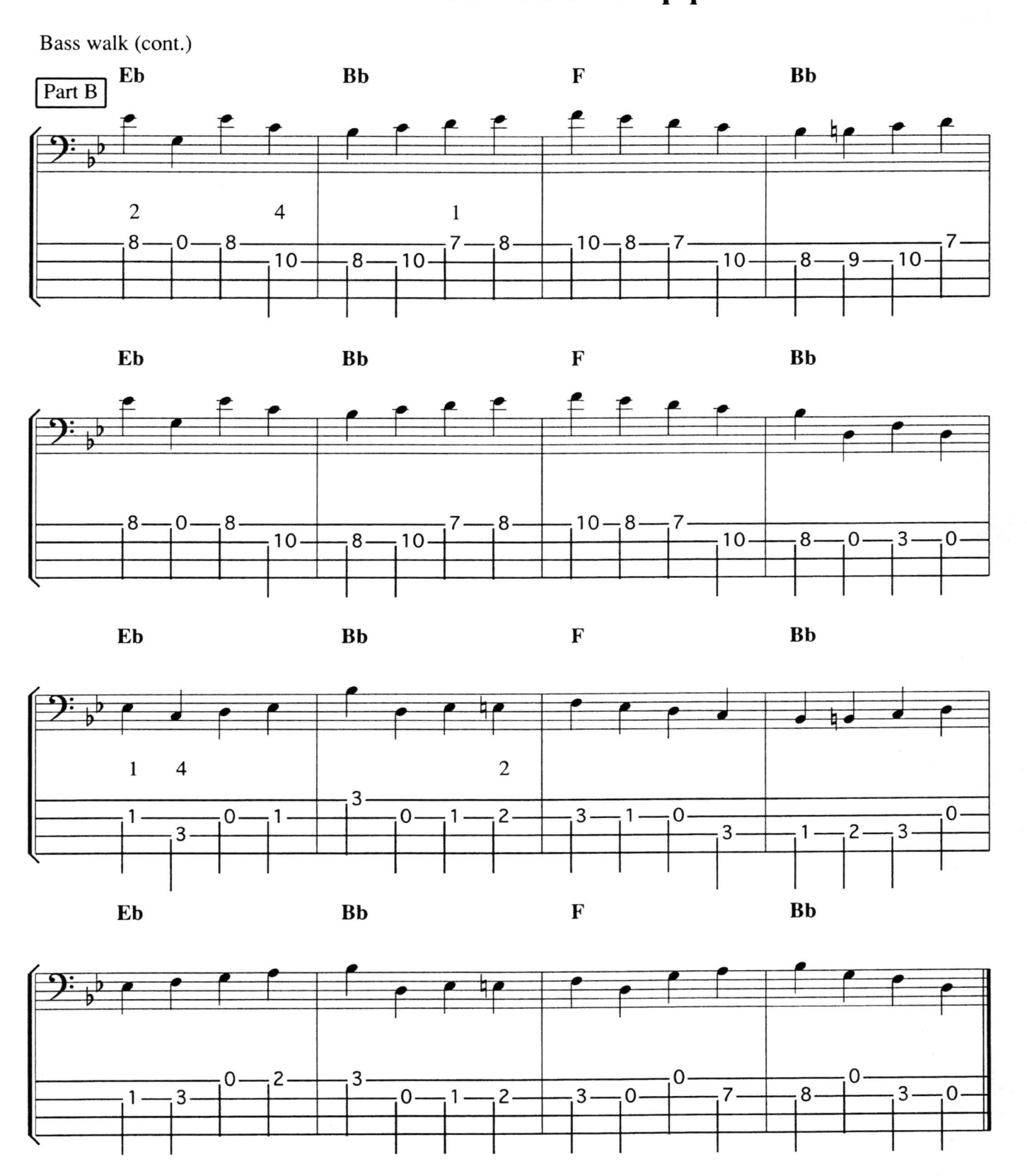

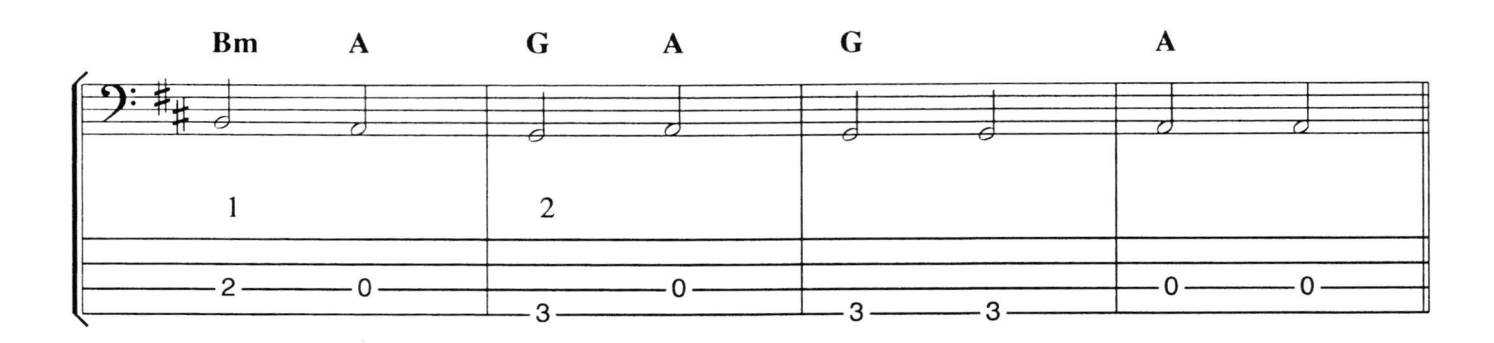

Pretty Peg

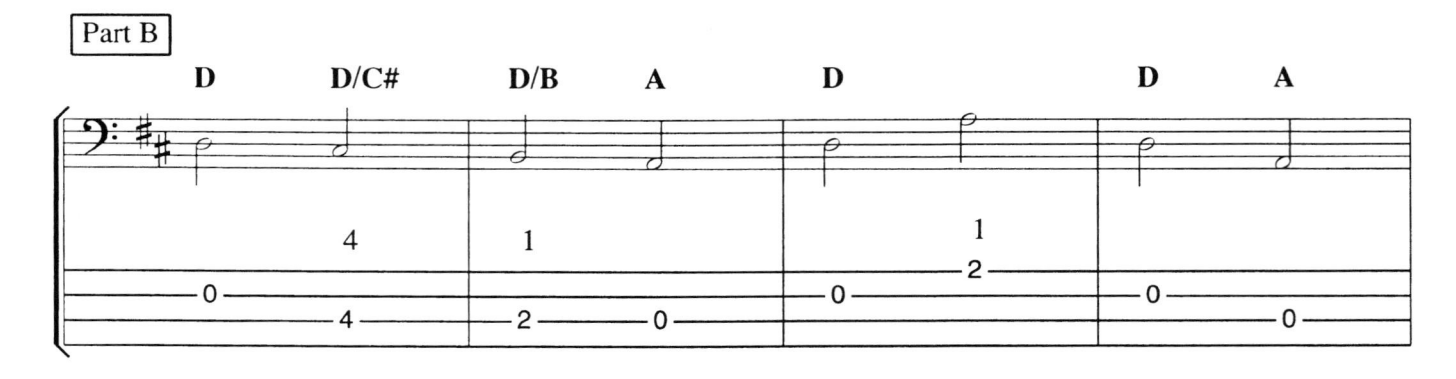

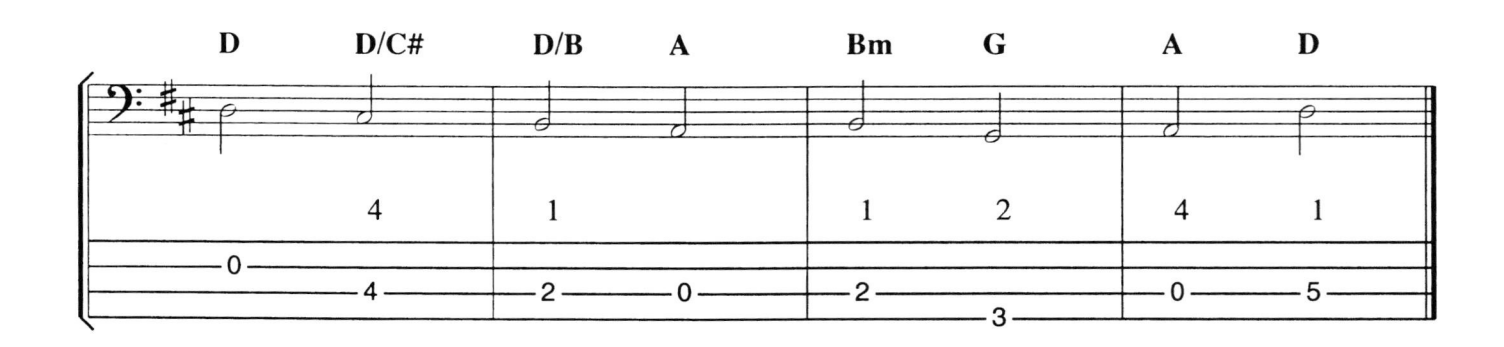

Pretty Peg

Bass 2*

*Bass 2 is not on CD.

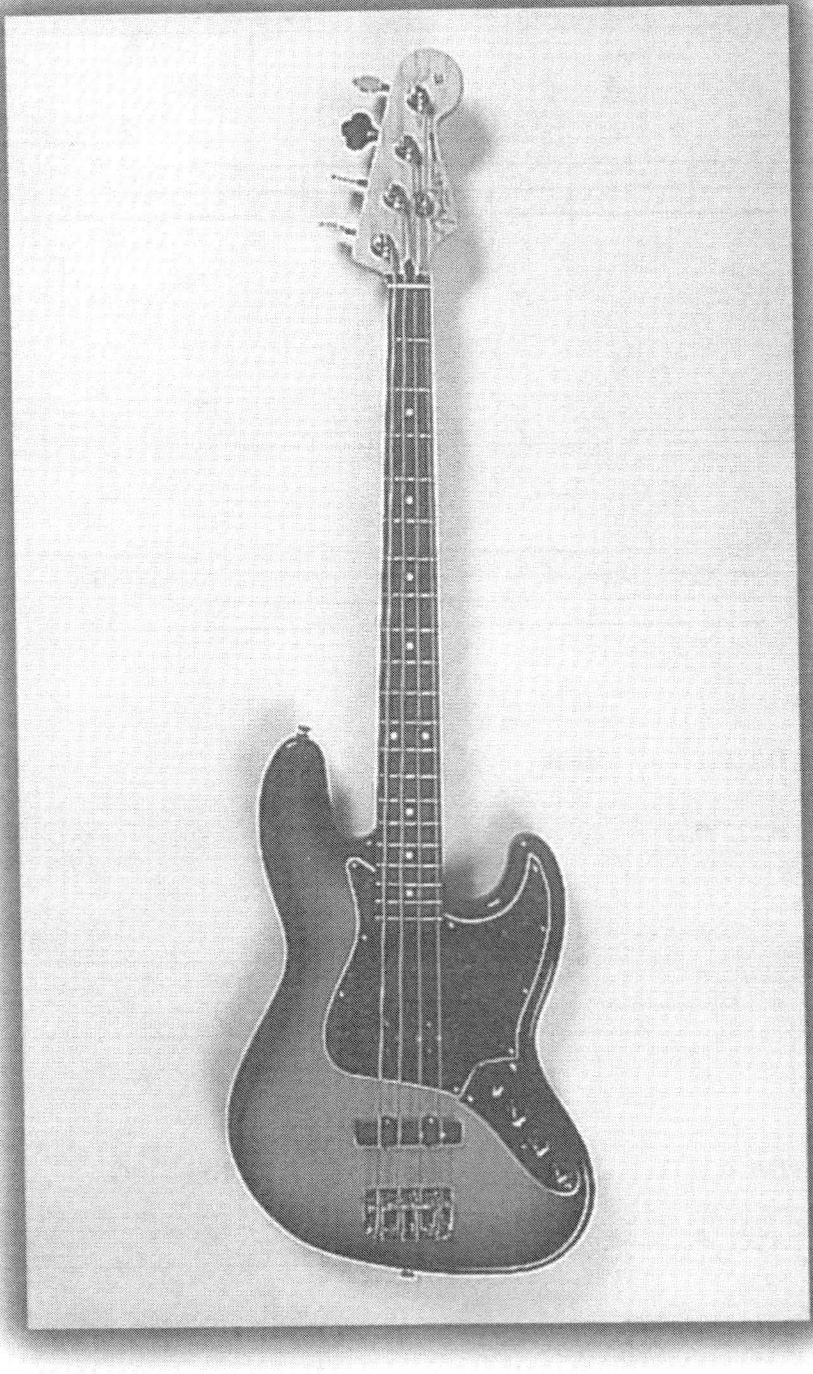

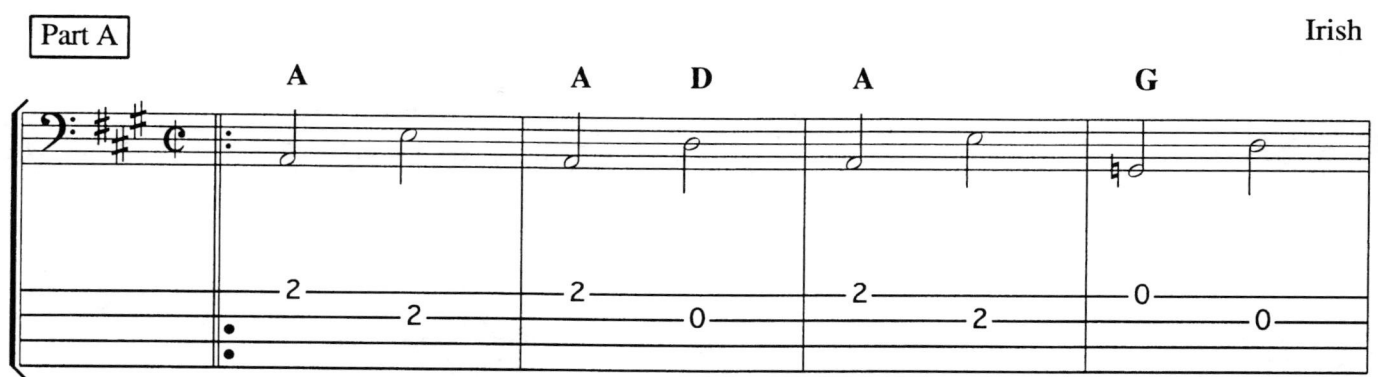

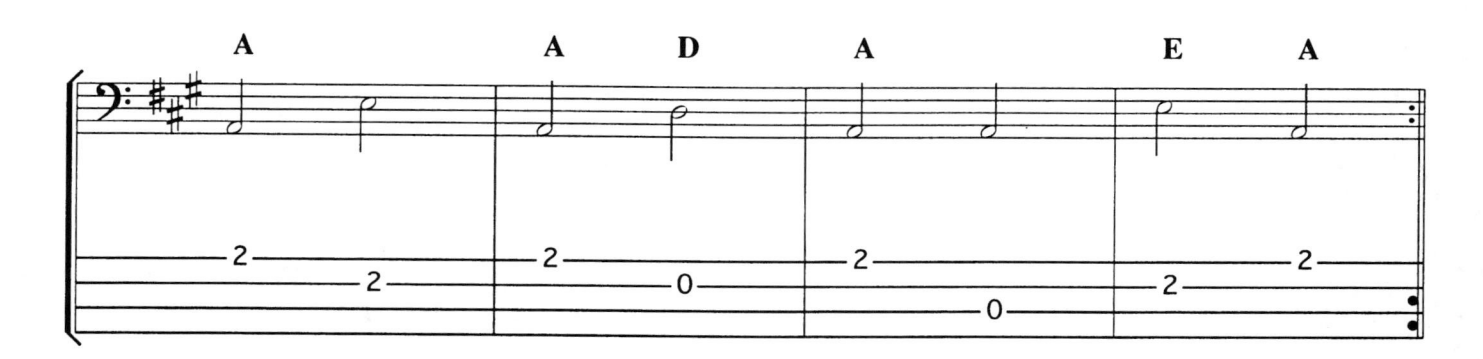

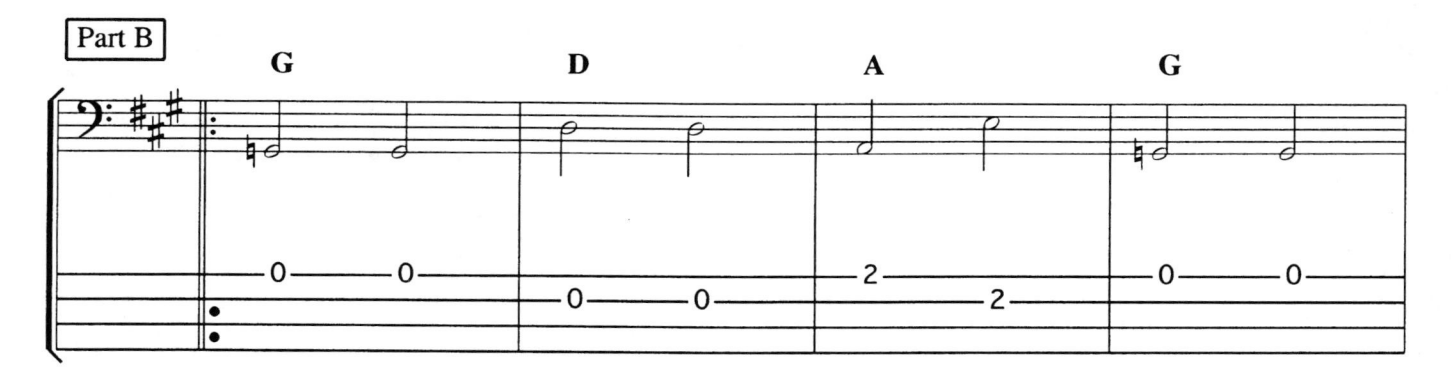

Red-haired Boy

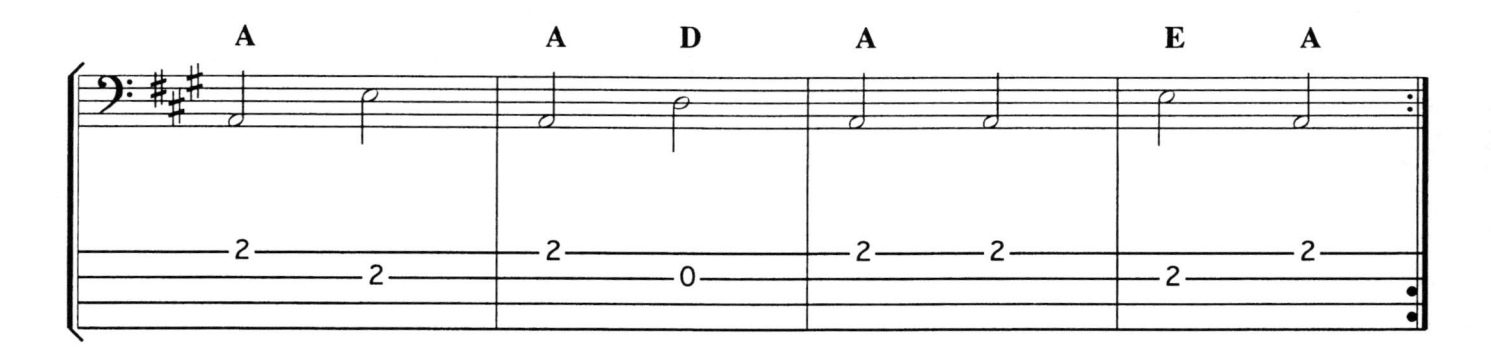

Bass 1

Irish

Red-haired Boy

Bass (solo)*

[Part A]

[sheet music]

[Part B]

[sheet music]

*Bass solo is not on CD. (This solo is intended for electric bass.)
(All notes are tapped: L1 = left hand, 1st finger; L2 = left hand, 2nd finger; R1 = right hand, 1st finger)

Red-haired Boy

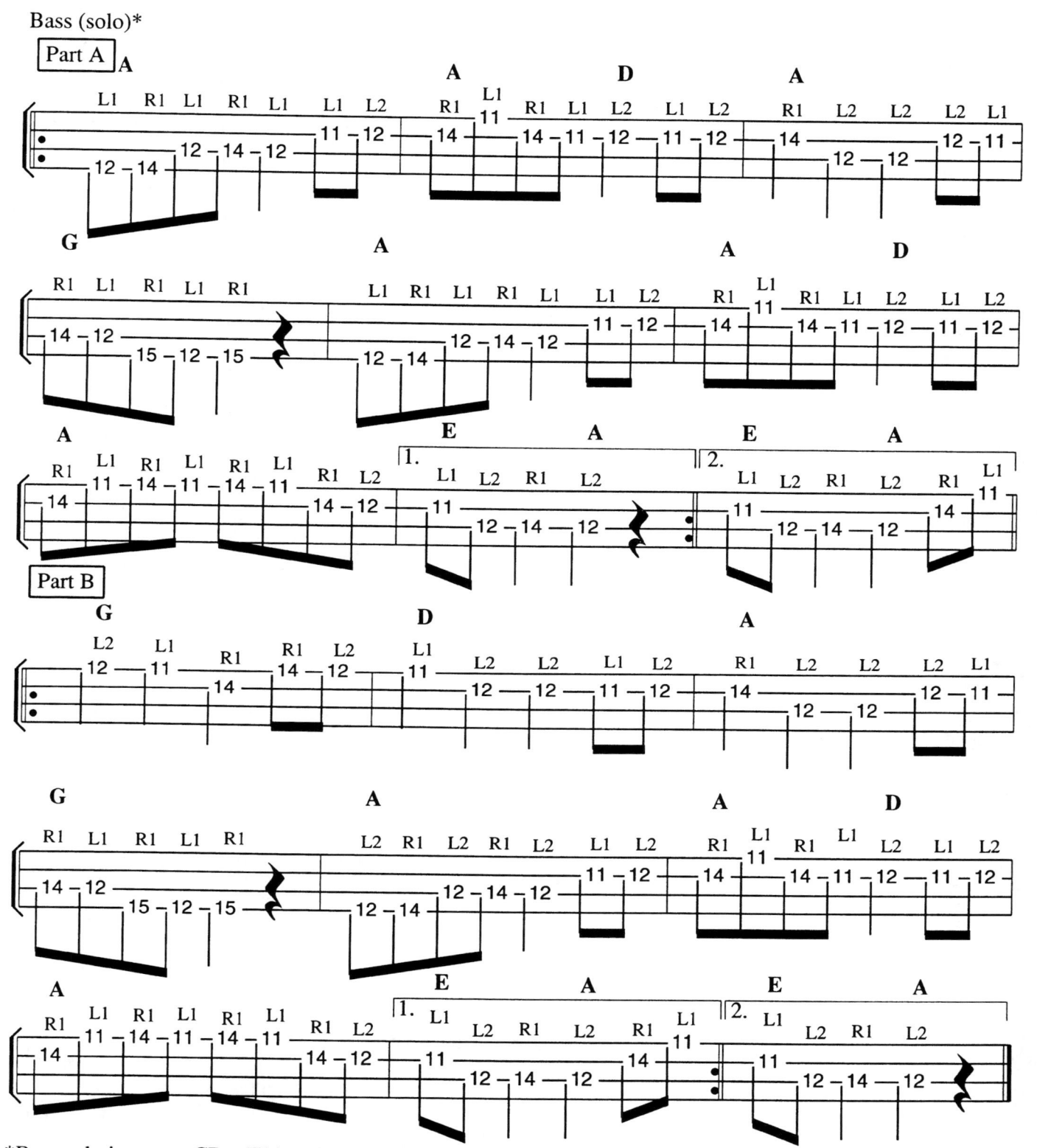

*Bass solo is not on CD. (This solo is intended for electric bass.)
(All notes are tapped: L1 = left hand, 1st finger; L2 = left hand, 2nd finger; R1 = right hand, 1st finger)

Red Wing

Bass 1

North American

Part A

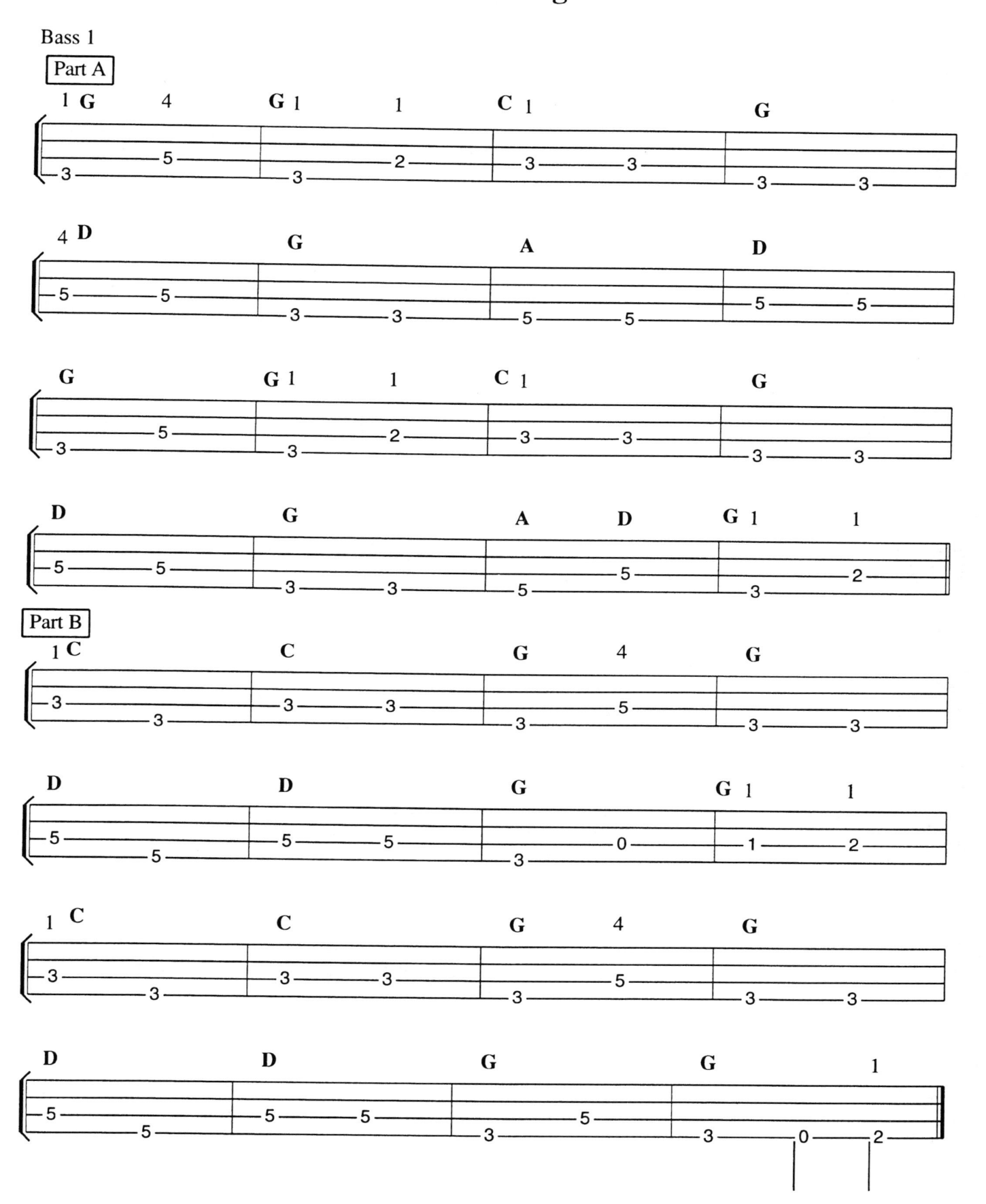

Red Wing

Red Wing

Bass 2*

*Bass 2 is not on CD.

Red Wing

Bass 2*

Part A

*Bass 2 is not on CD.

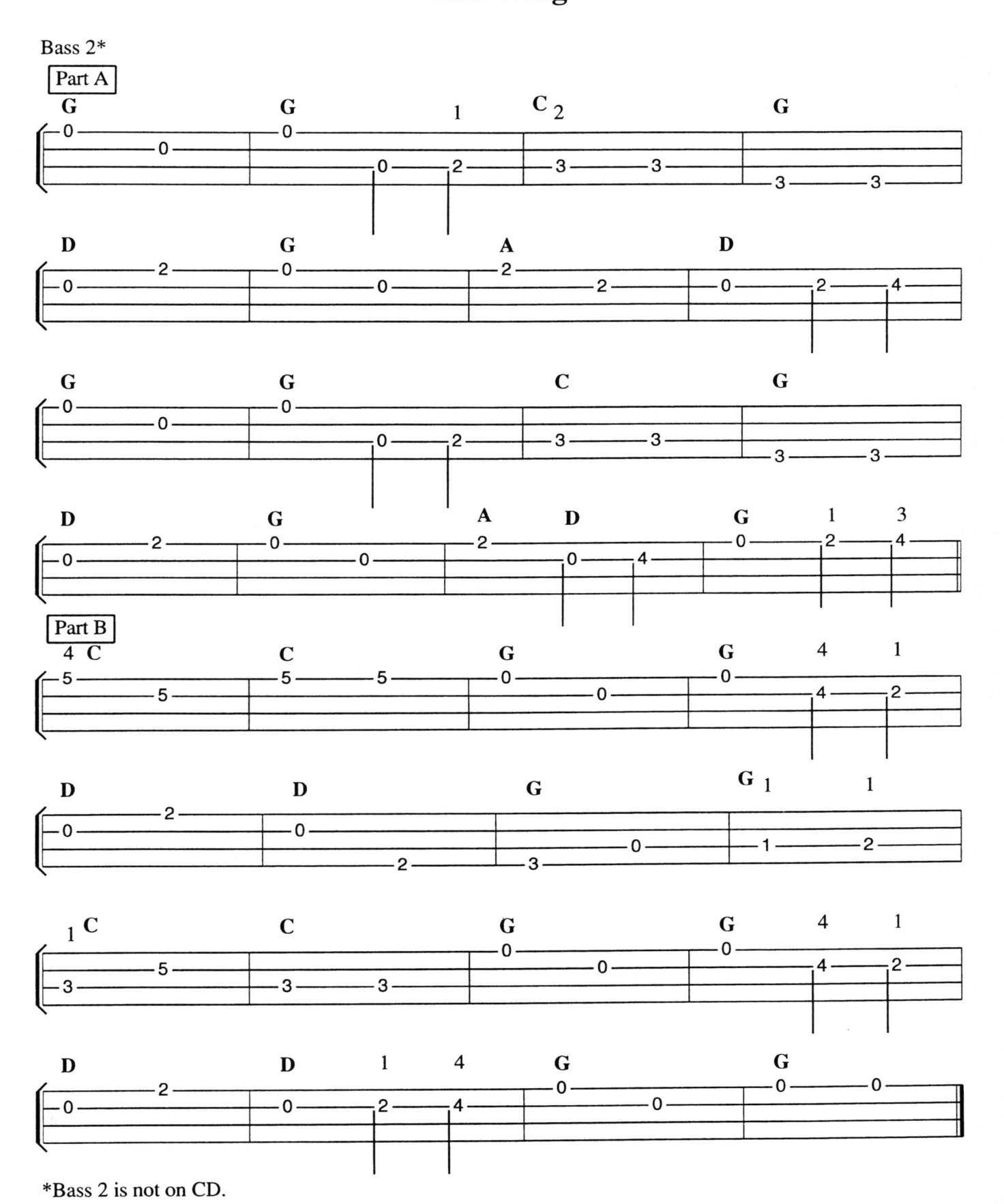

Red Wing

Bass solo*

*Bass solo is not on CD.

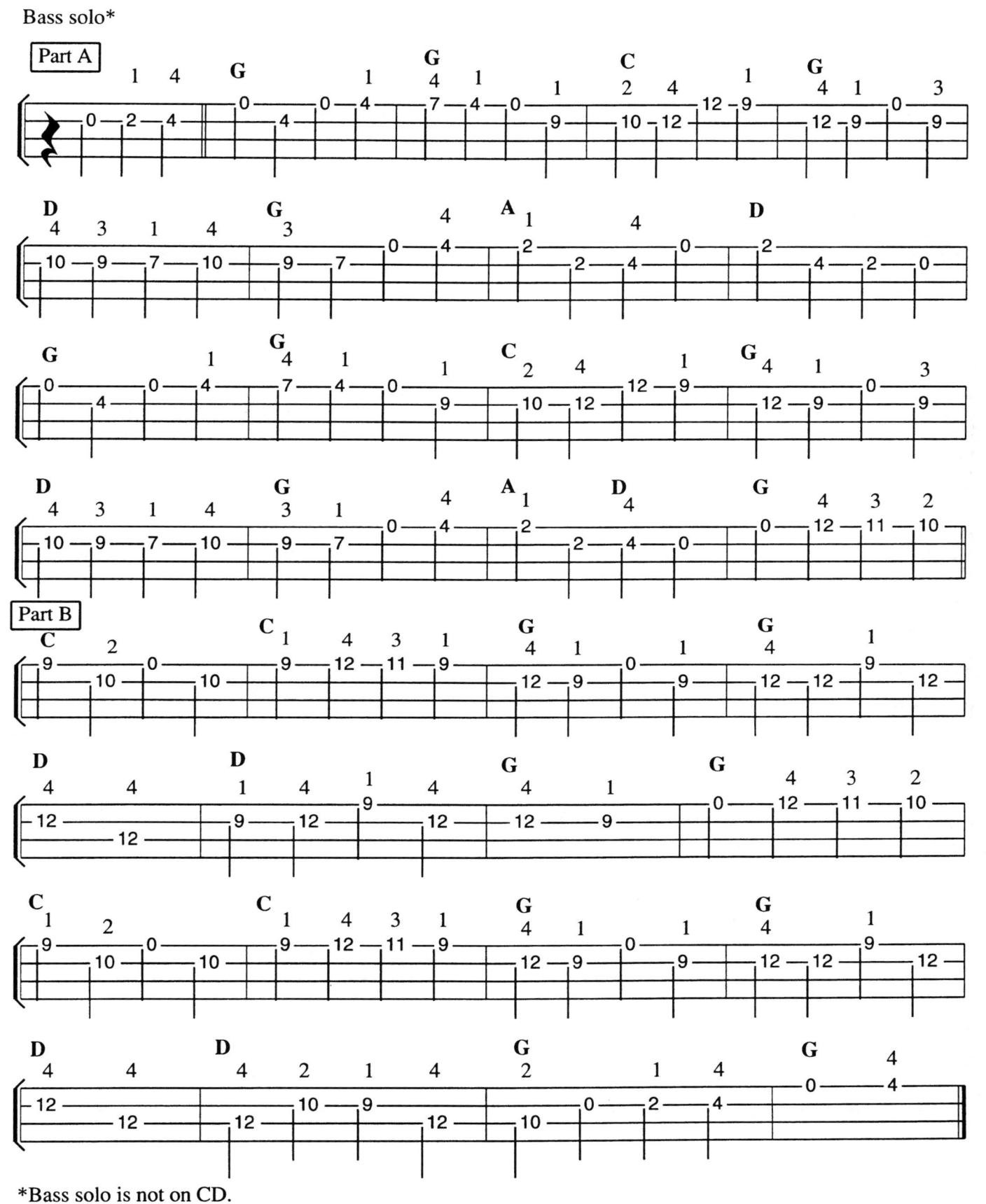

Red Wing

*Bass solo**

Disc 3
Track 3

Sailor's Hornpipe

Bass 1

English

Part A

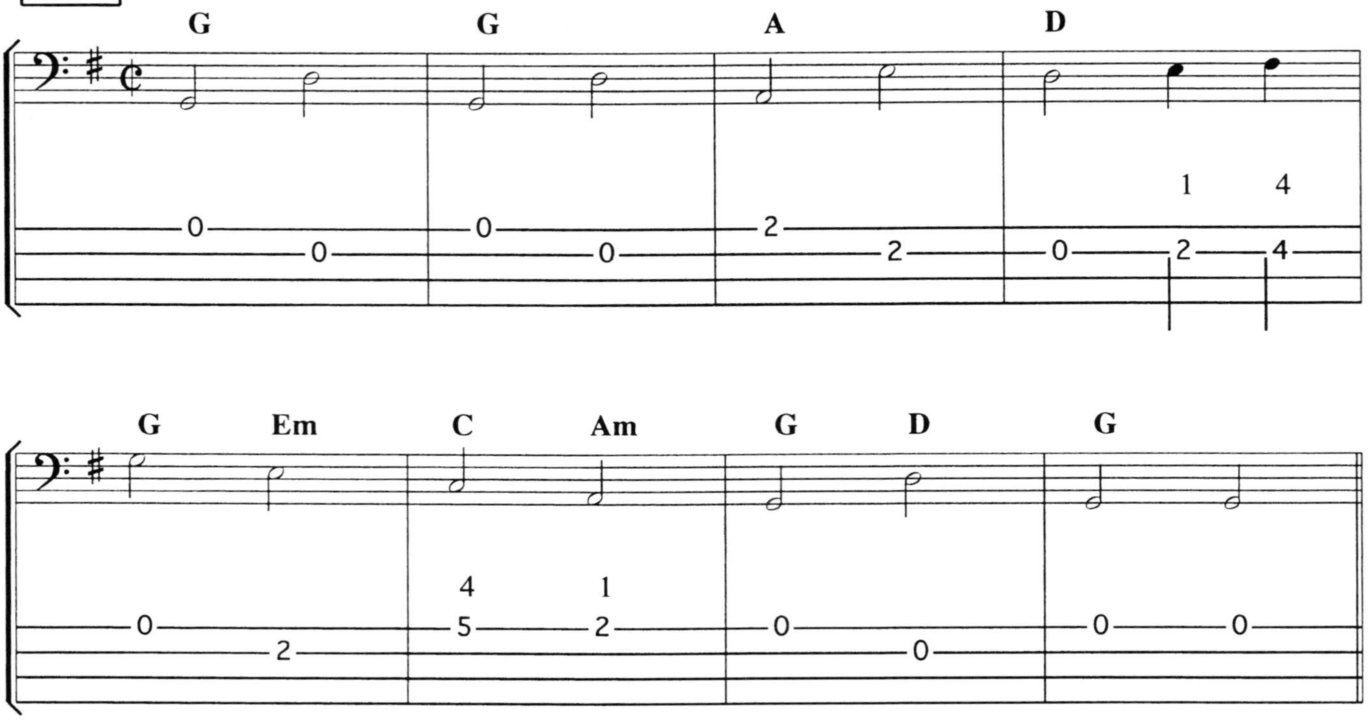

Part B

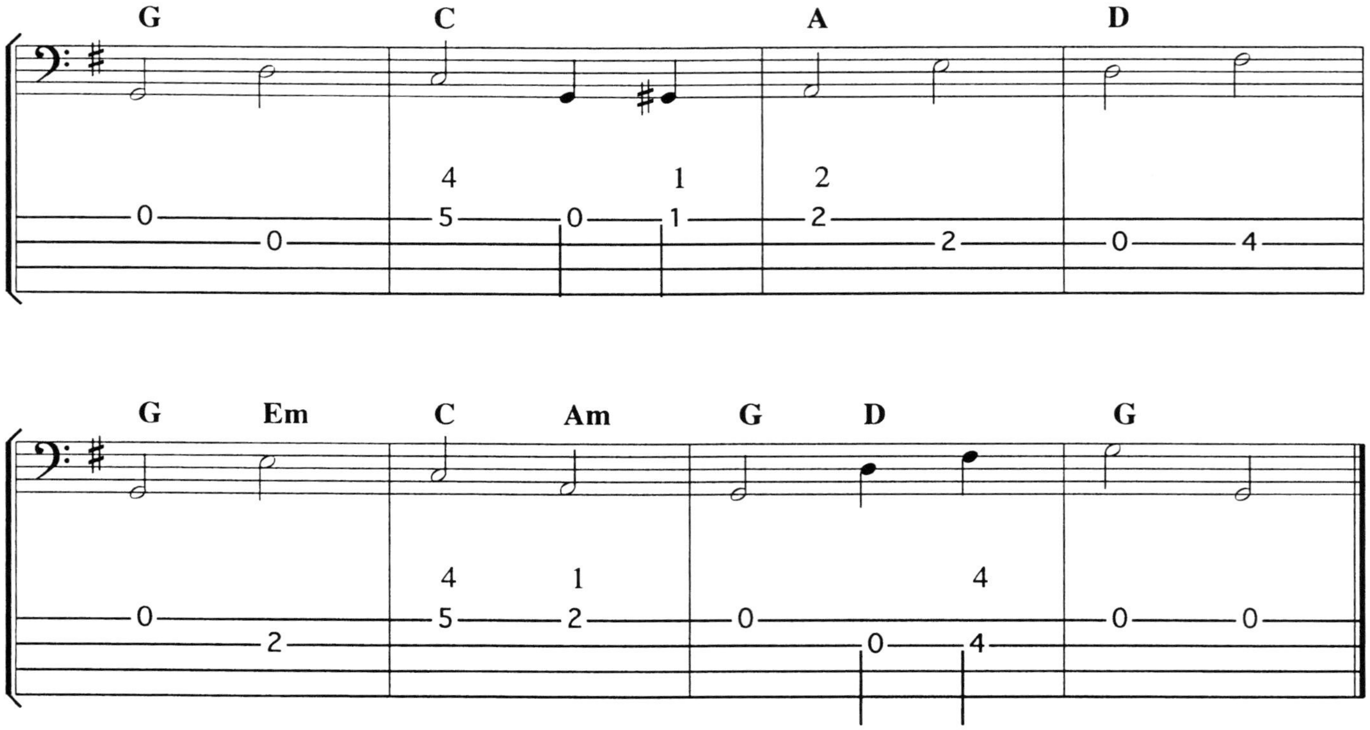

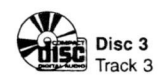

College Hornpipe

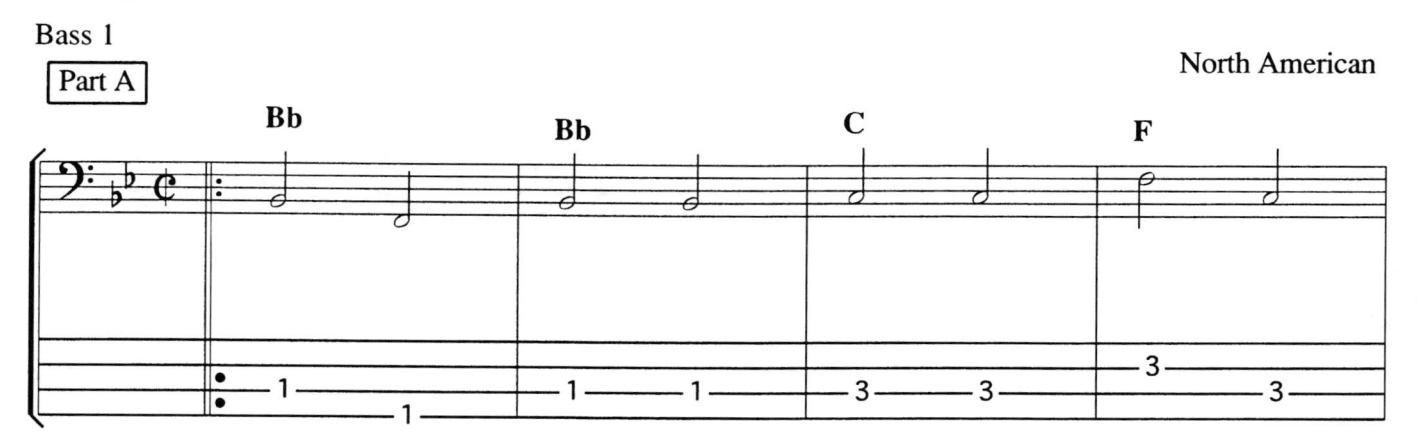

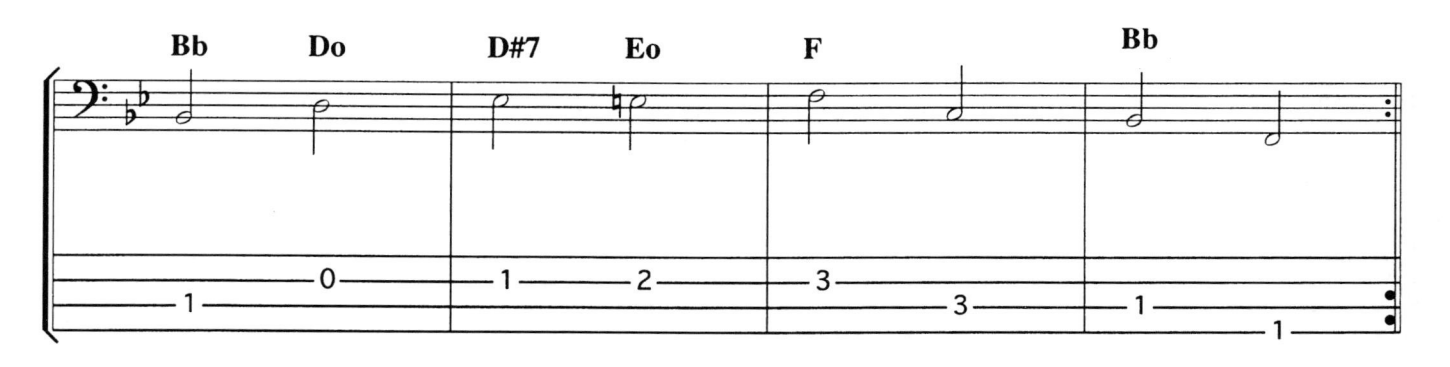

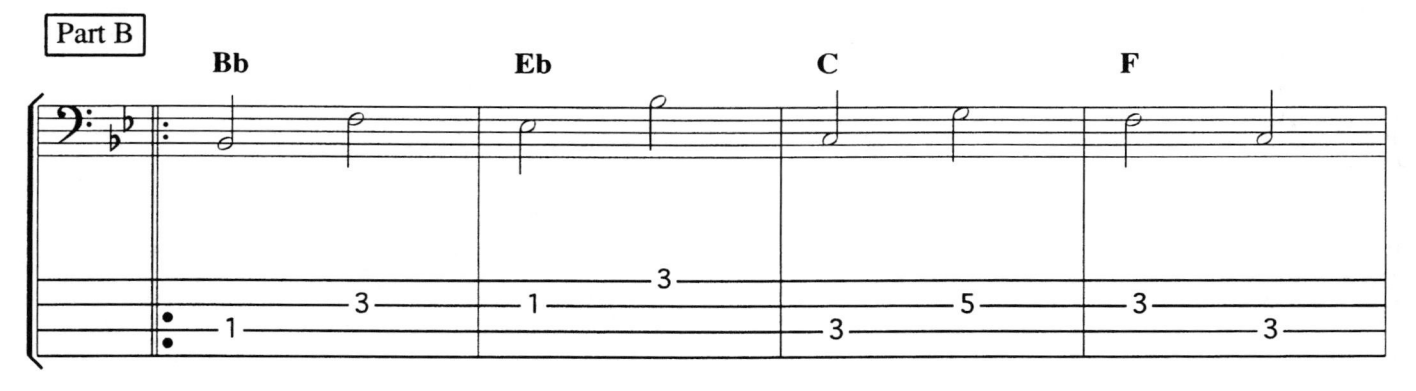

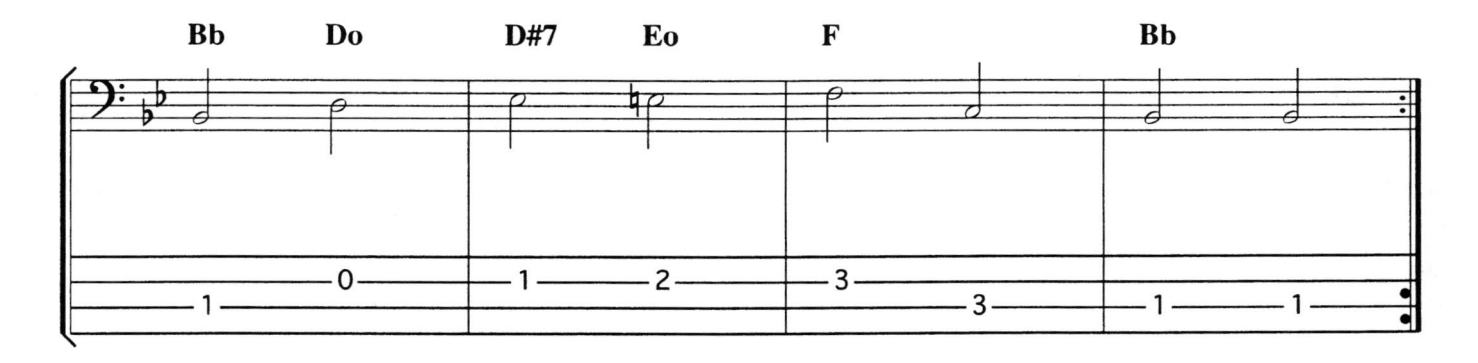

Bass 1

Part A

North American

Disc 3
Track 4

Saint Anne's Reel

Bass 1

Irish

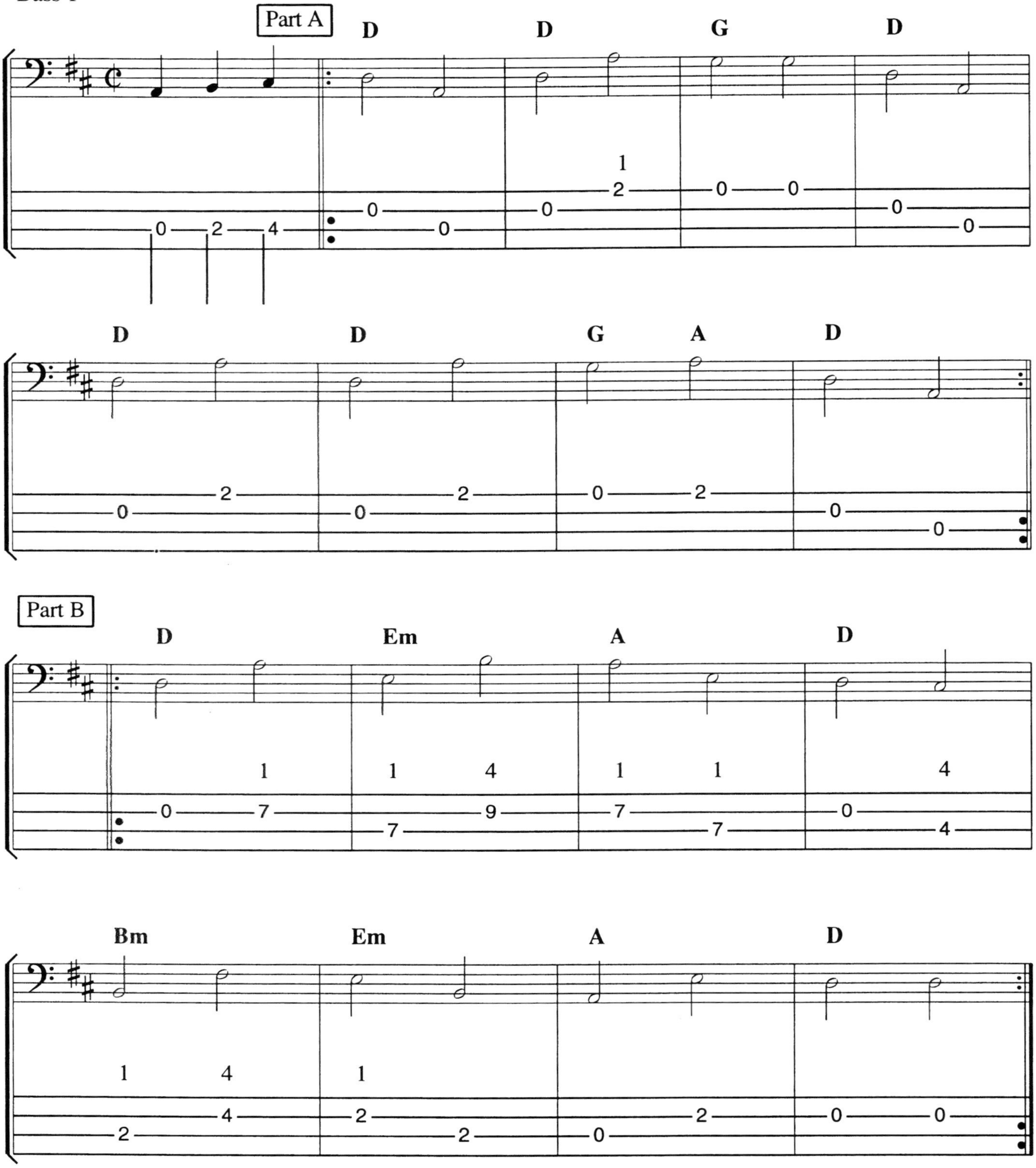

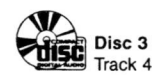

Sally Ann

Bass 1

North American

Part A

Sally Goodin'

Bass 1 (except banjo)

North American

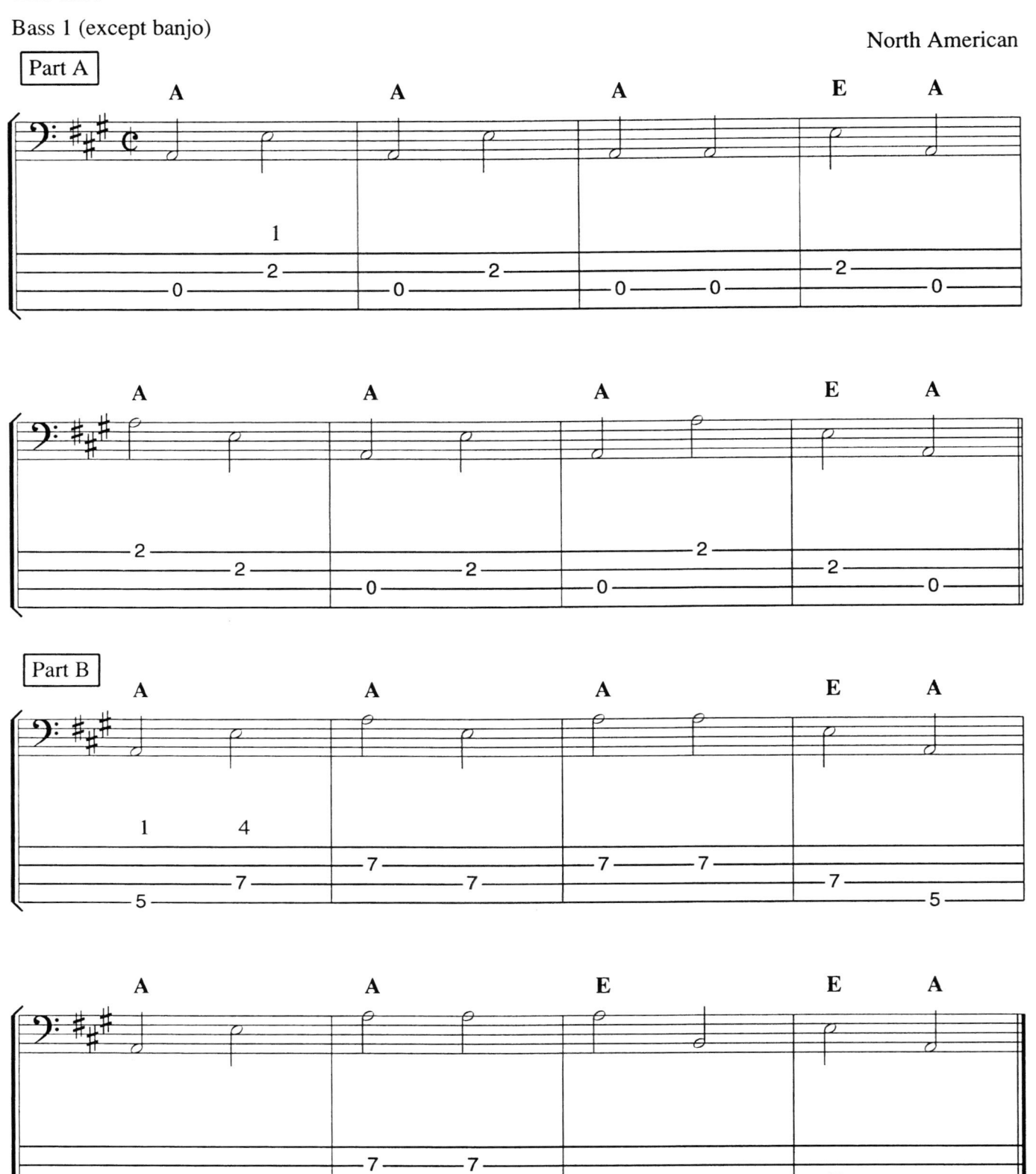

Part A

Sally Goodin'

Bass 1 (for banjo)

Sally Goodin'

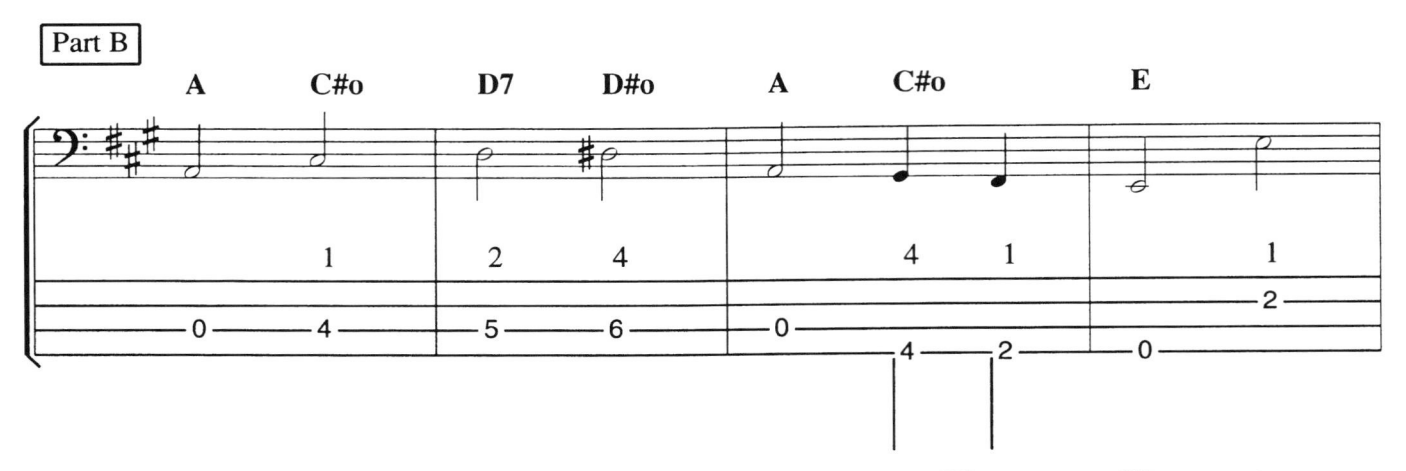

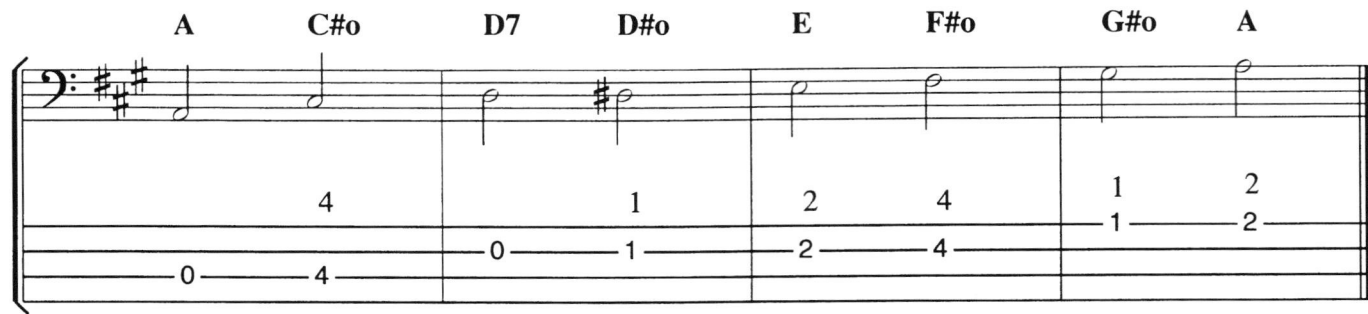

This page has been left blank to avoid awkward page turns.

Sally Johnson

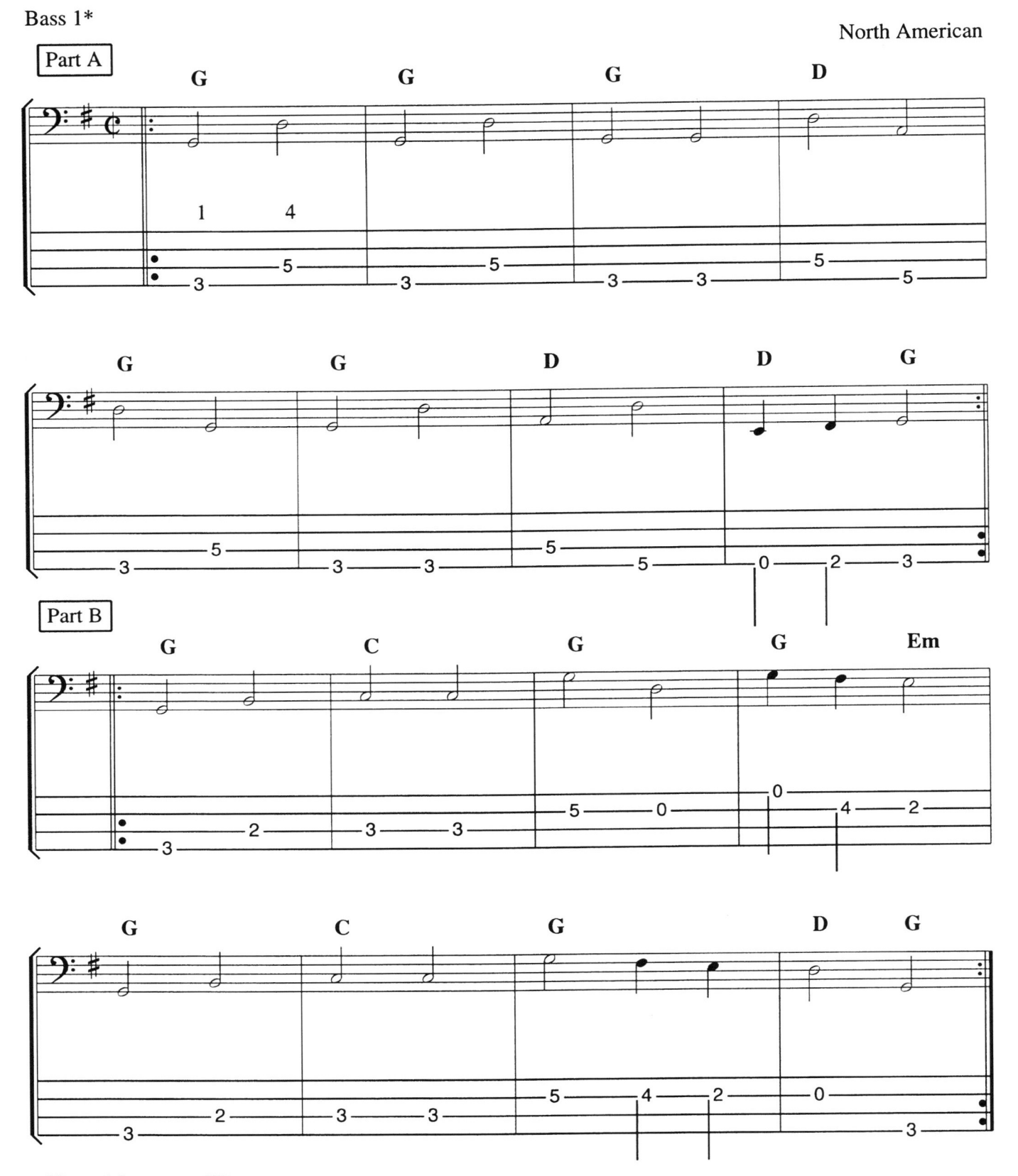

Bass 1*

North American

*Bass 1 is not on CD.

Sally Johnson

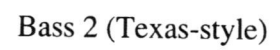

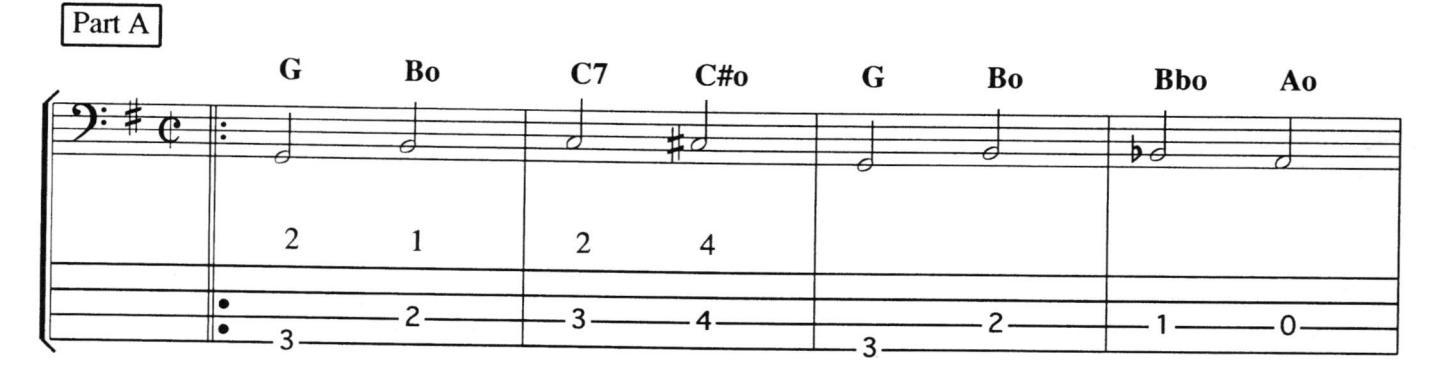

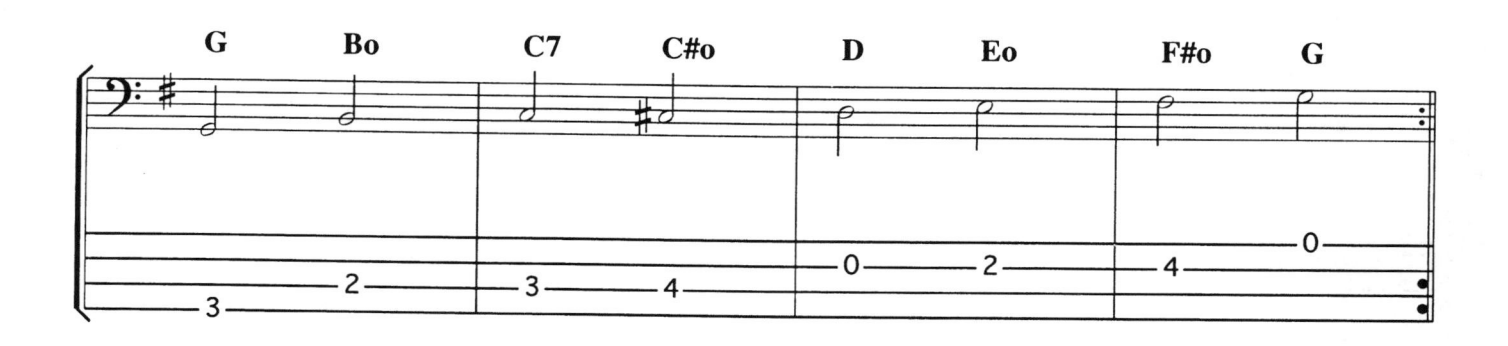

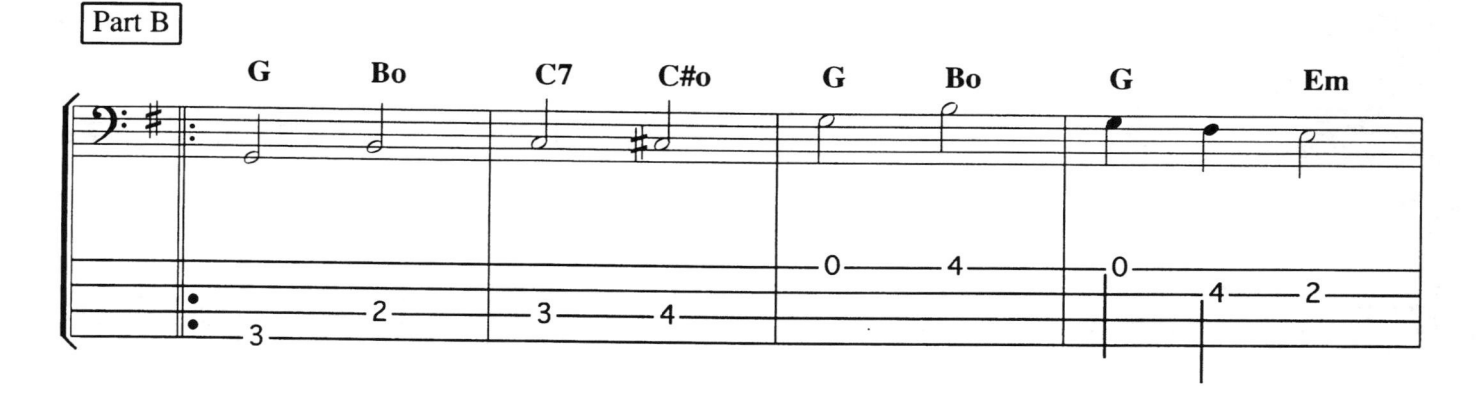

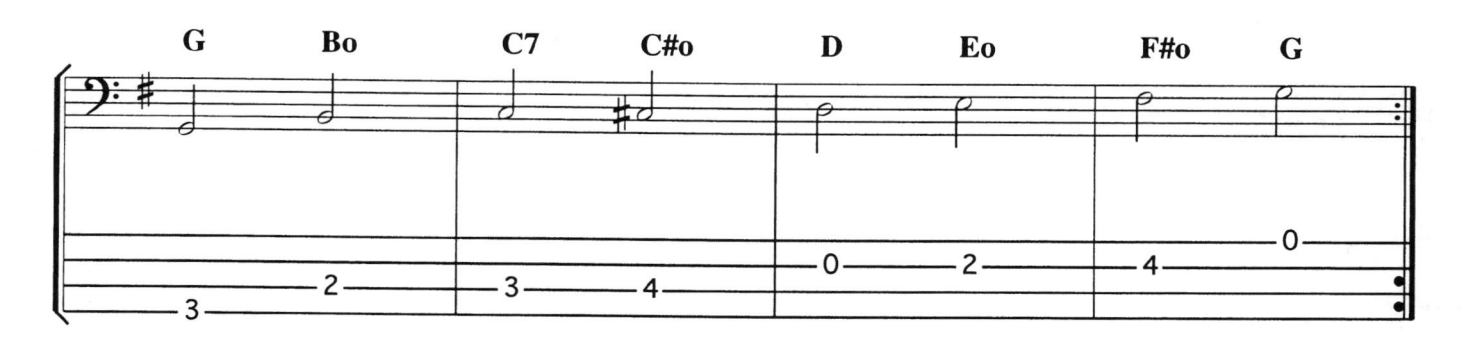

Salt Creek

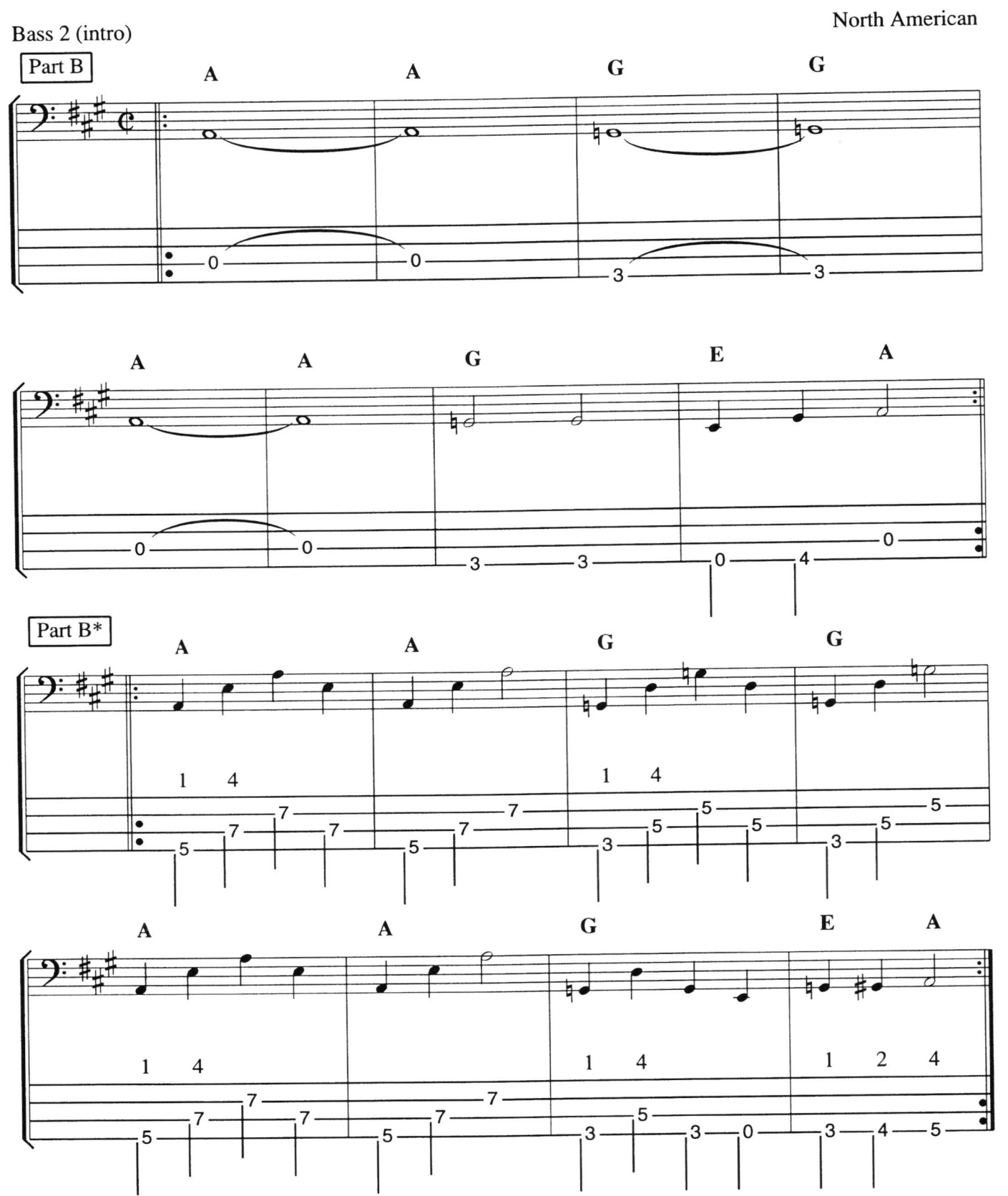

North American

Bass 2 (intro)

*Part B is not on CD. Part A is used for the first B part (double mandolin part at beginning of CD track).

Bass 2 can also be played 1 octave higher.

Salt Creek

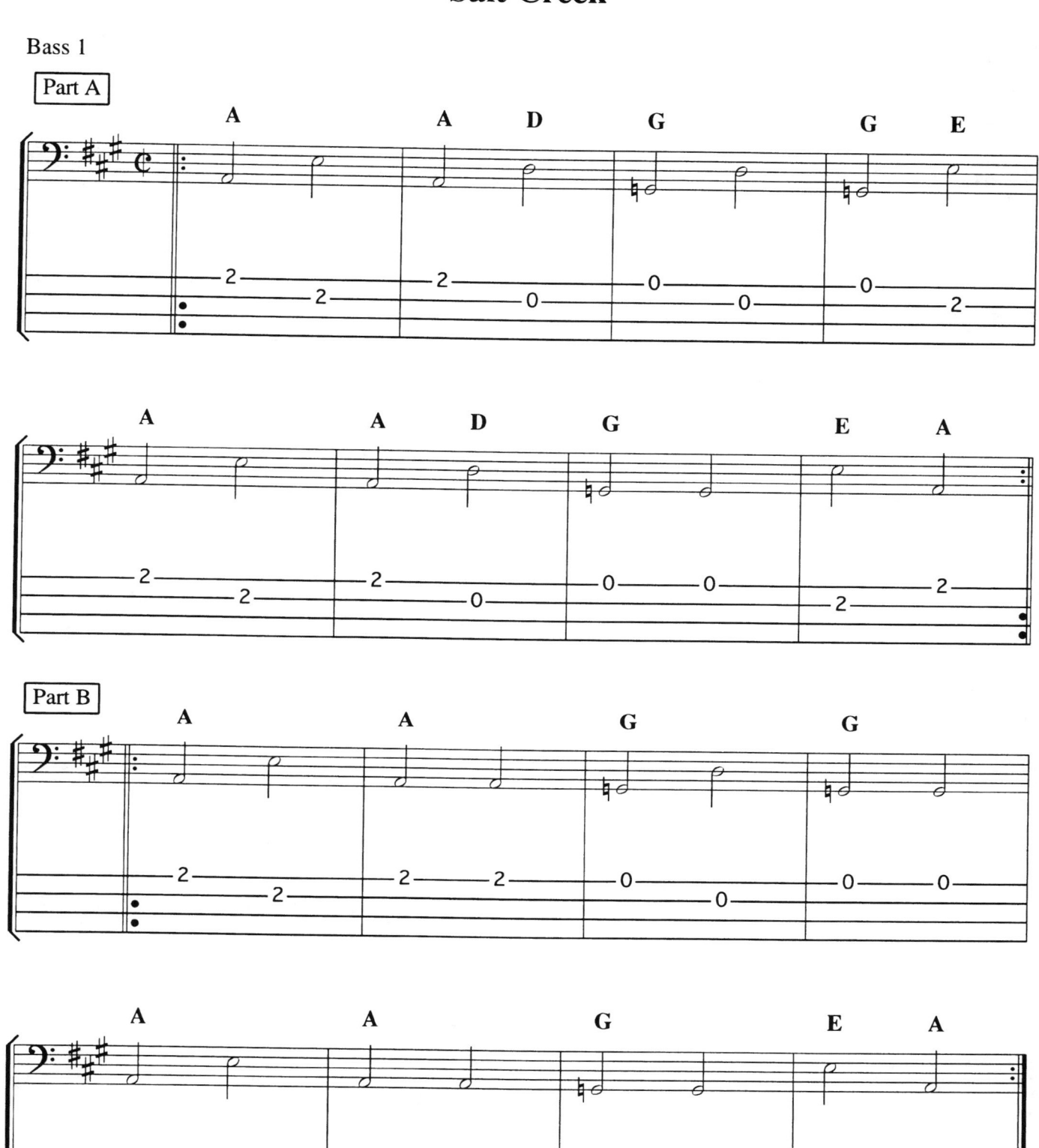

Soldier's Joy

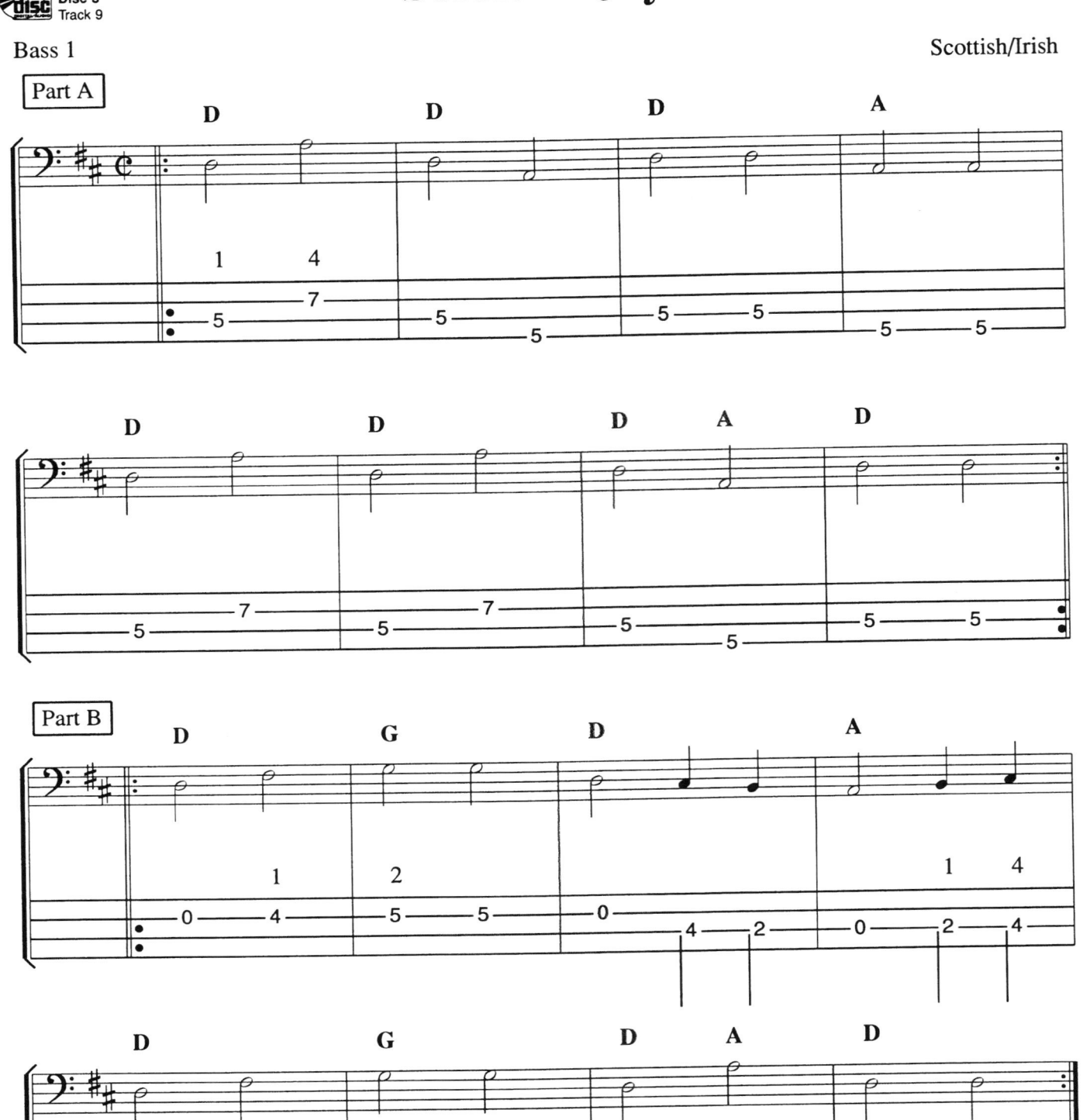

Bass 1

Scottish/Irish

Soldier's Joy

Bass (solo in D)*

*Bass solo is not on CD.

Soldier's Joy

Bass (solo in G)*

*Bass solo is not on CD.

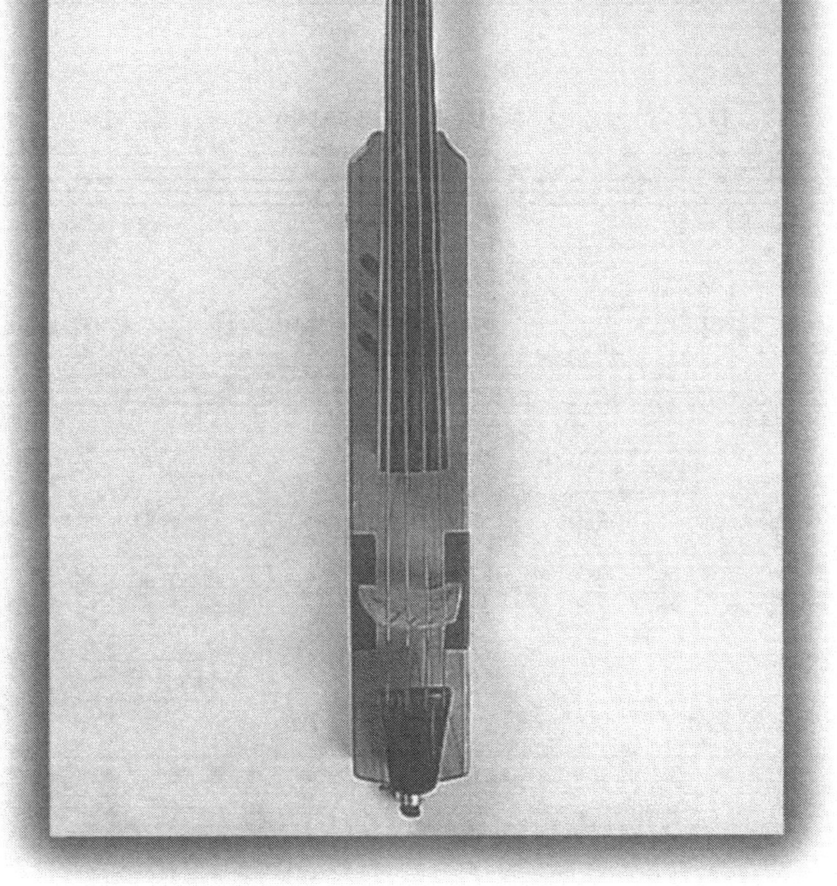

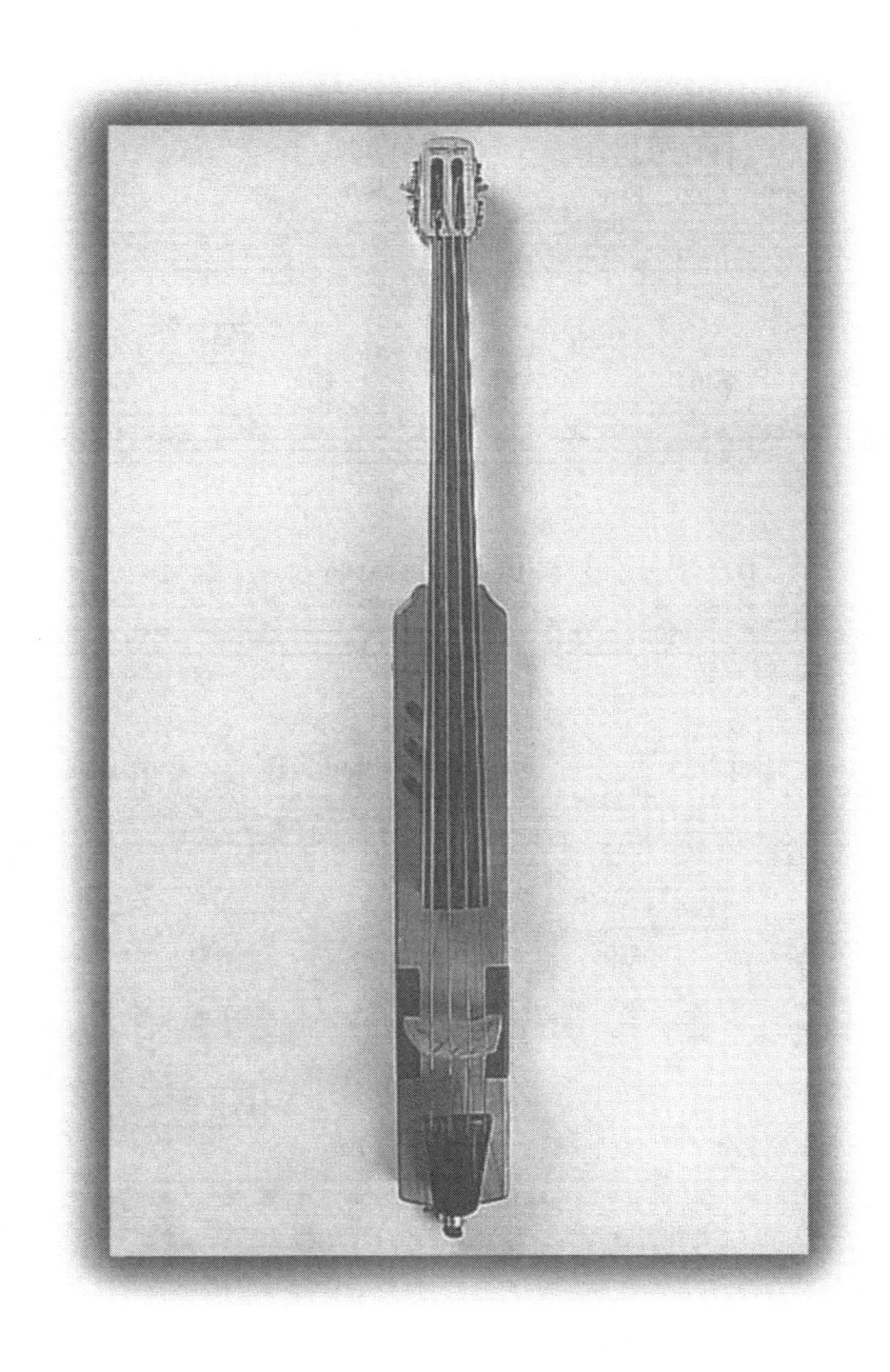

Swallowtail Jig

Irish

Bass 1

*During first fiddle part, play first part A without ties.

Swallowtail Jig

*During first fiddle part, play first part A without ties.

Temperance Reel

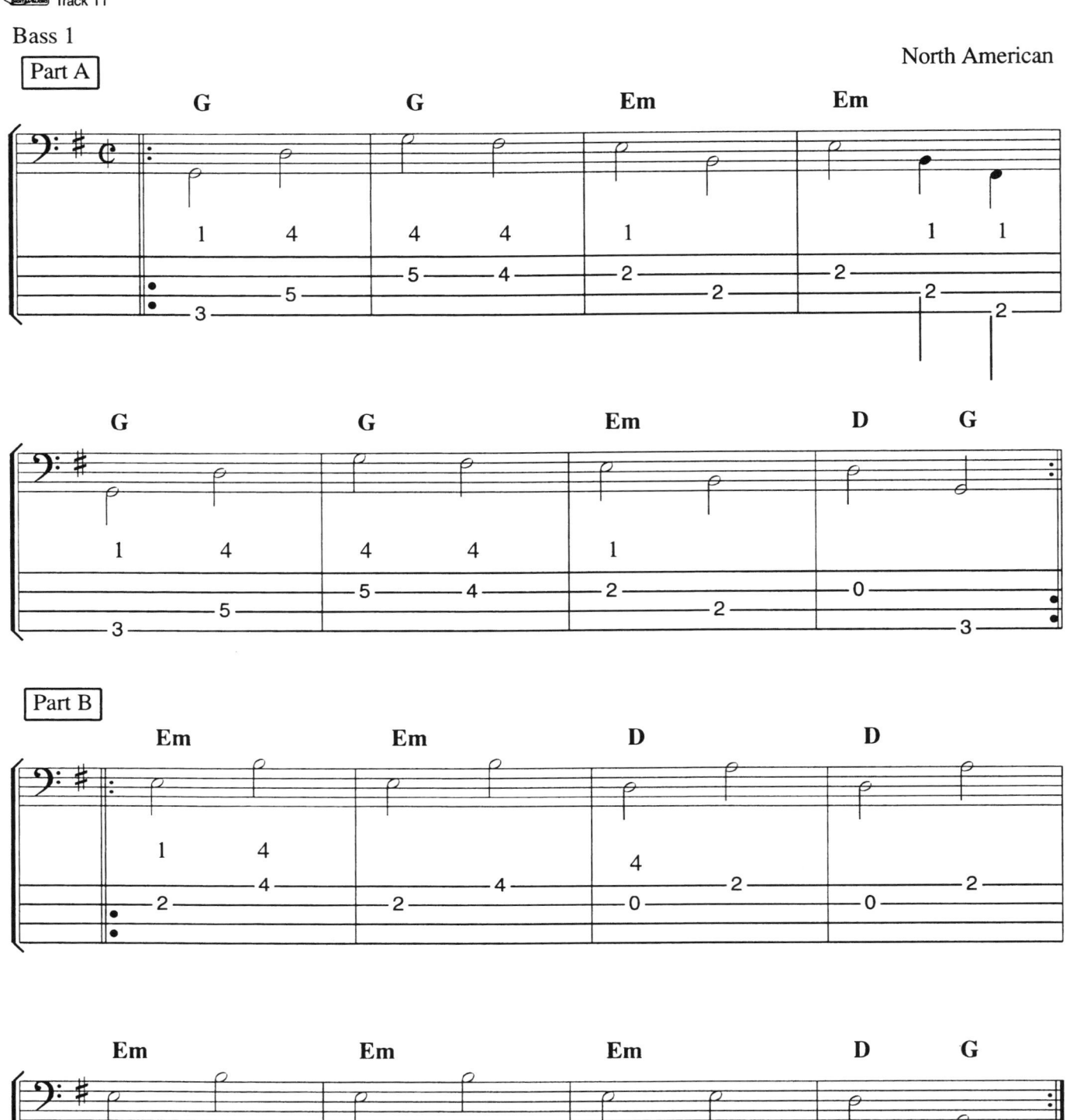

Bass 1

North American

Part A

This page has been left blank to avoid awkward page turns.

Tom and Jerry

Bass 1 (for mandolin/guitar/banjo)

North American

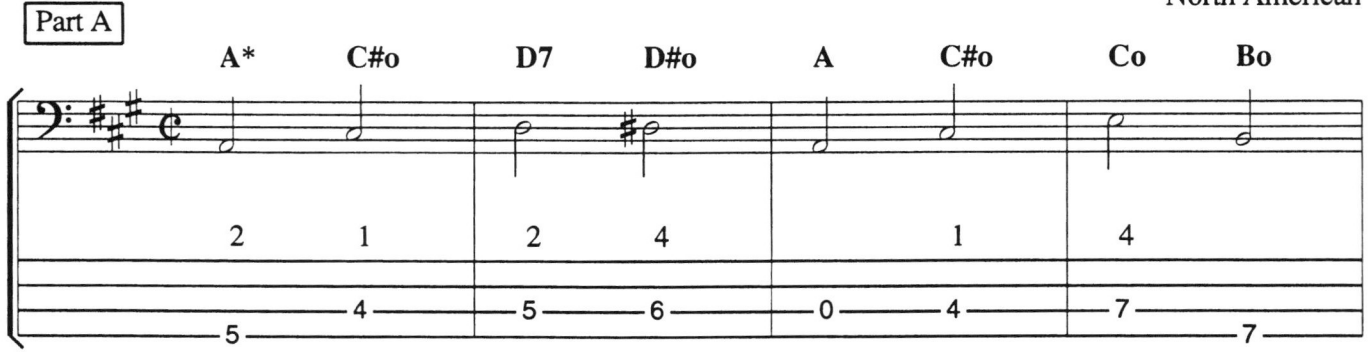

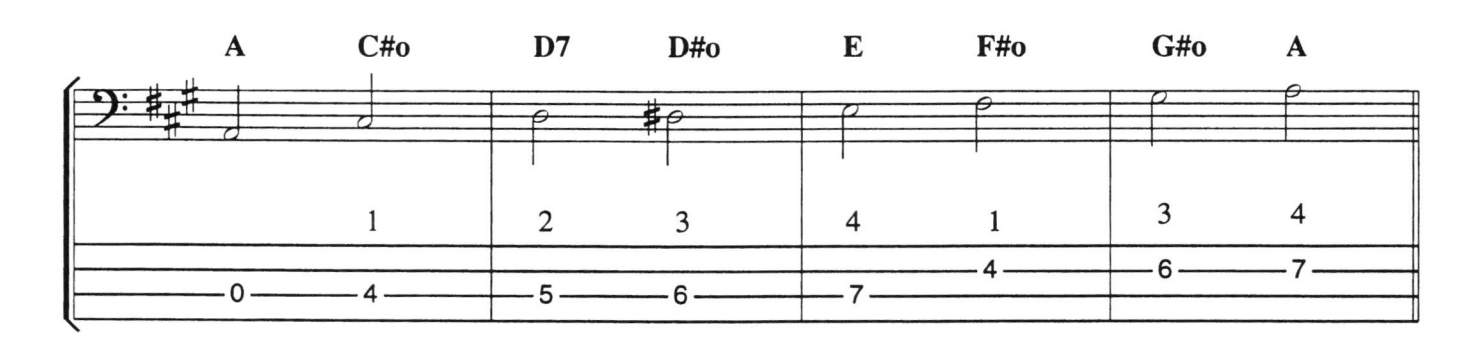

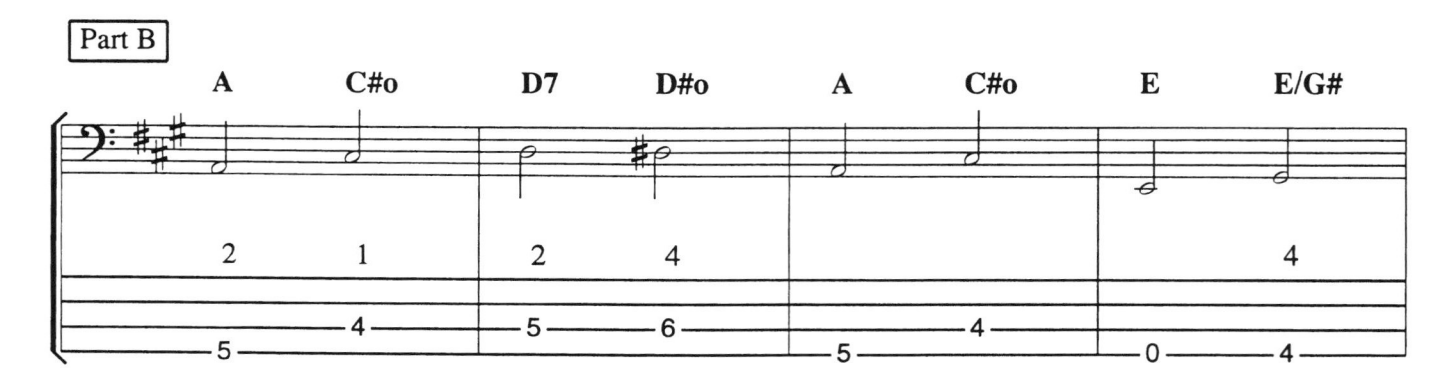

Part A

Part B

*See appendix for simplified chord sequence.

Tom and Jerry

Bass 2 (for fiddle)

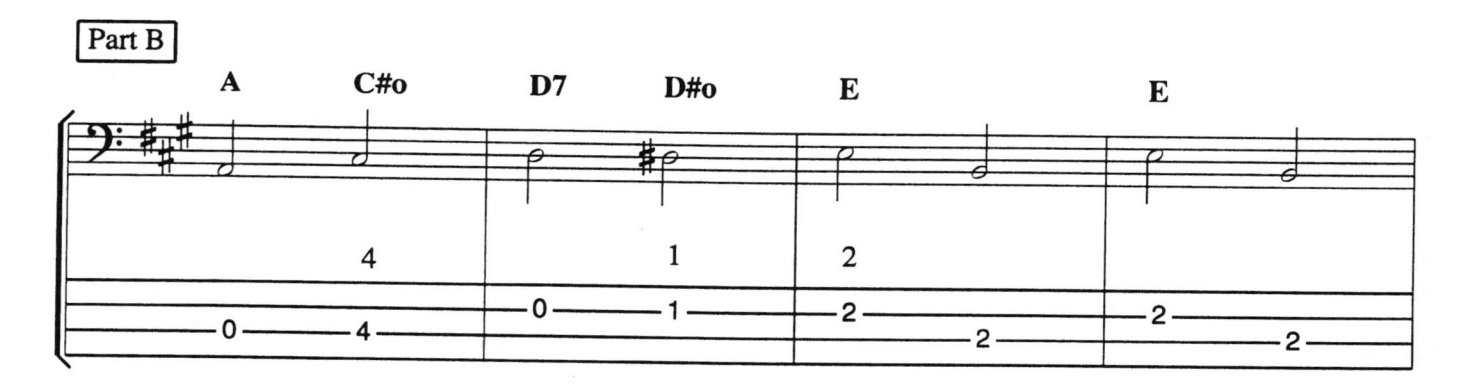

*Part B occurs only 2 times during fiddle solo (at 2:55 - 3:14 and 3:24 - 3:33).

Turkey in the Straw

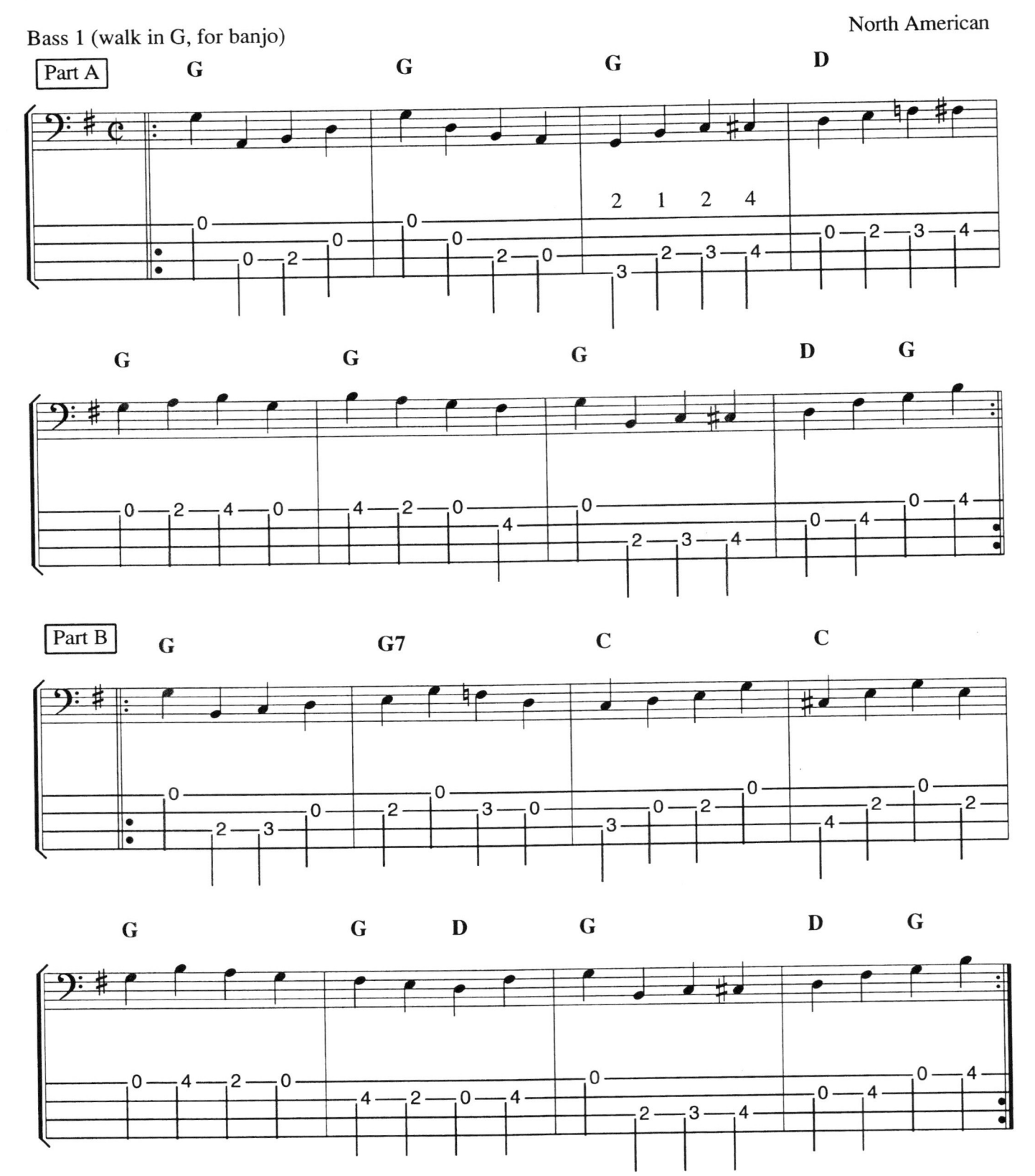

Disc 3 Track 13

Bass 1 (walk in G, for banjo)

North American

Turkey in the Straw

Bass 2 (key of G, for mandolin/guitar)

Turkey in the Straw

Bass 3* (key of G)

*Bass 3 is not on CD.

Turkey in the Straw

Bass 4 (key of C, for mandolin/guitar)

Turkey in the Straw

Turkey in the Straw

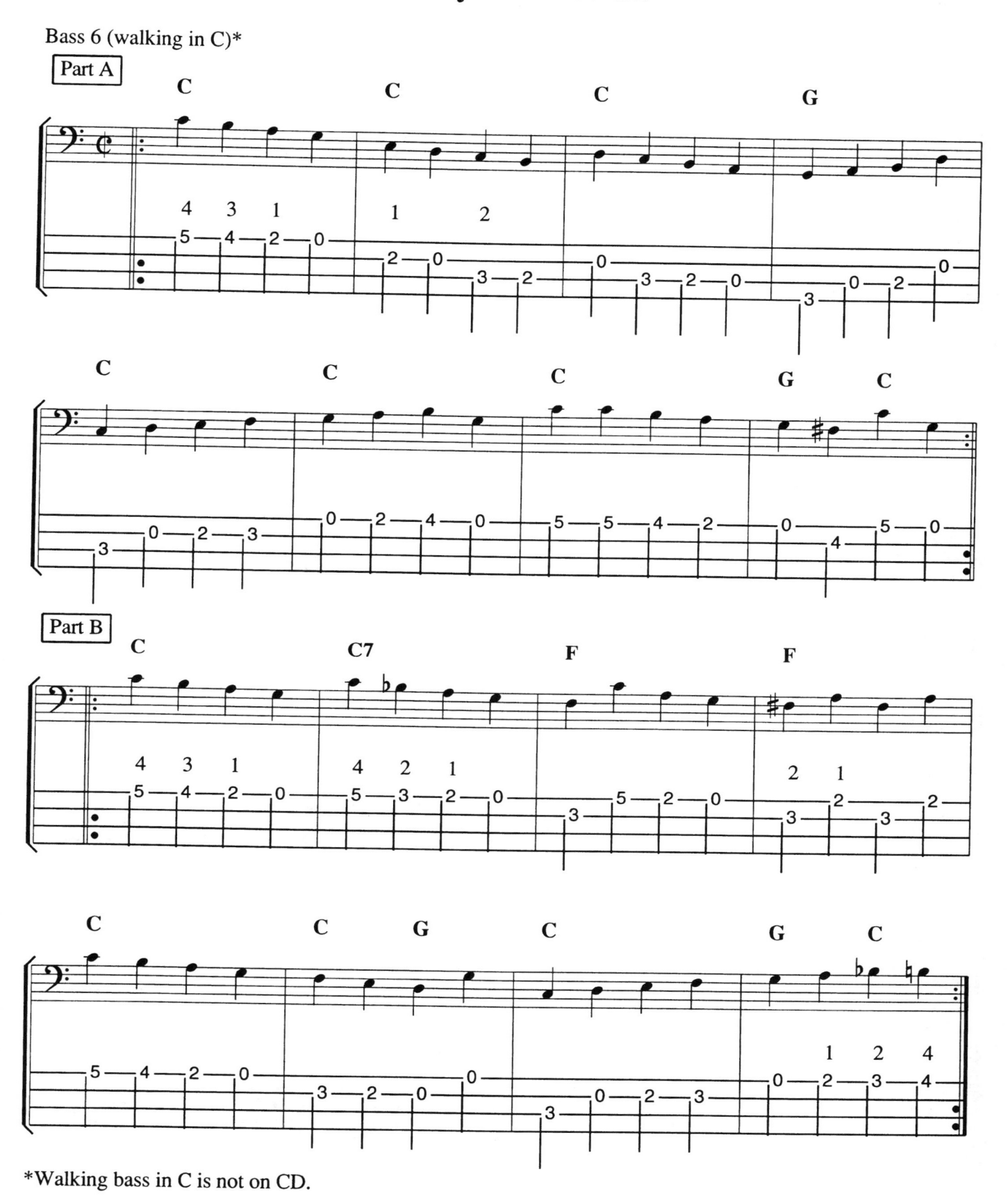

Bass 6 (walking in C)*

*Walking bass in C is not on CD.

Uncle Joe

Bass 1

Scottish

Uncle Joe

Under the Double Eagle

Bass (intro)

North American

146

Under the Double Eagle

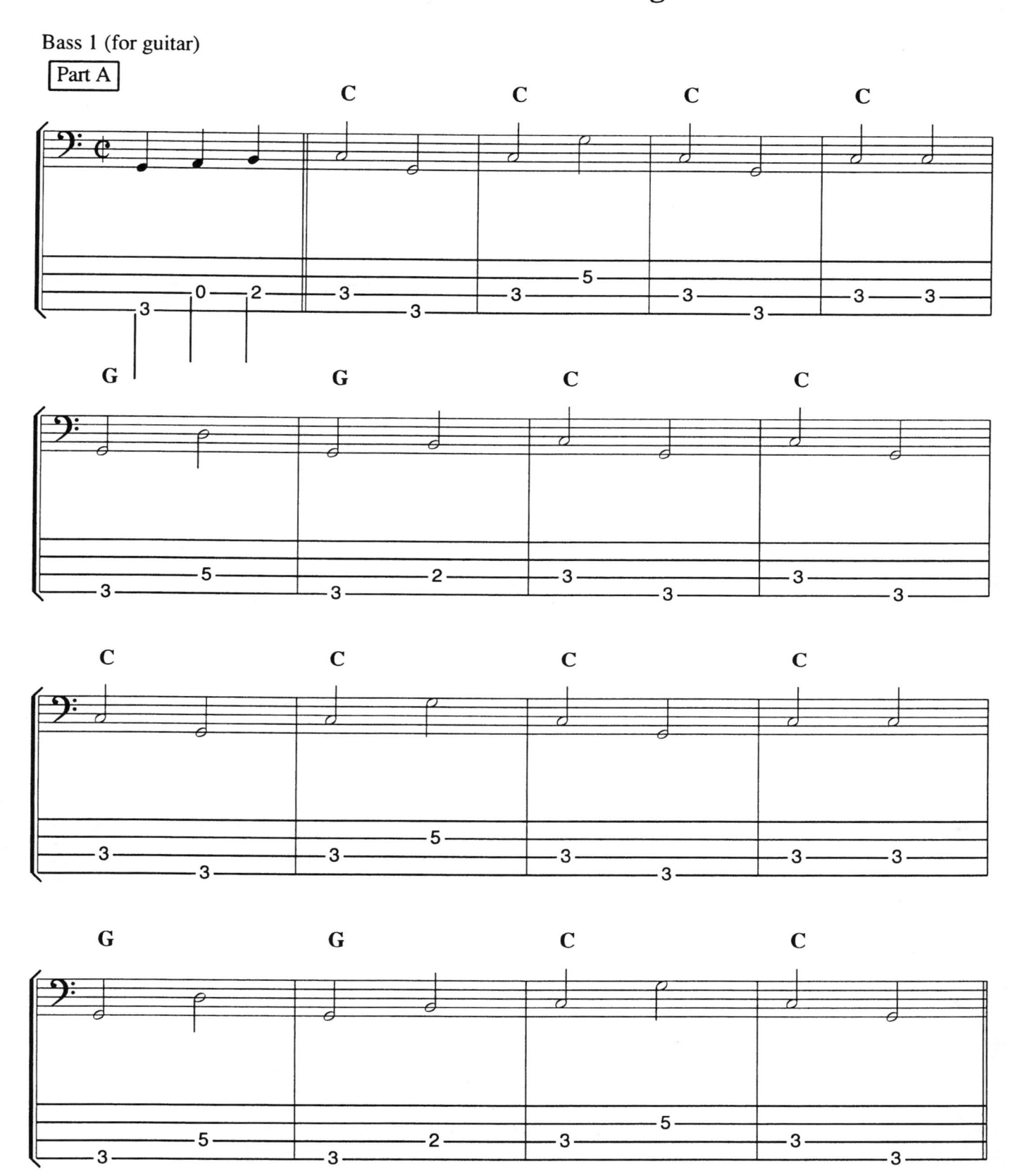

Bass 1 (for guitar)

Part A

Under the Double Eagle

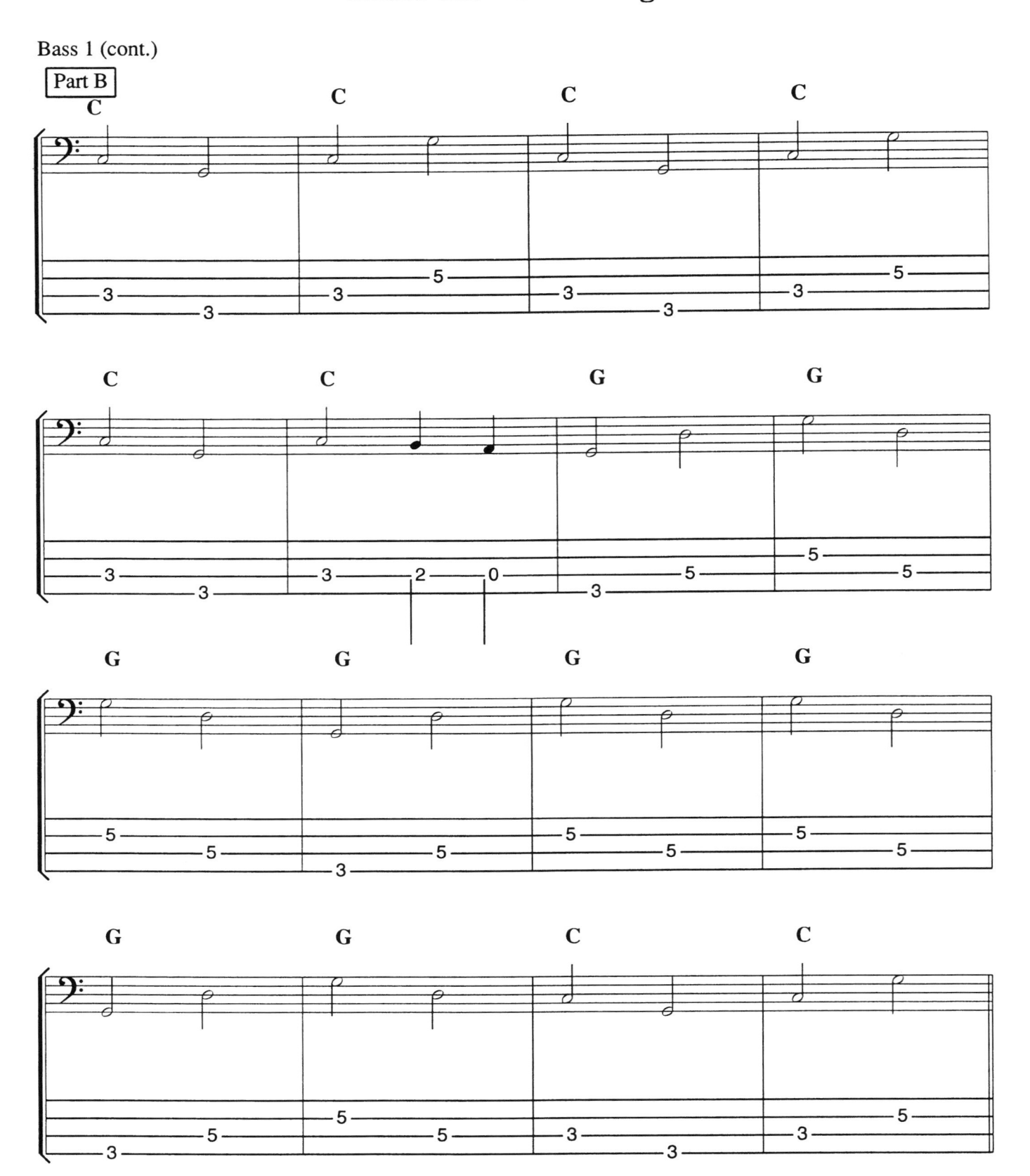

Bass 1 (cont.)

Under the Double Eagle

Bass 1 (part B cont.)

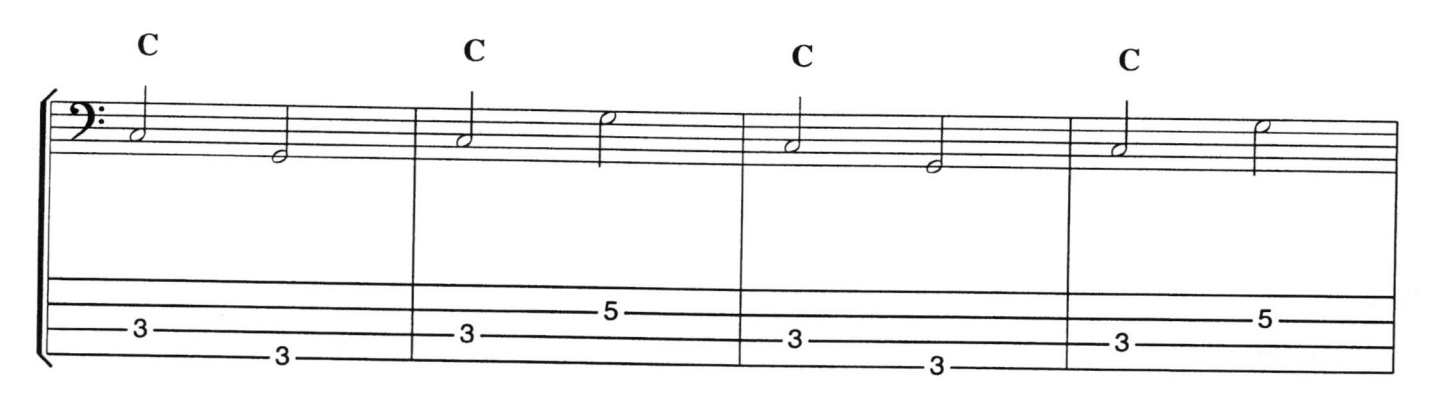

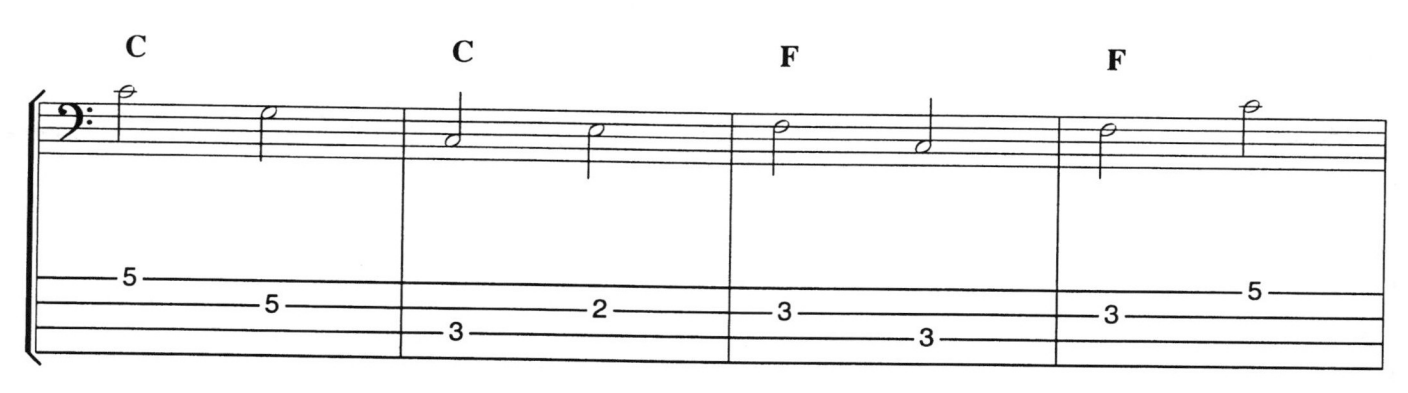

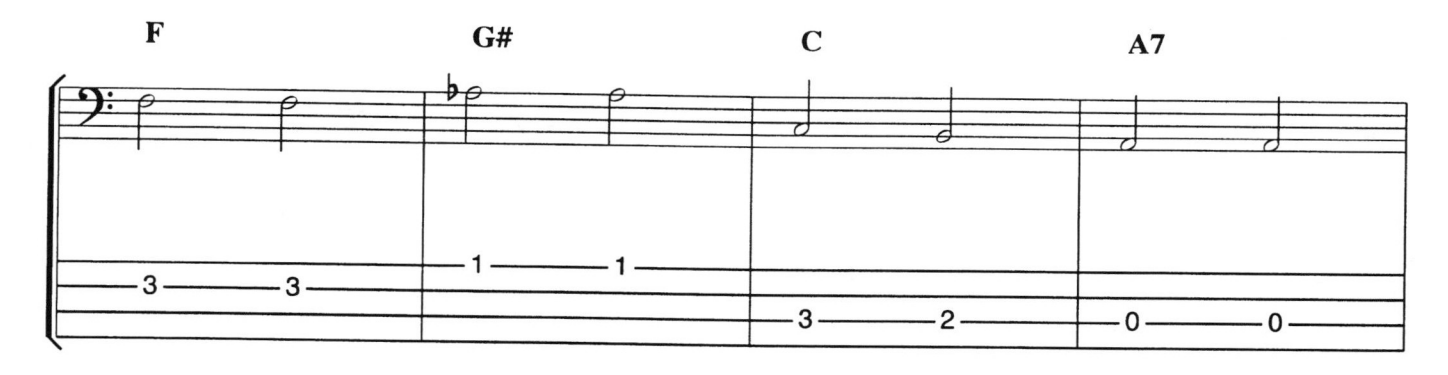

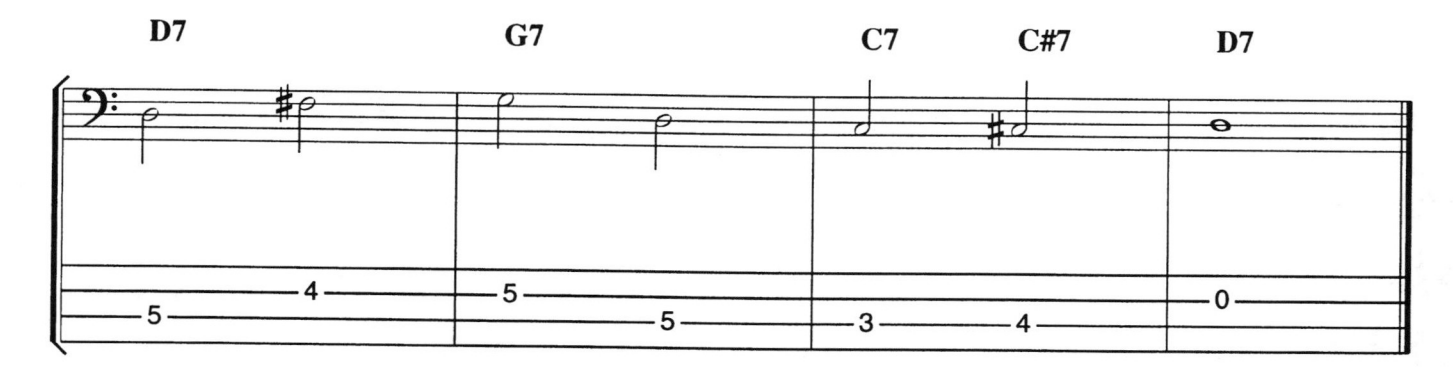

Under the Double Eagle

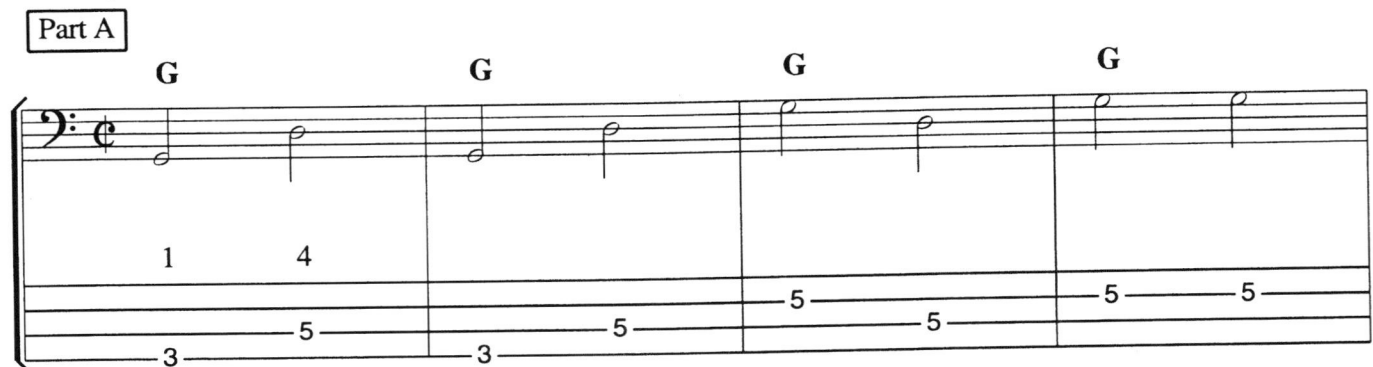

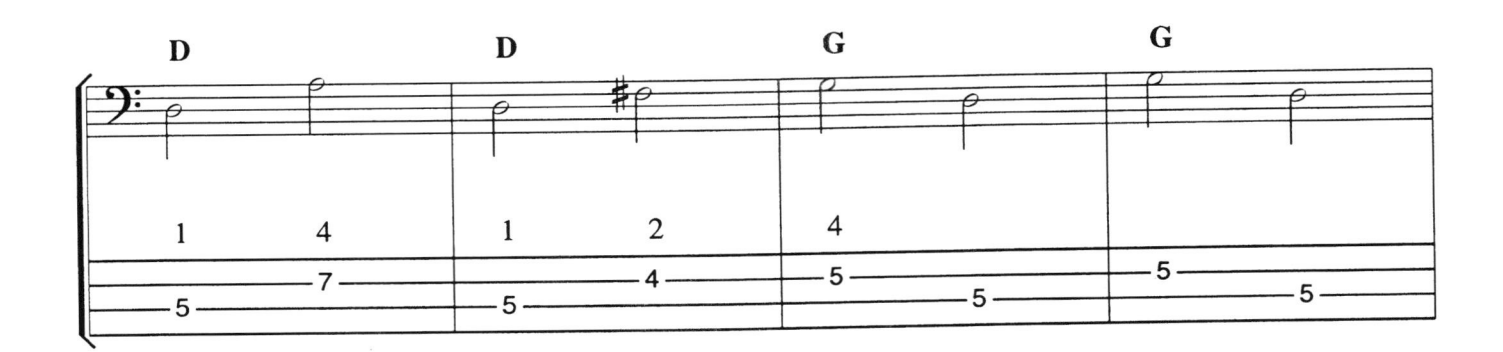

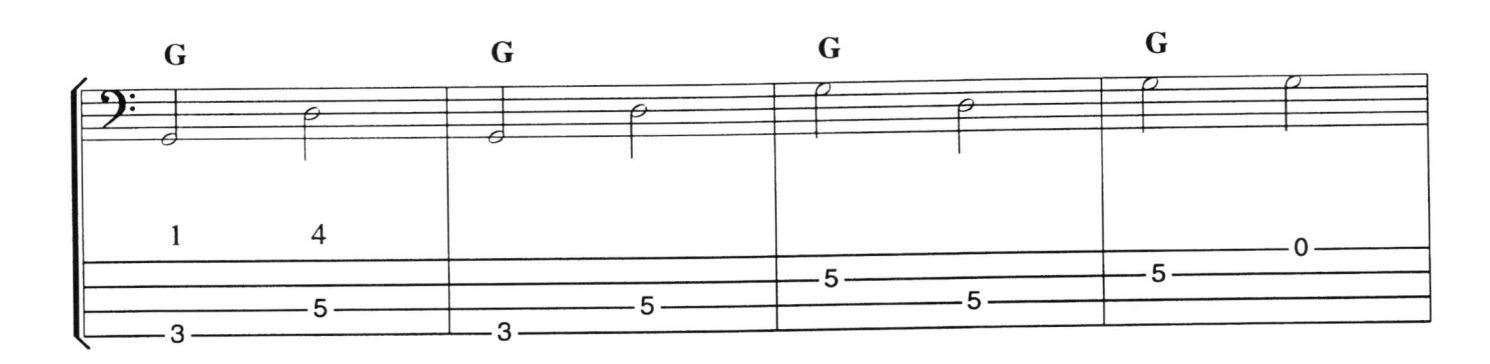

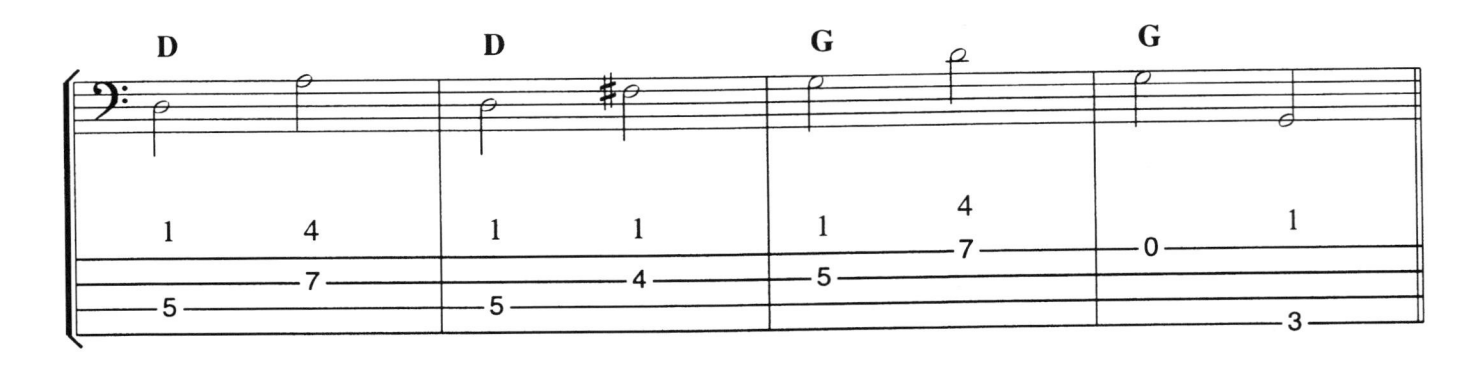

Bass 1 (for mandolin)

Under the Double Eagle

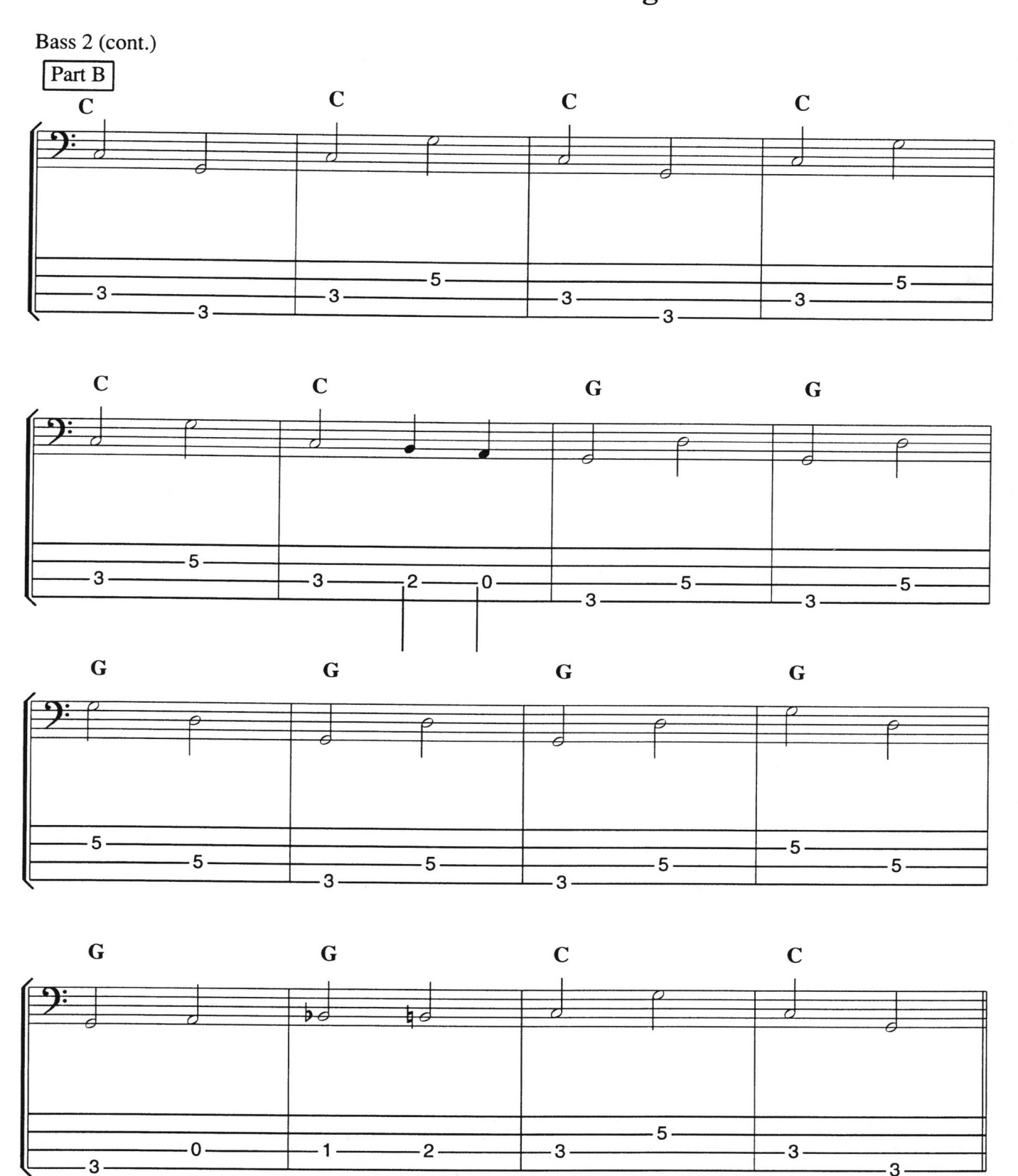

Bass 2 (cont.)

Under the Double Eagle

Bass 2 (part B cont.)

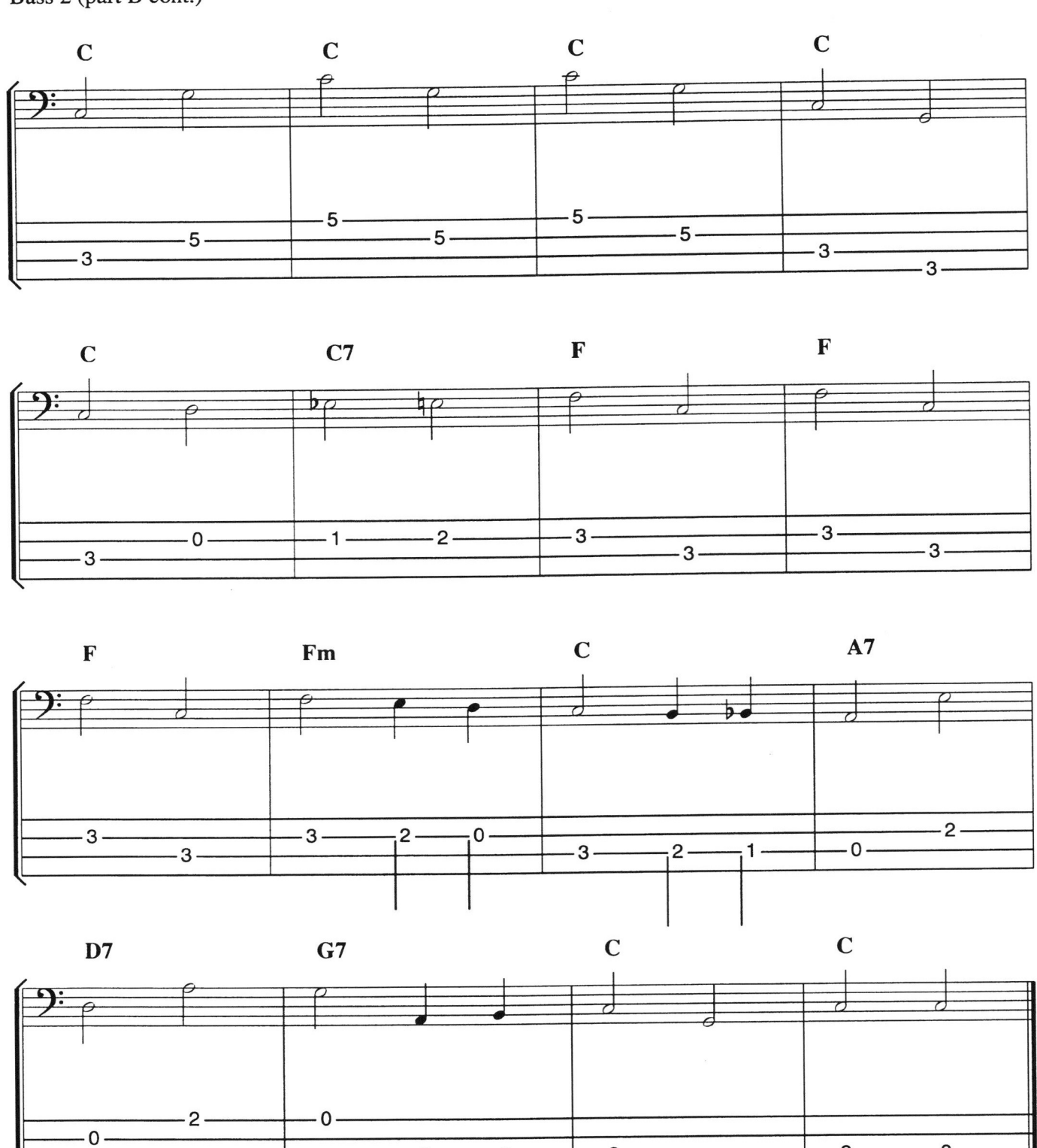

Under the Double Eagle

Under the Double Eagle

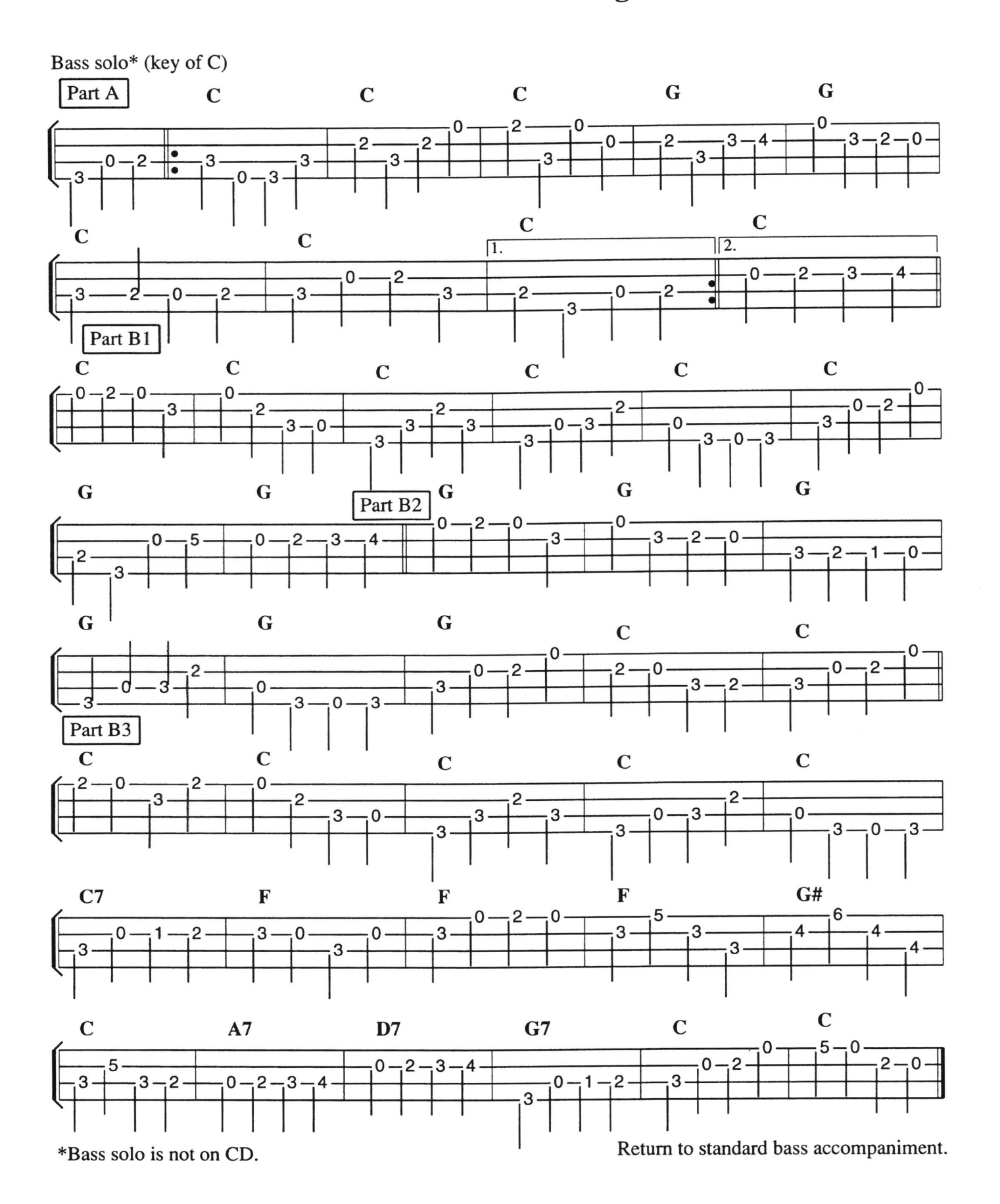

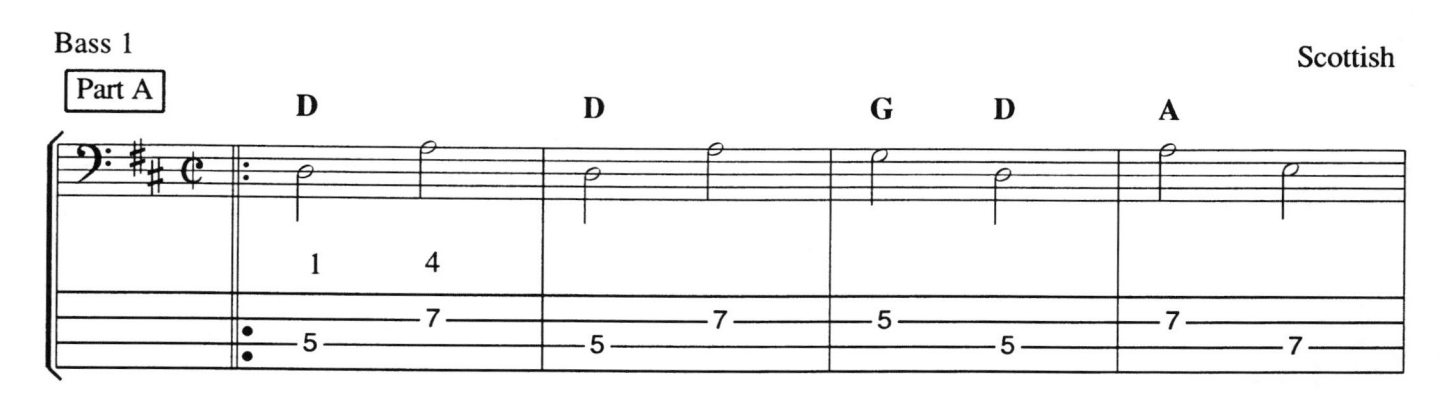

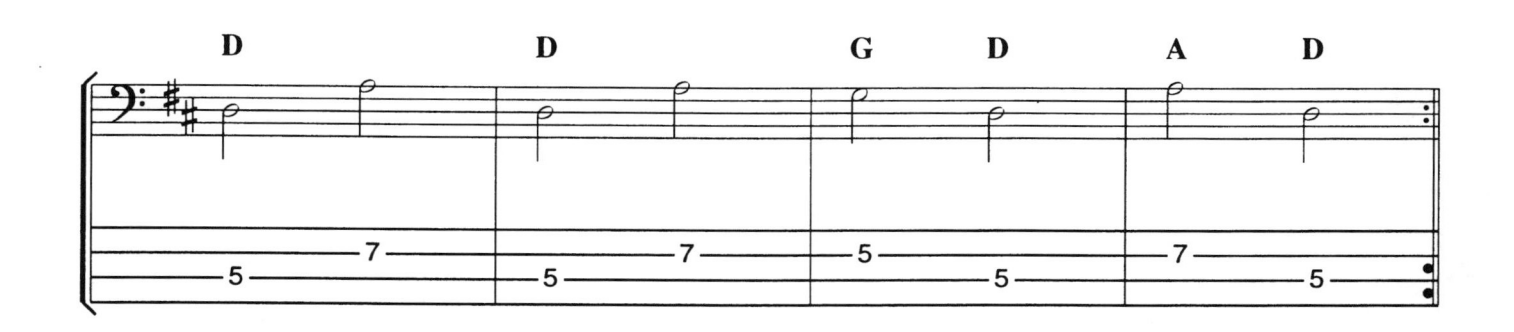

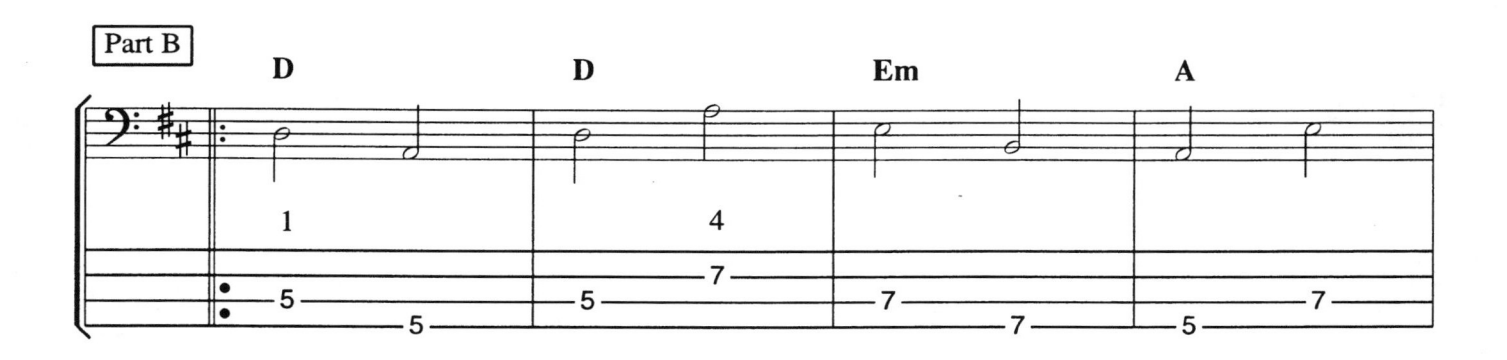

Whiskey Before Breakfast

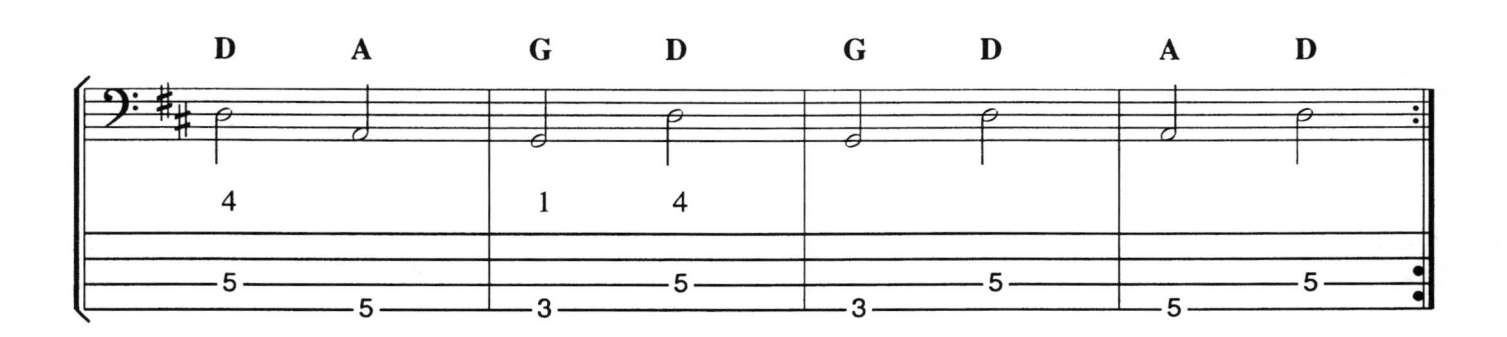

Disc 3 Track 16

Bass 1

Scottish

[Part A]

Whiskey Before Breakfast

Bass 2*

*Bass 2 is not on CD.

Whiskey Before Breakfast

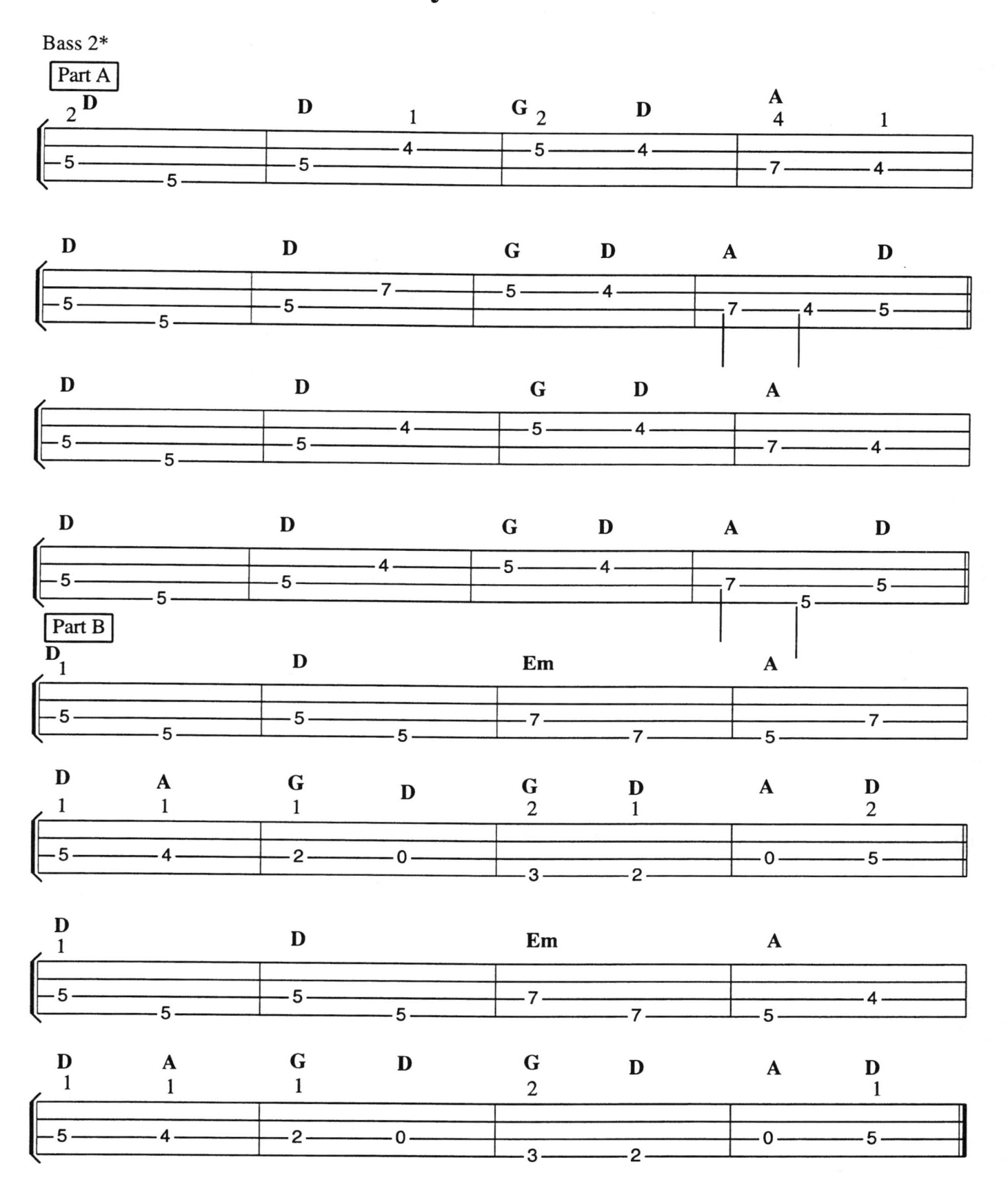

Bass 2*

*Bass 2 is not on CD.

Appendix

The Bass in Traditional Music

The bass is a fundamental instrument in most traditional music styles. It is to an ensemble of musicians what a solid concrete foundation is to a house. It is not necessary to be flashy to be an outstanding bass player in many styles of music. The most important thing a bass player can do is to be solid and consistent for your ensemble.

Many of the tunes in this book contain 1 or all of the following aspects of bass playing: 1) basic, 2) active and 3) solo. Basic bass accompaniment can be as simple as 2 notes per measure (root note and 5th note of scale—see table below). This basic type of accompaniment is ideal for most traditional music styles. More than this can easily become too much. All 50 tunes contain a basic bass part. A more active bass accompaniment can add a great deal of "spice" to a tune. However, an active accompaniment, when overdone, can crowd the arrangement of a piece of music. Bass players should carefully construct their accompaniment using both basic and active components so as to enhance the music they play. Many of the tunes in this book contain an active bass part.

The 3rd aspect of bass playing, or soloing, is challenging yet gratifying. Though bass players typically will not solo as much as they will accompany, it is, nevertheless, very fulfilling to be prepared to be a soloist. This book contains several bass solos that should be enjoyable for most bass players.

Playing Accompaniment

Since accompaniment is an essential part of the bass player's role in an ensemble, it is important to understand some of the basic notes available for accompaniment. The most common note for a bass player is the root of a scale (or chord). The root of an "A" chord is an "A" note while the root of an "F" chord is an "F" note (see triad table below). The second most important note is typically the 5th note of the scale. If a bass player is looking at a 2-beat measure that contains an "F" chord, the bass player can choose to play an F followed by a C, F followed by another F, F followed by an A, or perhaps an A followed by another A. The most typical choice would be F followed by C.

The basic bass parts in this book focus heavily on root/5th accompaniment while the active parts focus on root/3rd/5th (with occasional notes from the rest of the scale). Solos can contain all the notes of the scale including chromatic notes as well.

The following table lists most triads (a triad is a basic 3-note chord). The 3 notes that make up each triad are listed under root, 3rd and 5th.

Triad Table

Triad	Root	3rd	5th
A	A	C♯	E
B	B	D♯	F♯
C	C	E	G
D	D	F♯	A
E	E	G♯	B
F	F	A	C
G	G	B	D
A♭	A♭	C♭	E♭
B♭	B♭	D	F
D♭	D♭	F	A♭
E♭	E♭	G	B♭
G♭	G♭	B♭	D♭
A♯	A♯	C♯♯	E♯
C♯	C♯	E♯	G♯
D♯	D♯	F♯♯	A♯
F♯	F♯	A♯	C♯
G♯	G♯	B♯	D♯
Am	A	C	E
Bm	B	D	F♯
Cm	C	E♭	G
Dm	D	F	A
Em	E	G	B
Fm	F	A♭	C
Gm	G	B♭	D
A♭m	A♭	C♭	E♭
B♭m	B♭	D♭	F
D♭m	D♭	F♭	A♭
E♭m	E♭	G♭	B♭
G♭m	G♭	B♭♭	D♭
A♯m	A♯	C♯	E♯
C♯m	C♯	E	G♯
D♯m	D♯	F♯	A♯
F♯m	F♯	A	C♯
G♯m	G♯	B	D♯

How to Read Bass Tablature

(and music and measure symbols)

1. The four* lines on a tablature staff represent the four strings of the bass.

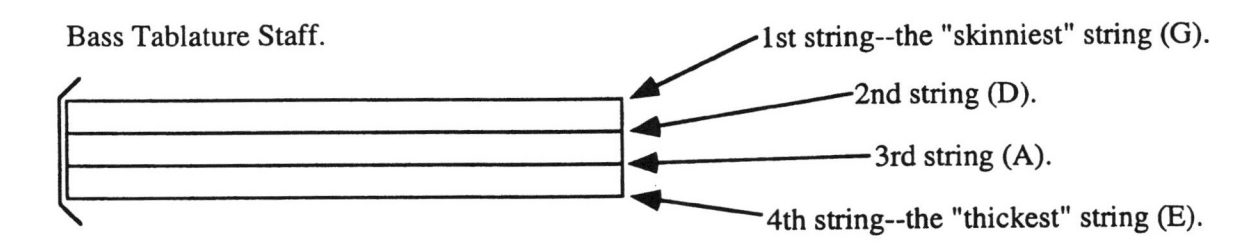

Bass Tablature Staff.

- 1st string--the "skinniest" string (G).
- 2nd string (D).
- 3rd string (A).
- 4th string--the "thickest" string (E).

*Some basses have 5 and even 6 strings. This book focuses on 4-string basses (acoustic and electric).

2. Types of measure lines.

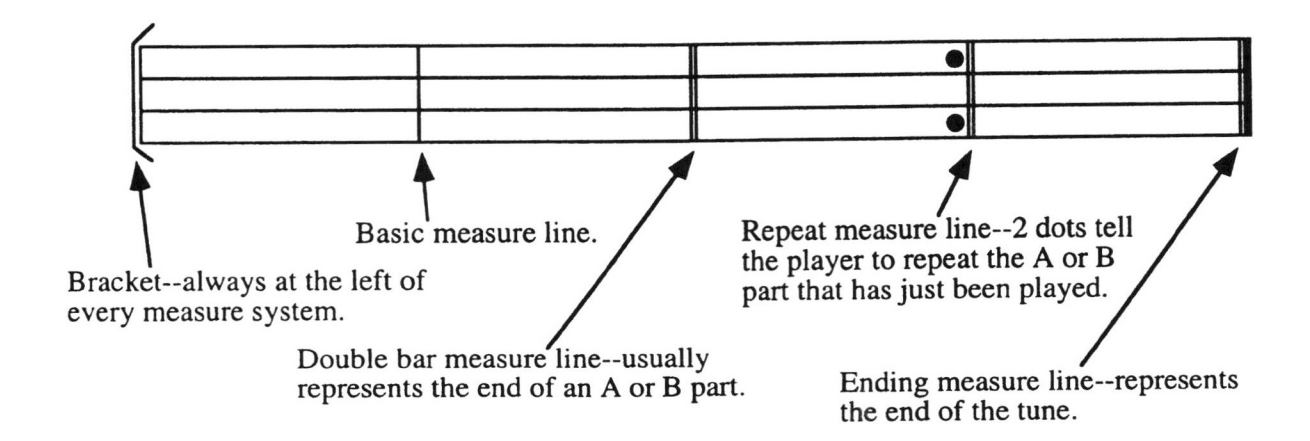

- Bracket--always at the left of every measure system.
- Basic measure line.
- Double bar measure line--usually represents the end of an A or B part.
- Repeat measure line--2 dots tell the player to repeat the A or B part that has just been played.
- Ending measure line--represents the end of the tune.

3. Tablature staff numbers represent fret to be fingered.

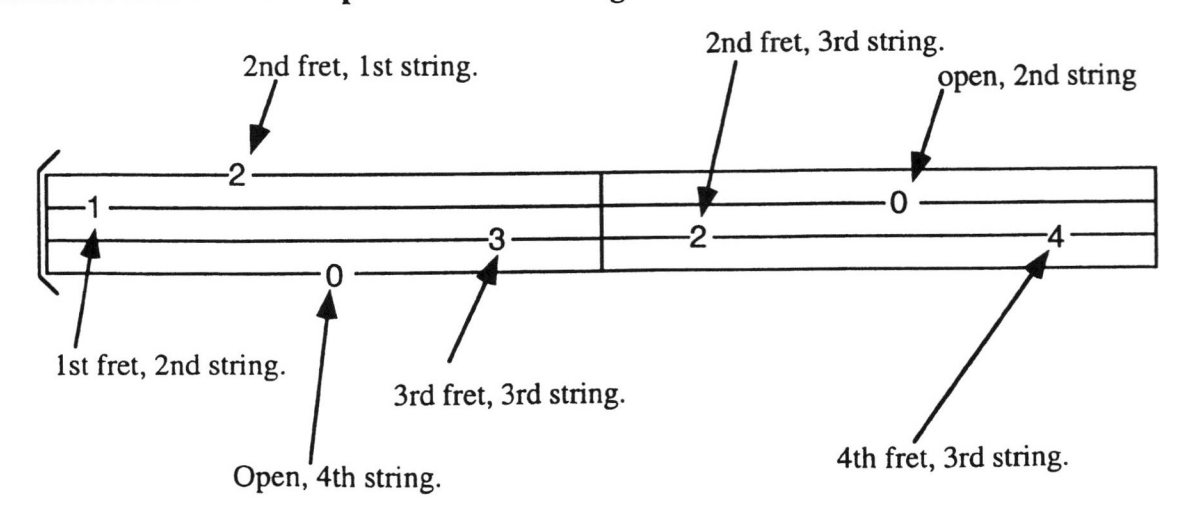

- 2nd fret, 1st string.
- 1st fret, 2nd string.
- Open, 4th string.
- 3rd fret, 3rd string.
- 2nd fret, 3rd string.
- open, 2nd string
- 4th fret, 3rd string.

4. Stems, beams and note values.

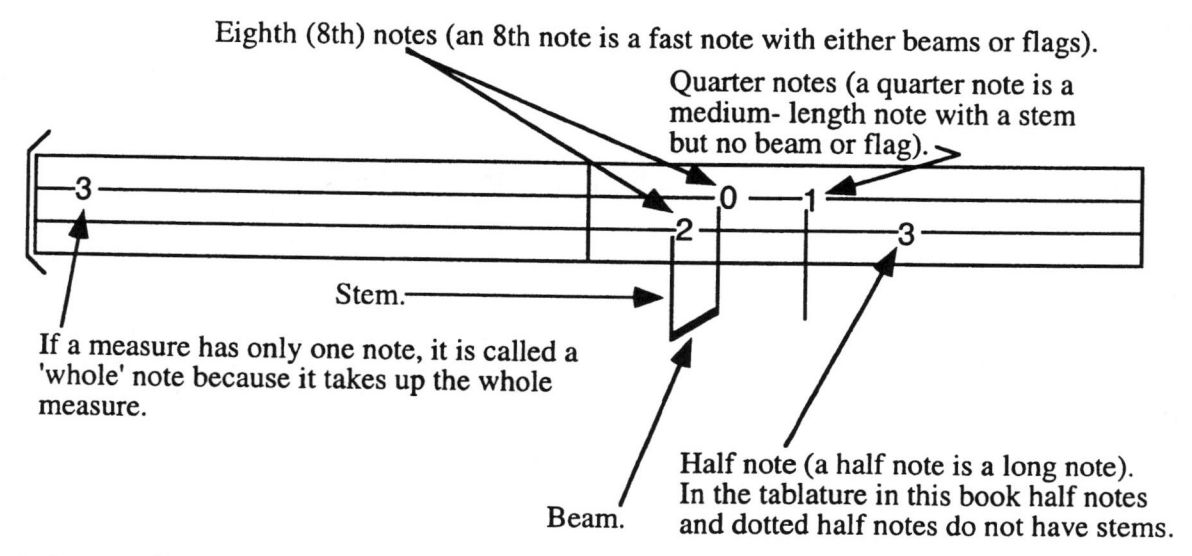

Eighth (8th) notes (an 8th note is a fast note with either beams or flags).

Quarter notes (a quarter note is a medium-length note with a stem but no beam or flag).

Stem.

If a measure has only one note, it is called a 'whole' note because it takes up the whole measure.

Beam.

Half note (a half note is a long note). In the tablature in this book half notes and dotted half notes do not have stems.

5. Rests (a rest tells you to stop playing for a brief time).

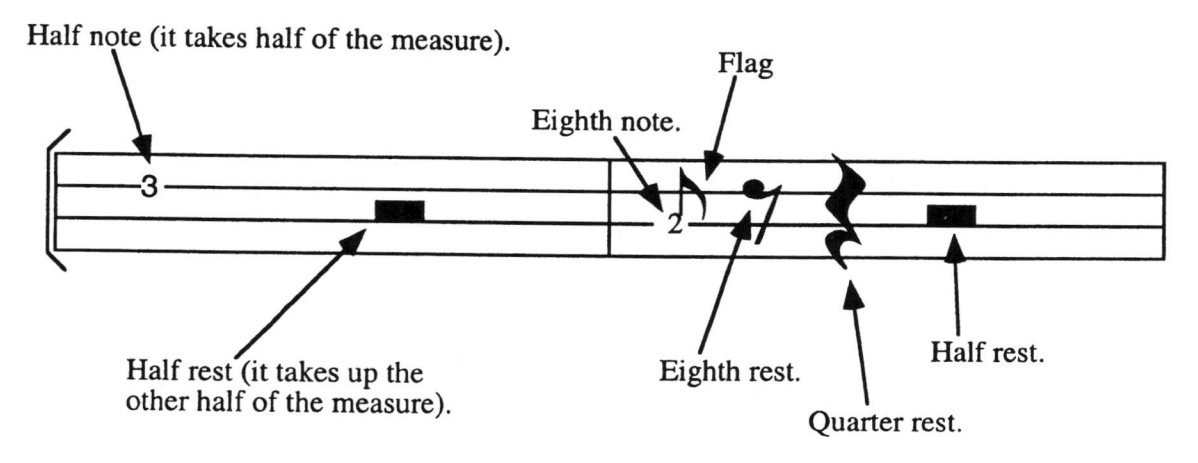

Half note (it takes half of the measure).

Flag

Eighth note.

Half rest (it takes up the other half of the measure).

Eighth rest.

Half rest.

Quarter rest.

6. Numbers above notes represent which finger is to play the note below.

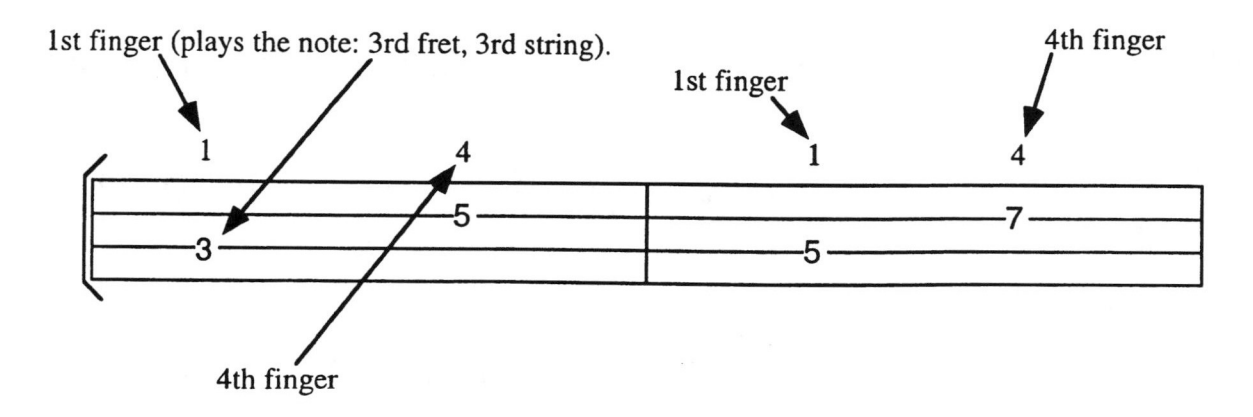

1st finger (plays the note: 3rd fret, 3rd string).

1st finger

4th finger

4th finger

161

Angus Campbell

Chords
Part A
|: A | A | D A | E |
| A | A | D A | E A :|
Part B
|: A | A | E | E |
| A | A | D A | E A :|
(capo 2)
Part A
|: G | G | C G | D |
| G | G | C G | D G :|
Part B
|: G | G | D | D |
| G | G | C G | D G :|

Arkansas Traveler

Chords
Part A (key of D)
|: D Bm | A D | A | A | D Bm | A D | D G | A D :|
Part B
|: D G | D A | D A | Bm A | D G | D A | D G | A D :|
Fiddle, Mandolin & Bass
Part A (key of C)
|: C Am | G C | G | G | C Am | G C | C F | G C :|
Part B
|: C F | C G | C G | Am G | C F | C G | C F | G C :|
Guitar will use these chords
Part A (key of G –Banjo solo)
|: G Em | D G | D | D | G Em | D G | G C | D G :|
Part B
|: G C | G D | G D | Em D | G C | G D | G C | D G :|

Aura Lee

Chords
4/4
Part A
|: A | D | E7 | A :|
Part B
| A C#7 | F#m |
| D Dm | A |
| A C#o Bm F#m |
| B7 | Bm7 E7 | A |

The Battle Cry of Freedom

Chords
Key of F
Part A
| F | F | B♭ | B♭ | F | F | F | C |
| F | F | B♭ | B♭ | F | F | C | F |
Part B
| F | B♭ | F | F | F | B♭ | F | C |
| F | F | B♭ | B♭ | F | F | C | F |
(capo 5) for Key of F (C position)
Part A
| C | C | F | F | C | C | C | G | C | C | F | F | C | C | G | C |
Part B
| C | F | C | C | C | F | C | G | C | C | F | F | C | C | G | C |
Key of G
Part A
| G | G | C | C | G | G | G | D |
| G | G | C | C | G | G | D | G |
Part B
| G | C | G | G | G | C | G | D |
| G | G | C | C | G | G | D | G |

Beaumont Rag

Chords
Key of F
Parts A & B

: C7	C7	F	F
C7	C7	F	F
C7	C7	F	F7
B♭	F D7	G7 C7	F :

Key of C
Parts A & B

: G7	G7	C	C
G7	G7	C	C
G7	G7	C	C7
F	C A7	D7 G7	C :

Billy in the Lowground

Chords
Part A

|: C | C | Am | Am |
| C | C | Am | G C :|

Part B

|: C | C | Am | F |
| C | C | Am | G C :|

Blackberry Blossom

Chords
Part A

|: G D | C G | C G | A D |
| G D | C G | C G | D G :|

Part B

|: Em | Em | Em | B7 |
| Em | Em | C G | D G :|

Bonaparte's Retreat

Chords
Part A

|: D | D | D | D :|

Part B (melody 1 -simple)

| D | D | A | A |
| D | D | A | D |

Part B (melody 2 -fancy)

|: D | A | D | A D :|

Carthage Waltz

Chords
Part A

G	D	C	G
Am	Bm	Am7	D
G	*D D G	Am7	D

Part B

*G C C	G	*G D D	G
G	C	G	Em
Am	G	D	G

*1 strum per chord (all other chords: pick/strum/strum)

Cherokee Shuffle

Chords
Part A

|: A | A | A | F#m |
| D | A | D E | A :|

Part B

|: D | A | D | A | D | A |
| A | F#m | D E | A :|

(capo 2)
Part A

|: G | G | G | Em |
| C | G | C D | G :|

Part B

|: C | G | C | G | C | G |
| G | Em | C D | G :|

Cluck Old Hen

Chords
Part A
|: A | A D | A | E A :|
Part B
|: A | A G | A | E A :|
(capo 2)
Part A
|: G | G C | G | D G :|
Part B
|: G | G F | G | D G :|

Cotton-eyed Joe

Chords
Key of A
Part A
|: A | A D | A | E A :|
Part B
|: A | A | A | E A :|
Key of G (or Capo 2 for key of A)
Part A
|: G | G C | G | D G :|
Part B
|: G | G | G | D G :|
Key of D
Part A
|: D | D G | D | A D :|
Part B
|: D | D | D | A D :|

Cotton Patch Rag

Chords
Parts A & E
| C | C7 | F F/E | F/E♭ D | G | G | C | G |
| C | C7 | F F/E | F/E♭ D | G | G | G | C |
Part B (can be used as Parts A and B for Guitar, Mandolin & Banjo)
| C | C7 | F | F | G | G | C | G |
| C | C7 | F | F | G | G | G | C |
Part C
| Am | Am | Dm | Dm | G | G | C | G |
| Am | Am | Dm | Dm | G | G | G | C |
Part D
| A7 | A7 | D7 | D7 | G | G | C | G |
| A7 | A7 | D7 | D7 | G | G | G | C |
Part F
| C | C | B | B | Dm | Dm | C | G |
| C | C | B | B | Dm | Dm | G | C |

Cripple Creek

Chords
Part A
|: A | D A | A | E A :|
Part B
|: A | A | A | E A :|
(capo 2)
Part A
|: G | C G | G | D G :|
Part B
|: G | G | G | D G :|

Devil's Dream

Chords
Part A & B (key of D)

|: D | D | Em | Em |
| D | D | G D | A D :|

Fiddle parts
Parts A & B (key of G)

|: G | G | Am | Am |
| G | G | C G | D G :|

Guitar and 1st Mandolin part
Parts A & B (key of A)

|: A | A | Bm | Bm |
| A | A | D A | E A :|

2nd Mandolin part
For chords on Banjo, use key of G chords (w/capo 2 for key of A)

Down Yonder

Chords

G	G	G	G
C	C	C	C
G	G	G	G
G	G	G	G
A	A	A	A
D (tacet)	(cont.)	D (tacet)	(cont.)
G	G	G	G
C	C	C	C
G	G	G	G
A	D	G	G

Eighth of January

Chords
Key of D
Part A

|: D | G | A | D :|

Part B

|: D | D | D | A D :|

(capo 2)
Part A

|: C | F | G | C :|

Part B

|: C | C | C | G C :|

Chords (Texas-style)
Key of D
Part A

|: D | G | A | D :|

Part B

D F#o	G G#o	D	A D
D F#o	G G#o
A Bo	C#o D

(capo 2)
Part A

|: C | F | G | C :|

Part B

| C Eo | F F#o | C | G |
| C Eo | F F#o | G Ao | Bo C |

165

Forked Deer

Chords
Part A
|: D | G A | D | A |
| D | G A | D G | A D :|

Part B
|: A | A | A | D |
| A | A | D G | A D :|

(capo 2)
Part A
|: C | F G | C | G |
| C | F G | C F | G C :|

Part B
|: G | G | G | C |
| G | G | C F | G C :|

Gardenia Waltz

Chords
3/4
Key of G (1st part)
G	Bm	Em	G	G	Bm	Am7	D
Am	AmM7	Am7	Am6
D	D+	G	D
G	Bm	Em	G	G	G7	C	Am
C	Cm	G	E7	Am7	D	G	G

Key of D (2nd part)
D	Bm	F#m	Bm	D	D#o
Em7	A7	Em	C	D	A7	A
A/C#	D	A
D	Bm	F#m	Bm	D	D7	G
Em	G	Gm	D	B7	Em7	A7
D	D

Grandfather's Clock

Chords
Part A
| G | D | G | C | G | D | G | D | | G | D | G | C | G | D | G | G |

Part B
G	G	C	G
G	Em	Am7	D
G	D	G	C	G	D	G	G

Part C (Banjo)
|: G | C G | G (tacet) | (tacet cont.) :|
| G | D | G | C | G | D | G | G |

Green Willis

Chords
Part A
:| D | D | A | E A |
| D | D | A | D :|

Part B
|: D | D | Em | A |
| D | D G | A | D :|

(capo 2)
Part A
|: C | C | G | D G |
| C | C | G | C :|

Part B
|: C | C | Dm | G |
| C | C F | G | C :|

Indian's Farewell Waltz

Chords
Part A
Dm	Gm	Gm	A
C	C	Dm	A
Dm	C	Dm	Gm
Dm	A	Dm	Dm

Part B
| F | C | F | Gm |
| Dm | C | Dm | Dm |

(capo 5)
Part A
Am	Dm	Dm	E
G	G	Am	E
Am	G	Am	Dm
Am	E	Am	Am

Part B
| C | G | C | Dm |
| Am | G | Am | Am |

Irish Washerwoman

Chords (6/8)
Part A
|: G | G | D | D |
| G | G | C D | G :|

Part B
: G	G	D	D
C G	C G
C D	G :

La Bastringue

Chords
Part A
: D	A D	A	D
D	A D
G	A D :

Part B (repeat 1st line 2 times)
|: D | C | D | A D :|
| D | C | D G | A D |

Leather Britches

Chords
Part A
|: G | G | G | D |
| G | G | D | D G :|

Part B
|: G | C | G | D |
| G | C | D | D G :|

Texas-style
Parts A & B
: G Bo	C7 C#o
G Bo	D
G Bo	C7 C#o
D Eo	F#o G :

Liberty

Chords
Part A

|: D | D | G | G |
| D | D | A | D :|

Part B

|: D | D | D | A |
| D | D | A | D :|

(capo 2)
Part A

|: C | C | F | F |
| C | C | G | C :|

Part B

|: C | C | C | G |
| C | C | G | C :|

Martin's Waltz

Chords
3/4
Part A

D	F#7	G	E7
A7	A7	D	A7
D	F#7	G	E7
A7	A7	D	D

Part B

A	C#m	F#m	A
E7	E7	A	E7
A	C#m	F#m	A
E7	E7	A	A7	(Return to Part A)

Mason's Apron

Chords
Parts A & B

|: A | A | Bm | Bm |
| A | A | D | E A :|

(capo 2)
Parts A & B

|: G | G | Am | Am |
| G | G | C | D G :|

Mississippi Hornpipe

Chords
Part A

|: G | C | G | D |
| G | C | D | G :|

Part B

: G D	Em Bm
C G	Am D
G D	Em Bm
C G	D G :

Mississippi Sawyer

Chords
Part A

|: D | D | G | G |
| D | D | A | D :|

Part B

|: D | D | A | A |
| D | D | A | D :|

Old Dan Tucker

Chords
Part A
|: C | C | C | G C :|
Part B
|: C | F | G | C :|

Old Joe Clark

Chords
Parts A & B
|: A | A | A | G |
| A | A | A G | A :|
(capo 2)
Parts A & B
|: G | G | G | F |
| G | G | G F | G :|

President Garfield's Hornpipe

Chords
Part A
|: B♭ | B♭ | F | F |
| B♭ | B♭ | F | B♭ :|
Part B
|: E♭ | B♭ | F | B♭ |
| E♭ | B♭ | F | B♭ :|
(capo 3)
Part A
|: G | G | D | D |
| G | G | D | G :|
Part B
|: C | G | D | G |
| C | G | D | G :|

Pretty Peg

Chords
Part A
| D | D A | Bm | A |
| Bm A | G A | G | A |
Part B
D D/C♯	D/B A	D	D A
D D/C♯	D/B A
Bm G	A D
(capo 2)
Part A
| C | C G | Am | G | Am G | F G | F G |
Part B
| C C/B | Am G | C | C G |
| C C/B | Am G | Am F | G C |

Red-haired Boy

Chords
Part A
|: A | A D | A | G |
| A | A D | A | E A :|
Part B
|: G | D | A | G |
| A | A D | A | E A :|
(capo 2)
Part A
|: G | G C | G | F |
| G | G C | G | D G :|
Part B
|: F | C | G | F |
| G | G C | G | D G :|

169

Red Wing

Chords
Part A

G	G	C	G
D	G	A	D
G	G	C	G
D	G	A D	G

Part B

C	C	G	G
D	D	G	G7
C	C	G	G
D	D	G	G

College Hornpipe

Chords
Part A

|: B♭ | B♭ | C | F |
| B♭ Do | D#7 Eo | F | B♭ :|

Part B

|: B♭ | E♭ | C | F |
| B♭ Do | D#7 Eo | F | B♭ :|

(capo 3)
Part A

|: G | G | A | D |
| G Bo | C7 C#o | D | G :|

Part B

|: G | C | A | D |
| G Bo | C7 C#o | D | G :|

Sailor's Hornpipe

Chords
Part A

G	G	A	D
G Em	C Am
G D	G

Part B

G	C	A	D
G Em	C Am
G D	G

Saint Anne's Reel

Chords
Part A

|: D | D | G | D |
| D | D | G A | D :|

Part B

|: D | Em | A | D |
| Bm | Em | A | D :|

(capo 2)
Part A

|: C | C | F | C |
| C | C | F G | C :|

Part B

|: C | Dm | G | C |
| Am | Dm | G | C :|

Sally Ann

Chords
Part A
|: A | D | D | A |
| A | Bm | E | A :|
Part B (repeat 3 times)
|: A | Bm | E | A :|
(capo 2)
Part A
|: G | C | C | G |
| G | Am | D | G :|
Part B (repeat 3 times)
|: G | Am | D | G :|

Sally Goodin'

Chords
Parts A & B
|: A | A | A | E A | A | A | A | E A :|
(capo 2)
Parts A & B
|: G | G | G | D G | G | G | G | D G :|
Texas-style
Parts A & B
: A C#o	D7 D#o
A C#o	E
A C#o	D7 D#o
E F#o	G#o A :
(capo 2)
Parts A & B
|: G Bo | C7 C#o | G Bo | D |
| G Bo | C7 C#o | D Eo | F#o G :|

Sally Johnson

Chords
A part
|: G | G | G | D |
| G | G | D | D G :|
B part
|: G | C | G | G Em |
| G | C | D | D G :|
Texas-style
Part A
|: G Bo | C7 C#o | G Bo | Bbo Ao |
| G Bo | C7 C#o | D Eo | F#o G :|
Part B
|: G Bo | C7 C#o | G Bo | G Em |
| G Bo | C7 C#o | D Eo | F#o G :|

Salt Creek

Chords
Part A
|: A | A D | G | G E |
| A | A D | G | E A :|
Part B
|: A | A | G | G |
| A | A | G | E A :|
(capo 2)
Part A
|: G | G C | F | F D |
| G | G C | F | D G :|
Part B
|: G | G | F | F | G | G | F | D G :|

Soldier's Joy

Chords
Part A

|: D | D | D | A |
| D | D | D A | D :|

Part B

|: D | G | D | A |
| D | G | D A | D :|

(capo 2)
Part A

|: C | C | C | G | C | C | C G | C :|

Part B

|: C | F | C | G | C | F | C G | C :|

Swallowtail Jig

Chords
Part A

|: Em | Em | D | D |
| Em | Em | D | Em :|

Part B

: Em	Em
Em	Em D
Em	Em	D	Em :

Temperance Reel

Chords
Part A

|: G | G | Em | Em |
| G | G | Em | D G :|

Part B

: Em	Em	D	D
Em	Em
Em	D G :

Tom & Jerry

Chords
Parts A & B (simple)

|: A | A | A | E | A | A | A | E A :|

Parts A & B (w/D-chord)

|: A | D | A | E | A | D | A | E A :|

Parts A & B (w/E-chord 3rd and 7th measures)

|: A | D | E | E | A | D | E | E A :|

Texas-style
Part A & B

|: A C#o | D7 D#o | A C#o | Co Bo |
| A C#o | D7 D#o | E F#o | G#o A :|

(capo 2)
Parts A & B (simple)

|: G | G | G | D | G | G | G | D G :|

Parts A & B (w/C-chord)

|: G | C | G | D | G | C | G | D G :|

Parts A & B (w/D-chord 3rd and 7th measures)

|: G | C | D | D | G | C | D | D G :|

Texas-style
Part A & B

|: G Bo | C7 C#o | G Bo | B♭o Ao |
| G Bo | C7 C#o | D Eo | F#o G :|

Turkey in the Straw

Chords
Key of G
Part A
|: G | G | G | D |
| G | G | G | D G :|
Part B
|: G | G7 | C | C (C#o)* |
| G | G D | G | D G :|
Key of C
Part A
|: C | C | C | G |
| C | C | C | G C :|
Part B
|: C | C7 | F | F (F#o) |
| C | C G | C | G C :|

*chords in parentheses are optional for the measure (these chords can be heard on CD).

Uncle Joe

Parts A and B
|: D | D | D | A | D | D | G | A :|

Under the Double Eagle

Chords
(Guitar solo)
Part A
|: C | C | C | C | G | G | C | C :|
Part B
C	C	C	C	C	C	G	G
G	G	G	G	G	G	C	C
C	C	C	C	C	C7	F	F
F	G#	C	A7	D7	G7	C* C#	D

(Mandolin solo)
Part A
|: G | G | G | G | D | D | G | G :|
Part B
C	C	C	C	C	C	G	G
G	G	G	G	G	G	C	C
C	C	C	C	C	C7	F	F
F	Fm	C	A7	D7	G7	C	C

*If you decide not to change to key of G, end on C chord.

Whiskey Before Breakfast

Chords
Part A
|: D | D | G D | A |
| D | D | G D | A D :|
Part B
|: D | D | Em | A |
| D A | G D | G D | A D :|
(capo 2)
Part A
|: C | C | F C | G |
| C | C | F C | G C :|
Part B
|: C | C | Dm | G |
| C G | F C | F C | G C :|